CHILDREN OF CHANCE

CHILDREN OF CHANCE

Elizabeth Pewsey

British Library Cataloguing in Publication Data

Pewsey, Elizabeth
Children of Chance
I. Title
823 [F]

ISBN 0-340-61360-2

Typeset by Hewer Text Composition Services, Edinburgh
Printed and bound in Great Britain by Mackays of Chatham plc

Hodder and Stoughton Ltd
A division of Hodder Headline PLC
338 Euston Road
London NW1 3BH

For Paul

PROLOGUE

No bride.

The chapel was full. The groom waited, stiff-backed, twisting his grey hat round and round in his hands. The best man turned his head to look for the tenth time towards the open doors at the west end of the chapel. The ribbons of the posies attached to the ends of each pew rustled lightly as a priest came past. He bent his head to speak to the groom's aunt. Her face was hidden by the brim of her hat; its pale grey feathers quivered as she listened.

She said something in a low voice to the woman sitting next to her and she in turn beckoned to the groom, who was looking towards them as they spoke. He came over, sleek and watchful. Then he went back to take up his position. The feathers on the groom's aunt's hat became still; the priest returned down the aisle and out of the west door.

Towards the back of the congregation, Cleo and Sylvester watched him go out.

'Is he marrying them?' she asked. 'He looks a bit cross for a wedding. And I thought there was going to be a bishop.'

'There is a bishop. He's waiting for the bride.'

'So are we.'

'How late is she now?'

Cleo looked at her watch, a big man's one, out of keeping with her silk suit. 'More than half an hour.'

'It's not like Prue.'

'Perhaps there was a last-minute problem with the dress.'

'You helped her get dressed before you came to the chapel.'

'Yes, and it's a very plain dress, very simple, nothing to get caught or tangled up. She was ready when I left her.'

'Was she all right? Did she say anything?'

'Very keyed-up, a sense of anticipation . . . She was excited. She didn't say much, though.' Cleo eased her toes out of her elegant

1

court shoes. 'If she doesn't come soon, I'm not going to be able to stand up when she walks down the aisle.'

Sylvester yawned, raising his hand to his mouth and stretching his legs out into the aisle. He glanced round the chapel, and then pulled himself up. 'Cleo, where's Valdemar?'

'He isn't here,' said Cleo. 'You know he isn't.'

'Yes, he is,' Sylvester insisted in a loud whisper that made the people in front turn round to see what was going on. 'He arrived late last night. I saw his car in the stables.'

'Maybe he decided to give it a miss, like Geza, and just come to the reception afterwards. It's not his family, after all.'

'No, but he's been here most of the summer, and his uncle is giving Prue away. Nice of him to do that; I would have been pleased to, but Mountjoy's better. It'll impress the neighbours.'

The congregation was becoming restless. People were relaxing, turning round to talk to people in the pew behind, gossiping, hinting at the unmentionable. Unspoken thoughts lay behind the pleasantries and compliments on hats and outfits. Perhaps, oh just perhaps, the bride wasn't going to come at all. Scandal! A previous marriage. Bigamy. Some dreadful disease, only now diagnosed.

There was a bustle at the back of the chapel; the organist abandoned his dispirited twiddling and launched into a march. Everyone stood up. A hush fell over the congregation as they waited for a radiant bride to appear at the west door on Mountjoy's arm.

There was no radiant bride among the group of people gathered at the door; no bride at all. The mitred bishop spoke urgently to the priest, who shrugged his shoulders and made his way down the aisle for a second time. He turned to face the congregation, raising his arms to quell the rising whispers.

He began abruptly, a look of distaste on his bland, round face.

'I am afraid the wedding has been, um, postponed, owing to, um, an indisposition of the bride. In fact,' he concluded in a rush of honesty, 'there is no bride.'

1

'Prue!'

Prue stopped. The voice rang out from behind her, but there was no-one there. A brisk tinkle from a bicycle bell directed her attention to the road; there, leaning against a red London bus, was Cleo, on a bike. The traffic started to move; Cleo heaved the bike on to the pavement.

'Sorry,' she said automatically, as a pedal dug into a passerby. 'Prue, what are you doing in London? Why didn't you tell me you were here?'

'Job-hunting. I need a job.' Prue gave a quick smile, not the lovely slanting smile that Cleo was used to, but a small, unhappy smile. 'And somewhere to live.'

'In London? Prue, you'll hate it. And what have you got there, in that black case?'

Without waiting for an answer, Cleo pulled Prue along the street. 'Quick, in here, there's a table free. Look, you grab it, I'll lock my bike. Order coffee.'

Prue pushed open the door to the little coffee bar and looked around for somewhere to put her carrier bag and the black case. There wasn't an inch of unoccupied space, so she jammed them under a tiny table, and was at once accosted by a black-browed Italian woman who demanded her order and simultaneously wiped the table with ferocious energy.

'Not possible, just coffee, this time of day,' she said, pointing to a notice above Prue's head.

'Oh,' said Prue. 'I don't want anything to eat.'

Cleo slid into the other seat. 'Coffee, and two of those pastries, the ones with almonds on top. My treat, Prue.'

'Thanks,' said Prue. 'I'm not really hungry, but we have to have something . . .'

'You're thinner than ever. You need to eat a lot of gooey pastries, fill you out a bit.'

Prue laughed, more openly this time; it was good to see Cleo again. 'Five minutes I've been here, and you're already telling me what to do for my own good.'

'Nobody else is going to, are they? You'll end up a stick insect like your aunt if you aren't careful.'

Prue's face froze. Cleo was horrified; what had she said to upset her?

'Prue, whatever is it, what's the matter?'

'Sorry,' said Prue. 'It hit me, suddenly. It was you talking about my aunt. She's dead.'

'Dead?' Cleo's voice was shocked. Not that she cared in the slightest about Prue's aunt as a person: she had only met her once, and thought her entirely depressing. Poor Prue, having to spend her holidays with such a misery. No, it wasn't that. When Prue said, baldly, she's dead, Cleo grasped at once what it meant for her. 'Because she was all the family you'd got, wasn't she?'

Prue nodded.

'When did she die?'

'At the end of term. I left early. Of course, you weren't there, you went immediately after A-levels. Sister Domenica told me I was to go home, my aunt wasn't very well, and when I got there, she had died.'

Cleo took life as it came, but she was too young to have had much to do with death, which was much less easy to handle. Her mind turned to practical matters.

'What about money? Has she left you the house?'

Prue shook her head. 'No,' she said. 'It wasn't hers, she rented it. That's why I've got to find somewhere to live. I can't pay the rent, you see, and they, the landlord that is, wants to let it to someone else.'

'It would be too big for you in any case,' said Cleo sensibly. 'But the money would have been useful. Did she leave any money?'

This time Prue nodded. 'Quite a lot.'

Cleo beamed. 'There you are, then. When that comes through you'll be fine.'

'No, I won't. She left it all to her church, to the Reformed Brethren.'

Cleo was speechless. She stared at Prue. Prue gazed back at her, big unblinking blue eyes with something very like panic in them.

'What, all of it?' asked Cleo. 'Nothing for you? What are you going to live on, how could she do that? They can't just take it, not when it leaves you without a bean.'

'They can and they will,' said Prue. 'The solicitor spoke to them about it, and they said I was a daughter of Lilith, and a corrupted soul. That was because I went to a convent, I expect; they always hated that.'

'What about furniture? Silver? She must have left you *something*.'

Prue was feeling better, it was a relief to talk to someone about it.

'No, they've got their horrid little hands on that too. I had to fight for my books; they were going to carry them off and burn them, because they were full of sinful knowledge. I managed to hang on to some clothes and some letters and photos and things of my parents.'

'What's in the black case?' asked Cleo. 'The one my toes are jammed up against under the table.'

'There isn't much room,' agreed Prue, trying unsuccessfully to move the case with her foot. 'It's a french horn. It was my father's.'

'And not of any interest to the Brethren?'

'You wrong them, it was of great interest to the Brethren: they thought they could sell it, french horns are quite valuable apparently. Although I can't see who'd want it; better new, I'd have thought.'

'How did you get to keep it?' Cleo was fascinated by the picture of churchy greed which Prue was painting. 'Did you just carry it off?'

'Yes, I did. The solicitor said it had clearly been my father's, so it belonged to me, but they weren't having that; prove it, they said.'

'How did you manage to get the horn, then?' Cleo was persistent. She liked to get the details right.

Prue laughed. 'They had one of the brethren – who by the way are mostly women, just to confuse – posted outside the house to make sure I didn't carry anything off. So I let it down on a piece of string at the back of the house, through the lavatory window, and I climbed out after it.'

'Why didn't you just go out of the back door?' said Cleo, puzzled.

'The back door was locked. That was them, of course. And the windows downstairs are all screwed shut; my aunt was terrified of burglars creeping in while she was asleep. Good thing she never had a fire. Most of the upstairs windows don't open, either, but the loo had to. Very hygiene-conscious, my aunt, very worried about smells.'

'Why didn't you bring the french horn to school? You could have learned to play it.'

'No,' said Prue. 'She wouldn't have paid for the lessons. Remember when I started the violin? Besides, I never knew it was there. I found it in the loft, after my aunt died. Together with a mangle.'

'A mangle!'

'Yes, they pounced on that.'

'The Brethren? Whatever for? Do they wash a lot? Baptisms, wet clothes, that sort of thing?'

'Of course not. It was a museum piece; they took it off to sell it. They're very keen on money. I think they're dishonest, too. I'm sure some of the furniture they whisked away was really mine, from my parents, but they weren't going to wait around and find out.'

'Why didn't the solicitor stop them?'

Prue shrugged. 'Not worth his while.' He was a pleasant man, Mr Truelove, middle-aged and unconcerned. He had advised Prue to take the french horn and go, wipe the dust from her feet. 'Where would you put the furniture? After all, you have nowhere to live.'

Cleo delved into the big Liberty bag she carried everywhere with her.

'What are you looking for?' asked Prue, as pencils, a grubby handkerchief, a sheaf of photos and postcards and a bunch of keys flew on to the table.

'Thank you,' said Cleo, retrieving them from Prue and stuffing them back into her bag. 'I'm checking that I've got my purse.'

'I can pay,' said Prue.

'You can't, don't be silly, you haven't a penny.'

'I have,' said Prue with pride. 'You're not going to believe this. I won some money.'

'How?'

'It was a mistake. I bought a raffle ticket. Someone came to the door just before my aunt's funeral; she had such a nice face, I couldn't possibly say no. My aunt thought raffles were the devil's work, but I won fifty pounds.'

'That isn't going to take you very far,' said Cleo.

'It's better than nothing. The solicitor asked the Brethren to give me what he called a token sum, to tide me over, but they refused, I knew they would.'

'Tell me about this job?'

'There isn't a job, yet. That's why I'm in London, to go to some agencies and see if I can find one.'

'Why London?'

'There's more work in London. And I don't ever want to see Witherton again; even the people who aren't Brethren look as though they're about to join.'

'Where are you going to live?'

'I've got the name of a church hostel . . .'

Cleo sunk her head in her hands.

'Prue, no! You can't. Ghastly mousy girls who go to church.'

'I'm a ghastly mousy girl who goes to church.'

Cleo looked at Prue with her red-gold hair and face from a Botticelli painting, and smiled.

'No, you don't qualify. You may feel mousy, and you may go to church – although you don't ever *have* to go again, do you realize? – but you don't look the part.'

The Italian woman brought them their coffee and almond-covered cakes. Cleo pulled hers apart with her fingers. Prue ate hers slowly, without any particular relish.

'Don't you like it?' said Cleo, licking the crumbs from her fingers.

'Yes, I think so,' said Prue.

'Eat it then, it isn't poisoned, it'll do you good. No wonder you're looking half-starved. Listen, Prue, haven't you got anyone to go to, no family at all?'

Prue put the rest of her pastry down on her plate; she didn't feel at all hungry.

'Absolutely no one. My mother was an only child; my father just had the one sister, my aunt. My grandparents died before I was born, so . . .' Her voice tailed away. Cleo looked at her in silence, trying to imagine what it would be like to be Prue, no parents, no family, not even the threadbare security of a religious aunt.

'It's a very good thing I saw you today,' she said finally. 'Why didn't you ring me up?'

'I tried,' said Prue. 'No answer. Have you been away?'

'Yes,' said Cleo apologetically. 'Mum and I went to stay with some cousins . . . Anyway, I'm here now, so that's all right. You aren't alone in the world at all. There's me, and Mum; she's not going to believe all this.'

Prue and Cleo had been friends since they started school together when they were seven. Cleo's mother was a painter. Cleo was her only child; her father had died when she was just a baby. She was at boarding school because her mother had to work, and that meant travelling.

Prue was there because it had been her mother's school, and she had wanted her daughter to follow in her footsteps. Not at seven, her mother would never have parted with her at seven, but her aunt was very happy to send her away.

'Of course, it wouldn't have been my choice,' her aunt told her friend as they did their Saturday turn in the dark hall which was home to the Brethren. 'Catholic, images everywhere, it made me feel quite ill when I went there. Fortunately, I won't have to go again. They arrange a special train for them at the beginning and end of term, and I shan't go to all those days they have, quite unneccesary in my opinion. No, I had no choice, it's in my brother's will, he left the money for it, although money got in wicked ways can never do good. He was a musician, you know, indulgence of the senses, I'm glad to say there's none of that in Prue. She did ask for singing lessons, and one of the nuns said she had a good ear, should play an instrument, but I soon put a stop to that. Pass those hymn books, dear, there are none at all along this row.'

'I've got to get a job, too,' Cleo said, blowing the grains of chocolate across the froth of her coffee.

Prue was surprised. 'Why? You don't need to work, you're going to Oxford.'

'Not until October. I'm broke, and my poor mum can't afford to feed and clothe me the way I want. Anyway, she's going to America for most of the summer.'

Clever Cleo had gained a place at Oxford, to her mother's delight. Equally clever Prue hadn't been allowed to take up a place at Cambridge. Her aunt didn't believe in what she called higher education for girls.

'You convinced me she should stay for her A-levels,' she complained to the nuns, 'and the ideas it's given her! She's certainly not going to mix with all those students, look what they get up to. No, she can do secretarial training in the holidays, there are plenty of good jobs these days, and she'll be married before she's twenty. She's a pretty child; pity she's odd like her father was, but it can't be helped.'

Sister Domenica had pointed out that if you wanted to be a paleoanthropologist, secretarial work wouldn't be very rewarding. Aunt Josephine hadn't known what the word meant, and she was shocked when Sister Domenica explained.

'Bones! Of men, too, I dare say, with nothing on!'

'Very ancient bones, Miss Pagan, millions of years old in some cases.'

'If Prue wants to get mixed up in that kind of thing, and I have to say I don't approve at all, quite unsuitable for a young girl, but if she must, then she can find a job working for a man at a university. Bones, indeed!'

'Wish you were coming up to Oxford. I won't know anybody there,' said Cleo.

'You soon will. You always make friends. Watch out!'

Cleo caught the saucer of her coffee cup with her side sleeve and slopped coffee on to the table.

'Doesn't matter,' she said cheerfully.

'It does,' said Prue severely. 'You're as clumsy as ever. Have a tissue. And look, some's gone on your jeans.'

Cleo dabbed at her jeans, not to much purpose. 'I'll pull my shirt out, that'll hide the mark.'

'You'd better wash them as soon as you get home,' said Prue. 'Cold water first, then a good hot wash.'

'Don't be silly, straight into the washing machine when I get round to it. Once a fortnight, if I remember.'

They paid and left the café. Cleo hurled herself at her bike, swearing furiously as the key wouldn't turn in the lock. Prue watched her for a minute and then took the key from her. 'There. You were forcing it.'

Cleo wound the chain up and thrust it into one of the panniers. 'Listen, a brilliant idea. Come with me to Mrs Dotteridge's.'

'What's that?' asked Prue, swept along in Cleo's wake.

'A superior job agency, out-of-London jobs, live-in, just the thing. Me for the summer, you too, only of course you can stay longer. Mrs D will love you, you're so neat and tidy, tidy-minded too. If she can find jobs for me, which she usually does, then she's bound to have something for you. With luck there might be two jobs near each other. I fancy Scotland. Moors, lochs, pipers . . . Come on, Prue, it's only a few streets away.'

Prue picked up the french horn and her carrier bag and set off after her friend. Half an hour later, Cleo gave a triumphant cry and darted across the road, hauling her bike after her. 'This is it.'

A brass plate said, 'Dotteridge and Farmody. Placement Agency.'

'Isn't that wonderful?' Cleo said. 'Placement. Placements is what we want. Does that stain show? Do I look respectable?'

Prue shook her head. Cleo was wearing faded and slightly torn jeans, and a huge dark red shirt with what looked like paint on it.

'Never mind. Have you got a comb?'

Prue handed one to her and she dragged it through her thick wavy black hair.

'Thanks.'

Prue's own hair was tied back in a pony tail with a small brown velvet ribbon. Her dress and coat were clean, fitted her and went with her flat polished shoes.

I look like a nun out for the day, she thought, as she followed Cleo through the door and up the linoleum-covered stairs.

'Hasn't changed here since about 1930,' said Cleo in a loud whisper. 'And I reckon Mrs D's been here as long. She's a terrific snob, don't let her harass you.'

There was a panel of opaque glass in the top half of the door. Cleo peered through it. 'There's a light on, she's in.' She rapped loudly on the door, and then stood back, pinning Prue against the wall with her arm.

'Wait for it. Ah, here she comes.'

Prue heard a strange wheezing and thumping noise, as though something was being dragged along the ground. A shadow loomed across the glass.

'Who's there?' a voice said.

It sounded like a man. Prue wondered what on earth Cleo was up to; she should have gone to the Knight agency, branches in every part of London, temporary work at top rates. But it was too late to make an excuse and go, the door was opening.

A huge figure surged out into the passage, blocking the light from the room inside. Mrs Dotteridge looked like a very ancient cabbage.

Smells rather like a cabbage too, thought Prue. Or was it dog? Sure enough, a grubby-looking dog with one eye was sniffing suspiciously round her ankles.

'Off, Tiger,' boomed the cabbage. 'Come in, Cleo, glad it's you. Who's this?'

'School friend,' said Cleo, giving Prue a push into the room.

Ghastly, thought Prue. No air, fug of dog and cabbage and smoke. She began to cough. The cabbage looked at her with a beady, merry eye.

'Healthy, is she? Don't like the sound of that cough.'

'Hay fever,' said Cleo promptly. 'Every summer for a week, then it's over, isn't that right, Prue?'

Prue nodded. She didn't trust herself to open her mouth, knowing that she would only cough again.

'Sit down, sit down. Right, how long for, Cleo? Going off to Oxford, aren't you?'

'Yes.'

'What about her?' Mrs Dotteridge gestured towards Prue. 'She going there too, or is she a thicko?'

'Prue's very clever,' said Cleo quickly. 'She isn't going to university for family reasons. We both want summer jobs, only Prue's could last longer. My term starts in October.'

'I know, I know.' Mrs Dotteridge heaved her bulk out of the chair which she had lowered herself into and stumped over to a filing cabinet.

'Skills? Typing, languages, flower-arranging, anything useful?'

Prue shook herself. It was like a dream, this stuffy room with such a preposterous woman; this wasn't how you got a good job. What was Cleo thinking of?

'Good German, reasonable French,' she found herself saying. 'As well as the usual secretarial skills. I can't do flower-arranging.'

'Pity. Got a catering firm in Barrow, want a factotum, as they call it. Need to help with all kinds of functions though, hence the flower-arranging.'

'No, Mrs D,' said Cleo. 'Not Barrow. What kind of function would they have in a place like Barrow, anyway? Look again. Outside London, but pleasant countryside. Rivers and lakes to swim in, things to see.'

'You young girls want everything.' More wheezing. 'No, that's abroad, can't recommend these foreign jobs, could be anything.

11

Secretary in a brothel, I wouldn't be surprised.' She wheezed and erupted into a ghastly groan as her fingers moved surprisingly quickly through the files.

How can she have all those jobs? thought Prue. Who would ever come to her?

'Here we are. Two jobs. Same village, one in a house, one in a castle. North of England. That's the kind of place I like to send my young ladies to. Class counts, even these days. 'Course, rich, these people. Have to be to afford my fees.'

She gave a loud cackle which turned into a wheeze, and thumped the files down on her shabby brown desk. 'Let me see . . . This one for you, Cleo, Mountjoy Castle. It's not a big castle, but genuine, old, in the guidebooks if you want history. Help Lord Mountjoy with old family papers; Lady Mountjoy not too well, so secretary cum personal assistant for her, what gobbledegook. Two or three months, perhaps longer. Live in as family, nice and friendly, Cleo, you'll like that. Him, her, nephew there for most of the summer, no children of their own, if I remember rightly, so this nephew's probably the heir. Also a young boy, relation no doubt – do you like children? Staff kept.'

She shuffled through the files on the table, and little puffs of dust flew up. Breathing heavily, she chose another one and flicked it open. 'And for you, what's her name, Cleo?'

'Prue.'

'Prudence, yes, you look like a Prudence. Funny how parents often choose such suitable names for their offspring, can't have a clue what they're like when they're just font-sized. Amazing how often it turns out right. Do you know anything about music?'

Prue was about to shake her head when Cleo answered for her.

'Prue's father was a musician.'

'Was he, now? You surprise me. Just the thing, then. Midwinter Hall. Sylvester Tate. The cellist. Heard of him?'

Prue shook her head, then changed it to a nod as Cleo kicked her.

'With a musician for a father, you would have. World-famous cellist, of course, best of his generation they say. Bachelor, but, my dear, between you and me, you don't have to worry about that, no problems there at all. I can be positive about that. I wouldn't send a girl off anywhere where there might be trouble of that kind. I know quite well what men are like, but you're safe with Sylvester.'

'Good,' said Cleo, while Prue gave her a puzzled look. What was Mrs Dotteridge talking about?

'There's a housekeeper, a very capable woman I understand, quite a character in fact. He needs help with a book he's writing and general secretarial duties, arranging appointments and so forth.'

She came to a sudden halt and banged the file shut. 'There you are,' she said, handing the files to Cleo. 'Here's what to say about yourself. Use the Felicity Paramour letter for Prue; you'll find it in the grey file, third drawer down under pending. You know where the typewriter is. Prue, if you haven't got a book to read, you can go to the newsagent's and buy yourself a newspaper or a magazine.' Her sharp black eyes fell on the carrier bag and french horn. 'Are those yours?'

'Yes,' said Prue apologetically.

'Find yourself a proper suitcase, that's my advice. Very unstylish, those bags of yours. Well, if you're going to the newsagent's, go.'

Prue found her voice. 'Thank you, Mrs Dotteridge. I've got a book.' She produced a paperback from her bag.

Mrs Dotteridge squinted at it. 'Never get a husband if you go round reading that kind of thing,' she said with a hoarse, heaving laugh. 'Virgin's read, that's what that is. Still, old bones can't hurt you. Now, be quiet until Cleo's finished, I've got some phone calls to make. Don't listen, nothing to do with you, and I don't care for eavesdroppers.'

Prue opened her book, mesmerized. If I had done what all my instincts were telling me to do, she thought later, and had rushed out of that little hell-hole, so exactly like a bad dream, then it would all have been so different.

But she stayed.

2

'Now,' said Cleo, as they emerged blinking into the sunlight. 'How are we going to get you home?'

Prue put down her bags. 'Cleo, I haven't got a home.' She felt very tired, too tired even to be despondent. Hungry, too; it was afternoon now, and she had had no breakfast, or lunch, just half an almond pastry. She had no job, no 'Here's the address, start at nine tomorrow', just a letter off to an unknown part of the north, with perhaps a job in what, two, three weeks? And, a more immediate problem, nowhere to live.

'Stop worrying,' said Cleo. 'They'll get the letters tomorrow, straight on the phone to Mrs D, saying "Yes, please," and we're off.'

'They may not want us at all,' pointed out Prue. 'They may be away. There may be dozens of people applying for the jobs.'

'No,' said Cleo confidently. 'It's meant for us, I just feel it. We're destined to go there, so there's no need to fret. And home is with me, now at any rate, then we'll get you sorted out.'

Prue picked up her bags. 'I won't say thank you for saving my life, because you know how grateful I am, and besides, I have no choice but to come with you. It's that or a Brethren hostel.'

'I'd rather have the arches at Charing Cross,' said Cleo.

Prue went on the underground while Cleo cycled. 'Are you okay on the tube?' Cleo asked her.

'Yes,' said Prue. 'I like it. I may get lost, but I'll get there in the end. Barons Court, on the District Line. That's the green one, that's easy.'

'You have to change.'

'Yes, I can manage that, Cleo, really I can!'

Cleo had her doubts. Prue was full of brains, and, when not oppressed by school or her aunt, full of vitality and mad ideas, day-dreaming one minute, then sending all her friends into fits of laughter with her funny observations. Streetwise she was not; and Cleo could see her going round and round on the Circle Line, talking to strangers instead of treating her fellow travellers with a knowing Londoner's disdain. Still, she had to learn, might as well start now. Cleo felt as anxious as a mother the first time her child walks alone to school.

Prue was naive and unworldly; yes, totally, but just wait until she finds her feet, thought Cleo as she threaded her way through choking streets on her bike. Ghastly to be alone like that, she's scared stiff and so she ought to be, I'd be in a blue funk, but it's the best thing that could happen, that evil old dink popping off; don't know what she died from, but I hope it hurt, and I hope she hasn't gone to a better place. 'Bloody Brethren,' said Cleo out loud, alarming a passing motorist. 'God's got a lot to answer for.'

'There,' said Prue. 'No problem. I got on the wrong train, I will admit, but I leapt off just in time. There were people busking; pity I can't play this horn. Bet you could earn quite a lot doing that.'

'Hang that bag over the handlebars,' said Cleo. 'It's about ten minutes' walk from here. Where are the rest of your things?'

'There's a bag of books at the left luggage at Victoria. I'll have to go and get them.'

'What about your clothes?'

'They're there,' said Prue, gesturing towards the carrier bag.

Cleo stopped. She held the bike with one hand and opened the carrier bag with the other. 'Toothbrush, washing things, some underwear . . .'

'And a shirt and skirt.'

'So where are the rest of your things?'

'I haven't got any,' said Prue, quite cheerfully.

'The Brethren can't have taken your clothes!'

'No, though I'm sure they would have if I'd given them the chance. I gave them to Oxfam. Cleo, don't look at me as though I'm an idiot; they didn't fit.'

'Ah,' said Cleo. 'Yes, you've grown, haven't you? Trust you to do that differently from everyone else. I stopped growing when I was fourteen. That's a nuisance.'

'I'm going to spend some of my raffle money on clothes.'

'You'll have to. It's a pity, because you need every penny . . . I can't lend you any of mine, they won't fit. Nor will anything of

Mum's, she's quite short, and roundish. Never mind, I'll think of something.'

That morning, setting off for the last time from Witherton via the lavatory window, Prue had felt mortified by her lack of clothes, her one good outfit provided by a thoughtful sister at the convent who knew how difficult it was to get Prue's aunt to buy her clothes. And what she did buy usually came from the Brethren jumble sale; the Brethren had minds above fripperies like clothes, so their cast-offs were mostly unwearable.

Now, walking along a London street in the sunshine with Cleo, with somewhere to stay, at least for one night, Prue didn't mind about the clothes. Even if she couldn't buy more than one or two things, it would be fun to have something new. A short skirt, maybe not as short as some she had seen on the tube, but certainly not hovering below her knees.

'Here we are,' said Cleo. She pulled her bike up a short flight of steps belonging to a large old Edwardian house.

'Goodness,' said Prue. 'Is this where you live?'

'Yes,' said Cleo, 'along with a lot of other people. Mum's got a studio on the top floor. Come on. I leave my bike here, in the hall.'

She led the way up several flights of stairs and then opened a dark door on the top landing. Prue walked out of the gloom into a room bathed in light.

'Oh,' she said. 'How lovely!'

'Painters need light,' said Cleo. She pointed up to the glass cupola in the centre of the ceiling. 'That helps, and the windows along there. It was built for an artist back in the 1890s; a lot of artists lived around here then. I'll show you the rest of it, not that there's much to show.'

There were two doors at the end of the studio; one led to a tiny bathroom, the other to a room just big enough for a bed and a desk under a sloping roof with a window in it.

'This is my room,' said Cleo. 'It was a kind of cupboard originally, used for storing canvases.'

'Where's your mum's room?' asked Prue.

'She sleeps in the studio,' said Cleo. 'There's a bed behind that screen. And the kitchen is that area behind the cupboards over there.'

Prue was entranced. Paintings and drawings everywhere, an easel, a drawing table laden with paints, jars of brushes and pencils, a little basket of charcoal . . . Prue sniffed.

'I like the smell. Is that the paint?'

'Linseed oil and turps, I expect,' said Cleo. 'I never notice it, you don't after a while. Now, tonight you can sleep in Mum's bed, she's away, so that's no problem.'

'Where shall I put the horn?' asked Prue. 'Are you sure your Mum won't mind?'

'Of course not, she'll say you must stay as long as you want. But there's no space at all except in the studio, and it's not fair on her; she often needs to work at night and she can't do it if someone else is in here.'

'What about daylight? How can she work at night?'

'Oh, not her big paintings, but drawings and illustrations. She teaches in the daytime, part-time at two schools; that and the illustration work pays the bills. She's quite well-established as a painter, but you can't count on selling pictures unless you're very famous.'

Prue looked at Cleo, so competent and, yes, grown-up, that's what she was. While she, Prue, felt like a schoolgirl still.

'Not surprising,' said Cleo. 'Look at all the things you've missed out on, can't be helped, and think of the fun you'll have catching up. You'll have to cram three years living into six months, wow! And nobody to tell you no, or warn you that it isn't suitable or nice, or that you'll get hurt if you do this or that. Perfect freedom.'

All very well, thought Prue, but it's still strange after all these years, with nobody to please, having to make my own decisions. She shivered. Cleo cast an expert eye over her.

'Coffee,' she said briskly. 'And a sandwich. If you don't get some food inside you, you'll pass out. Then you can have a bath and I'll ring a few people.'

An hour later Prue was sitting in Cleo's half-bath in a cloud of bubbles.

'You can either sit with your top half out of the water,' Cleo explained, 'or lie down, with your legs hanging out. You'll get the knack of it.'

Prue swirled the water idly with her hand; snatches of conversation floated through from the studio, where Cleo was on the phone.

'No, Lottie, she isn't a hippy . . . No, she hasn't got dirty feet, she's spotless, straight from the nuns . . . Of course she likes cats, she's wonderful with cats. Nothing pleases her more than talking to cats and looking after them . . . No, Lottie, well, perhaps that's a slight exaggeration . . . Honestly, Lottie, I thought it would be such a help for you, those poor cats having to go into a cattery instead of staying peacefully in their own home . . . I know it's a luxury cattery, but you wouldn't want to be in one, would you? . . . Her name's Prue, Prue Pagan. Yes, P-A-G-A-N . . . What? Yes, her father was a musician, he played the french horn, I know, because Prue has it with her . . . No, she doesn't play the horn, but her father's name was Piers, so it must be the same one . . . Oh, good, oh, Lottie, I am so grateful, the kindness of you, yes, quite homeless, no one in the world, except me . . . Yes, I'll tell her.'

Cleo's head appeared round the bathroom door.

'That was a piece of luck, Prue. I've fixed you up with somewhere to stay for a few days, not very near here, but that can't be helped. She's going away, and the student who lodges with her and feeds the cats is away as well until the end of the week. So you're going to go and look after them, and stay there. You'll be in clover, it's a wonderful place. Now for some clothes.'

Cleo disappeared as Prue was opening her mouth to point out that she didn't have a clue about cats, but surely they couldn't be much trouble. Ten minutes later, when she was regretfully deciding that she really would have to get out of the bath, Cleo was back.

'Here's a towel,' she said. 'All fixed. I've got a friend who's about your size. Fortunately she's very rich and fashionable, so she buys masses of clothes and never wears them for more than a few months. She won't be in, but she's leaving a parcel of clothes with the porter where she lives. We can pick them up tomorrow on our way to Lottie's.'

'I'm not sure that they approve of me,' said Prue doubtfully. She looked at the two sleek beasts who gazed back at her with huge golden eyes. 'They're staring at me, and I don't think they like what they see.'

'You're imagining it,' said Cleo. 'The brown one is Links and the grey one – Lottie says it's blue, not grey, I can't think why – is called Rechts.'

'Left and right,' said Prue. 'What strange names.'

'They sit on the piano when Lottie plays,' said Cleo. 'One on the right and one on the left. They always have, since they were kittens.'

Prue edged round a fat sofa, keeping her eye on the cats. The brown one yawned and stretched, his claws digging into the rug. He wandered over to Cleo and gave a loud yowl.

'Are they Siamese?' said Prue. 'Aren't they very highly strung?'

'No,' said Cleo. 'On both counts. They're Burmese, and they aren't highly strung at all. Tough as old boots, these cats.' She picked the brown one up and turned him upside down to tickle his stomach. 'See, loud purrs, just a softie.'

Prue was unconvinced, but she could always stay in a different room from them.

'Don't even think of it,' advised Cleo. 'They love to annoy, and they'll come and find you. Just talk to them a bit and give them the odd stroke. If I know Lottie, there'll be menus in the kitchen of what they eat and when, so you don't have to worry about that.'

'Is she German?' asked Prue as she followed Cleo into the kitchen.

'Austrian. Jewish, a musician, was going to be a concert pianist, but the Nazis came. She was lucky, ended up in Switzerland, but none of her family survived. Parents, four brothers and sisters, aunts, uncles, cousins, grandparents. She was the only one left. Bit like you, really.'

Prue went cold. Far worse to have had a family, a big family, and to have lost them all and in such a terrible way, than never to have any family except an aunt. 'How did she manage?'

'She came to England after the war and settled here. Gave piano lessons, then she went into management. Now she's an impresario, puts on concerts all over the place, very successful. Such luck, because it seems she knew your father, that's why she's letting you stay here. She said yes as soon as she knew who you were.'

Cleo went back out into the hall. 'Her office is in there. Don't worry if the phone goes, there's an answering machine. This is her private phone; you'll have to answer that one, because it might be me. I'll show you the rest of the house and then I'll have to go. Mum will be back, and I promised to help her with a few things. Hang on, though.'

Cleo dived back into the kitchen. 'I thought so, that's good, because you won't have to buy food. Look!'

Cleo had opened the door of a large fridge. 'Packed with goodies, lucky you.'

Prue was horrified. 'I can't eat her food.'

'It isn't her food, it's for you; look, she's left a note. Lottie wouldn't eat any of these things, she lives on a strange diet of yoghurt and lentils and things.' She glanced at Prue's disapproving face and grinned. 'You've got to learn to take what's on offer, Prue. You look just like one of the nuns when I took too large a helping at lunch.'

She shut the fridge with a bang. 'You're doing her a favour, remember, looking after her precious cats. Besides, the food will only go to waste if you don't eat it, and remember what the nuns said about waste . . .'

'Wanton waste makes wicked want,' said Prue, laughing. 'It's going to be wicked greed for me, and who knows, I might even get to like the cats.'

That night, Prue lay in a wide and wonderfully comfortable bed. She looked around the attractive room, with its thick carpet, polished furniture, her own bathroom opening off it. Then she thought of her room in her aunt's house, her narrow bed in a bare, narrow room unchanged since her early girlhood, when she arrived tearful and in despair, aching with longing for her parents.

'No point in crying,' her aunt had said crossly. 'They've gone to a better or a worse place, as the Lord decides. Perhaps it's all for the best, before your father, may God preserve his soul, slipped any further down the broad path to destruction.'

Prue, not understanding a word of what she said, had simply gone on crying. Now some of that loneliness came back. It was all very well, Cleo's unquenchable optimism. She had a home, and a mother, and cousins, and a place at university. She, Prue, hadn't. What was she going to do with her life? Marriage, that was what her aunt had planned for her.

Would anyone want to marry her? Cleo, now, all the girls at school agreed that Cleo was attractive to men. 'Blatant,' said Cissie, as they sat on their thin, hard beds, illicitly whispering after lights out about the houses in the country they would live in when they were married. Georgian houses, of course, with roses and labradors round the door.

Prue sighed and turned over in bed, then sat up as the door

slowly opened. Panic-stricken, she made herself turn the light on.

Two tails were visible at the end of the bed. Prue sank back on to her pillows, relieved.

'What a fright you gave me,' she told them severely. The cats jumped up on to the bed, roaring, and settled themselves down in two furry heaps, one on each side of her pillow.

Rather comforting, thought Prue, and fell asleep.

Prue passed the next few days as though in limbo, content to push all the disagreeable worries about her future to the back of her mind. I can think about that tomorrow, she promised herself. She read books, lying on the sofa with the two cats on either side of her, watched television – a new world to her, as neither the nuns nor her aunt had allowed it – and ate delicious things from the fridge. Although Lottie wasn't there, her house felt like a home, and that was something that Prue had never experienced before. People rang up from time to time: friends of Lottie's, whose messages Prue wrote dutifully on the pad by the phone, and Cleo, who chatted for hours about nothing in particular and than rang off suddenly with shrieks of horror about the phone bill.

Prue fed the cats, and went into the hall to pick up the newspaper and post. Then she noticed the date on the paper, and her stomach gave a jolt. Thursday! The student would be back tomorrow; she wouldn't be needed any more. Her mouth went dry. All these wasted days! She should have been out looking for a job, not idling here in luxury. The nuns were right, look what happened when you gave in to temptation even for a minute.

The phone rang and Prue answered it, feeling quite numb.

'Hello,' she said. Someone ringing from a call box, pip, pip, pip.

'Prue? It's Cleo. Pack your bags, we've got the jobs. Meet you at King's Cross tomorrow morning. Train's at 6.35, horribly early, but there you are. We go to Gossiby via Eyot. Don't worry about the cost, Mrs D's given me vouchers. They'll pay.'

'Oh,' said Prue. 'Tomorrow.'

'Come on, Prue, super job, look good on your CV, worked at a castle.'

'You're working at the castle. Mrs Dotteridge wanted me for Midwinter Hall.'

'Didn't I tell you? I swapped us round when I did the letters.

You'll like being in a family, do you good. And I'm used to artists, I'll take the cellist. Money running out, see you tomorrow.'

Prue stood by the open train door, watching the big hand of the ornate station clock as it ticked round, then glancing down the platform.

'Close all doors, close all doors, please.'

The guard came towards her, banging the doors shut. 'Are you catching this train, miss?' he asked as he reached Prue.

Prue nodded.

'Hop on, then. It's leaving. Close the doors!'

Prue hung on to the train door. 'No, not yet! My friend's coming on this train.'

'Can't hold a train for someone's friend. We'd be here all day if we waited for passengers. Now, on the train if you're going, or stand clear.'

He blew his whistle.

'Her luggage is in the compartment,' said Prue quickly. 'So is mine. If we aren't catching the train, I'll have to get it out. And there's a big suitcase in the guard's van.'

Annoyed, the guard furled his green flag again. 'Get her luggage out, then, and leave it on the platform for her. She'll have to come by the next train. Where are you going?'

'Gossiby.'

'Eyot, then.'

'Yes, we have to change at Eyot. There isn't another train that connects until this afternoon.'

'Can't help that. Your friend should have been here in good time. The railways aren't responsible for people who can't be bothered to be on time for their trains.'

'She was,' said Prue. 'In time, I mean. We were here ages ago. I think she just wanted to go to the Ladies.'

'Perfectly good toilets on the train. Now, pass her bags out; this train is going to leave.'

Prue climbed reluctantly on to the train and made her way down the corridor to her compartment. As she struggled with her friend's shapeless bag, she heard a yell and the sound of running feet. The carriage door slammed, the whistle blew, and the train jerked forward.

'Cleo,' said Prue. 'Thank goodness. The guard was saying I had to take your luggage off.'

'Tiresome man,' said Cleo, shoving the bag forcefully back on to the luggage rack before collapsing in a corner seat, breathing hard. 'Phew, it's hot, we should have the window open.'

'Where were you?' asked Prue. 'You nearly missed the train.' It was a dark thought, that she might have arrived without Cleo; of course, she could have coped, but it was undoubtedly better to have Cleo on hand. Dashing off like that, leaving seat and luggage and no doubt her ticket as well, lucky Cleo, with no thought for the next half hour, let alone for the morrow.

'Necessities,' said Cleo. 'Something to eat and drink from the Greek deli just outside the station; you can't eat railway food, it's stale and unwholesome. And magazines, must have something frivolous to read.'

Cleo sat back with a contented sigh, and swung her feet on to the other seat. 'I suppose your bag is full of heavy books about bones.'

'Mostly,' said Prue with a grin. 'Except for one, which I took from Witherton by mistake, my Burden Bible.'

'What's a Burden Bible?' asked Cleo, yawning as she settled herself even more comfortably.

'I got it when I was little. I was a Pilgrim, it's a kind of Sunday school. If you went to church twice every Sunday for fifty-two weeks in a row, they gave you a Burden Bible.'

Cleo sat up, incredulous. 'Fifty-two weeks in a row? What about holidays?'

'My aunt didn't believe in holidays.'

'Did you sing hymns or just pray?'

'Both.' She began to laugh as she remembered it. 'Jesus wants me for a sunbeam,' she sang.

Cleo collapsed in laughter. 'Jesus never wanted *me* for a sunbeam, that's for sure.'

'No, and I can't say I ever felt very sunny.' She stood up suddenly. 'I know what I can do.'

She pulled her suitcase down from the rack. Cleo's friend had thoughtfully provided it along with her cast-off clothes; Prue thought it very smart.

'What are you up to?' asked Cleo suspiciously, looking at the wicked expression on Prue's face.

'Here it is,' said Prue, waving a dingy little book in front of Cleo.

'My Burden Bible. I'm going to throw it out of the window. Look, a river, perfect!'

Prue lowered the window completely and hurled the book out. The train was running alongside a river; the book landed midstream, open and face down. As the train gathered speed, Prue and Cleo watched it bobbing towards the weir.

'Well done!' said Cleo. She dug a magazine out of her bag and inspected its cover. 'Here, Prue, this will take your mind off bibles and hymns. Look, "Enjoy a better sex life with your boss". Juicy stuff. Put your feet up and get ready to be a sunbeam at the castle.'

3

At the little country station, the air was still and heavy with heat.

'Why is the station called Gossiby and Mountjoy?' Prue had asked the ticket collector on the train from Eyot.

'Gossiby is the village, and Mountjoy is the castle. Midwinter is nearer, but the castle was more important when they built the railway. You must have heard of Mountjoy Castle. Worth a visit if you're staying in these parts.'

There was no one at the station. The guard helped Prue and Cleo make a heap of their bags and coats on the platform; then he climbed back on board and the train rattled off into the distance. The sound died away, the station was silent. Prue looked at their bags.

'What do we do now?'

Cleo looked around. 'Someone was supposed to meet us. Come on, there must be a telephone near here. Which way do you think the village is?'

Prue shouldered her big bag and gathered up the french horn and her carrier bags. 'Let's go and look.'

Outside the station there was a tiny space for cars, a track leading away across a field and a narrow road curving down a hill. From behind the gate into the field a large sheep glared at them, then went back angrily to pulling up little mouthfuls of the short, dry grass.

'I think we'd better try the road,' said Prue.

She was right. A quarter of a mile along the road they came to a sign saying Gossiby and Midwinter, and a pub called The Silent Woman.

Prue looked at the inn sign, a faded painting of a woman in a long dress with her head under her arm. She was puzzled for a moment, and then she grinned.

'Not very funny,' said Cleo crossly. 'Goodness, you can tell we've come to the end of civilization. And it's so *hot*!'

There was an old stone trough outside the pub. They dumped their bags on the ground and perched on the rough stone.

'It says Gossiby and Midwinter, but they must be miles away, the road just goes on and on. I wish this pub was open, then we could phone.'

'Listen,' said Cleo. 'A car!'

She stepped out into the road and waved as a battered Ford drove up. It stopped and a young man got out.

'Wow,' said Cleo under her breath, as she took in his lean, fit body, evident under a skinny tee-shirt, a thick head of tousled copper curls, a Byronic profile and a slightly soft, sulky mouth.

'You Cleo?' he asked Prue.

Cleo flashed him a generous smile. 'No, I'm Cleo,' she said. 'This is Prue.'

'Hi,' he said. 'I'm Luke. Sylvester sent me to meet you, take you to Midwinter Hall.'

'What about Prue?'

'What about Prue? She looks okay to me,' said Luke, with an appraising eye.

'I'm all right,' said Prue with dignity. 'You go to Midwinter Hall, Cleo. I'll walk until I find a phone box.'

'You'll walk a long way then,' said Luke. 'Nearest one's four miles in the other direction, and it's been out of order for days. Hop in. Where are you going?'

Cleo answered for her. 'Mountjoy Castle. We were told it's near Midwinter Hall.'

'So it is, as the crow flies. Not by road it isn't, though. It's on my way, I'll drop this Prue off. Going to visit, are you? They don't usually come on the train, people for the castle. Posh cars, most of them.'

'I'm going to work there.'

'Wish you luck, then,' said Luke, slinging Prue's things into the back and slamming the door. He started the car with a roar. 'They're really peculiar up at the castle. Live in a different world, if you ask me.'

'What do you mean?' asked Prue. She was beginning to wish that Cleo hadn't changed their names round.

Luke shrugged. 'They're just different from the rest of us. Different ways of doing things, different view of life. Don't look so alarmed,' he added, grinning as he saw Prue's face in the mirror.

'They won't rape you or eat you. It might just take you a while to adjust.'

'Is Sylvester Tate okay?' said Cleo. 'Do you work for him?'

'I'm helping out for a vacation job.' He gave the wheel a swift jerk and turned a sharp corner on to an even narrower road to the left. 'Hope you aren't car-sick,' he said, as the car swung round a series of tight bends up the hill. 'Look over to your left, that's Midwinter Hall.'

Set on the side of the hill, Midwinter Hall looked mellow and peaceful in the golden sunlight. Prue caught a glimpse of a little fountain in front of the house; then, as they went on up, she twisted her head round so that she could see the neat grounds behind the house.

'It looks a lovely house,' she said rather wistfully.

'If that's to your taste, you're in for a shock,' said Luke. 'There's the castle.'

It stood grey and powerful on top of the hill. It wasn't a big castle, as castles go, and it might now be just someone's home, but you could see it hadn't been built for peaceful purposes.

'Owned all the land round here, the Mountjoys used to. Unruly lot, always fighting the Scots or anyone else they didn't like the look of. They're more civilized now, but I reckon they've all got wild genes.'

He drove with a bump over a ramp and through an archway into an empty courtyard. 'I'll get your bag for you,' he said, opening Prue's door as he went past. 'There.'

'Where do I go?' said Prue, looking up at the great stone building.

'Try that door over there, the one by the dungeon steps,' said Luke as he got back into the car. 'It'll be open, they never lock it.' Before Prue could say another word, or Cleo offer any encouragement, he had backed the car, turned round and roared through the arch.

Prue stood and looked after them. The sound of the car grew fainter; she stood alone in the silent courtyard. Stone walls with pock marks from ancient battles surrounded her; as she looked up, narrow slits were visible at intervals. There was a wide flight of stone stairs leading up to another arch and several heavy wooden doors in arched doorways.

Despite the walls, it wasn't oppressive in the courtyard. There was a round, covered well, and a tree with spreading leaves provided speckly shade over the cobbles, which had grass growing between them.

Prue went back out through the arch. On closer inspection she could see that this was only part of the castle; there was a bigger keep beyond, and to one side a more modern building, still stone, but with pretty towers and bigger windows which looked out over a lawn. A gravelled drive led away round the other side. To stables? wondered Prue.

She went back into the first courtyard and, summoning her courage, pushed at the door Luke had pointed to. It swung open with a loud creak which made her jump. Stone steps led up into darkness; feeling her way, Prue started up them.

A small slit in the massive wall let in some light as the stairs curved round. At the top, there was another door. It led out on to a rampart which ran above the courtyard. Prue walked slowly along, looking down into the yard to see if anybody had heard her and come out of one of the other doors. Because she wasn't looking where she was going, she tripped over the milk crate which had been set beside another door. Two milk bottles rolled across the stone flags and fell with a resounding crash into the yard below. Prue held her breath, waiting for a door to fly open, an accusing voice to ring out.

Nothing.

She looked down at the crate. A note was tucked into one of the remaining bottles. She bent down and unrolled it. 'Four pints. Put it in shady place, back late.' Prue stuffed the note back into the bottle. The door was a most ordinary-looking one; it could have graced her aunt's redbrick terrace house. There was a bell beside it; Prue hesitated for a moment, then rang it. Perhaps the castle was broken up into apartments, holiday flats, something like that. At least whoever lived here would know where she would find the Mountjoys.

No reply. Prue looked up and down, uncertain what to do. Here she was, a heavy bag, a french horn, miles from anywhere, in this strange and apparently deserted castle. She put her bag and the horn down for a moment; then the door suddenly opened. A stocky young woman stood there, dressed in a short skirt and aertex shirt. She stared at Prue.

'What do you want?' she said rudely. 'Was that you making all that row? We have to pay for broken milk bottles, you know.'

'I'm sorry,' said Prue.

'Well?' said the young woman. 'If you've come to sell something, you're wasting your time. I never buy from strangers at the door.'

Prue pushed a stray strand of hair behind her ear and smiled. 'No, I'm not selling anything, I'm looking for the Mountjoys.'

'Why?'

'I've come to work for them.'

'Oh, you're that one, are you,' said the woman, her voice noticeably milder. 'Come in. You don't look the sort, I must say; Mrs Dotteridge said she was sending a practical, lively person. You look a bit dismal, if you don't mind me saying so.'

'I do, actually,' said Prue.

'Do what?'

'Mind you saying so. I'm not dismal, just hot and a bit fed up because I had trouble getting here and then there didn't seem to be anyone about.'

'Why did you have trouble getting here? You came on the train, didn't you? We sent a taxi to meet you.'

'Well, it wasn't there.'

'Bloody man,' said the woman without rancour. 'Know what he was up to. So, how did you get here?'

'Someone called Luke, who works at Midwinter Hall, gave me a lift. My friend's working there.'

'Yes, I know Luke. That's all right, then.'

All the time she was talking, the woman had been leading Prue through a labyrinth of passages and little rooms. 'You came in the tradesman's entrance. You should have gone in through the main door.'

'I'm sorry.'

'Do you apologize all the time? It's hardly important, is it?' She opened a final door and pushed Prue through it.

Prue found herself looking down into a huge hall. The gallery ran round three sides of it; the fourth side was dominated by an enormous fireplace and chimney. Vast pictures hung along the gallery walls, too dark and gloomy for any subject to be seen. Every few yards there was a bust on a column; they all had the same bony noses and blind marble eyes. The woman led the way past them to the wooden stairway which led down into the hall and leant over the balustrade.

'Mountjoy, your girl's come,' she bellowed.

She gave Prue another push. 'Go on, he's down there somewhere. See you later, I expect. My name's Sophie.'

With that, she abruptly disappeared through another door which was directly behind her.

'Watch out for the second step,' said a man's voice. 'It's rather uneven.'

Startled, Prue tripped on the step and put out a hand to balance herself.

'Mind the bear!' said the voice.

Prue didn't mind the bear. She and the moth-eaten creature rolled together down the final few stairs and ended in a heap on the carpet.

Prue stared into the bear's glazed eyes. I've been attacked by a bear, she thought, and her infectious giggle, never quelled despite the best efforts of aunt and nuns, bubbled out of her.

A large man, at least in his fifties, thought Prue, like a bear himself, loomed over her as she sat on the floor getting her breath back.

'What a lovely laugh,' he said. 'Welcome to Mountjoy Castle.'

At Midwinter Hall Sylvester, expansive in a loose flowered shirt and an enormous pair of baggy shorts, was cross-examining Cleo.

'I was expecting one Prue Pagan. I spoke to Miss Dotteridge; definitely Prue Pagan. I was delighted, I knew Piers Pagan in my student days; he used to coach at the college. One of the best horn players around; tragic, when he died. I said to myself, this Prue must be a relation, it's not a usual name, and her father was a musician. So why are you here?'

Cleo looked Sylvester straight in the eye.

'Miss Dotteridge made a mistake,' she said with a big smile. 'Prue wouldn't want to work for a musician, she would have made that clear at the agency. Reminds her of her dead Pa, she's always been anti-music.' She paused. 'Besides, she was brought up by a prim aunt who thought all musicians had loose morals.'

'And you say she's working at Mountjoy Castle?' Sylvester shook his head. He noticed one of the chintz curtains hanging slightly unevenly and went across to the window to twitch it into place.

Cleo looked around the room, rather startled by it. Every surface was crowded with pieces of china, clocks, framed photos, little glass objects, tiny scraps of lace mounted on black velvet. Svelte bronze women with floating draperies supported table lamps, and there was a fine bronze of a cellist. The walls were covered as well, with gold-framed paintings, one or two unexpectedly modern canvases, more photographs, a framed order with a large Elizabeth R on it. Two or three gold putti flourished trumpets or balanced on wings; there were more on the ornate marble chimneypiece. Underfoot, the thick pale blue carpet felt us though it had two or three layers of underlay and was heavy to walk on. The blue was picked out in the glazed chintz curtains and the blue chair and sofa covers. Tassels, too, Cleo noticed; tassels on the curtains and on the Knole sofa, tassels on the cushions and attached to some miniatures which hung by the fireplace. Altogether an overpowering room, thought Cleo – and very nick-nacky for so large a man.

Sylvester swung round. 'A prim aunt wouldn't like Mountjoy Castle for Prue Pagan, if she knew anything about anything. My word, not the place for a young girl, I'd say. Able to look after herself, this friend of yours, is she? Character, good head on her shoulders, that kind of thing?'

Cleo was surprised, and thought for a moment before she answered, 'No, actually. She's very clever, but not, well, she isn't exactly clued-up about life. She's had a very restricted upbringing, you see, the nuns, and her aunt was very religious in a secty way.'

'Oh dear.' Sylvester heaved a big sigh. 'Does she have a boy-friend? Good with men?'

Cleo laughed. 'Goodness, no. No boyfriends. Not ever; total innocent about men.'

Sylvester looked more concerned. 'Is she a plain child? Peaky face, brown hair, sticky-out teeth, that kind of thing?'

'No,' said Cleo. 'As it happens, she's very attractive, but what does it matter? She's going to work mostly for Lady Mountjoy; it's not a beauty contest. Is Lord Mountjoy an evil lecher or something? Miss Dotteridge is usually very on the ball about that kind of thing.'

Sylvester appeared lost in thought. 'Mountjoy's all right,' he said finally. 'Got what I'd call a lecherous eye, and has certainly had his good times – getting on a bit now, though, and devoted to his wife. He won't do your friend any harm. No, it's some of the others. I'm not going to say any more; it would only alarm you, and forewarned is forearmed. I spend a lot of time up at the castle; we can keep an eye on her, you and me. Wouldn't like Piers's daughter to have a bad time. Now, come and meet Lily.'

'Lily?'

'Cook, housekeeper, what-have-you. Runs me. Runs this place. She made me get a secretary. I'm writing a book you see, got a contract and all that; never get it done without help, she says. We all do what Lily tells us, it's easier that way.'

The kitchen was large. An old range running along one wall and stone flags on the floor went with a floor-to-ceiling dresser hung with china. A fine old refectory table ran the length of the room; there the old-world charm stopped and the working part of the kitchen was white, stainless steel and functional.

'I'd get rid of the range and have the floor redone, myself,' Lily said to Cleo as she sat her down at the table. 'Run along, Sylvester, get on with your writing. Cleo needs a bit of time to settle in.'

There was a tray on the dresser ready laid with a teapot under a lace tea-cosy and a delicate cup and saucer.

'No good looking for the biscuits,' said Lily, without turning her head to see Sylvester looking in a cupboard. 'I've hidden them; you had your week's ration yesterday. Take your tea and go.'

Sylvester shrugged his huge shoulders, winked at Cleo and went out with his tray.

'You'll get used to him,' said Lily. 'Would you like some coffee?'

'Yes, please,' said Cleo. 'Can I make it?'

'Beans in the freezer over there, brown and purple bag. The grinder's in the cupboard under the drawers.' Lily took down two china mugs and plonked a cafetière on the table. She moved the kettle from the side of the Aga to the centre of the plate. 'Won't take a moment to come to the boil. Now, tell me about yourself. Sylvester said he thought you were a musician's daughter, but you aren't, are you? That's the other one? Knew you'd be coming here.'

Cleo was amused. 'How? Did you speak to Miss Dotteridge?'

'No, can't abide the woman. She sent a girl up here last year, hopeless. No idea how to occupy herself in the country. Fell in love with Sylvester, if you please – well, that was a waste of time, though he thought it was very funny – then went off and got herself pregnant.'

'What happened then?' asked Cleo.

'Moved in with a mechanic in Eyot. Wasn't the father of the baby, but it didn't seem to bother him.'

'Who was the father? Why didn't she move in with him?'

'Can see you've got an orderly mind; I like that in a young girl, shows sense. She said this man in Eyot wasn't the father, wouldn't say who the father was, but we all knew, of course. Still, she's happy now, but Miss Dotteridge should never have sent her. Normally very good at sending the right people to the right places, Sylvester says, but she slipped up there. Now there's this muddle, and I can see there's going to be trouble.'

Cleo pressed the switch on the grinder which roared into action as she spoke, drowning Lily's words. 'Sorry,' she said as she tipped the coffee into the pot and poured the water on. 'Missed what you said.'

'It doesn't matter,' said Lily. 'Strong-minded, this friend of yours?'

'Sylvester was asking me all kinds of questions about Prue,' said Cleo. 'Why the interest? What is this place where she's working – Castle Dracula?'

Lily twitched her nose. 'Not far off, at that. Definitely some blood-sucking goes on up there. You didn't answer my question.' She sat down at the table with her mug cradled in her hands and shot Cleo a penetrating look.

Cleo wriggled slightly and took a sip of coffee. 'Is Prue strong-minded? I dunno. She can be very obstinate, I think, when it's a moral question; she's got a very clear sense of right and wrong. I suppose I know her better than anyone, we've been friends for years, but I'm not sure that I really know her at all. With her peculiar upbringing she's never been able to let go and be herself; she's always had to please someone, either her aunt or the nuns.' She reached out absent-mindedly towards the sugar bowl and crunched some brown crystals. 'Due for a break-out, must be, eighteen and knows nothing about life outside the convent and her aunt's dreary little town, never been out with a boy, never even been to the cinema.'

'Lord help us,' said Lily, shaking her head. 'Nuns!' There was a world of scorn in her voice. 'Family? Dad, Mum, brothers?'

'None of those. Her parents both died when she was little. Her aunt brought her up; she was a religious nut. Fortunately, she's dead, died last month. That's why Prue's able to take this job.'

Lily's bright and knowing eyes invited Cleo to say more.

'It was her church that made her aunt so odd, very low, bare table for an altar, severe and depressing. You know the kind of thing. She disapproved of her brother, that's Prue's father, who was a musician. She took it out on Prue, was desperate that Prue shouldn't be like her father: Bohemian, musical, different.'

'Musicians are different. You'll know about artists, though, with your mother a painter. Wasn't the aunt musical, like her brother?'

'Prue said there wasn't money for lessons for both her father and her aunt when they were children. Naturally, what money there was got spent on the boy.' She paused, remembering Prue's wretchedness when the violin she had started to play at school had been taken away from her. 'The nuns thought Prue might be musical, but she wasn't allowed to learn.'

'Poor child. Now, tell me about yourself.'

To her surprise, Cleo did. At the end of half an hour, Lily had taken her life to pieces, examined it and slotted it away in what was clearly a powerful mind. Cleo normally felt a kind of mild tolerance for women of Lily's generation; they'd missed all the fun, she felt, young at a time when life must have been so dreary. Lily didn't fit easily into that pattern, Cleo realized. And she doubted if those sharp eyes and that sharp mind missed anything at all.

'What's Sylvester like?' she asked as she cleared away. Lily was diving into cupboards and the fridge.

'Stickler for punctuality, Sylvester, that's one thing you've got to remember. He wants you to start work at ten, be there. Lunch today will be at ten past one; lunch is always at ten past one. You can help me; then take a bicycle and ride up to the castle, see how young Prue's getting on.'

'I can't do that,' protested Cleo, as she began to pull the leaves off a lettuce. 'She may be working.'

'No. Lady Mountjoy isn't well, rests every afternoon. Mountjoy goes out with a gun. Done it all his life, never changed. Doesn't often shoot anything, mind; just likes being out, I reckon.'

'He might have left her something to do.'

'No, lives in the present, he does. Lady M won't have much for her yet, take my word for it. I've got some jars of chutney for Sophie – she cooks up there, not much older than you, you can take those with you. Tell her I want the jars back when she's finished with them.'

The back door to the kitchen opened with a bang.

'Lo, Lily. Hi, Cleo,' Luke plonked a thermos down on the table. 'Ta, Lily, saved my life, that did. Bloody hot out there. Did I hear

you've got something to go up to the Castle kitchen? I'll take it.'
He crossed the kitchen to the fridge and got out a can of Coke.

'No, you won't. Cleo's going up after lunch. You've got plenty
to do here. I'd lay off that Coke, too; rot your teeth.'

'Give us a break, Lily.' Luke shook the can to make it hiss as he
opened it. He downed it in one go; Lily swept the empty can away
from him and pushed him out of the kitchen. 'Okay, Lil, I'll return
to my back-breaking labours.' He winked at Cleo, who smiled back
at him.

'And don't call me Lil.'

Lily was well into her fifties, but she moved like a girl. Small and
wiry, she darted around the kitchen, far more deft and competent
than Cleo.

'Nice body,' said Cleo as Lily handed her oil and vinegar to make
a dressing.

'Go easy on that vinegar, Sylvester doesn't like it too sharp. Luke?
He swims a lot, always gives a man a good shape.'

'Has he worked here long?' Cleo asked casually.

Lily cackled. 'Interested, are you? Oh, I can see there's going
to be fun and games here this summer. He's at Oxford; this is his
vacation work. His Dad's gardener up at the Castle.'

Cleo was pleased. 'I'm going to Oxford in the autumn.'

'Are you now? Then you'll have something else in common,
won't you?'

She scooped mayonnaise on to a bowl of chopped potatoes, and
snipped chives on top.

'As well as what?'

'Never you mind. Hop along, tell Sylvester lunch is ready.
Through the hall, door next to the plant. You'll hear him.'

Cleo heard the plangent tones of a cello as soon as she went
down the passage towards the hall. She knocked; no response, so
she popped her head round the door. 'Lily says lunch is ready.'

Absorbed, Sylvester gave the merest nod of his head and went
on playing. As Cleo went back across the hall she looked at
the clock. Just after one. Sure enough, on the dot of ten past,
Sylvester appeared in the kitchen looking very pleased with himself.
He hummed as he sat down and unfolded his napkin. 'Looks
delicious as always, Lily. Now, are we going to do some work this
afternoon, Cleo?'

'No,' said Lily, stretching over and taking the potatoes away from

Sylvester. 'That's quite enough of those. There are a couple of things Cleo's going to do for me after lunch, and she's going to say hello to Prue, make sure she's okay up there.'

'Good,' said Sylvester. 'Tell her to come and visit soon, I want to meet Piers Pagan's girl. Then she'll know she's got some back-up here, when the going gets tough up at the Castle.'

Cleo stared at him. 'What do you mean, gets tough up at the Castle? What is this? If there's going to be any funny business where Prue's concerned, she can't stay.'

'Leave her to fight her own battles,' said Lily. 'She'll come to no harm for the moment. For the future – well, time will tell. Have another tomato.'

4

'It's a very overpowering place,' Prue said to Cleo. 'And I'm not quite sure why I'm here, but I expect I'll find out.'

'Sylvester is worried about you.'

Prue looked puzzled. 'Sylvester?' Then, 'Oh, how slow I am, your cellist. Why should he worry about me?'

'He knew your father. Everybody seems to have known your father.'

'More than I did,' said Prue.

Wouldn't it make a difference, she thought, to be able to ring home, tell your parents you'd arrived safely, describe the castle, the people, know they were interested in every word you had to say . . . Then she laughed.

'What's funny?' said Cleo.

'I was just imagining having a mother and father, ringing them up, telling them about all this. And then I remembered the girls at school, spending their time not ringing their parents, thinking they were being spied on if their mothers so much as asked how they were.'

'That's where all the family fantasies come from, from people who haven't got them. I always think, how lovely to have a brother, what a special friendship that would be.'

'Yes,' said Prue.

'Only people who do have brothers spend all their time arguing with them, and mostly despise them thoroughly. Best on your own, Prue.'

'I suppose so,' said Prue.

'Now,' said Cleo, brisk and practical. 'I'll have to report back to Lily and Sylvester, just wait till you meet them, then you'll understand. What about this cook?'

'Sophie. She's young, which is all right, but a bit terse. She's out this afternoon, or you could have seen for yourself.'

'Lily sent these up for her, shall I just dump them on the table?'
'Oh, yes, I should think so.'
'Come for a walk. You don't seem to be very busy.'
'I'm not, but I don't think I'd better.'
'Soon, then.'

It was nearly a week before Cleo was able to entice Prue away from her work. Prue, always dutiful, had been diffident about sloping off, although she still wasn't sure just what her working hours and duties were. The Mountjoys were vague on the subject, it was all very casual.

Only person to ask is Sophie, she thought, and just have to risk getting her head bitten off again.

Sophie sat at the kitchen table reading *Today*. 'Look at this,' she said. 'Vicar has three wives. Amazing what some people get up to, imagine the energy. You go, Prue. The castle falls asleep in the afternoons when it's only Mountjoy and Magdalena here; he goes for a walk and she has to rest. Wait until some of the family come up, then it's all go.'

'What are you going to do?' Prue asked her.

Sophie pursed her lips and hummed a few bars of a hymn. 'I'll wander down to the village later, I dare say; Magdalena wants me to see Jacob – the vicar, you know, about flowers for Sunday. Are you churchgoers – no, you two must be Catholic. You've been at a convent, Magdalena told me.'

'We aren't Catholic, though,' said Prue.

Sophie raised her head, listening. 'Bicycle. Either Luke come to see what I'm up to, or your friend.' She folded the newspaper and tucked it in the drawer of the kitchen table. Then she stretched her arms above her head and yawned.

Prue went to the door.

'I'm sure that path is steeper than it was last time,' Cleo said. 'I'm hot and grubby.' She looked over Prue's shoulder into the kitchen.

'Hi, I'm Cleo. You're Sophie. Okay if I leave the bicycle down there in the courtyard? I did last time, there wasn't anyone here to ask.'

Sophie shrugged. 'Up to you. Don't know why you came on it anyway, can't really ride on that track. Luke usually just walks up. Don't bother about locking it, no one here goes in for petty crime.'

'I like cycling,' said Cleo, unperturbed by Sophie's remarks.

Prue and Cleo walked slowly along the track which led from the castle down to the village. It ran between ancient high hedgerows tangled with hawthorns and wild roses. Deep ruts from wetter days had dried into thick earthy hummocks. Their sandals sent up little spurts of dust as they walked; around them fields were parched and pale with weeks of sunshine and no rain.

'This should all be green and misty,' said Cleo. 'It's like the end of the world, this heatwave.' She glanced at Prue. 'Doesn't seem to affect you, the heat. You look very bouncy.'

'I like it hot,' said Prue, glad that she had given in to Cleo; it was good to be away from the castle for a while, and to have someone to talk to.

'See what you mean about Sophie,' Cleo said. 'Is she always as abrupt as that?'

Prue swung herself up on to a stile and paused, perching on the wooden rail.

'She is brusque, but she seems quite friendly underneath. I think she's got a secret, though.'

Cleo pushed Prue off the stile and hauled herself over. 'Got a secret? What do you mean?'

'Just that. Is she Luke's girlfriend?'

'Hope not,' said Cleo. 'I fancy him like mad. Super body, yum.'

Prue was shocked. 'You shouldn't talk like that. And yes, he is Sophie's boyfriend, I think. She asked me this morning if I'd ever been in love, and I said no, and she laughed and said I was lucky, that being in love was hell.'

'Mmmm,' said Cleo. They had come to a gate across a farmyard. 'Do we just go through here?'

'Yes,' said Prue. 'I came this way earlier this week, with a message; watch out for the geese, they rush at you.'

As she spoke, a large goose shot out of a barn and advanced purposefully towards them. Prue stamped her foot, the goose stopped in its tracks and let out a malevolent hiss. A flurry of hens rose clacking into the air. A dog barked; a horse put its head over a stable door to see what was going on. Inside the house a baby began to wail.

'Come on,' said Prue, 'we go out this way. What a commotion.'

'I hate the country,' said Cleo as they came out on the village

41

green. 'Nature's all very well, but it's vicious and noisy as far as I'm concerned.'

'The air's wonderful.'

Cleo took a deep sniff and wrinkled her nose. 'Cows, silage, no, give me traffic fumes any day.'

The village's main and only road ran straight between the high banks of the village green. The river cut the green in half the other way. Prue leaned over the thick stone walls of the bridge and looked down into what was now hardly more than a stream. 'You could paddle in this,' she said.

Cleo joined her. 'Lily says it's a torrent after storms in the hills.'

Prue sighed. 'Can't imagine it; can't imagine storms for that matter. It's all so peaceful.'

'Can't loll about here all day,' said Cleo briskly. 'We'll go to the village shop, Lily asked me to get something for her, and besides, I need some chocolate.'

Cleo was a lifelong chocolate addict. Best of all she liked bitter black chocolate, but when the desire for chocolate was strong, she'd even chew the thin covering of pale chocolate off the back of a biscuit. She was pleased to find one of her favourite brands tucked among the Smarties and Milk Bars. The shop was empty; the shopkeeper Bill was out of sight, in his little snug behind the shop. Prue idly read the local newspaper upside down while Cleo hunted for more chocolate.

A booming voice made the girls jump. 'Errands for Lily?' said Sylvester. 'And is this Prue? My word, you remind me of your father. I'm delighted to meet you. Have they eaten you alive up at the castle yet?'

Startled, Prue's eyes opened wide and she stared at Sylvester. 'My father?'

'Yes, you're Piers Pagan's girl, I discussed that with Cleo here.' He gave her a shrewd look. 'Yes, you do look like him. Lovely man, lovely musician. What do you play?'

'I'm not musical,' said Prue.

'Poo,' said Sylvester robustly. 'Piers Pagan's daughter, and not musical? I don't believe it. Do you remember him?'

Prue's eyes grew thoughtful. 'I remember him playing the horn, and my mother singing. I can't see them vividly any more, though. I used to, when I was little. My father was very kind.'

'Kind? Yes, he was, a generous man and a generous musician.

Everyone liked him. You've got his smile, Prue. If you've got his nature as well, you won't go far wrong.'

He rattled a can of coins for the blind which was on the counter. 'Where's Bill?'

The shopkeeper emerged from the back, blinking in the sunlight which streamed through the door.

'Hello, Bill,' said Sylvester. 'Come to pick up my paper – thank you,' he added, twitching it out of Prue's hand. 'And I'll pay for this young lady's chocolate.'

'I can pay for it,' said Cleo.

'Course you can, but now you'll have to offer me some. I love dark chocolate, and Lily's banned it.'

'Seventy-eight p,' said Bill.

'Here you are, Cleo. Do you want a bar of chocolate, Prue?'

'No, thank you. I can't eat it very often, it brings me out in lumps. Anyway, it's too hot for chocolate.'

Sylvester laughed. 'Never too hot for some things, and chocolate's one of them. Won't talk about the others.'

'Don't be vulgar, Sylvester.' A tall, spiky woman edged in beside the wool display. She stared at Prue and Cleo. 'Who are you?' she said rudely. Without waiting for an answer she turned to Sylvester. Her eyes travelled up and down his large frame, taking in the old plimsolls encasing his big feet, a huge flappy pair of colonial shorts and a vivid African bush shirt. 'You're getting very sloppy, Sylvester.'

Sylvester politely jammed the door further back to make more room. 'You'd dress like this if you had to wear the ridiculous clothes I do at concerts. I feel comfortable in these.'

'You upset the natives.'

Sylvester was in point of fact a source of joy and delight to the villagers; they loved to have something to gossip about.

'Seen Mr Tate's latest?' they would say over a pint in the Midwinter Arms. 'Bright blue, electric blue, just like my Katie has for school.' Others would nod knowingly into their beer, storing up the details for friends and relations who hadn't seen Sylvester's new track suit.

'Bill likes my shorts, don't you, Bill?'

Bill was a tall, thin man who admitted to being sixty and was probably nearer eighty. He approved of Sylvester's shorts since he himself wore shorts all the year round, even when the village cracked with ice and frozen snow. He nodded and shot an unamiable look towards Daisy, who took no notice; she had now turned her full attention on Prue and Cleo. 'You're the girls from London, of course. Come to work for the summer. I'm Daisy Pugh, the vicar's wife. Will we see you in church on Sunday?' She didn't wait for them to speak, but answered herself. 'No, of course not, you're Papists, aren't you? Been to a convent, I hear. Well, you'll know how to behave, I dare say, which is more than you can say for some of the young people round here.'

Cleo looked grave. 'That's what people usually think, but naturally now we're away from the convent we behave dreadfully. We're so repressed.'

Prue gave a violent shake as she tried not to laugh, and Sylvester swept Prue and Cleo in front of him as he lumbered out of the shop. The handbell attached to the door on a string clanged loudly behind them.

Daisy rummaged for her newspaper. 'Sylvester's getting very peculiar,' she said to Bill. 'It's being a musician that makes him odd.'

Daisy approved of people who worked hard, dressed suitably and got on in the world. She mistrusted artists; they were driven by daemons. Daemons to Daisy were like germs on a clean kitchen floor. Uncontrollable, the enemy, dangerous. And yet Sylvester with all his odd ways managed to make a lot of money. 'He's very arrogant, of course,' Daisy went on. 'I know he can play the cello, but . . .'

Bill darted out from behind the counter. 'Your paper's here, Daisy, no need to mess everything up. And Sylvester's is a rare gift; he's one of the greats, Daisy, as you very well know. If you're paying for the paper, you owe me for those three bottles of wine as well.'

'I'll pop in later with the money,' Daisy said with dignity. 'I just want to catch up Sylvester and those girls. We must fix up some tennis or something, young girls like some fun.'

Bill went back into his lair, shaking his head. 'Fun! Well, there's going to be plenty of fun here this summer, you could tell them that, couldn't you, Lord Jim?' Bill's dog twitched his tail and the pair of them settled down to watch the cartoons on the telly.

They sat on the flagged terrace which ran along the back of

Midwinter Hall. The surrounding fells were softened by the haze of heat; closer at hand, lawns ran down to fields and then a wood.

'What's on the other side of the wood?' Prue asked.

'A lake. A tarn, really. Good for swimming, and for skating when it freezes in winter. Not for me, of course: I'd fall over and break the ice.'

It was impossible to think of dark, icy winter time in the blaze of summer. Lily had made a jug of iced tea. Cleo lay on the grass on her back, her short skirt rolled back so that the sun could brown her legs.

'Careful of the sun,' Sylvester said. 'Don't want you red and peeling all over my papers.'

'I never burn,' said Cleo without opening her eyes.

'Got Valdemar's colouring,' remarked Lily.

'Mmm,' said Sylvester, looking again at Cleo's peaceful pose.

'Who is Valdemar?' asked Prue. She made strange noises as she sucked the last dregs of her tea from the bottom of her glass with a straw, and grinned when she saw Sylvester's startled face.

'That's disgusting, Prue, they wouldn't have put up with that at your convent.'

'No,' said Prue, merrily, 'but now I can do it if I want to.'

'Lax,' said Sylvester. 'Who is Valdemar? One of the Mountjoys. You'll meet him in due course, I expect. He's nearly always up here in the summer.'

Lily cackled. 'Course she'll meet him. Destiny, I'd say. Lord, it's almost worth taking that job at the castle to be in the thick of it.'

Sylvester tutted. 'Don't threaten, Lily. You know I can't do without you, and you couldn't stand the Mountjoys and their ways for five minutes.' Prue looked at the pair of them. Like ancient statues, she thought suddenly. Knowing, and mischievous, laughing at the helpless mortals. She turned her head and looked up towards the castle. Up there, you could look down on the valley and laugh at little beings coming and going on their sunlit way. Or you could look the other way, over to the darker fells behind and beyond the castle. Fiend's Fell, Wild Fell, Helm Fell: she was learning their names.

'Getting to know the fells, young Prue?' said Sylvester. 'They haunt you. I see them in my dreams when I'm at the other end of the earth. Each has its own character, you know.'

'I can see that.'

'Don't fill the girl's head with nonsense, Sylvester,' said Lily. 'Pour yourself some more tea, Prue, and tell us what you're doing for Lord Mountjoy.'

'He seems very nice,' said Prue.

Sylvester and Lily looked at her.

'I shouldn't talk about my work to other people.'

Sylvester grinned at her. 'My dear, by the afternoon everything you've typed in the morning is known by the whole village. We have no secrets here, or rather no small secrets. Big secrets, yes, but all the day-to-day things, well, they're common knowledge.'

Prue hadn't lived in a village before, but she had seen Sophie gossiping at the kitchen door to Mr Ivyson who delivered the milk; then there was the postman, and the coal man; Bill must know a lot of what went on. They probably knew about her as well; look at Daisy's remarks about the convent. It didn't bother her especially; the nuns had walked in and out of her room, her things, her mind, her feelings for years. Not to mention her aunt's relentless interrogations about how she spent every hour of her holidays. 'I like the Mountjoys,' was all she said.

Mountjoy had intimidated her at first; he was so big, and that powerful boom of the English upper classes had alarmed her; and he was very masculine. Used to the nuns and a man-hating aunt, Prue was ill-at-ease with men. Funny, though, she didn't find Sylvester alarming at all, even though he was very big as well. Magdalena Mountjoy seemed kind, although clearly not well, Prue didn't think she'd ever seen anyone so tired. 'It's nothing terrible,' she had assured Prue, seeing the expression on her face. 'Just my age, the doctors say. I'm supposed to take more exercise, but that's a ridiculous suggestion when I can hardly get up in the mornings.'

Prue was touched by Mountjoy's evident concern about his wife. However, if Magdalena Mountjoy was too tired to do more than dictate one or two letters to her in the morning and ask her to fix some appointments, and Mountjoy was out walking every afternoon, then she wasn't going to justify her wages.

'Is Magdalena any better?' asked Sylvester, stroking a large tabby cat which had strolled along the terrace and jumped on to his lap. 'She should see a specialist, Dr Gregson is no better than a witchdoctor. She needs someone who'll know what's wrong.'

Lily snorted. 'Nothing wrong with Magdalena,' she said firmly. 'I know exactly what her problem is, even if no one else does.'

Cleo sat up and brushed some dried grass off her legs. 'Psycho-logical?' she said. 'A woman's illness?'

Lily laughed. 'Get on with you. All in the mind? Oh, no.'

'What, then?'

'Who lives will see.'

Prue and Cleo climbed the stone staircase that twisted in a tight spiral up to her room. Cleo took a deep breath as she reached the top. 'You'll keep fit, Prue, that's one thing. Goodness,' she added, looking round. 'How very Rapunzel!'

Prue laughed. 'Yes, only my hair isn't long enough to let down, and if it were, whoever would climb up it?'

Cleo hauled herself up into the window embrasure, with its two-foot-wide ledge. 'Amazing view!'

'Isn't it,' agreed Prue, kneeling beside her. 'I'm going to put a cushion here on the ledge and then I can sit and read.'

Cleo pushed one of the narrow leaded windows further open and peered out.

'Careful, Cleo,' said Prue. 'It's a long way down.'

'Yes, it would have to be a very determined lover. Easier to come up the stairs.'

Prue laughed. 'Only there aren't any princes or lovers.'

'Wait and see,' said Cleo darkly. 'There's always the postman. Where do the others live? Where's the bathroom?'

'Next floor down,' said Prue. 'Blue door. Then below that's an office. I have the whole tower to myself. It's at the end of the part of the castle where the family live, so they aren't very far away.'

'If I were Lady Mountjoy, I'd have this room for myself,' said Cleo. 'You can't call it a bedroom, really; has to be a bedchamber. They must have had that bed specially made; look at the way the curved bedhead fits into the wall. Must have built it up here, too, can you imagine getting it up that spiral staircase?'

They clattered down the stone steps to Prue's office. Cleo turned her nose up at the ancient typewriter. 'Tell them to get you something more modern,' she said. 'Can't expect you to work on that.' She looked out of the window. 'Is this your boss?'

Prue joined her and looked down. 'Yes.'

'Good-looking. Wonder if he's a pouncer. You'd better introduce me, I can always tell, then you'll know what to expect.'

Prue wondered why Cleo always thought of sex when she saw a

man. To her, Mountjoy was an employer, a man almost old enough to be her grandfather, and one who was happily married.

'Yes,' went on Cleo, watching him. 'Sexy walk and a lecherous eye.'

'Oh, stop it, Cleo,' said Prue, annoyed. 'Why can't you ever see people just as people? Why do you always go on about their bodies and whether they're sexy or not?'

'Because that's the way the world ticks. Very dull, otherwise. Tired wife, mmm, wonder if he's sleeping with this Sophie in the kitchen.'

'Nobody's sleeping with anybody in the kitchen.'

Cleo laughed. 'No, very uncomfortable, unless they play games, cook and master, you know. Doesn't look the sort to me, but you can never tell.'

'You said Sophie was Luke's girlfriend.'

'Wish she weren't. Look, he's coming this way. Introduce me.'

Prue opened her mouth to protest; would Mountjoy want to meet her friend? Such niceties never crossed Cleo's mind as she ran down the remaining steps and out into the courtyard. By the time Prue jumped off the bottom step, Cleo was already talking to Mountjoy. He laughed at something she said, and smiled at Prue; then he turned and walked with Cleo towards her bicycle. Prue followed them.

Mountjoy wheeled the bicycle to the courtyard entrance for Cleo and said a friendly goodbye. He turned and almost bumped into Prue. She backed away; he was hot from his walk, his shirt slightly darkened with sweat; he smelt slightly, but not, Prue suddenly realized, unpleasantly. He didn't notice her embarrassment, smiled at her and waved a hand towards the door.

'Just going to have a shower. Then we'll go to the East room, where the family papers are. I'd like you to sort them out a bit while you're here, they're not very organized. Wait for me in the hall.'

'Quite different from Sylvester,' said Cleo appreciatively.

Prue had liked Sylvester. 'You can swap back if you like,' she offered.

'No thanks,' said Cleo. 'Mountjoy's too old for me, though I bet he was good in his time. I'd rather be at Midwinter Hall where I can lust after Luke.'

She was gone before Prue could expostulate. Prue knew Cleo in this mood; it was amazing how Cleo clicked with men. How did she do it? Was it just thinking about them the way she did?

Prue thought about Luke as she walked down the passage to the hall, a notebook and pen in hand. He seemed nice enough, lively, clever face, but nothing to get steamed up about. Prue's own half-admitted tastes ran to fair men.

Perhaps life would be easier without sex, thought Prue, committing an act of hubris that would undoubtedly bring the retribution of the gods upon her. Eros, lurking in the dark corners of the paintings on the walls, looked down at Prue. He was there in the seemingly chaste marble women on their plinths, in the hot roving eyes of the men drinking a toast in the picture which hung in the hall, and in the lascivious scenes sprawled across the tapestries, the subjects of which made Prue blink as she realized what they were.

'Come along,' said Mountjoy cheerfully, as he led the way back along the gallery and into a stone passage. 'Watch your step, the flagstones are very uneven. The Muniment Room is in here,' and he pushed open a heavy, ancient wooden door with huge metal hinges. 'All the family papers are kept in here. There are contracts, deeds, grants from the crown, that kind of thing as well, but you won't be concerned with them.'

A beam of sunlight shafted into the room, showing the dust.

'Dusty!' said Mountjoy. 'Hope you're not allergic to dust. I've never got round to sorting this lot out. Well, I haven't got the mind for it, get impatient with bits of paper. Anyway, my nephew, he'll be here at the castle quite soon, he wants me to get these in order. He has plans for the castle, not sure what, but it's easier to do as he wants. Very commanding sort of fellow; you'll like him, I dare say. Women seem to.'

Prue looked around her in dismay. There were papers everywhere, letters, accounts, inventories. Judging by the handwriting, some of them were quite old.

'You need an expert for these, not a secretary,' she said.

Mountjoy poo-poohed her. 'No, no. You'll be able to sort things out, different handwriting, different kinds of document, that sort of thing. These are mostly eighteenth and nineteenth century; my father had a very good man who worked for him, kept all the stuff from this century in apple-pie order. Well, he could afford to employ someone just for that. And there was a librarian, archivist chappie, whatever you call them; he worked on all the older papers. They are important, some of them, historically I mean – some letters and so on were in an exhibition in the British Museum last year.' Mountjoy spoke with pride. Prue could see that 'all this' mattered to him. 'I never had a son, you see. No one to take all this on; Valdemar's my sister's child, he'll inherit, but he's not interested in the past, only in the future. Quite right, really, we don't count for anything these days.'

Prue gathered some papers up to clear a space at a big desk tucked under the window. 'I'm not qualified to do this. I'll do what I can, but . . .'

That's right, do what you can. I can see you're clever. I'm not, but I like to have clever people around me. Magdalena's clever, very clever.' He sighed.

Prue coughed as a flurry of dust rose into the air. 'Miss Dotteridge said there was a little boy at the castle. Is he your nephew's son?'

Mountjoy looked at her, his mind elsewhere. 'Little boy? Oh, Thomas! No, Valdemar isn't married. He should be, getting on, forty now.' His eyes came back into focus. 'Thomas, that's who you mean. Hortense's son. Hortense's my niece. Thomas is at school in Eyot. He sings; he's a chorister, at the Cathedral. Be home for the holidays soon, liven the place up.'

'But his parents don't live here?' Prue was interested. It was a shame to think of the Mountjoys rattling round in this huge place on their own; it was obviously meant for family life. I hope he doesn't think I'm being inquisitive, she thought. I am, but maybe he likes talking about his family.

He didn't seem to mind. 'Hasn't got a father. Hortense, his mother, lives in India, does good works.'

Mountjoy closed an old volume he had been looking at with a bang, and a cloud of dust blew into his face. 'Best thing to do, borrow the little vacuum cleaner Sophie uses for the car, clean up before you begin. It's too hot to be breathing dust.'

Prue was glad to get out into the fresh air. Heavy with heat, it was still better than the fusty dustiness of the Muniment Room. Mountjoy headed off to see Magdalena. Prue decided to go to the kitchen and get a drink of water. If Sophie was there, she could ask her about the vacuum cleaner.

Sophie was in the kitchen, and in a foul temper. She turned the tap on so hard that the water shot out of the glass she was holding and soaked her tee shirt. She swore.

Prue blinked at Sophie's vehemence. 'It'll dry very quickly in this weather.'

'Yes,' said Sophie rudely. 'Okay for you to say that, you aren't sodden. Here, drink your bloody water.'

Prue realized that Sophie's temper wasn't really directed at her. She reached out for the glass of water and drank, glad to wash the dryness from her throat.

Sophie noticed the dust on Prue's shirt. 'You've been in the Muniment Room, haven't you? Mountjoy's been trying to get someone to tidy those papers up for years. Dull job, I can tell you.'

'Family papers can be quite interesting. They might be full of scandalous stories; people who've lived in a castle like this can't be dull.'

'These ones can. No one in this family has done anything important or interesting for centuries. Inbred, sickly . . .'

'Mountjoy doesn't look inbred or sickly.'

'No, but he can't have any children, can he? Low fertility, not enough sperm, that's his problem. It's because his mother's his cousin or aunt or something. I tell you, these people just aren't like the rest of us.'

Prue was fascinated, but she felt she ought not to be talking about the Mountjoys in this casual way. Mountjoy's sperm was surely a private matter.

Sophie let out a screech of laughter. 'Private or privates? Listen, duckie, no room here for nice feelings. Every man or woman for themselves; they'll trample all over you if they get the chance, don't forget that.'

Prue couldn't believe that; the Mountjoys were charming, friendly and courteous. Her only concern was that she wouldn't be earning her wages. Sophie laughed at that idea as well.

'You'll earn every penny, let me tell you, and a lot more besides. You've only been here a few days, and with Magdalena not very well it all seems very quiet. Just wait. Thomas breaks up soon; well, that boy's a real handful. Then Valdemar will be up; orders, orders, I can't tell you how bossy he is. Bringing his girlfriend, too; don't know how she puts up with him, but she's been with him for ages. People say they'll get married one of these days, but I can't see Valdemar getting hitched.'

Sophie seemed to have talked herself out of her temper; Prue ventured a question. 'Are you going out with Luke?'

Sophie's retort was swift and terse. 'Mind your own bloody business.'

Prue blinked and drew back; clearly, cosy chats with Sophie weren't going to be a feature of her time at the castle. She got up. 'Sorry. I wasn't prying, it was just I thought . . .'

'You didn't think. Luke fancies me, okay? That's as far as it goes. He's a bore if you want to know, should find himself a nice girl and stop pestering me. Now do me a favour and buzz off. I'm late with things, and Magdalena wants an early supper in her room. You'll have dinner with Mountjoy in the dining room.'

Prue was edging towards the door, but she stopped when she heard that. 'What about you?'

'I usually eat with him, but since you're here, I can go out. It's Women's Institute tonight.'

'Do you go to that?'

Sophie stared at her, her slightly crossed eyes disconcertingly angry. 'No. Grow this in a yoghurt pot, I do like your sponge, Mavis, what would I do with all that crap? No, I certainly don't go to the WI.'

Prue thought she heard an extra mumbled sentence, 'but everyone else does, thank God.' She must have misheard; why would Sophie say that?

What a strange person Sophie was, Prue thought as she headed for her tower. It was a pity. It would be good to have someone to talk to at the castle, someone near her own age. If she was going to spend all day in the dust with dead Mountjoys, a bit of liveliness in her off-duty hours would have been welcome.

Oh, well, she doesn't seem to like anyone very much, said Prue to herself as she searched in the big grey metal cupboard for a box of envelope files she had not noticed on a shelf.

Dinner at eight, Sophie had said. That gave her time to make a start in the Muniment Room. Bother, she had forgotten to ask for the vacuum cleaner. She would just have to put up with the dust. No way was she going to venture into Sophie's lair again with her in that mood; what on earth was the matter with her?

5

Sophie wheeled the trolley into the dining-room. In winter a dark room, now, in high summer, it was flooded with evening sunlight. The golden glow suited the room, bringing light to dim corners and giving the furniture a rich sheen.

Prue stood by a deep sash window and looked out over the shadow-streaked lawns. She hadn't yet got used to the scale of everything at the castle, the size and number of rooms, the grounds, the sheer age of the building with centuries of family possessions still in daily use.

'You can lay the table, Prue,' said Sophie. 'Table mats in the top drawer there, knives and forks in the third drawer down. Napkins at the bottom. Mountjoy likes the candles lit; pointless at this time of year, but he'll only make a fuss if it isn't done. Hopes to drive away the evil spirits, I reckon. Food's all here.' She gestured towards the trolley. 'The hotplate's on; it'll need turning off when you've finished. Salad and a pudding underneath, cream in a jug on the side. Mountjoy will see to the wine, the glasses are over there. I'm off, shan't be back till late. See you tomorrow.'

Sophie shot out of the door, only to pop her head back round it again. 'Leave the washing up, I'll do it in the morning.' She noticed what Prue was doing. 'Three places, Prue, not two.'

'You said Lady Mountjoy was eating in her room.'

'Yes, but Sylvester's here. Bye.'

Why? wondered Prue. He hadn't mentioned he was coming. Oh, well. She shrugged her shoulders and got another mat out of the drawer.

'Bustle about, young Prue,' a voice boomed out. 'Don't keep us waiting for our victuals.'

'Hello,' said Prue.

'Hello,' said Sylvester. 'I know what you're thinking. Why should you wait on me? Or even Mountjoy here. You girls are all getting a bit bolshie; we'll have women conductors on the podium, that'll be the next thing.' He heaved with laughter at his own joke.

Mountjoy took the remark seriously. 'Women just can't do that kind of thing, Sylvester. They don't have the authority. Like the army, it's no good denying it; men have the habit of command. Not all men, I grant you that, but some men. It's lacking in women. I daresay it's to do with genes or hormones.'

Sylvester, who thought that purple pigs were more likely to fly across the sky than women conduct important orchestras, paid no attention. He rarely paid any attention to Mountjoy, treating him with the broad tolerance he felt for small children and animals.

'What are we eating? Smells good.' He lifted the lid of the dish that Prue had put on the table. 'Cold soup, chicken casserole, good, good. That Sophie of yours can cook, Mountjoy. I'll swap her for Lily; bet she wouldn't nag me the way that old witch does.'

'Lily's a treasure,' said Mountjoy, pouring some wine for Prue. 'Marvellous woman, knows everything.'

Sylvester took a generous mouthful of soup and crumbled a roll with an enormous hand. 'She knows too much altogether. Past, present and future sees. Lily's in league with the devil, if you ask me. Prue, pass the pepper. And eat up, we need you to be alert and attentive after dinner. You're going to take notes for us.'

Unused to alcohol, Prue sipped her wine a little doubtfully. She decided she liked it, and drank some more, then held her glass up against the candlelight. Such a wonderful, warm, rich colour, she thought dreamily. She listened contentedly to Mountjoy and Sylvester's easy conversation. What a long way away Witherton seemed; how pleasant to be with these people who were so very different from her aunt and her joyless circle.

Magdalena Mountjoy looked drawn and exhausted. Her dark hair, an inheritance from a South American mother, had only a few strands of grey; its youthful colour went oddly with her pale, shadowed face. Forty-five, she looked ten years older, even in the gentle, flattering light of a summer evening. She was resting on a chaise longue when the dinner group came in. She waved a hand towards a door on the other side of the room. 'Prue, be very kind, will you, and make coffee for us. Sylvester, don't sit on that chair, you'll damage it.'

Mountjoy drew up a chair close to his wife; Sylvester planted himself in a substantial armchair, an injured expression on his face.

Prue went to make coffee. The door led to a little room equipped with a tiny sink, two gas rings and some shelves. No instant coffee, but Prue found a bag of coffee beans in the fridge – why the fridge? she thought. Are Magdalena's wits going? Prue wasn't very knowledgeable about coffee. Her aunt had disapproved of it.

Now what? She looked uncertainly at the beans. In tiny gold print on the side of the packet were some instructions. Good. Grind the beans . . . all very well, but how? There was a quaint-looking machine clamped to the edge of a shelf. Prue swung the handle; it looked more like a meat mincer than a machine for grinding coffee. She could always ask, she supposed, but they would stare at her, amazed that she didn't know how to make coffee. Besides, she was beginning to realize just how many things she didn't know about. If she asked all the time, she would drive everyone mad. No, she had to tackle things for herself, and she would start with the coffee. How much coffee? It didn't say. Oh well. She tipped a few beans into the grinder and cautiously turned the handle. It worked; a spoonful of ground coffee scattered over the shelf. So far, so good. Now, what to put it in? That was it, a little drawer which fitted under the grinder. Next, coffee pot? Jug?

'Hurry up with the coffee,' said Sylvester from the other room. 'We need you in here; also, I want some coffee. Make sure it's strong, young Prue, none of your weedy brews.'

Prue realized she hadn't put the kettle on. That at least wasn't a problem. She squinted again at the instructions on the side of the coffee packet, gave up and poured some more beans into the grinder. She decanted the ground coffee into a bowl and ground some more.

'What on earth are you doing?' Sylvester had come in search of his coffee. 'Good heavens, what a mound of coffee. Got carried away with that little gadget, didn't you? Just like your father, never do anything by halves. And don't giggle, how can I concentrate?'

'What do you make your coffee in, Magdalena?' he called across the room.

'Cafetière.' Magdalena's voice was wan compared to Sylvester's vigorous booming tones. 'Cupboard by the sink.'

With Sylvester's help the coffee was ready in no time. Prue put cups and saucers, beautiful, cloudy blue porcelain ones, on a tray together with sugar, cream and some small biscuits which Sylvester had discovered. She carried the tray into the sitting room and carefully poured the coffee. Then she perched herself in a corner of the room away from the others.

'Come nearer,' said Magdalena, laughing slightly at her. 'We won't eat you.'

Prue smiled back at her. 'No, I'm fine here, thank you.' She still didn't know why she was there, what they wanted her to do.

Magdalena was talking, her voice quiet and low, little animation on a face that Prue felt sure was meant to be full of life. How awful to be ill, tired day after day, and not to know what was wrong with you, if Sophie was to be believed.

Prue tried to concentrate, but the wine had made her sleepy. Yawning, she looked out of the window, watching the long shadows cast by the trees across the lawns; a faint smell of cut grass wafted in through the open window.

'Got those dates down, Prue?' said Sylvester suddenly.

Prue started. She had no idea what they were talking about; she went scarlet and wrote squiggly nothings down in her notebook, hoping she looked as though she had been paying attention.

Magdalena came to her rescue. 'If it's from the ninth to the twenty-third, we'll have to check on the insurance; I think it runs out on the twentieth.'

Sylvester nodded. 'Make a note of that, Prue. Mountjoy, you arranged the insurance, didn't you?'

Mountjoy agreed, his eyes never leaving his wife's face. They went on with their discussion. Prue concentrated; it was some kind of a music festival, obviously an annual event. Sylvester wanted her to note down what was agreed. 'Action Points,' he said dramatically. 'Otherwise it's all talk, and nothing gets done.'

They began to argue about where the events would take place. The festival was centred in Midwinter and the neighbouring village of Gossiby, with most events in local churches. Normally, Prue gathered, the Castle was the headquarters; now Mountjoy was worried about Magdalena's health; she would try to do too much. Sylvester and Mountjoy began a slightly acrimonious discussion about other possibilities.

Prue looked across at Magdalena. Her eyes were shut; she was paler than ever. Sylvester and Mountjoy went on talking. They didn't seem to have noticed. She's going to faint, thought Prue; dropping her notebook and pen, she reached the sofa just at Magdalena struggled to her feet, stood waveringly for a moment and then collapsed.

*　　*　　*

Consternation.

Prue stood stock-still, waiting for Sylvester and Mountjoy to do something. Then she realized that they were so busy being concerned that they weren't capable of doing anything practical. She put her hand on Mountjoy's sleeve. 'Quickly, your doctor's phone number.' He looked at her in surprise. How useless men are, thought Prue.

'372,' said Sylvester. Prue got to the phone before he did, and dialled. 'What's his name,' she hissed at Sylvester, her hand over the receiver.

'Dr Gregson,' said Sylvester.

'He's away,' said Mountjoy. 'Damn the man, just when we need him. There'll be a locum.'

There was: Dr Mukherjee would be up at once.

'Bloody foreigner,' said Mountjoy furiously. He was supporting Magdalena, who was gradually reviving.

'I think she's going to be sick,' said Sylvester anxiously.

Magdalena shook her head slightly. 'No, just very dizzy,' she whispered.

'Tell you what,' said Sylvester. 'Dr Gregson hasn't been any use, has he, clucking about time of life and your age. I know what he's like; maybe this chap's a bit more up-to-date.'

'Not chap,' said Prue. 'It's a woman.'

Dr Mukherjee had only arrived in the village the day before. Of course the whole village was agog at the news; fancy the health people sending someone like that. She'd give them herbs and strange potions: it was all the government's fault . . .

Mountjoy and Sylvester blinked at the astonishing physical beauty of Dr Mukherjee; nothing could be more different from grumpy, middle-aged Dr Gregson.

'Efficient, too,' said Sylvester as she swept them out of the room and shut the door on them.

'I do hope she knows what she's doing,' said Mountjoy in a worried voice. 'She can only just have qualified.'

'Then she'll have it all at her fingertips,' said Prue. You'd think they'd be grateful to have any doctor up here so swiftly, she thought, let alone one who clearly knew exactly what she was doing.

Sylvester and Mountjoy stared at her in surprise, but before they could say anything, the door opened again. Dr Mukherjee eyed the two men. 'You must be the husband,' she said to Mountjoy. 'Pack some things for Mrs Mountjoy, please. I'm taking her to the general hospital.'

'Hospital?' Mountjoy went pale, hardly noticed the indignity of being addressed as 'the husband'. 'Is she seriously ill? Will you be able to find out what's wrong with her?'

Dr Mukherjee fixed a cold dark eye on him. 'Your wife is not actually ill.'

'But she fainted; you can't say she isn't ill. Dr Gregson said . . .'

She smiled at him, the smile of a woman generations older than him.

'I know what Dr Gregson's diagnosis is, I have the notes. He is wrong, there is basically nothing the matter with Mrs Mountjoy. I am taking her to hospital as a precaution and so that we can run one or two tests on her. Now, if you could get her things, I would be grateful.'

Mountjoy went. Sylvester cleared his throat. 'Just one thing, doctor; it's Lady Mountjoy, not Mrs Mountjoy.'

'Thank you,' said Dr Mukherjee. 'I will remember that. You can help me take her to the car, if you would.'

The sound of the car engine died away and the silence of a summer evening fell once more over the castle. Prue and Sylvester climbed the shadowy stone stairs which led to Lady Mountjoy's room. Prue picked up her notebook and pencil; Sylvester gathered up the coffee cups, and the cold unfinished coffee. 'We'll wash these up, and then find ourselves something stronger to drink. Is Sophie around?'

Prue shook her head. She didn't know when Sophie would be back. When Sylvester left, she would be alone in the castle until Sophie returned. Could she lock the doors? Did Sophie have a key? Could you really make the castle secure?

Sylvester laughed at her fears. 'Good gracious, nobody around here ever locks their doors, walk in and out of any house you like. Only you don't, of course. Take it from me, you're as safe here with everything open as you would be in London with bolts across the door. Besides, Sophie will be back soon, nothing to stay out late for. Where did she go?'

Prue didn't know. It seemed she had a key; the one which hung behind the kitchen door was gone.

'There you are,' said Sylvester. 'Lock all the doors if it makes you feel happier. Ring me up if you hear strange noises in the night, but you won't. Have another brandy and it'll be morning before you know where you are. I'll send Cleo up first thing to see how things are. I wonder what's going on with Magdalena? She looked rotten. See you in the morning.'

Prue slept fitfully. She dreamt vividly; dark figures pursued her down stone passages, faces came alive from the tapestries and taunted her. The castle in her dreams was lit by smoking torches which cast a dull uneven light. Whispers echoed in the corners, then faded away into the darkness. She was in the gallery looking down into the hall. There it was bright, with hundreds of candles glowing against angled mirrors. People came and went, talking to each other, ignoring her. Prue opened her mouth to call to them; nothing came out.

'Someone knocking,' a voice said, quite distinctly, in her ear. Prue woke up with a start, to find herself in her round room, the pale light of early dawn at the window. And someone was knocking. Sophie must be back, must have forgotten her key after all.

Prue tumbled out of bed and ran down the stairs, pulling on her dressing gown as she went. Strange; whoever it was, was knocking on the big doors that led into the courtyard, not at the kitchen door.

Prue drew back the bolts with difficulty. They had been stiff the night before, 'Never closed,' Sylvester had said. 'But if it makes you feel better . . .'

It did, but now she had to open them, and who was it waiting so impatiently at the other side, anyway? With a final pull the last bolt slid back and she could heave the doors open.

Of course it wasn't Sophie. Sophie was miles away, snatching a rare night away with her lover, with no intention of leaving her bed at dawn. This was a man. Prue stared at him; he looked like one of the figures she had seen in the half-shadows in her dream. Was she still dreaming? Was this one of those peculiar dreams when you think you are awake, but what seems to be the normal world is still a dream? She almost put out a hand to touch him. He was tall, very tall, and very dark. His voice was a pleasant baritone where you might have expected a bass. He was frowning, clearly irritated, and he couldn't be bothered to hide it.

'What is going on? Why are these doors shut? They're never shut. And who are you?'

The passenger door of the car opened and a woman got out. The man must be about forty, Prue thought, and this woman was in her mid-thirties. They were lost, perhaps, or . . .

They weren't lost.

'Don't bully the child,' said the woman. 'This must be the girl who was coming to work for Magdalena and Mountjoy. I'm sorry we woke you up, my dear; usually we just drive in.'

As if they owned the place, thought Prue indignantly.

They almost did. The man was Valdemar, Mountjoy's nephew; the woman was Sylvia, his long standing companion.

'Mountjoy asleep?' Valdemar enquired after he had parked the car in the stables and heaved a lot of luggage out of the boot.

Prue explained. Sylvia was quick with sympathy. Poor Magdalena; poor Mountjoy, who must be so worried about her. Valdemar was more concerned about his breakfast. 'Go and tell Sophie to get up. We've had a long journey, we need something to eat.'

'Where have you come from?' asked Prue in her best party-manners voice. And why have you arrived at this time of day, was her unspoken question.

Valdemar took no notice of her enquiry, but Sylvia told her that they had driven from London; Valdemar always drove at night in the summer to avoid the traffic.

'I'll get Sophie,' said Prue, suddenly aware of her flimsy dressing gown.

'I'll just put some clothes on . . .' She fled.

'Bloody Sophie,' said Valdemar angrily, as he banged the cupboard door in the kitchen. 'Where the hell is she? I've told Mountjoy he should give her the push. She may be able to cook, but she's a liability, never here when you want her.'

Prue felt tense and ill at ease. This man was everywhere, restless energy burning out of him. He was too big for the kitchen; it was like having a panther prowling up and down. Not domesticated at all, thought Prue. I wish he'd go away.

Sylvia came to her rescue. 'Val, darling, take yourself off. Prue and I will make breakfast and bring it to you.'

'I'm quite capable of making my own breakfast. I can't bear women who think only they can perform perfectly simple tasks like making toast. What annoys me is that Mountjoy pays for Sophie to be here to cook, and she bloody well isn't.'

'She isn't paid to cook at five in the morning,' said Prue.

Valdemar flashed a contemptuous look at her. Sylvia's mouth twitched. 'Well said. Not such a little mouse after all. Since Sophie isn't here, Val, there's no point in going on about it. Either sit down or go and pace up and down somewhere else.'

'What happened then?' asked Cleo later that day when Prue had walked down from the castle with a message to Lily from Sophie.

'Don't rush back,' Sophie had said. 'Nothing for you to do here.'

Prue remembered Valdemar's fury at Sophie's absence. 'Mountjoy's nephew might be angry if I go.'

'Valdemar? None of his business. Anyway, he's out, gone to pick up Thomas from school, they won't be back until this evening. You buzz off, see your friend; God knows you need friends in this place. Just bring those things back from Lily by five o'clock, I need them for dinner.'

'Won't Mountjoy and Magdalena be back?'

'No; she's coming out tomorrow, he rang from the hospital just now. Go.'

'What happened then?' echoed Prue. 'Well, they had breakfast and then he, Valdemar, went off to swim in the lake and Sylvia went to bed.'

'So Sophie wasn't there at all?'

'No, she tipped up at about half-past eight.'

'Did she look satisfied? Sated? Night on the tiles?'

'Honestly, Cleo, how do I know? She looked sleepy, that's all I can say.'

'That's good news, because I happen to know that Luke was here last night; he can't have been out on the gad with Sophie,' said Cleo triumphantly.

'Perhaps Sophie was here with him.'

Cleo thought for a moment and then shook her head. 'No. He was in the kitchen here at about half-past ten, elevenish, having a yak with Lily.'

'I don't yak,' said Lily, who had just emerged from the garden door to find Prue and Cleo lying on the grass. 'What are you two doing here? Haven't you got any work to do? Gossiping, I dare say.'

Prue sat up. 'Lily, do you know where Sophie went last night?'

Lily passed her a bowl. 'You can pick some raspberries for me, we can have them for lunch. I don't know what Sophie was up to, how should I? I was at the WI yesterday evening. It was a talk on local birds, very interesting.'

'Can you imagine living in the country and going to the WI?' said Cleo. 'The tedium!'

'You're a townee, Cleo,' said Prue.

'I felt like that about the country when I worked in London,' said Lily. 'I wouldn't go back to that now. Give me the WI any day.'

'What did you do in London?' asked Prue.

'This and that,' said Lily vaguely. 'Sophie wasn't at the WI either, she never comes. Doesn't like Daisy, of course, and Daisy was in the chair last night. Jacob was away, some clergy conference, she said, so we finished quite early. Good chance for her to get a few extra glasses in.'

'Now who's gossiping?' said Cleo, scrambling to her feet. 'Come on, Prue, you can help pick raspberries. Lily, tell us about Mountjoy's nephew. Prue won't say anything about him. I think she must be a bit struck.'

'I'm not,' said Prue indignantly. 'You wait until you meet him; you won't like him, either.'

Lily led the way to the raspberry beds. Sylvester's large tabby cat was asleep under one of the bushes; Lily put her big basket down beside the animal and set to work filling her bowl. Cleo stood beside her.

'You do the lower ones, I'll get the ones at the top. Come on, let's have the lowdown on this Valdemar man. What a peculiar name.'

'It's an old family name,' said Lily. 'There's been a Valdemar every generation for centuries. Each worse than the one before, if you ask me. No, I tell a lie; the real villain lived in Mountjoy Castle in seventeen something. He was up to all kinds of mischief.'

'What kind?' said Cleo, always inquisitive.

'Excesses,' was all that Lily would say.

Prue sucked her finger where a branch had scratched it. 'And this one? Does he go in for excess as well?'

'He's a complex man. Dashing. Immoral, ingenious.'

'A rake, in fact,' said Cleo. 'That's not special.'

'His intellect rules his passions. That makes him infinitely more dangerous than other men of his kind.'

Cleo was intrigued. Prue was only half-listening now, her mind lulled into a happy ease by the warmth and the hum of a bee dancing in and out of the bright flowers which grew on the old wall of the fruit garden.

'What about Sylvia?' Cleo went on. 'She's his mistress. Is that just for now?'

'Oh, no, that's a long-standing affair. Years, now. Like a wife really, but she hasn't tamed him. She's his civilized self; with her he's charming, urbane, very much in control. I don't know if Sylvia sees much of his darker side. She probably doesn't, probably better not to.'

'Does he go raking when he's here?'

Lily plucked a particularly large and juicy raspberry and ate it. 'These are all ripe. I came here two days ago, there were hardly any to pick. Now they're ready; if we don't pick them and enjoy them now, they'll rot on the bushes.'

'You didn't say,' said Cleo. 'How is this man when he's here with his uncle? Lightness or darkness?'

'There's women here counting the hours till he comes again; then there are others who'll have nothing more to do with him, who wish he'd never set foot in the county.' Lily handed Cleo her bowl. 'Go and tip those into the big basket. Mind the cat, he seems a sleepy fellow, but he'll scratch you soon as look at you.'

'Like Valdemar, then.'

'I'm not going to say another word about that man.'

Cleo balanced the bowl of raspberries on her head and walked like an African woman on neat feet towards the basket. 'Is Prue safe then, up at the castle?' she said softly.

Lily gave Prue a witchy look. 'No. Being eighteen isn't safe. Being alive isn't safe. Prue's all right for the moment, though; nobody would notice her.'

Cleo looked at her friend. Prue felt the hairs on the back of her neck tingling and looked round at Cleo and Lily. She didn't like being looked at; like a goldfish in a bowl, she said. 'And you were talking about me, weren't you?'

'No,' said Lily, always ready to lie in a good cause. 'We were talking about the Mountjoys.'

Prue didn't believe her, but it didn't matter, she was too warm and relaxed to mind. Usually she felt uneasy when she knew people were talking about her; she took it for granted that anything people said would be unfavourable. That was years of her aunt making sure she knew how unworthy she was. Unworthy of what was never clearly stated, but Prue knew that she was on the wrong side of whatever line was being drawn. Her aunt had done well; perpetual low esteem and uncertainty had made Prue very biddable. Now, only slightly guilt-ridden, she looked from her half-empty bowl to the full basket of raspberries.

'Oh dear, I haven't been much use, have I?'

'More to life than picking raspberries,' said Lily.

'Yes, like eating them.' Prue adored raspberries. 'Come on, let's go and have some.'

'Save some for Sylvester,' said Cleo. 'They are his, after all.'

'He'll only want a few,' said Lily. 'He likes them, but they disagree with him. I'll give you some to take up to the castle, Prue, and there are some other things Sophie has asked for. Magdalena will be wanting fruit when she gets back from the hospital.'

How does she know? thought Prue. From what Sophie said, Magdalena hadn't had a proper appetite for weeks. Lily was so sure; was that age, being so knowing? Prue wondered how much Lily did know. Lily said it was easy enough, no magic, just watch and remember, let your mind float a little, the answers were always there. Lily's real magic, of course, was knowing the questions in the first place.

Prue went towards the house with a light step. Goodness, she was getting lazy, idling in the sun like that.

She smiled to herself as she went into the kitchen with Lily. 'Imagine what my aunt would have said. Actually, she wouldn't have said anything, she'd have been speechless with horror at such idleness. She thought that if young people weren't gainfully occupied, they were thinking sinful thoughts.'

'Get on with you, you wouldn't recognize a sinful thought if it bit you, though it's probably time you had a few,' said Lily. 'Look at Cleo here, she's got a head full of sinful thoughts. Quite right, too, at her age. Now run along to the sitting room, Prue. Across the hall, the door on your right,' Lily went on briskly. 'There's a white dish with sugar in it. Sylvester always takes it off the tray, and he'll have left it in there. He shouldn't have sugar at all, but there you are.'

Prue skipped across the hall and into the sitting room. And there, sitting calmly on the sofa, was a man. A young man, with silver blond hair, a beaky nose, and an agreeable smile on his face.

Little prickles ran down the back of Prue's neck and across her shoulder blades. She stared at him; he rose politely.

'Am I in your way? I was waiting for Sylvester.'

6

Velvety voice, thought Prue. Her blue gaze swept over him, and she smiled at him, delighted.

'Sylvester's out, I think.'

'Oh,' the man said. 'I'm sorry, I don't know your name. I'm Seton.'

'I'm Prue. Prue Pagan.' Again, the lovely, slanting smile.

Beautiful smile, thought Seton. His own mouth turned up at the sides, in what Prue thought was a most appealing way.

'What an unusual name. And are you?'

'Am I what?'

'A pagan.'

'Of course not. It's an odd name, and people always make fun of it.'

He smiled again. 'No, it's not odd, and I wasn't making fun of you. Are you a friend of Sylvester's? No, you must be the girl who's come to help him with his book.'

Prue shook her head. 'No, I'm a friend, not of Sylvester, but of the girl who's come . . . Cleo.'

Inspired, Prue picked up the sugar bowl and gestured to the door. 'Cleo's in the kitchen, with Lily. There are raspberries. Do you like raspberries? Come and have some.'

And he came, held by Prue's smile and her blue gaze.

'Oh, lord,' said Lily as Prue led him into the kitchen. 'Look what the cat's brought in!'

'Lily,' said Prue reprovingly. 'He's come to have some raspberries.'

Prue went to the sideboard where she had seen Lily getting the bowls and took out another one. She put it on the table, and fetched a spoon. 'That's for you,' she said to Seton. 'The raspberries are good, we picked them just now.'

'Thank you,' he said.

'Seton's got perfectly good raspberries of his own, acres of them, I dare say. Got acres of everything, haven't you, Seton? When did you get back? We weren't expecting you this side of the autumn.'

'Do you live near here?' said Prue, pleased. 'Oh, this is Cleo.'

Cleo said hello. Seton held out his hand. 'No, I'm covered in raspberry juice,' she said.

'Seton lives in Gossiby,' Lily said. 'He's what's called a land-owner.'

'You seem very put out, Lily,' said Seton, sliding along the bench and tucking his long legs under the table. 'Aren't you pleased to see me? Cast any good spells lately?'

Lily snorted and passed him a dish of raspberries. He poured a generous helping of cream over them, sprinkled sugar on the top and set to. Prue toyed with her own raspberries, her eyes flickering over to Seton's side of the table. Cleo ate her raspberries quickly, watching Prue watching Seton. Lily was busy around them, opening cupboards, consulting the list which Prue had brought from Sophie, packing things neatly in a bag.

'There,' she said. 'If you've finished, Prue, you get along back to the castle with this lot.'

'Oh,' said Prue. She didn't want to go back to the castle. She liked being here; she wanted to stay here, sitting near Seton. She liked looking at him. She watched his hands; they made her feel shivery, they were somehow interesting. And his hair was silky, and so fair; she wanted to touch it. Also the grey eyes, trustworthy, kind eyes, Prue thought. She was fascinated.

Lily was firm. 'No, off you go. Sophie will need these things earlier than she thinks. And Cleo has one or two jobs to do for Sylvester.'

'I haven't,' said Cleo. 'Not that I know about, anyhow.'

'I know about them,' said Lily.

Seton rose. 'Did you walk, Prue? I'll run you back.' He opened the door for her.

Lily could do nothing, which made her cross. 'Drat the man,' she said.

Cleo was surprised at Lily's hostility to Seton.

'What's wrong with him?' she asked. 'You must have a reason for shoving Prue out like that; you could see she was smitten.'

'Smitten! Yes, exactly.'

'Is he married? Queer? A criminal? He's not my type, but Prue's obviously fallen for him. Do you think he liked her?'

'Liked her! What's liking to do with it? Oh dear, why did he have to come back now? It's the worst thing that could have happened. I should have known, I should have foreseen it.'

Cleo's face brightened as she heard whistling in the yard. She bounded over to the door and swept a bow at a rather surprised Luke. He smiled at her a little warily, and edged past into the kitchen.

'Bumped into Sophie in the village, Lily. Says you've got some stuff for her. Shall I take it up?'

'Too late,' said Cleo. 'Prue's taken it.'

Luke shrugged his shoulders. 'She's off with Seton. Saw them getting into his car. Not like Seton to go out of his way for anyone. He taken a fancy to that Prue?'

Lily pursed her lips and said nothing. Cleo sent him a smouldering look. 'Mmm, must be the heat. Very sexy, all this warmth, don't you think?' Luke sat down on the other side of the table, ignoring Cleo. Cleo wasn't having that.

'Cheer up, Luke,' she said. 'Tell you what, when you clock off this evening, let's go down to the pub and I'll buy you a drink.'

'Yes,' said Lily, suddenly energetic again. 'You do that, Luke, otherwise she'll get under my feet. Sylvester won't be back till late, got a concert, and I've got things to do.'

'Getting the cauldron out, are you?' grumbled Luke. 'Oh, all right, better than hanging around at home. Dad's a right misery at the moment. Moaning on about changes coming at the castle, saying it'll never be the same again and all that; whinge, whinge.'

'You come by for Cleo at about half-past seven, Luke.'

The pub was a real eye-opener for Cleo, who was used to London pubs. The Midwinter Arms couldn't have changed much since the eighteenth century. And, thought Cleo, some of the people in it looked as though they had been there ever since.

She wasn't the only woman; this was the unofficial ladies night, when wives and daughters and sweethearts were left in the snug while their menfolk gravitated across the passage to the public bar. One broad wooden bar stretched across the end of each room, and across the passage. The section across the passage was hinged, and was the only way into the two rooms for the staff.

The barman slowly polished a glass, never taking his eyes off Cleo, who was sitting with Luke at the bar. The other women in the room were talking vigorously amongst themselves but, with an expertise born of years of gossiping, they were able to hear what was being said at the bar.

'Aren't you going to introduce us to the girlfriend, Luke?' said the barman.

Luke sighed. 'Lay off, Alfred, I'm not in the mood. Alfred is the village funny man, Cleo. Part-time policeman and part-time publican.'

Alfred beamed all over his little red face. 'Part-time Alfred, that's me. I like a joke, you see, I've got a good sense of humour. Luke here, he hasn't got any sense of humour at all.'

One of the women came to the bar from her table. 'Two more of the same, Alfred,' she said. 'Hear there's doings up at the castle, Luke. Lady Mountjoy rushed to hospital in the middle of the night, and no one at the castle. Well, only that slip of a girl who's just come.'

Luke shrugged. 'I'm not interested in the castle.'

'What, wasn't Sophie there?' another woman shrieked across at her friend.

'Vicar was away last night, gone to a conference in Durham.'

A very aged woman who sat hunched over a port and lemon cackled. 'I went to Durham once. Get up to all sorts in Durham, you'd be surprised.'

'You wouldn't be surprised, Agnes, would you? You'd be up to it yourself, we all know what you were like!' This from the woman at the bar, in a tremendous bellow. 'Deaf,' she confided to Cleo. 'But she doesn't like to miss out on the repartee, so we just shout a bit.'

Cleo smiled, uncertain what to say. Out of the corner of her eye she could see that Luke was going red, she wondered if he was going to lose his temper. Goodness, he was sensitive about Sophie. Who clearly wasn't interested in him.

Another woman, younger than the rest, came in through the open door. She was striking-looking, not very tall, but with turbulent red hair and enormous green eyes. Her red halter top clashed with her hair, and her faded denim shorts were grubby – as were her bare brown feet. She stared at Cleo, and sauntered over to the bar.

'Hi,' she said to Cleo.

'Hi,' said Cleo.

'This is Julie,' said Luke. 'Cousin of mine, wild as they come. Julie, this is Cleo.'

'Working for Sylvester,' said Julie. 'I know.' She was staring intently at Cleo. 'Lovely colour hair. Natural. I'm a hairdresser,' she added to explain her interest. 'Slate blue eyes, too. It isn't a usual colouring. Do you get it from your Ma?'

Cleo was taken aback, unused to such immediate personal questions.

'No, actually, my mother's fair. My father was dark.'

'Dead then, your pa?' This seemed to quicken her interest in Cleo, who was beginning to wriggle on her stool.

'Leave her alone, you and your nosy questions, Julie. Get back to the old hens, let her have her drink in peace. She doesn't want you interrogating her and then telling the whole village about her.'

'Long words, can tell you're educated,' said Julie pertly. She took the drink Alfred had put ready on the bar for her and slid down from the stool.

'Drink up, Cleo,' said Luke abruptly. 'We're going.'

'Sorry about that,' said Luke gloomily. 'Stupid idea, the pub in weather like this.'

'It was my idea,' said Cleo mildly. 'I was thinking of a peaceful country pub with a garden, perhaps a river . . .'

Luke laughed. 'Soft southern pubs, not down-to-earth northern ones.' He sighed. 'May as well get back, I suppose.'

'No, let's go for a walk,' suggested Cleo. Bother the man, thinking about Sophie all the time; languishing, that was what he was doing. Feeble. If Sophie wasn't interested in him, then lots of others would be. Her, for one. Julie for another, if Cleo was any judge of the look in her green eyes.

'All right,' said Luke unenthusiastically.

He led the way through a farmyard, opened a gate on to the fell and they set off up a steep stony track. There was a network of these tracks, far older than the neat and orderly roads in the village. These were winding, cross-country ways, with paths leading off them down to farms and barns. They were tracks for sheep and horses and ox carts, now deeply rutted by tractor wheels. Many of them were deeply sunken below the level of the land around, with high hedges; ancient, untouched hedges full of pink and white wild roses.

Cleo snuffed the air with the wariness of a city-bred girl, suspicious of malodorous underlays to the sweet summer smells. Luke, used to it all, strode on, eyes on his feet, oblivious to his surroundings or even, it seemed, to Cleo.

She broke into a jog and caught up with him. 'Are we going towards the castle, by any chance?' she panted.

Luke came out of his reverie. 'I don't know . . . yes, we are really. At least if we stay on this track, we'll reach the Lower Farm, then it's a short cut through the wood and you come out on the East Lawn.'

'And is the East Lawn where you want to be? Is that where Sophie takes a solitary walk in the evenings? I would have thought she would have been busy in the kitchen.'

'I expect so. Do you want to see Prue? Will she be with the Mountjoys or with Sophie?'

Cleo shrugged. 'I don't know. Come on, then, perhaps you can catch a quick glimpse of Sophie through a window, your fix for tonight.'

Cleo was cross; she wasn't used to a man being so completely unaware of her. In London, she would have written Luke off as a bad go and looked for someone else. Here, there weren't very many interesting men around; and besides, she did find Luke powerfully attractive. What could he see in Sophie? She even had thick ankles.

Prue sat on an ancient stone bench, sympathetically listening to Thomas grumbling about his train. He had quickly decided that Prue would be a good listener; she had kind eyes, nice ones, too, with funny gold flecks in them. And, he discovered, she didn't have a father either. As they discussed the awfulness of boarding school, Prue's gaze strayed over the lawns. Who was that coming?

Prue recognized Cleo from her walk before she could see her face clearly. She could tell that Cleo was cross, her body was always expressive. She interrupted Thomas. 'Look, there's my friend Cleo. Let's go and meet her.'

'I don't mind if we do,' said Thomas ungraciously. Then he saw that Cleo was with Luke and he brightened. 'She's with Luke. Terrific, he's the person I need.'

Thomas had driven Valdemar mad in the car on the way back from Eyot, singing a mixture of plainsong and pop, loudly and off-key, telling silly jokes.

'I thought you were supposed to be able to sing,' Valdemar said in irritation. 'For God's sake shut up, or I'll drive into something.'

'He's only letting off steam,' said Sylvia, who was very fond of

Thomas. 'It's the end of term, he's got something to make a noise about.'

'He can wait until he gets to the castle, can't he?' said Valdemar.

'What's for dinner?' asked Thomas. 'Is it going to be roast chicken? Sophie usually cooks me roast chicken on the first day of the holidays. I love roast chicken. Do you know, it said on the menu last week it was going to be roast chicken, and do you know what they gave us? Chilli con carne, which is the most revolting thing you could possibly imagine. They take all the bits left over from everybody's plates, you know, and stir in these peculiar beans, they get them cheap because they're so hard, and then they stir in lots of horrible red pepper and boil it all up, and then they expect us to eat it. HONESTLY!'

As Thomas's voice rose to a penetrating yell, Valdemar drew to the side of the road and stopped. He turned round to Thomas. 'Right. One more yell out of you, no, any sound at all, and you're walking.'

'You couldn't make me walk. You are mean, Val, Mountjoy would kill you if you just left me on the road. Don't you know there are all kinds of weirdos about? They like small boys in shorts, that's what Mr Praetorius says. He says we have to be specially careful because they come into Evensong to watch us sing, and then they might try to grab us afterwards. Do you know, Sylvia . . .'

Valdemar gave up, jerked the car into gear again and roared into the road, nearly flattening a nun on a scooter who was trundling sedately along.

'Thirty points for a nun,' carolled Thomas happily. 'Fifty points because she's on a bicycle. I think a scooter counts as a bicycle, don't you, Val?'

Val had been short-tempered all day, and even Sylvia's skilful, soothing handling hadn't put him in a good humour. Sylvia thought he might be in for one of his black moods, when temper and depression made him an impossible companion for days or even weeks on end.

'Stop at this petrol station,' she told Valdemar.

'For Christ's sake, let's get this child home before I murder him.'

'Sssh. He's only a little boy. You were like that once.' Sylvia slid out of the car and went into the shop. She came back with a large bar of chocolate and an ice cream. She handed them to Thomas, who took them with a coo of thanks and subsided in happy ecstasy on the back seat. Between mouthfuls, he crooned to the big black rabbit which was in a travelling basket on the seat beside him. 'Holidays, O bun,' he sang. 'No more school for you and me, home for weeks and weeks!'

'There,' she said, strapping herself in. 'That should keep him quiet for a while.'

Sophie had been quick to shoo him out of the kitchen. Thomas was disappointed that Mountjoy wasn't back. 'He promised that on the very first day of the holidays we would get the train set out and do a really super layout, and it *is* the first day of the holidays.'

Thomas moaned about his train set all evening, driving everyone mad. He got his roast chicken; there was a brief but awful moment at dinner when Valdemar had thought that he, too, was going to be given roast chicken with mashed potatoes.

Prue, seeing his face, gave a sudden snort of laughter, quickly suppressed before he noticed. She was alarmed by him. He was over-powering, crackling with electricity, his movements swift and vigorous; he frightens me, she told Cleo as they sat on the stone steps which led down to the lawn. Thomas had carried Luke away to the railway set; Valdemar said he had work to do and had vanished; Sylvia was having a cosy chat with Sophie in the kitchen.

'Frightens you? I should think so. Sex on the hoof, that man, wow!'

'Is he very sexy?'

'Oh, Prue, he radiates it. Can't you feel it when he's there? It's the energy and the look in his eye, tremendously sexy. Effortless, too, you can see he was born with it. Thomas is going to be just like him when he grows up. What relation is he to the Mountjoys?'

Prue tried to remember what Mountjoy had said. 'His mother is Hortense, who is Valdemar's half-sister; his mother married twice. So Thomas isn't really a Mountjoy at all.'

'You must have got it wrong. He's amazingly like Valdemar and like Mountjoy, too, though not so much. Where is he, by the way, Mountjoy? Is he still at the hospital?'

'They're keeping Magdalena in for another night; she's coming out first thing in the morning. He has a cousin there, stays with him, saves driving backwards and forwards from here. He really is devoted to her, you know. It's lovely to see them together.'

'You'd be surprised what devoted couples can get up to,' said Cleo with dark cynicism. 'There's someone in the bushes; is it Thomas come back to pester us?'

'Where?' said Prue. Certainly, the bushes were rustling as though someone was walking through them.

'It's Julie,' said Cleo, surprised.

'Who?'

'Girl we met in the pub. I took Luke for a drink, what a waste of time. I'm going to have to do something about that man, I do lust after him, and I'm not going to spend my summer in useless pining.'

Julie slouched across the lawn and flopped down on the step beside them.

'Hi again,' she said to Cleo. 'This the girl with the funny name, working for Mountjoy?'

'I'm Prue,' said Prue politely.

Julie's eye's slid over her. 'Not bad-looking, if you had a bit more go. Your hair's the wrong length, does nothing for you. I'll cut it for you if you like.'

Prue was taken aback and pushed her hair back off her face.

'Flick, flick, all you girls from posh schools are always flicking your hair back. Like the bloody masons, is it, that's how you recognize each other?' She lay back and shut her eyes.

Go away, thought Prue. And then, perhaps my hair is too long. Her thoughts slipped easily to the memory of Seton's hair shining in the sun.

'Do you think about sex all the time?' Julie said, her eyes still shut.

Prue jumped. 'I wasn't thinking about sex,' she said indignantly. 'I was just thinking about something I saw today that I liked.'

'Yeh, something to do with a man,' said Julie. 'Sex, like I said. I think about sex nearly all the time.'

'Just sex in general,' inquired Cleo, 'Or a particular man?'

'Could be a woman for all you know, I might be a lesbian. I'm not, actually. My mum would kill me for that; can't stand anything perverse, she can't. I was kissed by a dyke once, she wasn't bad, but it's no fun really. Thighs, that's what I think about a lot. Coming up here this evening, a crowd of cyclists went past.' Julie sat up and made a noise of rich appreciation.

Despite herself, Cleo was interested. 'Bums,' she said. 'Men have fantastic buttocks, makes me go all soft inside, a pair of really good buttocks.'

Julie poked Prue in the ribs. 'What turns you on, Prue? Go on, we won't tell.'

'I don't know,' said Prue, blushing. Thighs, bums; the truth was that Prue had never seen a naked man, and so could hardly be very specific anatomically about what turned her on. Until today, she wouldn't even have known what being turned on meant; if it was the way that Seton made her feel, then she did know now, and very exciting it was, too.

'You a virgin, then?' asked Julie, looking at Prue as though she was a rare specimen in a glass case. 'How old are you?'

'I'm eighteen.'

'You don't look it. You are one, though, aren't you? Oh well, that won't last, not in this village.'

Prue was furious now. Who was this vulgar girl talking about her as though she were an animal? She wasn't interested in men, or sex, not in general, just in one man, and that was quite different.

Her voice was high and cold when she answered.

'It's absolutely none of your business, my private life.'

Julie laughed. 'Come off it, love. You're in Midwinter now, no one has a private life here; we all know about everyone.'

7

'It's too hot,' grumbled Sylvester as he heaved himself out of his car. 'Cleo, earn your living, take this music in.' He thrust a tatty box at her and carefully took his cello out. 'My cello doesn't like this weather at all, it's hot and dry. Cellos like more humidity; I've had to keep it in the bathroom overnight, with the tap going. Dribble, dribble, all night long.'

'Is it a very valuable cello?' asked Cleo as she followed Sylvester into the house.'

'Immensely. It's my Vuillaume, if that means anything to you, ignorant girl. And irreplaceable, as far as I'm concerned. Now, you see, it's fine in here, cool, comfortable. They knew how to build in those days. Where's Lily? Lily!' he bellowed. 'I want some iced coffee. In the kitchen, to catch up on the news. Then I'm having a shower, and then we're going to get to work, Cleo.'

Catch up on the news? thought Cleo. What news? He's only been away about five minutes.

'More than twenty-four hours, actually,' said Sylvester, squeezing his bulk on to the bench in the kitchen. 'The whole world can change in twenty-four hours. Is Magdalena out of hospital? What's the diagnosis? What have you and Luke been up to? How's young Prue getting on?'

'Magdalena's back later this morning,' said Lily. She poured out a tall glass of iced coffee for Sylvester and one for Cleo.

'Can I have ice-cream on mine?' said Cleo, heading for the freezer.

Sylvester sighed longingly. 'Youth! You'll have to watch it, Cleo, or those pleasing curves will turn into vast hips and you'll waddle.'

'No chance, I'm wasting away. All I have is iced coffee and ice cream.'

'Wasting away?' Sylvester's dark brown eyes were sympathetic. 'Why?'

75

'I'm in love,' said Cleo sorrowfully. 'Or in lust, anyway.'

Lily made a derisive sound. 'She's hankering after Luke, who of course has no eyes for anyone except Sophie.'

'Ah, Sophie,' said Sylvester. 'Luke would be much better off with you, Cleo, but if you do finally get him to bed, don't let it interfere with your work for me. I can't bear unpunctuality, whatever the reason.'

'Turn your attention to Seton and do us all a favour,' said Lily.

'Seton,' said Sylvester, suddenly much more wide awake. 'Seton? Is he back?'

'Mmmm,' said Cleo. 'He was here. But he's not my type, too tall, too much of the blond hero. Although he could appeal to some women, I can see that. Besides, Prue's fallen for him.'

Sylvester exchanged a quick glance with Lily.

'Oh ho,' was all he said. 'And there you are, Cleo, wondering what can have happened since I went away. You see? Momentous events. Seton, eh? Oh dear, oh dear.'

'You haven't heard all the news, yet, either,' said Lily. 'Valdemar's at the castle.'

Sylvester hummed a tune and rattled his fingers on the table. Cleo and Lily watched him in silence. 'That is news,' he said finally. 'Is Sylvia with him?'

Lily nodded. She took up the empty glasses and carried them over to the dishwasher.

'That's something. He's not usually too bad when she's around.'

Lily sniffed. 'I don't think it makes the slightest bit of difference.' She banged the door of the dishwasher shut so that the glass and china inside rattled and clinked. 'Peter's in a taking.'

'Peter? Why?'

'Is that Luke's father?' put in Cleo.

'Yes, you haven't met him yet, have you? The castle's his life; he was born and bred up here, and his family has always worked for the Mountjoys. Now Valdemar's got this crazy plan, and Peter doesn't know what's going to happen.'

Lily sat down and put her elbows at the table, matching Sylvester opposite, who had his chin cupped in his immense hands, concentrating hard.

'Plan?' he said. 'What plan?'

'I told you that man was brewing something last time he was up. You said, oh, poo, nonsense, but you see I was right. He wants to

turn the castle and grounds into a kind of show, put Midwinter and
Gossiby on the map. Historical characters and I don't know what.'

'You're joking,' said Sylvester. 'Oh, you must be wrong, no one
could possibly have such a mad idea. Nothing short of nightly Roman
orgies would bring people up here, not in the kind of numbers
you'd need.'

'They do in America,' said Cleo. 'My mum did some work on
programmes for a firm there, they made a lot of money out of it.
Son et lumière, that kind of thing.'

'It's a non-starter,' said Sylvester firmly. 'Mountjoy must be desperate to let Valdemar come up with a half-baked idea like this.'

'Why should Valdemar have anything to do with the castle,
anyway?' asked Cleo.

Sylvester and Lily stared at her. 'He's the heir. He'll inherit when
Mountjoy pops off.'

'Oh, I see. He hasn't got any children, I'd forgotten. Doesn't
anyone else get anything at all?'

'Valdemar gets the lot. He probably wants Mountjoy to sign over
part of it to escape death duties, may already have done so.'

Sylvester took money seriously; his usually jovial face looked quite
foxy. 'Mind you, Valdemar's got a point. It costs a fortune keeping a
place like that going; roof repairs, death watch, woodworm, dry rot.
The place is a bottomless pit.'

'What does Valdemar do?' asked Cleo, rather bored by the
conversation, very interesting no doubt to Sylvester and Lily who
lived here, but not to her.

'Structural engineer,' said Sylvester. 'He specializes in enormous
skyscrapers, ugly buildings, in the States, Hong Kong. You know the
kind of thing.'

'He wouldn't want to give that up to run a decaying castle,
would he?'

Lily made a clicking noise. 'Course he would, he's a Mountjoy
through and through; they've got that place in their guts. If the
only way to keep it going is to turn it into an amusement palace or
whatever, then that's what he'll do. And to hell with all the rest of us.
None of the Mountjoys have ever given a damn for anyone outside
the family.'

The phone rang. Cleo leant back on her chair and plucked the
receiver off its hook. 'Midwinter Hall.'

'Who's that?' The crisp voice rang out.

Lily and Sylvester exchanged glances. Sylvester held out his hand for the phone.

'Valdemar? Sylvester here.'

'Ah, Sylvester. Who answered the phone?'

'Cleo. She's working for me, helping with the book. Why?'

'Just wanted to know. I thought I recognized her voice, don't know anyone called Cleo. Now, is that wretched girl of Mountjoy's there? Sophie says she hangs around at Midwinter Hall – I suppose she's friendly with this Cleo of yours.'

Sylvester's thick eyebrows rose. 'Are you talking about Prue? Prue Pagan?'

'Yes, Prue, don't know her surname. Mountjoy's rung, he's on his way with Magdalena. He needs this girl to go to the doctor's here, collect some things. The bloody creature's vanished.'

'Send Sophie,' suggested Sylvester.

'You know what Sophie's like, she'll go, but then she won't make lunch. You know how difficult she can be.'

'You surprise me. Sophie is fond of Magdalena, I can't see her not giving a hand.'

'The point is, she shouldn't have to. This other girl is being paid to work for Magdalena, so where is she?'

'It's a big place, Val. She'll be there somewhere.'

'I'm not a fool, Sylvester. Sylvia and I have looked everywhere; she isn't here. Sophie says someone went out very early, crack of dawn; in which case, where did she go, and why hasn't she got back?'

'I'm afraid I can't help you, she hasn't been here. Hold on.'

Sylvester covered the phone with a large hand and made faces at Cleo. 'Do you know where Prue is?'

Cleo shook her head. 'No, but they should; it's not like Prue to go off when she should be working. She's very conscientious.'

Sylvester gazed into the distance for a moment and then spoke into the phone again.

'Valdemar? Are you still there?'

'Yes, of course I'm here.'

'Does the doctor know what Magdalena needs? Is it waiting there to be picked up? Because, if so, I'll collect it and come up.'

'Ridiculous,' said Valdemar. 'You're a busy man, Sylvester, your time is valuable. You can't go running errands.'

Sylvester paid no attention. 'I'll be up in about twenty minutes. Keep looking for Prue; it's not like her to go missing.'

Sylvester put the phone down and heaved himself into action. 'Forget the plan for today, Cleo. You're coming up to the Castle with me. The idiots don't know where Prue is. Do you think she's run away?'

Cleo picked up her bag from the sideboard. 'What for? Where to?'

Lily was briskly clearing the table. 'Frightened by Valdemar, wouldn't be surprised; she'll be like a hypnotized rabbit with him. If she had any sense she'd run, but then who ever had any sense at eighteen? I'll come to the village with you, Sylvester, see if anyone there has seen her.'

Prue had been in the village, but too early for even the nosiest of villagers to be aware of her. It was Thomas's doing.

'Prue, have you ever seen an otter? There are otters in a stream up beyond Devil's Fell, Peter says. I've always wanted to see otters. I think otters are marvellous, don't you?'

Thomas had found a kindred spirit; ever since she had read 'Ring of Bright Water', Prue had longed to see otters. 'Perhaps Peter will take us one day,' she said.

'He won't,' said Thomas urgently. 'You have to go really early. He won't get up that early unless he has to, and he says certainly not to see a pack of pesky otters.'

Prue was no match for the wiles of a pleading small boy, and a small boy, moreover, with an abundance of easy charm.

Why not? she thought. They could go very early, be back before breakfast. Nobody could mind; in any case, she'd be back before they knew she'd gone. Thomas looked at her like an expectant puppy. 'Please, Prue. It'll be super.'

'Let's see if you wake up. It's just the beginning of the holidays, you may be tired.'

Thomas was ecstatic. 'Of course I'll wake up. I won't be too tired, I'll set my alarm. Shall I come and wake you up?'

Prue didn't feel quite so enthusiastic at five the next morning when there was a scratching on her door. 'I'm coming,' she said as she slid out of bed. She padded to the window and looked out over a magical countryside, wispy with mist, green and grey and very quiet and still. Oh, it was worth being up so early to see this, why didn't she get up at this time every day?

They slipped through the village and up the fell path, Prue

keeping up a steady pace, while Thomas pranced and danced around her. They reached a crossroads and Prue stopped. 'Where now, Thomas?'

Thomas balanced on one leg on a pile of stones. 'Mmm. That way, I think. That's east, isn't it?'

'Thomas, have you got a map?'

'I don't *need* a map. I *know* where the stream is. It's past Robinson's farm, which I'm sure is over there. Come on, Prue.'

Prue could see that Thomas had no more than a vague idea of where he was going. Why on earth hadn't she brought a map? The castle was full of maps, old maybe, but the fells wouldn't have changed much. Or a compass, she should have brought a compass. Not that she knew how to use one. Outdoor activities hadn't been high on the convent's list of useful skills. Their attitude was that outdoors was likely to be dangerous and best avoided. They did us no favours, thought Prue, as they climbed steadily uphill, now on a narrow sheep track. Since dangers clearly lurked everywhere, inside and out – unless, of course, you'd taken the veil – it would be better to have learned how to deal with them early on.

Three quarters of an hour later, Prue was sure they were on the wrong track.

'Thomas,' she called to the small figure ahead. 'Thomas, you said a couple of miles from the Castle. We must have come further than that.'

Thomas's face took on an injured expression; how could anyone doubt him? 'You're thinking of town miles, Prue, country miles are quite different. It takes much longer to go a mile in the fells, it's rough ground and up and down. We're nearly there.'

Prue didn't believe that for a moment, but Thomas headed purposefully off down a slope; slopes often led to a stream, that she did know, from geography lessons. She followed him.

There was a stream, she could hear it, just a soft sound of water on stones. The way became steeper as the path narrowed even further. Thomas took no notice of the boulders and rocks in his way. He clambered over them, urging Prue to follow him.

'I don't think this is a good idea,' said Prue. 'I don't think this is actually a path, and it's getting very steep.' She clutched a branch from an overhead tree to stop herself from falling forward. Thomas turned reproachful blue eyes towards her.

'This is a gully,' he said. 'Gullies are always a bit tricky. Come on, we're nearly there, we can't give up now. Look, there's the stream!' They were indeed in a gully, a shadowy place, with dappled sunlight showing fleetingly through the branches. It wasn't cool, the days of hot sun had even warmed this sheltered place.

There were no otters, although they found a pool which Thomas said would be perfect for otters. 'We're too late, they've been and gone,' he said sadly. 'We'll have to come even earlier next time.'

Prue shook her head. It was all very well, but how long would it take them to get back to the castle? She would be late, Mountjoy would be bringing Magdalena home, there were things to do, and here she was, miles from anywhere.

'Come on, Tom,' she said quite crossly. 'I have to get back, it isn't my holidays.'

The trouble was, they couldn't. They were both too inexperienced to know that a difficult climb downwards was as likely as not an impossible climb upwards. They couldn't do it. They were stuck.

'The stream is only a trickle, really,' said Thomas. 'But, do you know, just a bit of rain and it turns into a raging torrent. It would come up to here just as you were watching.' He held his hand above his head, and indeed Prue could see that there was a waterline visible.

'That's nonsense,' she said bracingly. 'Water takes time to rise, we aren't in the tropics.'

'It doesn't. We did it in geography,' Thomas explained patiently. 'Because the hills are rocky, the water doesn't get absorbed into the ground. It runs down on the surface and into streams, so they rise very, very quickly.'

True. Prue remembered that from her geography as well, the section headed 'Sudden Floods'. Prue peered up into the sky through the leaves. It seemed a clear blue, but there had been little puffy clouds growing on the horizon as they walked, clouds no bigger than a man's hand, she said to herself. How stupid to come out like this, with no map, not telling anyone where they going. Peter might remember telling Thomas about the otters, and draw the right conclusion; even then, Prue suspected that they weren't at the place which Peter had been talking about. She was sure they had come much further than that from the castle.

Thomas had been investigating. 'We can't get out that end,' he said cheerfully. 'The stream goes underground, and it's a kind of rocky bit and then it's a sort of cliff, sheer, about sixty feet straight down to the ground. The stream waterfalls out; it must be very exciting when there's lots of water.'

He looked expectantly at Prue. 'How are we going to get out?'

Prue could see that Thomas trusted her. She was an adult, adults looked after boys, he was safe. They weren't safe, though, because she couldn't think how they were to get out, and what if those clouds were even now gathering for a storm? It seemed to be growing darker, she was almost sure it was.

'Don't panic,' said a clear voice in her head. 'Think!' She couldn't think, because the clear voice was being drowned by headlines which shouted much more loudly: 'Two drown in lakeland tragedy, 18-year-old fails to save schoolboy. Mystery of drowning deaths.'

How Prue wished she had learned more when she was a Girl Guide. She had attended dutifully every week, practised tying knots, gained her sewing and knitting badges and knew how to put up a tent on the smooth convent lawns. What use was any of that?

At the castle, Valdemar was seething with annoyance and impatience. He hated to have his will crossed in any way, he loathed inefficiency and despised incompetence. Not to be where you should be at half-past nine in the morning was unquestionably incompetent.

Sylvester handed Sophie the packet for Magdalena. Then he turned to Valdemar.

'Stop raging, Val, use your wits. Either Prue has left, which seems unlikely, she isn't that kind of a girl, and besides you say all her things are here; or she's out somewhere for a purpose.'

'Purpose? She should be here, that's where she's paid to be, and she isn't. I could have sent Mountjoy a properly-trained, experienced woman to help him and Magdalena, but no, he has to go to that peculiar Miss Dotteridge, a byword for supplying useless girls. My firm would never use her.'

Sylvester growled. 'I've used Miss Dotteridge for years, and let me tell you, all her girls have brains. Cleo's got brains, Prue's got brains.'

'Brains? The girl's a half-wit. Anyway, you don't need women with brains to do this kind of work. Women with brains, and I can tell you there are very few of them, are nothing but a bloody nuisance. They have no idea at all of how the real world works.'

Sophie eyed them both with ill-concealed hostility. 'Your views are fascinating, Val, and completely irrelevant, apart of course from being totally wrong. The question is, where is Prue?'

'No, it isn't. I don't care where she is, she's quite old enough to take care of herself, I just don't like to see Mountjoy being taken advantage of.'

'Rich,' said Sophie, taking off her wide white cook's apron. 'If you want to talk about taking advantage of Mountjoy, you needn't start with Prue.'

Valdemar swung round. 'What are you talking about?'

'Nothing,' said Sophie. 'Nothing that you'd understand, anyhow. I'm going to wake Thomas up, he's so inquisitive he may know where Prue's gone.'

She was back in no time. 'He isn't there. Bet she's gone with him; he knows he can't wander on the fells alone unless Mountjoy's said he can. He's cajoled Prue into an expedition.'

'I hope they're back soon, in that case,' said Sylvester, still worried. 'I think it's building up to a storm, it was bound to happen after all this heat, could be a big one. They'll get wet.'

'Serve them right,' said Valdemar coldly. With Mountjoy away he slipped easily into being in charge at the castle, and he was still enraged; he hated anything to get out of control. How dare anyone disturb him like this? And he was disturbed. Thomas and Prue were probably perfectly all right, although he didn't credit either of them with any particular sense, but he wanted Thomas here, safe and sound, or at least to know where he was.

Prue and Thomas weren't perfectly safe. The clouds were building at a tremendous rate, great pillars of blackness rising into the sky and billowing together to form layer on layer of dark, storm-menacing clouds. Sylvester looked out anxiously at the darkening landscape. 'We've got to find them, Val. Prue hasn't been here long, I don't suppose she knows what to do if she's lost on the fells in weather like this. Thomas is better, but he's only a child.'

'So what do you want me to do? Call up Mountain Rescue? The idiot girl's gone out for a walk with Thomas, gone too far or lost her way. It's going to rain, she'll find shelter or get wet. As long as Thomas is with her, they'll be all right.'

'And what if they've wandered down Parkin's Gully?' asked Sophie. 'Just as an example of where a walk might take them. What then, with cliffs one side and a beck that turns into a raging torrent in half an hour. Three people drowned there last summer, do you remember, Sylvester?'

Sylvester did. So did Peter when summoned to advise. 'Wouldn't go near Parkin's Gully, not in this weather,' he said wisely. 'Not the right day for it at all. Wait until the storm's past; it'll be fine again tomorrow.'

'Yokels,' said Valdemar in exasperation. 'In words of one syllable, Peter, Thomas and that girl who's working for my uncle . . .'

'Prue,' said Peter helpfully.

'Yes, Prue. They are lost. On the fells. Do you have any idea where they might have gone? Sophie says they could be in Parkin's Gully. I can't imagine why they should be, but . . .'

'Oh, dear me no, they shouldn't be there, not in this weather. They might be that way, though; I daresay young Thomas went out to look for otters.'

'Otters?'

'Yes, Dead keen to see otters, he was. Told him there were some in the pool near Robinson's Farm. That's over that way. Same beck as runs into the gully, but the pool with the otters is further up.'

Valdemar became a man of action. 'Right. First, find out if Thomas is there. Sophie, who are these Robinsons? Are they on the phone?'

Peter answered. 'They are, but no good you telephoning them. Mrs Robinson will be in town, market day. Harry Robinson'll be out after his sheep; weather like this, no farmer'll be sitting inside waiting for the telephone to ring.'

'Then we'll have to go.'

Sylvester shook his head. 'Not in that car of yours, Val, it wouldn't make it there, because it's extremely tough ground. Take Mountjoy's Land Rover.'

'Good thinking, Peter, go and get the Land Rover out.'

Peter shook his head mournfully. 'I can't do that, it's in the garage. Blew a gasket last week.'

Valdemar looked blacker than ever. The room went quite dark as clouds blotted out the last trace of sunlight. There was a moment of quietness, then a brilliant flash of lightning and almost at once a tremendous crack of thunder. Simultaneously the heavens opened and great sheets of water swept down across the fells.

'Ah, storm's come,' said Peter, 'I said it was going to rain.'

8

Prue was becoming more and more alarmed at their predicament. It was bad enough to have got themselves into a place which they couldn't climb out of; it was going to be disastrous if the beck rose and carried them over the sheer drop at the end of the valley. Moreover, Prue could feel thunder in the air, and she hated thunder.

Prue knew it was irrational; there was no need to be afraid of any of God's workings, the nuns had told her again and again. Accept it as part of the majesty of His universe, offer up your fear as prayer. That had done no good; when large Sister Gabriel had hauled her up from under the bedclothes and demanded to know what she was doing, she had got into a lot of trouble for answering, 'Praying.'

Thomas was self-centred, like most small boys, but even he could see that Prue had no control over the situation at all. Looking at the water beginning to rush and swirl over the rocks beneath them, he realized that no one could really have much control of it.

'Forces of nature,' he said thoughtfully to himself. 'Prue, come on. If we stay here, we'll drown.'

Prue was afraid and angry: afraid of the rising water and of drowning, angry with herself for not being able to help Thomas and for longing for a handy bed or table to hide under when the thunder started. Thomas was too young to die! So was she, if it came to that.

Thomas's practical words brought her to her senses.

'Come on where?' she said, in almost a normal voice.

'Up,' said Thomas. 'We need to go up.'

'We can't,' said Prue impatiently. 'We tried, we just slip down again. There's nothing to hold on to.'

'Then we'll have to climb a tree.'

And they did. Thomas, of course, was a dab hand at climbing trees. Prue wasn't. She had never been a tomboy, and it would have been ten Hail Marys and no pudding for a week if she'd been found up a

85

tree at the convent. As trees go it was a comfortable tree, but Prue had no particular head for heights, and she felt even more unsafe perched up on a thick branch than she had down in the gully.

'I need to pee,' announced Thomas. 'Don't look. I'm going to see if I can hit that rock over there.'

Prue shut her eyes.

'Done it,' said Thomas triumphantly. 'I've been practising at school, but it's never gone as far as that before.'

'Don't be disgusting,' said Prue crossly.

'It's going to be difficult for you, isn't it?' said Thomas. 'I mean, it's much more difficult for girls. You'll have to sort of hang over the branch. I won't look,' he added kindly.

'I don't need to go to the loo,' said Prue firmly. It wasn't exactly true, but she could wait for a while. How long would they be up the tree? Were they safe up there, among the dripping leaves? She was cold; Thomas must be too. Would they get hypothermia? How long did it take to die of hypothermia? If they got too cold, would they just topple out of the tree into the beck below – a beck which was indeed rising fast and no longer looked liked a gentle summer stream?

'How long does it take for the water to go down?' she asked Thomas.

'It depends how much rain there's been further up. It's bucketing down; it might be a couple of days, I suppose.'

'A couple of days!' Prue was horrified. 'We can't stay up here for a couple of days.'

'They'll rescue us before then,' said Thomas. 'They're sure to.'

Prue kept her counsel on that one, but she didn't feel any of Thomas's confidence. If only they had told someone where they were going. Not that it would have helped much, since she was quite sure that they weren't wherever it was that Thomas had meant to be.

Had it been left to the search party from the Castle, they might indeed have had to stay up the tree for two days. Valdemar was still in a horrible temper, chiefly because there was no one to order about. Sylvester and Cleo had gone off to see if they could borrow a Land Rover or some other four-wheel drive vehicle in the village. Sophie was looking for dry clothes and making up a flask of hot coffee with brandy and putting doughnuts in a bag.

'Doughnuts!' Valdemar spat the words out as though Sophie was packing up a bag of toads.

'Doughnuts. Thomas loves doughnuts. He'll be cold and hungry; he'll need something sweet. Doughnuts will be fine.'

'The petty-mindedness of women never fails to amaze me. What the hell does food matter? We've got to find the bloody idiots, let them go hungry, wasting everyone's time like this.'

'I am doing something sensible, helpful and practical,' pointed out Sophie as she tucked everything neatly into a basket. 'You, on the other hand, are doing absolutely nothing at all except ranting and trying to throw your weight around. Why don't you go and find someone else to shout at? Sylvia's used to it, I dare say.'

'Sylvia's on the phone, she's talking to the police and the rescue people.'

'Ah, another trivial job. Good, they'll know what the latest weather forecast is.'

After that Sophie simply ignored Valdemar, which so nonplussed him that he went out into the pouring rain and paced up and down in the yard. He chafed at not being able to do anything, and was surpassingly nasty when Sylvester and Cleo finally rolled through the castle entrance in a very ancient and dilapidated old Land Rover.

'For God's sake! Is that all you could find?'

'It's Jack's,' said Cleo. 'It's very kind of him to lend it to us. All the other ones in the village are being used. Farmers work in the daytime, you know.'

Valdemar eyed Cleo with dislike. 'Move over, Sylvester,' he said. 'I'll drive.'

'I'm quite capable of driving,' said Sylvester. 'I know the country here far better than you do.'

'Then you can navigate. I hate being driven by other people.'

'Nonetheless,' began Sylvester as Sophie came out under a huge umbrella with her basket of goodies.

'Shut up, both of you,' said Cleo. 'Squabbling, when Thomas and Prue may be in danger.'

'The stupidity of men never fails to astonish me,' said Sophie as she handed the basket to Cleo. 'I suppose you've got enough petrol; Jack never puts much in.'

Sylvester peered at the gauge. 'Right down. Do you suppose it works?'

'Probably the only thing that does,' said Valdemar. 'Didn't it occur to you to get some petrol in the village?'

'Peter will have a can,' said Sophie. 'He's gone out towards

Fiend's Fell in case they're that way, but I know where he keeps it.'

The can was located, then they had to hunt for a funnel. Finally, they were ready. Sylvester refused to relinquish control of the wheel; Valdemar held ostentatiously on to the door as they jerked into gear. He put his head out of the window.

'You and Sylvia stay at the castle, do you hear?' he shouted at Sophie. 'Someone's got to be at home when Mountjoy and Magdalena get back.'

While all this was going on, others had been more effectively busy. Seton was working at his desk when Julie appeared at the door.

'Hello, Julie,' he said. He admired Julie's looks and found her very sexy, but he never did anything about it because he always had the feeling she was laughing at him.

'That Pagan girl, the one you fancy,' she began.

Seton carefully screwed the cap on to his fat pen and stood up. 'I don't know what you're talking about.'

'She's out with Thomas. Lost. Lily knows where she is; you know what Lily's like. There's a search party out, from the castle, but they won't find her.'

'It's quite a storm but I shouldn't think they'd be in any danger,' said Seton.

'Depends where they've gone. Valdemar's in a rage, I expect, you know how he feels about young Thomas.'

'No, I don't know how Val feels about anything. Did Lily send you?'

'No, Lily says to let it be; they're safe, she reckons. I think that Prue Pagan will be shit-scared. The fells get to you, when you don't know them.'

'How does Lily know where they are?'

Julie shrugged. 'How does Lily know anything? Anyway, why don't you go and rescue her? She'd like that. Up near Robinson's Farm, they are, trapped in Parkin's Gully.'

Seton stiffened and his voice lost its casual tone. 'Parkin's Gully? Why didn't you say so at once? Julie, are you sure? That's very dangerous, people are always getting killed there.'

'Perhaps there'll be two more dead, then. Bye.'

She left as suddenly as she had arrived.

Seton moved quickly. He dived into the downstairs cloakroom, which was full of old gumboots, walking sticks, macs and the other paraphernalia of country life. He dragged on a coat, bundled some macs under his arm and grabbed car keys from the hook. He went to the garage, threw everything into his Land Rover and ran back into the house for a map. Whistling for his dogs, he pushed them into the back, started the car and was off.

'So you were rescued by a dashing prince in an old mac,' said Cleo. She and Prue sat in front of a log fire in the huge stone fireplace of the castle great hall: summer can pass in a moment in the fells, and the storm had brought a chill to the air.

Prue ached with tiredness. Fresh from a hot bath she looked young, squeaky-clean and, thought Seton, very attractive. His feelings towards her were perhaps not a lot stronger than those he felt for a favourite dog; but then he liked dogs very much indeed.

Seton had paused at one end of the gallery above, to look down at the two girls by the fire. At the other end of the gallery was a taller figure, lost in shadow.

Valdemar watched Seton, then looked down at Prue. She was enveloped in an old dressing-gown of Mountjoy's; nothing of the come-hither about her at all. Good figure, although not much of it, and once or twice he had noticed a sparkle in her eye at variance with her quiet ways. She had probably never slept with anyone, but then she was really too young and inexperienced to be very rewarding, quite different from the familiar loin-tinglings stirred up by the luscious Cleo. He sensed a kindred spirit there; certainly that would be worth the chase. On the other hand, if Seton found Prue attractive, then why not get there first? Bugger Seton, he could go and hunt on his own patch.

The grinning little faces on the tapestries mocked him. They knew this was their patch, their game; all these people were their victims, as much as the languishing nude nymph whose tresses they tugged as she lay, very voluptuously, desire for her invisible lover evident in every neat little thread.

'How did he know where you were?'

'Someone had told him. It was amazing. I really was in a panic, and I think Thomas was too, though he didn't want to show it. Then there was this dog barking, and there was Seton calling down to us.'

'I thought you said you couldn't climb back the way you'd come,' said Cleo.

'We couldn't, not by ourselves. But we could with Seton helping us. He's very strong, you know, and so good with Thomas. Thomas was scared, and when he got to the top he started crying, said he couldn't help it, and, do you know, Seton knew just how to handle him, not to make him feel a coward or a failure. Thomas was quite cheerful when we met up with you.'

'I noticed,' said Cleo, thinking of the six doughnuts the boy had eaten. Cleo wouldn't forget that meeting in a hurry, Valdemar and Sylvester and Seton all shouting at each other like cockerels in a farmyard. Seton had been happy to bring Prue and Thomas back to the castle, but no, the rescue mission – the *official* rescue mission – was Valdemar's; they must take Prue and Thomas back.

They compromised in the end, Prue staying with Seton, Thomas stuffing doughnuts in the back with Cleo while Sylvester and Valdemar bickered in the front.

'And wasn't Magdalena kind?' said Prue. Despite the tiredness she had a tight radiance about her, caused entirely by Seton. Magdalena had come back to the castle while they were out on the fells, no longer looking ill, but rested, seemingly much younger and very happy. She greeted them with smiles, saw to it that Prue had a hot bath and something to eat, hugged Thomas who didn't want to leave her side, and left Sylvester and Seton helpless with laughter.

'She always used to be like that, Sophie says.'

Prue looked up, pausing in her neat brush strokes as she dried her hair.

'Who?'

'Magdalena.' Cleo stretched out her legs and admired her toenails, which she had been painting. 'I like this colour of Sophie's. I can't see her painting her nails, can you, but she must do. Yes, Sophie says Magdalena used to be very lively and attractive, witty, too. Then when she started to feel ill, she changed. Sophie hopes that whatever they've given her in hospital now has done the trick.'

'I wonder what was wrong with her.'

'Some deficiency, perhaps,' said Cleo. 'Anyway, it certainly cheers this place up when she's like this. It'll be fun working here, Prue, you'll see.'

'Not if Valdemar's staying. He doesn't like me.'

'Ignore him. He won't take any notice of you; you're an inferior being, as far as he's concerned. So you don't need to take any notice of him.'

'Sylvia's going, though,' said Prue. 'Her mother's ill, in France. She's leaving this afternoon. She must be worried.'

'Don't think so, specially,' said Cleo with the easy callousness of youth. 'I think her ma's been peculiar for ages, gaga, really, so Sophie says. Probably a blessing if she pops off, then Sylvia can concentrate on keeping Valdemar under control.'

Prue gave a great yawn. 'Goodness, what a temper that man's got. I don't know how she puts up with him.'

Daisy had often wondered that. She was on friendly terms with the castle, although not as friendly as she would have liked. The friendliness was due to her position as the vicar's wife, not because they liked her for herself. Of course, if Jacob had an ounce of ambition, if he would only bustle about and keep in touch with people who mattered in the church, and not bury himself away in a remote and powerless parish . . .

Daisy dreamed of mitres and palaces. In a different world, she would probably have made an excellent bishop herself. She would have been an ideal cleric – and it would have kept her off the drink, too.

Daisy drank to drown her restless energies and to keep at bay the demon longing for a life of her own. She had even, heaven forbid, thought of leaving Jacob, but he needed her; he would be useless on his own and no other woman would take him on, even if he had the nous to go after another woman. Daisy knew she had made all the running. Jacob had been almost surprised to find himself on the wrong side of the altar one chilly Saturday morning, exchanging his marriage vows with a triumphant Daisy in front of all her friends and relations.

Daisy's keen hearing picked up the first sounds of the approaching train and she picked up her bags, ready to be first on board. There wasn't going to be a fight about it, because she was the only person on the platform. Then, as the train pulled in, two more people came on to the platform; well, thought Daisy, just who I was thinking about, Sylvia and Valdemar. Surely Valdemar wouldn't be going anywhere by train? He drove everywhere, usually at great speed. Was Sylvia leaving him? No, even at this distance – for Daisy was right at the other end of the platform – she could see that their parting was entirely amicable, affectionate even.

'Mind the doors, mind the doors, please.'

Daisy hastily opened the nearest door and found herself in the luggage van. The train gave a loud screech and then jerked forward, nearly sending Daisy into a pile of mailbags.

'You can't stay here, love,' said the guard behind her. 'Plenty of seats further along.'

Daisy retrieved her dignity and her bags, and set off along the corridor, peering into the compartments as she went. She was sure Sylvia would be travelling first class, but there was no sign of her in the first-class section. There were very few people on the train, and Daisy passed one empty compartment after another. Ah, there she was.

Daisy pushed open the door and grinned at Sylvia, who was thinking that, with a whole train to choose from, why did anyone want to come into her compartment?

'Hello, Sylvia,' said Daisy. 'Fancy you being on this train. I thought you drove everywhere, or at least went first class.'

Sylvia smiled. 'No, I only go first class when the trains are crowded. No point in wasting money when you can have a compartment to yourself anyway.'

Daisy didn't take the hint, but plumped herself down opposite Sylvia. 'I like company on a long journey,' she said cheerfully.

I don't, thought Sylvia, putting her book down in a resigned way.

Daisy straightened herself out and opened a large zip bag which she was carrying. 'Gin and T?' she said hospitably. 'I always bring my own. The railways charge the earth for a mingy little measure, and there's usually no ice or lemon.'

Sylvia watched bemused as Daisy unwrapped heavy crystal glasses.

'I take two glasses in case I meet a friend,' Daisy explained. She poured out two liberal shots of gin. Ice came out of a little box and then Daisy produced a lemon and a sharp little knife. A dash of tonic from another chilled bottle, and without in the least meaning to have anything to drink, Sylvia found herself sipping the full glass which Daisy had passed to her. 'You're going to London,' said Daisy. 'So am I. I'm going on church business, Mothers' Union; they have a big get-together once a year. Very boring, actually,' she added with a flash of honesty. 'Still, London's London.'

Sylvia nodded.

'Of course, you live there, don't you, so it's not a treat for you. Just going home, I suppose. Is it work?'

'Work?' Sylvia was puzzled.

'Do you work? I mean, are you leaving the Castle to go back to work?'

'Oh, I see. No. I do work, but not in the summer, my clients are away then. I advise people on what pictures to buy,' she said, hoping to forestall any further questions from Daisy.

It was people that interested Daisy, not their work. 'So why are you going to London?'

'I'm not staying in London. I'm flying to Paris. My mother lives in France, and she's ill.'

'Oh, I am sorry,' said Daisy. 'That is a worry for you. Is she very elderly?'

As Daisy slipped into the practised words of a vicar's wife, consoling parishioners whose aged parents were a source of worry or irritation, Sylvia let the soothing words slip over her.

What would Daisy say if she knew the truth? wondered Sylvia. That my mother died years ago, that I go to France when I can stand Valdemar no longer, to a husband who is pleased to see me, undemanding, peaceful, easy to get on with, relaxing and pleasant to go to bed with?

And Sylvia asked herself, for the hundredth time, why she stayed with Valdemar, who had no idea the husband existed, instead of simply staying in France.

Daisy was still talking. 'All these girls go on and on about how good their boyfriends are in bed. Personally I think most of them are still virgins. I hope they are, anyway; don't they know that sex is essentially unimportant? Look at me and Jacob. Of course we know about that side of things, but as you get older, it isn't so important. You realize that affection and shared interests are what matter.'

Sylvia gave her a direct look. 'I don't know about that,' she said. 'I stay with Valdemar because he is so exciting in bed, and because he makes me feel exciting.'

And it's the truth, she thought, gazing out of the window. And it will shut her up. I've shocked her.

Daisy came back at once. 'You don't shock me saying things like that. I understand, we're all different. And Valdemar, even I can see that he's the kind of man . . .' Her voice trailed off. 'It's a shame,' she went on. 'He would have been such a good father, I think, but men like that are frightened of getting married, aren't they?'

Sylvia laughed. 'He doesn't need to get married. He's very

absorbed in his work, he has the Mountjoys for family and he has me.'

'And all the others,' said Daisy without realizing what she was saying.

'Others?'

'Oh, nothing, no one,' said Daisy quickly. 'It's just, he has a bit of a reputation in the village. There's nothing in it, I'm sure, only that some of the girls obviously like the look of him. And then there was that fuss in London, before you knew him, I think. A paternity suit, if I remember rightly. Nothing came of it.' She gave an apologetic laugh. 'Just gossip, of course. That's what happens when you live in the country.'

'Yes, I suppose so,' said Sylvia unenthusiastically.

'Valdemar's very fond of Thomas, though, that's why I say he would have made a good father. Well, Thomas's father's never paid any attention to him.'

'I thought no one knew who Thomas's father is.'

'No, Harriet would never say who it was, not to anyone. Mountjoy was very upset about it. Harriet said it was no one's business but hers.'

'And Thomas's.' Sylvia was thoughtful. Despite her irregular lifestyle, she came from a solid family; children were part of it, and they knew who their fathers were.

Daisy wasn't listening to Sylvia. 'Then Harriet went off to India to find herself, left Mountjoy to look after Thomas. They had a nanny for him, a nice girl, left very suddenly. They didn't replace her, because by that time Thomas was old enough to go away to school.'

Daisy chewed thoughtfully at her slice of lemon. 'Funny, it was Valdemar who wanted him to go to a choir school. Mountjoy was going to send him away to his old prep school down in the south, but Valdemar got very forceful, said it was far too far away, and the boy was musical, which is true, let him go and sing. So he did. And does. Simon Praetorius thinks very highly of him, I'm told.'

Sylvia frowned. 'The name is familiar, but I can't recall . . .'

'Master of the choristers. In Eyot. He's an old friend of Sylvester's, and of Valdemar's too, funnily enough. They were at Cambridge together.'

'Yes, I've met him. I didn't think Val knew him well.'

'Simon never goes to London if he can help it.'

Daisy replenished her glass. Sylvia's was still two-thirds full. Outside, a sparkling and sunny world sped by, cleansed and renewed by the tremendous storm of that morning.

'Don't you feel like a spaceman?' said Daisy unexpectedly. 'Cocooned in a train like this, out of time, really. You've left one place and haven't got to another, hanging between two worlds. I sometimes wonder if the world I've left behind and the one I'm going to actually exist, or whether the one stops when I leave and the other only begins when I get there.' She paused. 'You can't know, can you?'

Sylvia had no time for metaphysics. 'It has never occurred to me. Surely you can telephone along the way, just to make sure that everything is still there?'

Daisy's thoughts had moved on. 'Do you wonder what Valdemar's doing when you aren't there?'

'I don't think about it at all,' said Sylvia. 'I'm not much of a worrier about anything. I know more or less what he's doing, of course; he's very busy with some plans for the castle at the moment. He'll play some tennis and swim and get restless and go for long drives. He'll spend time with Magdalena, they get on very well together.'

'But you don't really know, do you,' said Daisy earnestly, 'where he is at any particular moment. Now, with Jacob, I do. I keep his diary. I know that at this moment' – and she glanced at the slim gold watch she wore for best – 'he's talking to the Parish Clerk.'

'If he exists,' said Sylvia. 'When you're not there, I mean.'

'What?' said Daisy. 'Oh, yes, I see what you mean!' And she laughed heartily. 'Have another drink,' she said.

9

Jacob, naturally, was not with the Parish Clerk. The minute he had delivered Daisy to the station he had set off in quite a different direction, all his clerical duties postponed for the day. Instead, he planned to spend as many hours as possible making love, which was quite his favourite activity; although not with Daisy, who found the whole business rather a chore.

Jacob knew it ill-became his cloth, but since at heart he was a pagan, he found that making love was the nearest thing he ever had to a religious or mystic experience. Had he married a wife of similar inclinations, there would have been no problem. Jacob was naturally monogamous; only his need for a rich and fulfilling sex life drove him to a kind of bigamy.

Promiscuous he was not. He would never have picked up a stranger for casual sex, nor was he the kind of vicar who goes to naughty parties or visits surburban houses of correction. No, he needed to love where he made love. He looked forward to a day spent in the company of a warm heart and a strong mind as much as to a pair of warm thighs.

And Valdemar? Just as well Sylvia wasn't a worrier. After he had left the station he drove back to Midwinter and shot up the drive to Midwinter Hall. Lily watched from an upstairs window.

'Talk of the devil,' she said to herself, for she and the woman who came in to do had just been talking about Valdemar, and not in a very complimentary way.

'I could fancy a night on the tiles with him,' said Mrs Grobbins, all of fifty-five with six children and a disreputable husband who barely made it home on Friday and Saturday nights. 'Not that I ever went with a smart man like that. I liked them tough and hearty and a touch of the fields about them.'

Which accounted for the fact that only one of her children looked in the least bit like her husband. 'Still, he's got something about him, hasn't he? Kind of basic under the fancy clothes.'

Lily had to admit that this was true. Look at the mischief it had caused over the years. You'd think at forty he'd grow up, stop looking at every woman as a challenge; but no.

'Wonder what he wants,' she said. 'You finish in here, Flo, and I'll go downstairs, see what's brewing. He may have come to see Sylvester, but I'd like to know why.'

Valdemar hadn't come to see Sylvester. He had come to see Cleo. He raised a hand at Lily.

'Don't disturb Sylvester,' he said. 'I can hear he's practising. I'll wait. Is there some coffee?'

He headed for the kitchen as though he owned the place, thought Lily indignantly. Valdemar always behaved as though he owned wherever he was; it was one of his attractions, being so much at his ease.

'Just as at home at Buckingham Palace or in Chinese go-down, I dare say,' Lily said to herself.

The kitchen was empty. Valdemar glanced round; drat the man, thought Lily. He's after Cleo.

'Looking for Cleo?' she said maliciously.

Valdemar's eyebrows rose; he wasn't used to being questioned.

'She's gone to the village. May be some time.'

The back door swung open and Cleo came dancing in. 'Lovely, lovely morning, Lily, and Luke smiled at me, that's a good start to the day. Oh.' She stopped abruptly as she saw Valdemar, who rose to his feet and said good morning.

'Hello,' she said. 'Are you looking for Sylvester? He's practising.'

'I heard,' said Valdemar. 'I'll wait for him. I'm sure he won't be long.'

Cleo listened to the distant sound of the cello. 'Yes, he will. He's working on the whole of that sonata, that's only the first movement.'

'Are you a musician?' enquired Valdemar.

'No,' said Cleo. 'I've heard that piece before, though. Lily, I'll go and get some of those letters done. No coffee, I'll take a Coke.'

Valdemar watched her reach into the fridge with a connoisseur's eye. Good legs, curvy, but Valdemar liked all shapes and sizes. She pushed her shiny dark hair back from her eyes, winked at Lily and left, hardly giving Valdemar time to get to his feet again.

Lily had expected Valdemar to decamp once Cleo had gone, but he didn't. He stayed and made himself very agreeable. He was what the eighteenth century would have called a proper man, and Lily, for all her age and experience, found it difficult to resist his appeal.

'That girl reminds me of someone,' he said. 'Who is she?'

'Her father's dead, her mother's some kind of an artist, in America for the summer. Cleo's a clever child, going to Oxford in the autumn.'

'Perhaps I've met her mother somewhere, and that's why she seems familiar. Thank you for the coffee, Lily. If Sylvester's going to be practising for a while, I'll catch him another time.'

'I'll tell him you called.'

As soon as his car turned out of the drive, Cleo was back in the kitchen. 'Lily, did he really come to see Sylvester?'

'That's what he said.'

'He's very tough, isn't he? Knows what he wants and gets it.'

'So they say.'

'Do you think he fancies me?' Cleo asked, frowning. 'Or does he look at every woman he meets like that?'

'Like what?'

'Oh, Lily, you know.'

Lily relented. 'I'd keep out of his way if I were you, that's as far as I'll go.'

'What about Sylvia?'

'Sylvia went this morning. To visit her old mother in France. Sylvia's old mother in France is often ill, and usually when Sylvia feels that Valdemar is getting out of hand.'

'So while the cat's away . . .'

'Sylvia's no cat, takes Valdemar as she finds him, I reckon, which is as often as not in someone else's bed. And he's no mouse, don't you make any mistake about that. He's dangerous, that man. Far too clever, and full of schemes.'

Cleo roared. 'You make him sound like a character out of a Restoration play, one of those wild men, all ruffled shirts and duels at dawn and tumbling maids before supper.'

'Just what he's like. Only modern and much more subtle, and a lot of trouble if you're not careful. If he's after you, watch it. I've never known him fail.'

Cleo stared at Lily. 'What, you mean to say that every woman he's wanted has gone to bed with him?'

'One way or another, yes, that's exactly what I mean. Pass the big wooden bowl, Cleo, it's in that cupboard behind you.'

Lily thoughtfully rubbed a clove of garlic round and round the bowl. 'If they aren't interested in him, it simply stimulates him and he becomes even more predatory.'

'Do you mean that you think that if he finds me attractive, then that's it? Just roll over and wave my legs in the air?'

'Don't be vulgar. No, I do not. I just know that you'll end up finding him fascinating and wanting to go to bed with him.'

'Nobody, nobody at all can be attractive to all women.'

Lily sighed. 'I'm not saying that.' She went to the fridge and took out the salad drawer. 'Look at these radishes, the size of them! There are lots of women who don't interest him; they're the ones who he probably wouldn't succeed with. He recognizes a spark in the women he goes after; probably most of them don't know they have it, and that's why he gets what he wants.'

She handed the radishes to Cleo to wash, and Cleo dumped them in the sink before attacking them vigorously with a brush. She held one up, admiringly. 'Rude, that's what these radishes are. Do you know what they remind me of? They remind me of . . .'

'Yes, I can imagine, Cleo, there's no need to be coarse. Trim them for me, will you? There's another knife in the drawer there.'

Cleo sat at the table, paring the radishes into fanciful shapes. 'Men,' she said. 'Why do they think they can get away with anything?'

'Most of them can. Val in particular has got away with an awful lot. He sees no reason to change his ways, even at his age.'

'It's ridiculous, I'm not going to take any notice of him. He can go and find some other willing victim.'

'Yes, so long as it isn't Prue.'

'Prue? Oh, surely not. I mean, yes, Prue can be very attractive, she's amazingly pretty when she's lit up, sparkling – but I don't think Val would ever see her like that. She's too nervous of him.'

'Sparkles, does she? Yes, I can see that.'

'When she first came to the convent, she was always sparkling and full of fun. I suppose she wasn't miserable about her parents any more, and the nuns were much kinder than her aunt. They were fond of her. But they didn't approve of the liveliness, it's not ladylike to dazzle. Besides, they encouraged Prue to be serious, because she's so clever. Lucky Prue, she's got it all, if only she knew. Most of the girls there were aiming for marriage, the right man, nice house; I can't tell you how draggy they were. It wore Prue down in the end; what with that and her aunt nagging away in the hols, she never had a chance.'

Cleo bit thoughtfully into a crisp radish. 'These are good,' she said appreciatively. 'Fortunately, I don't think all is lost; now her ghastly aunt's dead, Prue's becoming much more like she was before they all got to her. She worries about what's going to happen to her, though; she doesn't have a lot of confidence in herself.'

'The nuns don't seem to have quelled you,' said Lily drily.

Cleo laughed. 'No, well, they did their best. It was different for me. I had Mum, and my holidays were always fun. Mum and I did a lot together. We went abroad, and stayed with my cousins in Cornwall, and she has a lot of friends. Oh, there's no comparison with Prue's life. The sun never shone for Prue, not all those years. She never had a break. Nuns, aunt; aunt, nuns. No wonder she became booky, it was her only escape.' She looked thoughtful. 'You can say what you like about repressive girls' schools, they're very good places if you're like me. No distractions, so you get on with your work. Now, if I'd gone to a co-ed day-school . . .'

'Your mum's obviously got a lot of sense,' said Lily. 'But I hope Prue puts those years behind her, it isn't the best start in life, a childhood like that. Anyway, for now, she'd best not be dazzling, much better not to attract Val's attention. That goes for you, too, Cleo.'

'All I want to do is get my hands on Luke. Where's he gone, by the way? The castle, I suppose, to make gooey eyes at that horrible Sophie.'

'It's Sophie's day off, she's gone somewhere in Magdalena's car, so he can't be at the castle. He'll be in for lunch, anyway.'

'Oh, good,' said Cleo. 'Back to my work, then. Goodness, Sylvester is a slave-driver.'

'Get on with you,' said Lily, collecting a basin of kitchen bits for the chickens, who lived in a run near the vegetable garden. 'You've got it easy. Do his letters and then spend some time with your books. Take your mind off sex, that will.'

'Go and find Prue,' said Magdalena. 'She'll be in the turret room, I expect.'

Thomas lingered at the door.

'Run along!'

He came back into the room and stood by the sofa, twiddling the silk tassel in his fingers.

'Don't do that, Thomas, it'll fray. What is it? Is something the matter?'

'Oh, nothing,' he said casually. 'I just wondered, are you all right now? Not ill any more?'

Magdalena turned to look at him and saw the anxiety in his eyes. She put out a hand and tousled his hair.

'I'm fine. Absolutely fine. I wasn't really ill at all, there's no problem.'

Thomas grinned, hugely relieved. 'Good,' he said. 'That's okay, then. I'll go and get Prue.'

He stopped again at the door. 'Val won't be there with her, will he?'

Magdalena looked up from her work again. 'No, I don't think so. Why?'

'I'm keeping out of his way a bit. He's cross with me, isn't he? He's cross with Prue, too, which isn't fair. It wasn't her fault.'

'Don't worry about it,' advised Magdalena. 'Just go.'

Prue was glad to leave the Muniment Room. The aged typewriter made her wrists ache, and the room was dim, little light coming in even when there was full sunshine outside. As they came out into the sunlight, Thomas challenged her to a race, and set off at a good pace. Prue followed, and they arrived skidding at the other side almost together.

'Haven't you got any work to do?'

Valdemar was looking down from the ramparts, glowering at them.

'Magdalena wants Prue,' shouted Thomas. 'Come on, Prue, quick, before he gets nasty.'

'Nasty?' said Prue as they went in. 'You shouldn't say that about your uncle.'

'He's still fuming over yesterday. He thinks we made him look a fool.'

'I don't see why,' said Prue. 'It was very good of him to come and find us. It was just that Seton got there first.'

Her voice softened as she thought of Seton. Would he come to the castle today? He had said he would, as he went away the day before.

In the afternoon would be best, because then she could be free for an hour. She'd done a lot this morning so that she could have some time for him. But he might not come; he might be busy, he might not want to.

Magdalena rose as she came in and rolled her tapestry into a bag.

'Good. It's Sophie's day off, Prue, so we'll go to the kitchen and see to lunch. Sophie will have left things ready.'

'I'll come and help,' said Thomas eagerly.

'No, thank you,' said Magdalena. 'You don't help, you just eat everything.'

'I won't, I promise. It's very boring, just me, no friends here. You can't leave me by myself, I'll get lonely.'

'I thought you were going out with Mountjoy?' said Magdalena.

'This afternoon. Oh, look,' said Thomas as he opened the fridge. 'My favourite cheese.'

'Leave it alone,' said Magdalena. 'Prue, the phone's ringing. I switched it through, so you can answer it here.'

Prue picked up the receiver. 'Hello.'

It was Seton. At the sound of his voice, her heart started thumping; she took a deep breath, trying not to sound too pleased. Then her heart sank. He couldn't make it this afternoon.

'Oh,' she said.

'Are you free this evening?' he went on. 'Yes? Good. I'll pick you up at seven. We'll have dinner somewhere.'

Prue put the phone down, her eyes shining. Magdalena looked at her. 'For you, was it?' she enquired.

'Yes,' said Prue. 'Is it all right if I go out this evening? That was Seton. He wants me to have dinner with him.'

Magdalena laughed. 'Your time off is your own, Prue, you don't have to ask. You're grown up now, you know.'

'Grown up?' Such an idea had never occurred to Prue. 'I don't feel grown up.'

'Well, grown up enough to go out to dinner with Seton. You won't come to any harm with him, and I know he'll get you back at a reasonable time. No, you can do what you like, Prue, but let us know where you are or who you're with. We don't want another panic.'

'Oh, no,' said Prue, contrite. 'I am so sorry about yesterday.'

'You've already apologized, several times. Don't worry. I've got some things for you to see to this afternoon, they won't take long, and then you can go and make yourself smart for the evening.'

Prue thought about that as she ate her lunch. She was so wrapped up in her thoughts that she forgot to feel uncomfortable at being with the Mountjoys and Valdemar, and morever she quite cheerfully ate the egg salad which Magdalena had piled on her plate. Prue hated eggs.

Years of convent discipline helped Prue to get through her work for Magdalena efficiently and accurately. At four o'clock she put everything neatly in a folder on her desk, and ran out to the stables to get Sophie's bike – 'Sophie won't mind, I'm sure,' Magdalena had said – and lurched and jolted away down the perilous path to Midwinter.

Cleo was having a very organized afternoon. She had sorted out a boxful of Sylvester's papers, much to his fury.

'That's the trouble with people like you, tidy, tidy. Clear up your mother's paints, do you? Arrange them in rows according to colour?'

'Those are the tools of her trade,' said Cleo with dignity. 'I wouldn't interfere with your music, but this is just mess. You keep all your bills and things in perfect order; why are your letters and the notes for your book in heaps? You'll never get it finished if your papers aren't in order. A system, that's what you need. It'll save us no end of time, you'll see.' And she carried off another boxful, disregarding his roar of disapproval.

She dumped the box in the library where she had made herself at home, and went off to the kitchen; Luke might have come in for something.

'Hello, Cleo,' said Prue. 'I was just coming to look for you. Will Sylvester mind my being here again? Lily says of course not, but I don't want to get you into trouble.'

Cleo made a scornful noise and slid on to the bench. 'Move along, kiddo,' she said. 'Now, what's the excitement?'

'There isn't any excitement, I just wanted some advice. About clothes.' Lily and Cleo exchanged looks.

'You look just right for this weather,' pronounced Lily. 'Short-sleeved blouse, cotton skirt, very suitable. Not like Cleo here, flaunting herself in her tiny skirts and shorts. Good thing Sylvester's the way he is or he'd be all over her.'

Prue looked startled. 'It's not what I'm wearing now,' she began.

Cleo nudged her. 'Course not, we know that. Lily's teasing you. Come on, spit it out. What are you up to?'

'Seton,' said Prue, and stopped.

'Seton? Seton what?'

'Seton has asked me to have dinner with him tonight.'

'Has he now,' said Lily. 'Where, may I ask?'

Prue didn't know; he hadn't said, and she didn't care.

'It matters,' said Cleo. 'If it's a cycle ride by the river to the pub at Gossiby, that's different from dinner at somewhere grand with seven courses and a bill to match.'

'Oh, dear, should I have asked him?' said Prue. 'I never thought . . .'

'As long it isn't a quiet little dinner for two at home, with that big sofa conveniently by, not to mention that great four-poster bed upstairs,' Lily said, banging things together in the sink.

Prue was indignant. 'It isn't like that, Lily. It's just kind of him to take me out. He thinks I might be bored at the castle, with the people there much older than I am, and . . .' Her voice tailed off.

'Yes, and Seton's only twelve or thirteen years older than you are, isn't he?' said Lily. 'Now, Cleo will find you something to wear. It'll be a bit big for you, because you're slim, and Cleo's a big girl.'

'I am not!' said Cleo.

'You are bigger than me,' said Prue. 'You've got, well, chest, for one thing, and I haven't.'

Cleo, who had a generous figure and a magnificent cleavage in the low, clinging dresses she liked to wear, looked thoughtful.

'It's true, Lily. Joking apart, Prue's got very small boobs. I don't think my dresses would look right on her.'

'Boobs!' said Lily with distaste. 'What kind of language is that? Prue's got a nice little bosom, nothing wrong with her figure at all. I'm handy with a sewing machine; we'll fix her up with something.'

Cleo had other thoughts apart from dresses. She hung behind with Lily as they went upstairs to her room, Prue flying up the stairs ahead of them in her eagerness to find a dress. Lily might be so old as to hardly be human, in her fifties, past everything; however Cleo had discovered very quickly that Lily was most certainly a woman of the world and there was nothing about men and sex that she didn't know. It made Cleo wonder just what Lily's career in London had been, but at least you could talk to her without embarrassment.

'Prue isn't on the pill,' she hissed as they followed Prue along the passage.

'Of course she isn't, a nice convent girl like that.'

'But perhaps she ought to be.'

Lily paused. 'You go on, Prue,' she called out. 'I just want to get some soap from this cupboard.' She pulled open the door.

'I don't think Seton will lay a finger on her, not yet anyway. He's the kind who needs pushing, Prue's too inexperienced to push.'

'Look at her,' Cleo said. 'Entranced, glowing with it all. Give her a couple of glasses of wine and a quiet, dark place, she won't need to push. He's human, isn't he? Hasn't taken any vows of celibacy or anything?'

'All I know is, none of the girls round here, village or big houses, have ever had any trouble with him. Not like some I could mention. On the other hand, I could sense trouble for Prue the minute he arrived, that's why I was so cross he hadn't stayed away in America. She needs a nice boy her own age. Seton either won't be interested at all, which is most likely, and she'll be miserable, or he'll fall for her, which will mean a marquee on the lawn and wear your best hat.'

'Prue's far too young to get married, she's never even slept with a man. How could she possibly do that?' Cleo was appalled.

'Girls do, all the time, and what a mistake it usually is. Men ought to come properly labelled "Trouble" or look more like what their natures really are. If they were green with one red eye and blue feet we wouldn't look at them, and we'd all go on much better.'

'Lily, be serious! Prue might get pregnant.'

'Not tonight, she won't. I tell you, he's a gent. Prue's waiting, let's find her something to wear.' She shook her head and sighed. 'What it is to be young.'

To Cleo, evening out meant black. So at ten to seven Prue was lurking on the castle walls – transformed. Cleo and Lily had decided her hair was all wrong for a little black dress, so they had rushed Prue into the village where a laconic Julie had snipped and combed to good effect.

'There,' she said. 'If he doesn't fancy you now, there's no hope for him.'

'Who?' said Prue, pleased with her hair but deeply suspicious of Julie.

'Seton. It's him you're getting all tarted up for, isn't it? Need all the help you can get with that one; dead fussy, he is. One foot wrong, and that's it. Demure, that's my advice to you, be demure. If it's worth the effort, that is. Good-looking man, I grant you that, but he's never going to set the world on fire. You could do much better, I reckon, as far as fun is concerned.'

'Come on, Prue,' said Cleo. 'You've not got much time.'

'Enjoy yourself,' Julie called after them. 'Don't do anything I wouldn't do,' she added with a rich laugh.

Valdemar was sitting on the window-seat in Magdalena's room. 'There's a girl on the walls, what's she up to? She isn't going to hurl herself off, by any chance? What's she doing here, anyway? The castle's closed.'

Magdalena joined him. 'Who? Oh, it's Prue. Doesn't she look nice?'

'Prue?' Valdemar frowned. 'That can't be Prue, she's like a mouse.'

'Nonetheless, it's Prue. She's done something to her hair. Sensible child, it was awful before, just hanging down. I don't know where she got the dress from, because it doesn't look like the kind of dress she'd own at all. I expect she borrowed it.'

Valdemar was still watching. 'Granted that she looks much better than usual, why is she prancing about on the walls?'

'Val, she isn't prancing. She's waiting for Seton. She can see his car coming up the hill from there, and then she can be down there to meet him.'

'Seton?'

'Yes, Seton's taking her out to dinner. Very nice of him. It's rather boring for a young girl like that with all us older people. Good for her to be with someone nearer her own age.'

Valdemar's expression darkened. 'She should be working. There are all those letters and papers to go through in the Muniment Room; she's hardly made a start on them.'

Mountjoy came into the room and crossed at once to his wife, giving her a hug and ruffling her hair with his lips, a most uncharacteristic display of affection for a reserved man. He smiled at her, and nodded at Valdemar. 'What's bothering you, Val?'

'It's only Prue,' said Magdalena. 'She's waiting for Seton to collect her. She's all dressed up and looking very pretty; it annoys Val.'

'Not like you to resent a woman looking pretty, Val,' said Mountjoy, amused.

'Nothing to do with it. Bloody girl should do the job she's paid for, she clearly thinks this place is a finishing school. I've got a pile of work, she could have helped me with that this evening.'

'Don't be silly, Val,' said Magdalena. 'You just can't bear to think of an attractive girl going out with someone else.'

'I'm not interested in her, seems a very uninspiring specimen.'

Mountjoy looked over to the castle wall. 'Well, she's gone now, so you won't have to be offended by the sight of her any more.'

'I hope she has a good evening,' said Magdalena. 'Seton isn't exactly lively.'

'Nor is she,' said Mountjoy. 'She's a nice little thing, suit Seton very well, does as she's told. Time he got married. It's a nice property, and there's no other close family. Good thing for him to have some children to leave it to.'

'Nice, nice.' Valdemar flung himself down on a sofa, slouching, with his long legs stretching across the carpet. 'Two boring people, Seton especially. That man's got no vision.'

'Ah,' said Mountjoy, stepping over Valdemar's legs and sitting in a chair opposite. 'He doesn't like the plans?'

'Not at all. Totally unreasonable. Hasn't had time to look at the whole thing properly, just "No". He'll come round in the end, of course, they always do. Says he doesn't want the peace of the area disturbed, rural ways, different pace of life, all the usual rubbish. Can't see an inch in front of his nose: empty houses, young people all gone to the wicked city to work, nothing but old crones and toothless old men hanging round the village pub – only there won't be a village pub, either.'

'You're very vehement.' Magdalena seemed remote, uninvolved. 'Don't let it worry you. Things so often turn out differently from the way one plans.'

Valdemar shook his head. 'It's a practical problem. A business matter. I can't let the castle crumble away, just for want of effort.'

'Perhaps it should crumble away. It's a relic from the past, it belongs to another world.' Magdalena sounded suddenly weary. 'All the great rooms shut up, the cold, the darkness, the damp. Sometimes I think we're living in a mausoleum.'

'You're tired,' said Mountjoy, concerned. 'Val . . .' He stopped.

'What?'

'Nothing. I'll go and make Magdalena some tea.'

Left alone with Magdalena, Valdemar sat and looked at her. 'You've changed.'

She smiled. 'You never change, Val. Perhaps that's why you're so surprised when you occasionally notice that people around you have changed.'

'Something's happened. Something's different, that you haven't told me.'

'Don't try to bully me, Val.'

He got up to stand beside her, took her hand. She removed it and placed it in her lap.

'You look different. Serene. Drugs? Are they giving you drugs?'

'No. Leave it, Val, I'm tired. Ask Mountjoy to bring the tea to our room? Thank you, Val.'

As she drifted towards the door, she turned and looked thoughtfully at him. 'Time for you to find yourself a wife. Children. Those are what count, in the end.'

'Women's talk.'

Magdalena smiled and left.

Valdemar paced up and down, not giving a moment's thought to Magdalena's advice. Valdemar was a constructor. Buildings, rooted in the earth and rising high into the sky were his absolutes. The higher, the more overpowering, the better.

He had first felt the glory and power of a huge building when he sang in the cathedral as a boy. That had been his revelation, not the power of God, but the power of man that could build such tremendous monuments. He had set out to duplicate the work of the old cathedral makers, but his inspiration was not of the spirit but of the will. To Valdemar, the castle was another great shout of power, and therefore it had to be maintained, it had to stand. Great seats of power should stand forever, that was true immortality. Everything else was illusion.

He glanced up at the great bulk of the deserted keep; its shadow darkened the lawns below where the sunlight streamed across the greenness. His clever mind, drained of humanity by the structures which dominated it, plotted and planned.

He had driven Nature out with a very efficient pitchfork, and naturally Nature was going to have her revenge, sooner or later. The chaos he had spent his life fighting was creeping up on him. He should have listened more closely to the lessons in those long hours of services in the cathedral when he was a boy. As ye sow, so shall ye reap. Valdemar had done a lot of sowing.

10

Prue sank back into the comfortable leather seat of Seton's car. She liked watching his hand on the gear lever; she liked the rich hum of the car engine, the sound of the wheels on the road. Prue had never been in a car like this before. Powerful, she thought appreciatively. I expect it can go really fast, not on roads like this of course. She gave Seton a long sideways look. 'Where are we going?' she asked.

'Ghercombes,' Seton said, swerving to avoid a tractor which was lumbering towards them in the middle of the road.

'Ghercombes? Is it a pub?'

'No,' said Seton. 'It's a country house hotel. Very famous. Very good. The only trouble is, it's buried in the depths of the country.' He glanced quickly at her, wondered if he liked her new look, the smart hair cut, the elegant black dress. She looked vivid, that was the word. He thought perhaps he preferred the mousy Prue.

Like so many men, he imagined he liked girls to look natural. Like all men, he had no idea how much artifice went into looking natural. As his mother could have told him, Englishmen marry women who care how they look, clothes, shoes, hair, nails. Then they subdue them into dowdy country or suburban pleasantness and immediately take up with some extravagant creature, all glow and crackle and fashion.

Seton would do exactly the same; he would be fond of his wife, even more so than of his dogs, well, than most of his dogs. He would beget several radiantly beautiful children, the girls to go the way of their mothers, the handsome boys to marry attractive girls who would settle down in the country while their husbands . . . and so on. Unless some freak of the genes produced a sport, unless some most unusual disaster or crisis jerked one of them out of his peaceful, rutted ways.

He was pleased with the reception his old friends at the hotel gave Prue. Henry bustled up to greet them, cooing with pleasure,

111

fluttering over them as he ushered them to a vast, deep sofa and waved a waiter towards them. Then he hurried off to the kitchens to find Patrick, the chef, the genius whose cooking brought visitors from the other side of the world to this lonely spot.

'My dear,' he hissed. 'Seton is here with such a pretty girl, the one from the castle, I'm sure it is, and she's flashing such naughty looks at him.'

Patrick at once left his army of pots and pans and minions and swept out to greet Seton, immaculate in his whites, bending over Prue's hand in a courteous gesture, his shrewd eyes looking her up and down.

'Champagne?' said Seton.

Prue's eyes danced. 'I've never had champagne,' she said. 'I would like to try some.'

Henry clucked in horror, never had champagne! Then it must be the best. She must savour a unique first experience, 'as you must savour all delightful first experiences,' he added, looking, thought Prue, exactly like a sly cherub.

Seton was usually careful in his choice of wine, never extravagant, but of course he had to accept Henry's choice of champagne.

'And the menu,' he said, passing Prue an unostentatious typed sheet.

Prue looked at it, surprised. 'I thought they'd have a terribly grand menu in a place like this,' she whispered to Seton.

He laughed. 'They don't need it; the food is so good it doesn't need a magnificent menu. What would you like?'

Prue's convent French hadn't covered food like this, so Seton patiently translated the items for her.

No prices? she thought to herself. Goodness, it must be very expensive. But Lily had said how well-off Seton was, and he wouldn't have brought her here if he couldn't afford it.

Seton chose for her; girls of Prue's age needed decisions made for them. All right to choose for themselves when they turned into gluttonous middle-aged ladies with blue rinses, absorbed in food and health farms.

'Oysters,' he said. 'You'll love oysters. No, don't tell me, you've never had them. Splendid, it's going to be an evening of adventure.' He smiled at her and Prue gave him a dazzling, enchanting smile in return. He made her tingle; he knew she couldn't eat anything. How embarrassing, what could she say?

The champagne arrived. Prue took a sip, sniffed because the taste was unexpected, and sneezed loudly. Henry tut-tutted. 'My dear, you mustn't treat this champagne like that!'

'Bubbles up my nose,' said Prue, in fits of laughter as she searched for her hanky. 'It's gone everywhere, what a waste!'

Seton looked rather put-out and drank some of his champagne in a much neater manner. 'Mmm. Very good, Henry, but it's not going to be a habit.'

'Ah, but tonight you're celebrating,' cried Henry. 'We heard all about your daring rescue of Prue here – it is Prue, isn't it? Yes, of course. Good gracious, she could have been drowned. And young Thomas, that beautiful boy; it just doesn't bear thinking about.'

'Mmm,' said Seton again, in quite a different tone of voice. Henry glided away to greet some new arrivals, and Seton took Prue into the dining room.

By now Prue was sure she was in love with Seton, and she abandoned herself to enjoyment of the feeling. The candlelight flattered Seton's undoubted good looks, gave definition and interest to an otherwise slightly bland countenance. What with the champagne, Seton, the silver, the china, the sumptuousness of it all, Prue was intoxicated.

She wasn't sure about the oysters. She looked at them doubtfully, and then when Seton showed her how to tip them off the shell . . .

'Delicious,' he said enthusiastically. 'Where does Henry get such wonderful oysters?'

A waiter told him as he passed by on swift feet. 'France, sir,' he whispered. 'Flown over specially.'

'How do they cook them?' asked Prue.

'They aren't cooked. They're raw,' said Seton. 'That's why you have to be careful where you eat them. Do you like them?'

'I think so,' said Prue. She thought they were rather horrid but she wasn't going to say so. It was just that she wasn't used to them; look how everyone else was enjoying them.

Seton was so pleased with his oysters that he didn't notice Prue's slight lack of enthusiasm. 'That was just a little extra,' he told her, 'to whet the appetite. Now we can really begin.'

How can anyone possibly eat all these courses? thought Prue. Seton doesn't seem bothered, he can't eat like this very often. She had noticed Seton's firm, flat stomach.

Sylvester envied Seton his physique. Let's sing the body beautiful, he had said to him one day when Seton, unusually, had been in his shirtsleeves.

'You should take more exercise,' Seton had said. 'Go walking on the fells, like I do.' Sylvester thought that was a ridiculous idea, and said so.

'Besides, I've got a living to earn, not like you, sitting on your acres watching the money roll in.'

Prue liked the sorbet, lightly green and tangy on her tongue. At least she knew what she was eating. Or thought she did until Seton told her it was a basil sorbet. Basil? Veggie ice cream. Oh well, thought Prue and took another mouthful. This was certainly a whole new world.

Seton held the wine up to the light and admired its colour. Then he looked across at Prue. He stared. Never mind the wine, there was something very strange about her colour.

'Do you feel all right?' he asked her, puzzled. Prue, who was feeling very peculiar, didn't answer. She was gazing at an enormous red lump which was coming up before her eyes on the back of her hand. She felt a pain on her other arm – another angry red patch was beginning there. A cold trickle went up the back of her neck and she gave a funny little noise.

The room swayed slightly. 'How awful,' said Prue in a dreamy voice, 'I must have had too much champagne.' Then she slipped quietly and neatly to the floor.

The discreet dining room flamed into life. They hadn't seen such excitement there all year, not since the Luthiers had publicly ended their marriage at the dining table, and Maria Luthier had poured the chilled cucumber soup all over her husband before walking away with his wallet.

A bustling little man, almost totally bald, knelt down beside Prue. 'What a thing,' he said with great good humour. 'Most striking reaction, very rare to see a case like this.'

Seton was horrified; all these people looking at them, although most of them were pretending not to, just making sympathetic clucking noises into their plates.

'I would be grateful if you could give her some air,' he said angrily to the small bald man, two waiters and Henry, who had all joined Prue on the floor.

'This is Sir Desmond Fuseli,' hissed Henry. 'A physician. Consulted by royalty.'

'Oh, I'm sorry. She doesn't need a doctor, though. The wine has just gone to her head. I'll take her outside.'

'Dear me, no,' said Sir Desmond. 'That's not the case at all. This is a very violent allergic reaction. What's she eaten?'

Seton, Henry and the waiters all looked at each other.

'Oysters!' they said together.

'Oysters? She's been eating the oysters? There it is, then. Most interesting. I wonder if it happens every time she eats them.'

'She's never had them before,' said Seton.

'Ah. Take some advice. I know oysters are supposed to do wonders, lot of nonsense in my opinion, but next time you feed a girl oysters, make sure she's had them before and isn't allergic to them. Raw seafood – it doesn't suit everyone, you know. And now, you see, your pleasant plans are all spoiled, because I can tell you that it will be several days before this young lady is up to much at all, let alone what you probably had in mind.' Ignoring Seton's protestations, he told the waiters to carry Prue to a bedroom and said he would be up as soon as he had finished his sorbet.

'Prue.'

Prue opened her eyes – not an easy thing to do with such swollen eyelids. Someone was calling her. Where was she? All she could see was a gold cherub, a fat little body with wings and a sly, pouting face with pursed lips.

Am I dead? thought Prue for one wild and ridiculous moment. In heaven?

'Prue? Oh, you are awake. Good.'

It was Magdalena. Prue groaned and tried to sit up. 'I feel terrible,' she said. 'Where am I?'

'Still at the hotel. You couldn't come home last night – you were too ill. So I've come to get you now. I don't expect you feel in the least bit like moving, but you're in the bridal suite, and they have a honeymoon couple arriving today.'

Prue looked round the opulent bedroom. More cherubs held white and silver draperies over the end of the bed; she could see into the bathroom, all gold taps and rosebud tiles.

'Isn't it incredible?' said Magdalena cheerfully. 'Costs the earth, and it's nearly always booked up; only chance that it was the one empty room last night, the couple who had been here checked out early because they had decided to split up.'

'What, on their honeymoon?'

'Seems so.'

'I am sorry,' said Prue, returning to the comfort of her own faults. 'I'm such a nuisance. I think I should give up my job with you, everything has gone wrong.'

'Not at all,' said Magdalena. 'Part of your job was to cheer me up, and you certainly do that – one never knows what you're going to do next.'

'I'll get dressed,' said Prue, swinging her legs gingerly over the side of the bed. 'Where did this nightie come from?'

'The hotel have some. No, don't try and put that dress on. It's very pretty, but I've brought some other clothes for you.'

Prue looked at the black dress in horror. 'How dreadful! What on earth has happened to it? It's ruined!'

'I think you were sick in it. I expect it will clean.'

'It isn't mine, I borrowed it from Cleo.'

'Cleo will understand.'

Magdalena led Prue into the bathroom and handed her some clothes. She sat down in a heavily-brocaded chair to wait.

The phone rang. 'Prue?' a voice said. 'How are you?'

'Hello, Seton,' said Magdalena. 'It isn't Prue, she's in the bathroom. No, she hasn't recovered, she looks terrible. I'm taking her home. No, don't come and see her this afternoon, she won't want anyone to see her until she's herself again. She's puffed up like some strange reptile. No, I'm sure she does't blame you, and I wouldn't waste any time worrying about it, it was no one's fault. Why don't you take a gun and go and kill something? That'll take your mind off things. I'll let you know when Prue's in circulation again. Goodbye.'

'I thought I heard you talking to someone,' said Prue as she came out of the bathroom. She sat down in front of the mirror and started to tug a comb through her tangled wet hair.

'Do be more gentle,' said Magdalena. 'You must take care of your hair. It was the phone, Seton ringing up to ask how you were.'

Prue stopped combing, her hand suspended in mid-air. 'Seton? Is he very cross with me?'

'Cross with you? I should hope not.'

'Well, I did spoil his evening.'

'Nonsense. The oysters spoilt your evening. He wanted to come to see you this afternoon, but I said no.'

Prue's mouth drooped slightly.

'Have a good look at yourself,' advised Magdalena. 'Not your hair, the rest of you.'

Prue looked. 'Oh, dear,' was all she said.

'Puffy, you see,' said Magdalena. 'Never mind, it will go down quite soon.' This is how I may look when I'm old, thought Prue. Shapeless, little piggy eyes, skin like an old hearthrug.

'Exactly,' said Lily. 'Not many girls of your age ever think for a minute that they'll be old and wrinkly one day, and not so far in the future, either. You'd be surprised how soon it is that you'll wake up and be fifty. Gather your rosebuds, Prue, don't sit and moon about while you're young. Make the most of it. Plenty of time for wondering whether you should or shouldn't do something when you're too old to have the choice anyway.'

'I don't know what you're talking about,' said Prue crossly. Still rather puffy, she sat on a deckchair under an umbrella – sun won't do you any good, according to Lily – at Midwinter Hall.

'I'll take you down for the day,' Magdalena had offered. 'That way Val won't come and snarl at you.'

Prue's stomach gave a nasty lurch. 'Snarl at me? Why should he?'

'Thinks you're malingering, attention-seeking. He's got a pile of work sorted out for you to do. I've told him to find his own secretary. As soon as you're well enough you can do those papers for Mountjoy. They need doing, and you can be left in peace there in the Muniment Room.'

'I'm supposed to work for you,' said Prue.

'Yes, but there isn't anything at the moment that I can't do, I've got all my old energy back. Cleo is helping with anything that needs doing for the music festival. That's fair, because it's half Sylvester's affair anyway. It isn't officially, of course, but he loves organizing. He has to take over everything. Now stop protesting, just do as you're told.'

Prue was good at that, so she obediently settled down at Midwinter Hall, determined to be up early the next day to immure herself in a pile of dull and dusty papers.

Lily was contemptuous, and said so loudly at lunchtime. 'Pass the mayonnaise to Cleo, Luke; I don't know what's the matter with you. Family papers! They'd be better burnt. What's in those papers isn't fit for anyone's eyes, least of all an innocent like Prue.'

Cleo stopped gazing at Luke for a minute and turned her attention to Lily. 'Why? What are the papers about?'

'They're about the family. Not this lot, their ancestors, and I've already told you they were a wicked bunch.'

'Pity we didn't have a revolution in this country,' said Luke gloomily. 'The Mountjoys would have been beheaded and that would be the end of it. They're an anachronism, squatting up in that crumbling castle. Valdemar's the only one living in the twentieth century, but he's as bad of the rest of them when it comes to the family and the castle.'

'Who would be living in the castle now if they'd had their heads chopped off?' said Prue.

'Ridiculous conversation,' grumbled Sylvester, putting down the *Financial Times* and reaching out for the mayonnaise. Lily snatched it away and put it on the dresser.

'Give that back. I can't eat poached fish without mayonnaise.'

'Oh yes, you can. Don't argue, I'll tip it down the sink if you do.'

Cleo bent her head over her plate and winked at Luke. Prue flashed a slightly swollen but sympathetic grin at Sylvester.

'I'll tell you who'd be living in the castle. Val would, that's who,' said Sylvester.

'He wouldn't exist,' said Luke in the voice of one explaining something to a small child.

'Pipe down, brat,' said Sylvester with perfect good humour. 'If not this Val, then his twin. People like Val bob up to the surface whenever they live and whatever their circumstances. His ancestors must have been like him to grab the land and build the castle and keep their enemies out across the centuries. Val's just like a Norman baron; try competing with him for a contract and see where you get. Your Sophie knows all about that, sensible woman. Straight out of the jungle, Valdemar is, she told me. The only thing you can do is get out of his way.'

'She isn't my Sophie,' said Luke, rather sadly.

'Who is her boyfriend, then?' said Prue, and immediately wished she'd kept quiet. The others all turned and stared at her. 'Well, she's got one, hasn't she? I mean she goes out, and . . .' Her voice tailed away us Lily shook her head at her.

Luke swung his legs over the bench. 'I won't stay for pudding, Lil,' he said. 'Got to get on.'

'Do you need any help?' asked Cleo.

118

'No, he doesn't,' said Sylvester. 'I do, though. Have some fruit salad, and then we can get some work done.'

Cleo pulled an exaggerated face. 'Slave, slave, that's all I do. Meanwhile, my private life goes to rack and ruin. How can I work well, when I'm living in a torment of frustration? If Sophie's got a boyfriend, why can't she come clean about him? Then Luke could leap on me on the rebound. Lovely!'

'Cleo,' said Prue reproachfully and not very clearly, since her mouth was full of a particularly lush strawberry from the fruit salad.

'I know, what would the nuns say,' mimicked Cleo. 'They wouldn't, I don't believe any of them would know what I'm talking about.'

'Disgraceful, you are,' said Lily with perfect good humour. 'Talking about things which should be kept to yourself.'

'Why? I'm among friends.'

'Stop thinking about sex for five minutes and get on with Sylvester's book,' said Lily. 'His agent was on the phone again this morning, saying where is it? And Prue, find yourself an improving book and a place in the shade. Go and rest, get rid of those lumps, very uninspiring. Magdalena won't be picking you up for a couple of hours yet.'

'I go,' said Cleo dramatically, 'but I promise you, if I don't get to tumble Luke, I'm going on the prowl to Eyot. Must be some nightlife there, nothing ever happens here.'

'Don't speak too soon,' said Lily.

Sylvester thoughtfully ate a spoonful of fruit salad. 'I heard from Hortense today,' he told Lily. 'A letter. She's worried about Thomas. Says she thinks something is going on at the castle. Can we find out what it is, will it be bad for Thomas?'

Lily shook her head, and pushed the bowl of fruit salad out of Sylvester's reach.

'Course she's worried about Thomas. She's been worried about him since the day he was born, and she'll worry about him until the day she dies.'

'Guilt, perhaps, rather than worry.'

'No,' said Lily, thinking it over. 'Yes, she does feel guilty, not surprising in the circumstances, but she's worried, too. What happens if he ever finds out, if Mountjoy ever finds out . . .'

'These things blow over,' said Sylvester philosophically. 'Luckily,

Thomas is growing up okay. There could have been something wrong with him, but there isn't.'

'No. Why has Hortense suddenly got worked up about what's happening at the castle?'

'A soothsayer.'

'Soothsayer?'

Sylvester nodded. 'India's full of them, of course, and Hortense would be drawn to that kind of thing. This one warned her, described what Hortense at once decided must be Mountjoy Castle, and then told her some stuff about secrets revealed, young life at a crossroads; she feels that has to be Thomas.'

'Just as likely to be Prue,' said Lily. 'Poor Hortense, though, it's such a long way to have gone to get away from a mistake. Such a distant country, such different ways, and eating mangoes and so on.' She shook her head. 'She can't stay there for ever, she'll have to come back some time. Apart from anything, Thomas is longing to have a proper mother; he hardly knows her. Let her come back to a different part of the country, settle somewhere new, make a home for him . . .'

Sylvester ponderously swung his feet over the bench and stood up. 'People aren't the same when they've lived in India. It changes them, I've often noticed it. It's the heat. Look at us this summer, the heat's affecting us all.'

'Summer madness,' said Lily.

11

That night was the hottest and most sultry of the year, and the village, the Hall and the Castle hummed and stirred with life all night long. There was no darkness; the late-setting sun gave way to a huge and brilliant moon, which cast strange shadows across the fields and hedges and lawns. Animals were abroad; Sophie, on her way to a clandestine meeting in the forest, could hear rustlings and scuttlings. Things screeched, called, moaned. The earth itself seemed to breathe; everything was full of life. Lovely, soft earth, thought Sophie as she sank blissfully into a carpet of grass, waiting and listening.

Others were abroad, too.

Sylvester, unable to sleep, had taken his cello outside and was playing Bach to the moon. Lily, alert, was in the kitchen, waiting for when he would finish playing and come hunting for refreshments.

'Fruit juice is what he can have. You have to watch him or he'll be in here, bottle of wine, cheese, all sorts of things he shouldn't have.'

Cleo grinned sleepily at her. Restless with the heat, and woken up completely by the sound of the cello beneath her window, she had got up to get herself a cold drink.

'I think I'll go for a walk,' she said. 'It's a wonderful night. Magic!'

Lily snorted. 'Magic! Oh, yes, a magic night, all kinds of mischief going on. I can think of a few that won't be in their own beds tonight. I saw Sophie sloping off to the forest, for one.'

Cleo became alert. 'Sophie? Not with Luke?'

'No, no, Sophie wouldn't walk like a cat across the fields for Luke. Risky, though, she'll have to watch it.'

In the vicarage kitchen, Jacob poured Daisy yet another glass of cold white wine.

'Generous,' said Daisy. 'When it's usually, "Don't you think you've had enough?"'

'It's very hot tonight,' said Jacob mildly. 'And you seem to have one of your hay fever attacks coming on. Must be the dust from the fields and paths, I can't remember such a summer.'

'It's pollen, not dust,' said Daisy. 'I don't think your mind is getting any sharper as you get older.'

'It might have various causes, with allergies you can't tell.'

'Mmm,' said Daisy. 'Oh, well, I'll take an antihistamine, can't hurt. Shouldn't with alcohol, they say, but white wine isn't exactly alcoholic.'

Jacob thoughtfully found the packet of tablets for her, and handed them to her with another glass of wine. 'Take two, perhaps,' he said. 'Just to make sure.'

Daisy pressed the tablets out on to her palm, blinked at them and sucked them into her mouth. 'Ugh,' she said. 'They taste foul. Fill up my glass, would you . . . mmm, I must say, I feel very relaxed, even though it is so hot. Sleep in the spare room, tonight, Jacob, it'll be far too hot in bed with both of us, and you take up so much room.'

'Of course, whatever you say.'

'It'll do us both good to have a proper night's sleep. Sunday tomorrow, busy day.'

'Busy night, I hope,' said Jacob under his breath.

Why don't I leave her? Jacob asked himself as he unbuttoned his clerical collar. It was a question he often asked himself, but never answered. She would make a fuss, he knew that. Then, his bishop would move him to another parish; not that Jacob's little ways would worry him. Compared to what some of the clergy got up to, Jacob was refreshingly straight in his sins. But the parishioners wouldn't like it, clergy should set an example, and it wasn't good to see a marriage fail in front of their eyes. Jacob liked his church, his parish, the wonderful sex, his friends at the Hall and the castle, the music. No, he wasn't going to give all that up in a cloud of accusations and tantrums.

The house was quiet. An owl hooted outside, Mrs Grobbins' half-witted dog raised its peculiar voice in a strangled howl. Agnes' one-eyed tomcat wailed a challenge back and went off in search of the farmer's neat little tabby. Jacob tip-toed down the passage.

Snuffling snores wafted out from their bedroom. A glance inside showed Daisy sprawled not very elegantly across the bed, her long legs uncovered, the light on, a book on the cover, a prissy voice on the radio reading a story. Jacob sighed. Once, those legs had excited him; if he hadn't seen in them a promise which was never kept, he wouldn't be here now. He straightened his sleeping wife out; nothing was going to wake her for several hours. He drew the curtains, turned the light out and the radio off, and put the book neatly on the bedside table. Then he left, closing her door and then the back door as he went.

One of the vicarage hens cackled at him as he went past. Good Lord, even the hens were up and about; what a night. He and the tomcat slid along either side of the wall which led to the woods, the cat in the hedge, the vicar on the road, one striped, one not, both intent on the same purpose.

At the castle, some people slept. Thomas slept, with the blissful abandon of childhood, dreaming of electric trains and otters. Magdalena slept soundly as she did these days, relaxed and happy. Prue slept, her curtains drawn back, the moonlight streaming through the open casement, drowning her in light so that she looked unreal, a princess with spun-gold hair from a fairy tale.

Mountjoy was awake, cleaning a lock; he was fascinated by locks, always had been, and had collected them since he was a boy. This was a heavy, seventeenth-century lock. Lovely action there, he thought, his fingers deftly probing decades of grub out of the crevices. His eyes strayed to his sleeping wife. He gave a little sigh of happiness. The dog at his feet thumped a heavy tail and dropped back into his own deep slumbers.

In the other tower Valdemar prowled, his mind full of figures and plans. He never slept much, anyway, and would be up working for hours yet. He sensed movement and life around him; it didn't please him. He came into his own in the great dark stretches of the night, when he felt he was the only person in the world.

He stopped by an open window. He could see, far across the valley, lights on at the Hall; he could hear the faint sound of Sylvester's cello. What was creaking? There was a sound above the cello, close at hand . . . the window in the South Tower was moving to and fro. Bloody girl, couldn't even fasten her window. No good calling out, wake the household. She wouldn't hear, anyway.

Valdemar thought nothing of going into a comparative stranger's bedroom; normal manners and courtesies never counted very much with him.

123

He walked irritably across the courtyard and up the spiral stone staircase on the other side. Prue's door was unlocked. Without knocking or even glancing at the sleeping figure on the bed, Valdemar crossed to the window and tugged the catch into place.

Prue made a soft noise and flung herself on to her back. Valdemar turned; the moonlight still shone in her bright hair and now also streamed across one small bare breast. Valdemar stood like stone, breathing hard, suddenly full of urgent desire. Stupid girl, lying like that.

He left quickly, shutting the door noisily behind him, off, with long strides, to the village; not so much a tomcat, more a marauding panther, but still in search of the same quarry as the vicar and Mrs Grobbins' cat.

Julie slipped through the village, watched by eyes gleaming from observation posts at windows all down the village street.

'That Julie, off again. Her mum ought to watch her, she'll do it once too often.'

Julie knew she was watched, and it didn't worry her one bit. She had been watched since she was a wild two-year-old, having tantrums and being dragged home by her exasperated mother. She was used to it. Forest? she thought to herself. Castle grounds? By the beck on the high fells? Tom, or Dick, or Harry? Whistling, she headed for the castle, doubtful if Sophie would be there on a night like this, but she could look in on her way, catch up on the news.

Julie missed Valdemar by a whisker. She helped herself to a drink in the kitchen, and then went on her wild way to find the hot and eager young man waiting for her by the tarn. For the other two equally hot and eager young men waiting in vain for her elsewhere she didn't spare a thought. There would be other nights, other assignations.

Valdemar strode on, his blood still up. He thought of Seton, and then an unbidden recollection of Prue stirred him again. Why should Seton have that particular goody? Perhaps there was more to the girl than there seemed at first, perhaps enough interest for a few idle summer evenings.

Ah, but this was better. Cleo, walking swiftly along the lower path. Valdemar jumped down beside her. Again, he was struck by her looks. Surely he knew her from somewhere else?

'Wonderful evening. Just on my way to see Sylvester,' he lied.

Cleo gave him a long, cool look, her vivid blue eyes meeting his without embarrassment. 'Then you go that way.' She gestured along the path where she had come.

'You shouldn't be out by yourself, in lonely places so late at night. It could be dangerous. There are strange people about.'

'Hmm,' said Cleo.

Her olive skin was tanned with a fine sheen in the moonlight. Her dark hair gleamed, her teeth were very white. And what a body, thought Valdemar; he liked curves. He drew closer to her and ran a firm hand down her back to rest on her bottom.

'Mmm,' said Cleo.

'You know,' he went on, his head bent over her as he nuzzled the back of her neck, 'I'm sure we've met before. You seem so familiar.'

'Never,' said Cleo firmly, trying rather unsuccessfully to keep a check on herself. With his reputation, did she want just to be another local statistic? She decided she did, the air was too full of warm voluptuous scents and sounds. Luke was fast asleep; who else was there?

'Enjoying yourself in your usual way,' said a soft voice.

A slightly dishevelled Julie, languorous after a delightful but brief session by the tarn – 'I can't stop, Julie, my Dad'll kill me if he knows I'm out. That trouble with the police, now every time I'm out he thinks I'm in more trouble,' a last, tongue-thrusting kiss, trousers hastily done up and gone – came out of the bushes.

Cleo moved away from Valdemar, but he caught her by the arm.

'I wouldn't, Val,' said Julie. 'Not this one. This is one you'd really regret.'

'Oh, go away, Julie,' said Valdemar in an irritated voice. 'For God's sake, you've got the whole countryside to roam over. Why do you have to be here?'

'Fate,' said Julie.

'Take my word for it,' she went on, turning her attention to Cleo. 'If you're feeling sexy, and who wouldn't on a night like this, go and find someone your own age. Luke, now, he sleeps with his bedroom window open. His bedroom is on the ground floor. Very convenient.'

'Bugger off,' said Valdemar, losing his temper.

'Not my style,' said Julie, with a wonderful, inviting smile.

Cleo vanished into the shadows. Valdemar eyed Julie. 'Last summer, that was it, Julie. All right for a time, but nothing long-lasting.'

'Whoever said anything about long-lasting? I wouldn't have you long-lasting if you came in a fancy box with ribbons. Long-lasting? What's long-lasting will be your past catching up with you one of these days. All those wild oats, regular fields-full there'll be under your name. Come on, a kiss for old time's sake.'

She twined herself round Valdemar's neck. The musky smell of her was too much for him and he responded swiftly and almost involuntarily.

'This way,' whispered Julie. 'I know a place near here.' Julie always knew of a place.

'And you owe me, God,' she whispered to herself. And so do you, Valdemar Mountjoy, but I don't suppose you'll ever realize it. Just saved you from the burning pit, she thought as his hands felt her. Oh well, enjoy!

'Drat the girl,' said Lily as she poured a glass of juice for Sylvester.

He snapped the last clasp of his cello case shut and drained the glass in one gulp. 'More, please.' His slightly frizzy hair was damp; so was he. 'I'll take a shower and go back to bed, and don't you dare wake me up in the morning. What girl, anyway?'

'Girl?'

'You said, drat the girl. To whom were you referring?'

'Break my brains, you talking like that in the middle of the night. Cleo. Can't be sure what she's up to, but I've got a bad feeling in my bones.'

'Bones, you and your bones. Tucked up in bed, fast asleep, stop fussing.'

'Who's fussing? And she isn't. She's out, like everyone in the village under the age of thirty, and at least one who won't see forty again – he's the one that worries me.'

'Leave the girl alone,' said Sylvester, yawning hugely. 'Made me sleepy, midnight music. You were young once, remember? If she's out with a swain, why, more power to her elbow.'

'Swain, indeed. And elbows aren't the part of her anatomy that I'm concerned about. Get off to bed, you're no use to anyone.'

She hummed softly to herself as she flitted around the kitchen, remembering far-away times in the heat of other hot nights. How quickly it all passes, she thought; that's the really great sadness.

She flicked off the light and went upstairs. She could hear the shower running in Sylvester's bathroom. The door to Cleo's room was wide open; she looked in, but there was only an empty bed, the sheet thrown back, no Cleo.

'I hope she's enjoying herself,' Lily said to herself as she climbed into bed and reached for a book. And not with Valdemar, dear God, not with Valdemar. She read, not wanting to sleep until she heard Cleo come back.

Cleo had no immediate intention of returning to her own room. At the cottage she had stolen softly round. What if it's the wrong room, she thought, eyeing an open window: it could be Peter, that would be awkward. She flattened herself against the wall and took a quick look into the room. Not Peter. Goodness, what a gorgeous body. Luke was lying on his stomach, naked, a sheet just trailing across his legs.

Oh, my, what a wonderful bum, thought Cleo. Very quickly and quietly, she eased the window up and climbed into the room. With one quick movement she took off her dress and slid beside Luke. He grunted and rolled over. Cleo found an exciting bit of him and gave it a not too gentle squeeze.

Luke woke up with a start. 'What the bloody hell . . . who . . . Cleo!'

'Quiet,' said Cleo, brushing her lips across his soft and sleepy mouth. 'Sssh. I was lonely, and your window was open, so I came in.'

'Well, you can just go straight out again. I don't want you here.'

'Not true,' said Cleo, much gratified by what she could feel. 'I think I'm more than welcome. How long is it since you've been with a girl?'

'I'm not . . .' Luke tried to protest and struggled to sit up. That made matters worse, and exasperated with himself he pulled Cleo down on him. 'Oh, Christ, all right, oh, damn it.'

And what of Seton, on this night of mixing and matching? He, too, felt a quickening of the blood, but he sat down purposefully with his accounts, which soon quelled any other more interesting ideas he might have had. The thought did cross his mind that a warm body to share his big bed in the bedroom upstairs might be altogether delightful. It was easy to imagine Prue in it, so fair, so good, so willing to please, surely so kind. And she liked dogs. In his slightly muddled English way, Seton had crossed his Rubicon. It was time for him to marry, his duty, really. Look how well the estate was doing; he was worth far more now than he had been when his father died five years ago, and one had to think ahead. A son, at least one son.

Seton could see himself teaching him to shoot, visiting him at prep school, watching him playing in the First Eleven at public school. Of course, Seton wasn't bright enough to realize that girls like Prue weren't very likely to produce perfect little English gents; the genes were wrong, too much brain and, when she really grew up, too much character.

Seton went to bed happy, his mind made up.

12

Firm footsteps sounded up the worn stone steps to the Muniment Room as Seton went in search of Prue. He knocked on the open door, and looked round it.

Prue had woken early; after all, she hadn't been out most of the night. It was cooler, although the mist just drawing off the lawns promised yet another hot day. How lovely to drift from one long summer's day to another, thought Prue. Idle thoughts, she realized; it was years since she had indulged in idle thoughts. The nuns had resolutely fought her propensity to daydream and had made sure that she passed her time – even her leisure time – in a brisk and useful way.

And at home, in the holidays. Aunt Josephine's religious fervour must have developed her psychic powers; how else would she always know when Prue's mind was drifting away to a world of its own, and drag her back to reality with a complaint or a request, some extra duty, a pointless errand.

She might be free of all that now, but nonetheless she had a living to earn, a persistent, worrying fact that threaded endlessly through her mind. What would happen in the autumn? Where would she go, what could she do? Better get up, get dressed, have an early breakfast, finish those letters she had to do for Magdalena and then settle down to work in the Muniment Room.

She was still there, several hours later, when Seton found her. Her eyes were slightly screwed up as she tried to decipher a particularly spidery piece of handwriting. She had a dusty smudge on her nose; Seton found it delightful, just like a puppy trying to behave like a grown dog.

'You look very serious,' he said.

Prue jumped; her face lit up when she saw who it was. 'Hello,' she said, smiling.

Glorious eyes, thought Seton. That blue, and little golden flecks, terribly attractive.

'People are always saying I look serious,' Prue went on. 'I'm just concentrating, that's all.'

'You should smile all the time, you've got a lovely smile. What are you doing? You shouldn't be shut away like this on a hot summer's day.'

'It's what I'm here for.'

'I thought you were supposed to be a helping hand for Magdalena. Write a few letters for her, do the menus, flowers, that kind of thing.'

That, in Seton's mind, was suitable work for a young lady, sound fill-in work for the brief time between school and marriage, and all useful practice for managing one's own household.

Prue thought how handsome Seton looked. His muscular, well-made body looked good in a light summer jacket and trousers. His face hadn't yet taken on the bony, weathered look of his ancestors; time would fix that.

'When do you finish with all this?' Seton balanced one hip on a dusty table and waved a hand at the piles of papers and ancient leather-bound volumes.

'I should work all day and all evening,' said Prue contritely. 'I've had so much time off, what with one thing and another.'

Oysters, she thought. And being trapped in the gully; she mustn't cause any more disturbances this summer.

'No, I don't think that's being fair to yourself,' said Seton. 'It hasn't been your fault. You were ill, and I think you were quite right to go with young Thomas, he could have got into real trouble there. Jolly lucky you were with him.'

'Yes, but I wasn't much use,' said Prue with honesty. 'He was much braver than I was. What was lucky was your finding us, and knowing just what to do.'

Prue had no practice in flirting or attracting a man, but unwittingly she couldn't have done better: stroke, stroke; Seton purred.

'No, I'll have a word with Mountjoy if you like. Can't work all day and in the evening, have the union out.' He laughed, pleased with his joke. 'Come and have a drink. We'll go to the Duck and Feathers in Eyot, no oysters there, but it's a good place on a summer evening, river, that sort of thing. We might take a boat out.'

He touched her hand lightly, gave her an affectionate smile and went to find Mountjoy. He had come to see Mountjoy anyway, wanted his advice about a gun. 'The mechanism isn't right. Should I send it to old Murray to look at, or do you think it's something simple?'

'My dear chap, you know more about guns than I do, I'd say it was careless cleaning, but that wouldn't be like you, Seton.'

'Fellow who came to stay used it. I'll have a go at it myself if that's what you think it is. By the way, thought I'd take young Prue out for a jar this evening, if that's all right with you.'

'Nothing to do with me, ask Magdalena. She won't say no, but in any case the girl's evenings are her own. Do her good to get out, looking a bit peaky. Very conscientious little thing.'

'Who is conscientious?' Valdemar paused beside them, his body taut with purpose and energy. 'Morning, Seton. I'm on my way to look at those lower walls, Mountjoy.'

'Oh, good, good, but don't put yourself out, Val, you must have plenty of other things to worry about.'

Valdemar shot him a quick look from his hard blue eyes. Not like Mountjoy not to want to talk about the castle; what was going on? 'Seton, we must have a talk sometime about the plans. You'll think differently when you've had a proper look.'

Mountjoy smiled a little distantly. 'Plenty of time for that, Val. We were just talking about Prue. She's working very hard; Seton's taking her out tonight.'

'Working hard?' said Valdemar incredulously. 'That girl does bugger all. Slopes about the place, gets lost, fainting fits, blotches, useless specimen – as far as work's concerned, anyway,' he added, remembering her very becoming disarray.

Seton stiffened. 'I'll be off, then, Mountjoy. Morning, Val.'

'Don't forget your gun,' said Mountjoy, handing it over.

'No, better not, Might need it.'

He gave Valdemar another, very chilly look as he went.

'That man's a fool,' said Valdemar dismissively. 'Always has been. Mountjoy, I . . .'

Mountjoy cut him short. He was holding an old walking stick which he used to whack branches out of his way when out walking. Now he teased the ground with it, making a little pile of dust.

'No, Val, not now, not for the moment. Yes, I know it's important, but something's come up, I can't think about all this for the moment. Put it on ice, there's a good chap.'

Mountjoy whistled to his dog, brushed a few hairs from his faded green shirt and wandered off.

Valdemar watched him as he walked away across the lawn, a frown on his handsome face; what had come up? Valdemar was used to his uncle doing what he said; Mountjoy had as much charm as Valdemar, but lacked his remorseless energy and intelligence.

'Much easier just to do what he wants. He always gets his way in the end,' he had remarked to Magdalena after a particularly exhausting session with Valdemar. 'This place will be his one day, he might as well get on with it. He makes me feel old, and I don't like that. Plenty of other things for me to do.'

Sylvester came out from the castle, breathing heavily. 'Ah, Val, another lovely day.' Then, as he saw Val's furious face, he raised an eyebrow. 'Someone crossed you, Val? What a face!'

'What? Oh, it's you, Sylvester. Don't know what's got into Mountjoy, can't seem to get through to him these days. Time's not on our side, you know, we need to press on. I can't hang around here wasting my time.'

'I'm sure you'll find something to occupy you,' said Sylvester, with only a very slight note of irony in his voice. He drew out a large paisley handkerchief and mopped his brow. 'Mistake to walk, all this exercise isn't safe for a man of my size.'

'If you took more exercise, you wouldn't be that size,' said Valdemar with brutal disregard for Sylvester's feelings.

'That's what Lily says, you know. And if she can't make me change my ways, there's no chance whatever that you will. God made me large, suits me. My music might go if I were lean like you. Look at those sopranos who diet and aren't ever able to sing a decent note again.'

'You'll keel over with a heart attack one of these days, then you won't be able to play again. Would have thought you wanted to keep fit.'

'I am surprisingly fit,' said Sylvester, wondering what had annoyed Val; something must really have caught him on the raw for him to lash out like this. 'I have good strong muscles. You'll have to watch it yourself, you know. Forty, aren't you? Mmm, your thighs will get a bit plumper and you'll thicken round the waist. Can you still get into your old suits?'

'I have no idea, since I don't wear my old suits. Being rich, I buy new ones.'

'It comes to us all. Even my glorious Gabriel, whom I miss so much. Why he had to go to the East on tour during the summer I can't imagine. Even he, and you know how careful he is, is losing some of his superb tautness. I love him just the same, of course. I'm not the type to try and recapture my youth by chasing ever younger ones, that would be very undignified.'

That earned Sylvester a penetrating glance; was Sylvester needling him? 'How's Sylvia?' Sylvester went on blandly. 'Have you heard from her at all?'

'No,' said Valdemar curtly. 'Never do when she's away, I suppose she's busy with her bloody mother. She'll ring when she's on her way back.' He gave a melancholy figure drooping over an urn a swipe with his foot.

'Ridiculous gewgaws Mountjoy has all over the place. He found this in some yard. You would think he'd have better things to do than poke about among other people's rubbish. Thinks it came from here, part of the garden which was dedicated in memory of some uninspiring member of the family who got herself raped and killed a couple of hundred years ago. I had it cleared and integrated into the vegetable garden, good soil there, sentimental twaddle to find this dreary thing and plonk it here on the terrace. That's what's wrong with people like my uncle, no sense of today, let alone tomorrow. People spend their whole bloody time looking backwards and cooing over utterly uninteresting things which should have been forgotten minutes after they happened. There's that tedious girl poking around among those papers for Mountjoy; what a waste of time, probably all she's fit for, but for God's sake, what a useless activity. You're as bad, contemporary music hasn't got a hope. Nothing's any good until it's been embalmed and become historic.'

'Oh dear, you are extremely tetchy today,' said Sylvester. 'It's all nonsense, you know, you're as keen on family history as anyone. And you're planning this historic castle affair. That's hardly modern.'

'Of course it is. Completely up-to-date technology. Then we can make sure that the castle can be repaired as it should be, but here and now, a castle for the late twentieth century.'

'I think that may be a contradiction in terms,' said Sylvester. 'Is Magdalena in? Get yourself a drink, dear chap, and calm down. Doesn't do your blood pressure any good to keep on going off pop like this. Get Sylvia back, that'll put your hormones back in balance.'

Sylvester rumbled quickly away; better to leave Val to simmer down by himself. Provoking him was fun, but you never knew with a man like that. He mentioned it to Magdalena as he sat by the open window in her sitting-room, sipping a delicious cold drink.

'You're looking remarkably well these days, Magdalena. I'm glad to see you've got over that illness. It's very tiresome being ill. And you've put on a little weight, that suits you, you know.'

Magdalena smiled. 'Yes, I feel very well these days. And, of course, Mountjoy's happier now. He does fret so when he's worried about me.'

'You're very fond of him, aren't you?'

Magdalena nodded. 'Yes, he's a dear.'

'There was a time, of course . . . Seeing Val in a terrible temper a few minutes ago, I've sometimes thought it strange that you settled down with a man as equable as Mountjoy. Don't you ever hanker after a little more excitement?'

Magdalena fiddled with her glass. 'That's a disconcerting thing to say, Sylvester. No, I'm quite happy, we don't all need or want more than we have.' She moistened her lips slightly. 'Val is in a temper, is he? I wonder why.'

'Mountjoy seems to be a little evasive about this scheme Val has for the castle. Getting cold feet, is he?'

'No, that isn't it. Well, not exactly.'

Sylvester adjusted his bulk more comfortably on the crimson silk of Magdalena's sofa, which creaked slightly.

'Careful, Sylvester, I like that sofa.'

'Don't you start on at me. Lily nags all day long, don't eat this, you can't have that. Val let fly this morning with a few very nasty remarks about my size; if I weren't such a peaceable man, I might have become quite upset. I think Val needs a girlfriend.'

'I hardly think that's Val's problem, Sylvester. You know what he's like. Out with Julie last night, for instance. I don't think he's short of sex.' Magdalena gave a quick smile, but her voice was slightly bitter.

'I said a girlfriend, not sex. Someone he could spend a bit of time with, think about. Time he took an interest in someone. Sylvia's all very well, but she keeps hopping off to Paris. Do you know what the matter is with that mother of hers?'

'Oh, there isn't a mother, Sylvester. Val doesn't realize, he's too self-centred, and where Sylvia's concerned, it's out of sight, out of mind. Sylvia has a man in Paris, a lover perhaps, although I suspect it's a husband.'

Sylvester's face was a picture of astonishment. 'No, surely not! How did you find this out?'

'Lucy Praetorius told me. She was in Paris on some musical jaunt and she saw Sylvia at a friend's house. She got chatting to someone else there, asked about Sylvia's mother. It turned out Sylvia's parents have both been dead for years.'

Sylvester was hugely delighted. 'So that's how she's put up with Val all these years. I did wonder. Of course, if she's got another life somewhere else, and particularly if she's married, that's why the comments about Val and her getting married have never bothered her. Well, I take my hat off to her!'

Magdalena opened a drawer of the pretty little walnut bureau which stood between the windows and took out a silver-wrapped box.

'Have a truffle, Sylvester. I know you shouldn't, but I want one, and I'm not going to sit and eat it in front of you.'

'Delicious. I don't think I've ever seen you eat chocolates, Magdalena.'

'I'm eating a lot, probably need the vitamins or something,' said Magdalena vaguely, putting a second one in her mouth and sitting down again with the box beside her. 'Have another one.'

Sylvester munched as Magdalena ate her truffle thoughtfully, looking past Sylvester and into the distance through the window.

'I don't think Val should be here, Sylvester. Not now, not this summer. Can you think how we can get him to go?'

'That bad, is he?' Sylvester was surprised. With the Mountjoys family was family, and there were always a lot of family visitors at Christmas and in the summer. Val always came, with or without Sylvia. It would be dull without him, Sylvester had to admit; his dynamism and commending personality breathed life into the old stones. Tiresome, yes, but you couldn't help responding to his vigour.

'And there's the Festival coming up. Val's never missed that. He won't admit it, but I think music's as important to him as it was when he was a boy.'

'Do you think so? I think that part of Val died years ago; he's nothing but a machine now, not human. Music's so much to do with emotion, and I think Val's past feeling anything for anyone – except self-admiration, that goes without saying.'

'Exactly what I was getting at. Needs a girlfriend. Couldn't you invite some enticing creatures up for a visit? That might calm him down.'

Magdalena's face lit with sudden humour and she looked much younger for a moment. 'There's always Prue.'

Sylvester roared. 'He's so rude about her. It's a shame, she's just ready to unfurl her petals and ends up with you lot. You know, Lily's convinced that Seton is keen on her. She could do worse, although he is so dreadfully dull.'

'Perhaps Prue is a little dull.'

'Oh, I don't think so. No, I think we've only scratched the surface of Prue; she may surprise us all yet. She can't be her father's daughter and not be a good deal more interesting than she seems.'

'She'd better stay dull while she's here. She's going to be a beauty once she stops looking worried all the time, and Valdemar could change his mind. It has happened.'

'Poor Prue if it did. No, perhaps she's better off with Seton after all, at least for the time being. Lucky girl, how simple life is for someone like her.'

Life did indeed seem very simple for Prue, basking in Seton's attention and affection. She was definitely in love, no question about it, she told Cleo. 'We went in a boat, he's terribly strong, hardly any effort, the boat zoomed along. Then we moored under a tree and had a picnic. He's so nice to be with, so friendly. We talked about his dogs.'

Lily was weeding. 'That gardener, fine for the big things and cabbages – who wants cabbages? – but a little care and attention here around the house, useless.' She yanked at a recalcitrant piece of couch grass. 'Look at this, wind its way into anything, this would. Strangle us all in our beds.' She pulled herself straight, a bracing hand holding her back. 'I'm not as young as I was. All this bending. What was that about dogs?'

Cleo looked up from the pile of papers she was sorting and numbering. There was no breeze to disturb them; the air was completely still. 'Dogs,' she said, with a spluttering giggle. 'Prue, not dogs!'

Prue was indignant. 'Why not dogs? I like Seton's dogs. They're all working dogs, you know, and he trains them himself. There's Bess, she's the labrador, and . . .'

Cleo groaned. 'Spare us, Prue, the catalogue of Seton's dogs. What about him? Did you end up folded in his arms? Have you been to bed with him yet?'

'Cleo!'

Lily cast a quick, beady look at Prue, now bright red. 'Leave her alone, Cleo. Not everybody wants to hop straight into bed with a man they like.'

'Why not? And in my particular, immediate case, I can point out that there was nothing straight away about it, it's taken no end of time and trouble. And he's still gone on Sophie, the stupid man.'

Prue sat up. 'Cleo, you haven't . . . Oh, Cleo, you should be careful.'

'Careful? Life isn't for being careful, Prue. Don't you be too careful with Seton. If you fancy him, then do something about it.'

'I expect I will,' said Prue, stretching her hands in front of her.

Cleo heard footsteps and turned her head. 'Talk of the devil,' she said. 'Hello, Seton, we were just talking about you.'

Seton didn't like the sound of that. He had Cleo docketed in his mind as slightly dangerous; that was a friendship he wouldn't encourage once he and Prue were married. He merely nodded at Cleo, smiled at Lily, must always be polite to servants, and held out a hand to Prue, who was on her feet, head slightly on one side, smiling at him. 'Come along, Prue, or we'll be late.'

'Where are you taking her to?' said Cleo.

'We're going to a film in Eyot, and then some dinner somewhere. Yes, Prue?'

'Oh, yes,' said Prue – the bliss of another whole evening with Seton.

She hummed to herself as they drove along leafy green lanes.

'Happy?' asked Seton.

'Yes, this is heavenly,' said Prue. 'Here with you, wonderful summer's evening.'

'Much better to take the back way, no traffic to speak of,' said Seton, skilfully avoiding a combine harvester, two cows and a barking dog. 'Steady on,' he said encouragingly to his car as though it were a team of horses.

Besotted, Prue admired his driving; she admired everything about him. It was exciting to sit close to him during the film, although not as exciting as seeing her first film in a cinema. Very bold, she thought, watching hard to see if she could pick up some tips. It made her blink once or twice; they'd never shown anything like this at the film club in the convent. Her leg brushed against his. Seton put his hand on her knee; further up would be interesting, thought Prue, shocking herself.

They held hands as they walked back from the restaurant, then in the car Seton, after a brief fight with the gear lever, kissed her.

Prue responded at once, rather to Seton's surprise; flattering, but it didn't do for a girl to be too eager.

Ah, thought Prue, this was why Cleo was so keen on sex; while a little vague about exactly what going to bed with a man meant – despite Cleo's expert explanations in answer to her tentative questions in the convent about a thousand years before – Prue knew perfectly well that kissing Seton was only the beginning, and that even more delightful pleasures awaited her. When was it going to happen?

Seton disentangled himself. 'Mmm, that was nice,' he said, exactly as though he had just eaten a fresh bread roll.

13

Lily was furious. 'I saw it coming, it's a disaster. Where is it all going to end?'

Sylvester watched her with amusement. 'Now what's bothering you? You're becoming a very unrestful person, Lily. You mustn't crack up now, just when we're going to be busy with the music festival.'

'Music festival! It's people I'm talking about. Young Prue, getting in deeper and deeper with Seton, and it won't do.'

'Magdalena and I were talking about this yesterday.' Sylvester tipped some more of the evil-smelling polish on to the cloth. He rubbed it softly into the back of his cello, working with little circular movements. Sylvester always cleaned one or other of his cellos when he was making plans.

'It helps me think,' he told Valdemar, who had walked uninvited into the room and expressed his irritation with Sylvester's steady polishing. 'God, what an awful pong.'

He had overheard Lily's words, much to her vexation. No, she wasn't going to say any more, it was none of his, Valdemar's business, and the best thing he could do for everyone was to take his fine self out of Sylvester's room and preferably out of the county.

'Evil-tempered woman,' remarked Valdemar as she left. 'Don't know why you keep her on, Sylvester. Should have got rid of her years ago. Why is she fretting about that girl and Seton?'

'She thinks that Seton may want to marry Prue, in due course, after a seemly interval, naturally; Seton's not one to do anything rash.'

'It would be rash to marry that girl at any time! Who is she, an absolute nobody, educated in some half-baked girls' school, which means she isn't educated at all. Not much to look at, although she does have one or two redeeming features, I suppose, if that's to your taste. Seton can do much better. What does he want to get married for, anyway? Plenty of women around to go to bed with, no need to marry one of them.'

Sylvester carefully screwed the lid back on the little brown bottle of polish and wrapped the cloth round it.

'Disgusting stuff that, Sylvester. What is it?'

'Varnish restorer. The smell which offends you is, I think, the linseed oil. Not everyone likes it.'

'I should think not. Reminds me of someone, though, someone I knew a long time ago, she used to smell of linseed oil. You're a friend of Seton's, Sylvester, why don't you warn him off this girl? Mountjoy should sack her, that would put an end to it all.'

'I think the Mountjoys like having her around. It's more young life at the castle, and when you don't have children of your own, that can be important.'

'Thomas is enough young life for anyone.'

'That's why Seton wants to marry, of course, you do realize that. He wants to have children, a son especially.'

'More fool him. I've never felt the need to have children myself. Women like them, but they're nothing but a bloody nuisance. Perfectly sane people I was at Cambridge with, intelligent men, boring on about their children, schools. "Wilfred's behaving oddly, wonder if he's on drugs." Waste of time, the whole tedious business.'

'You might feel differently if you had children of your own.'

'You don't.'

'I should very much like to have had children,' said Sylvester, with enormous dignity. 'It's the one great sadness of being the way I am that I can't. Children are our future, you can't get away from that.'

'I've got my own future, don't need any brats messing up my life to interfere with that.'

Valdemar's indifference to all the things which make life difficult, interesting or meaningful to most people was a source of amazement to his friends and colleagues. They admired his brilliance, his singleness of purpose, his easy and enviable success with women, his certainty about himself and his life. The wiser of them shook their heads and predicted trouble, later rather than sooner, maybe; but you paid a price for such inhumanity in the long run.

'He isn't inhuman,' one of his many ex-mistresses said indignantly. 'Cold-hearted, yes, oh, and indifferent to your feelings. But you should see his face when he's listening to music.'

'Music? Veronica, what do you know about music?'

'Nothing, and I shall never go to a concert again, ever. You can't imagine how dreadful it is, all these people, nearly all men, in evening clothes, making this endless noise. Ghastly! But not to Valdemar. No, his face was quite, quite different, as though he was making love to someone he cared for, very revealing.'

'Did he look like that when he made love with you?'

'Good gracious, no. Terrific in bed, but that was energy and expertise and passion, nothing tender or beneath the surface. Give me funny old Philip any day. Not much of a clue, but goodness, he's full of warmth. No, Val was all style, then get your knickers off and thanks very much.'

'You were desperate about him at the time.'

'Yes, I was sure that I could unlock the secrets of his heart, make him fall in love with me, find the man who was there in the music – but no way.'

'He sang, didn't he, when he was a little boy?'

'I believe so. His best friend is a musician, up there in the north, where he goes to hang about in the family castle. Attractive man, Simon Praetorius. Trains the little boys who sing in the cathedral.'

'Choristers. Perhaps Val likes little boys.'

Veronica roared. 'No, definitely not. One knows, that isn't his problem. He's got a nephew, young cousin, something like that, a beautiful child – he sings. Come to think of it, that was Val's doing, if I remember rightly – but he drives Val mad. No spark of interest at all.'

'Oh well, if we can acquit him of pederasty, he can't be all bad. Incest? That would be exciting.'

'There's no one for him to be incestuous with, his mother died when he was a child. Oh, there is a half-sister, but she lives abroad. The only woman in his family is his uncle's wife – Magdalena Mountjoy.'

'Ah Magdalena. Hot stuff, she used to be. She must be about Valdemar's age, now. No, I can see, none of the usual sins. Just cold, bloody-minded, arrogant, contemptuous of other people's weaknesses and feelings. I stand by my opinion of him; the man's not human, not within the meaning of the act.'

'He may change, one day.' Veronica sighed and got up from the table, smoothing her skirt down. 'Look at this bill. I'll have to stop coming here, we eat practically nothing and it costs more and more.'

'That's why we come here, Veronica, keeps our figures under control. Don't forget your bag. I'm just going to powder my nose.'

Sylvester took his bow from the open cello case and pushed his chair into position.

'I'm going to practise, now, Val. Go away.'

'I'll stay,' said Valdemar. 'I'll sit here, then I won't disturb you.'

'It's the best thing about you, Val,' said Sylvester as he began to tune the cello. 'Liking music. We've got a very good Hungarian ensemble coming for the festival this year, the Budapest Chamber Orchestra – ever heard them?'

'Once, in Budapest. Superb soloist they had, Muronyi, some name like that. Part gypsy I expect, looked very wild and dramatic.'

'Geza. He's coming. Great fun. Now, quiet!' And Sylvester launched into a study played at dazzling speed; Val sat back and watched.

Cleo paused as she crossed the hall, listening to the astonishingly fast patterns of sound from the other side of Sylvester's closed door. Then she continued to hop from black square to black square on the chequered floor. 'He loves me, loves me not.'

A final hop brought her to a stop on 'Loves me not.' With a quick sigh she pushed open the door leading to the kitchen. 'Lily,' she said as she slid past the bucket and mop leaning against the inner door.

'Don't come bothering me now, I've dropped a dozen eggs. What a mess!'

'Yes, it is. Here, pass me that. Have you put salt on them?'

Lily cast her a scornful glance. 'You youngsters, think nobody else knows anything. Of course, it's psychological, what I really wanted to do was throw them at Valdemar.'

Cleo looked around, surprised. 'Lily, has the heat got to you? Valdemar isn't here.'

'Oh yes, he is, in with Sylvester.'

'Sylvester doesn't like anyone in with him when he's working.'

'Doesn't mind Valdemar, don't ask me why. He's brought some papers for Sylvester, from Magdalena; must be something to do with the festival, but he'll have another purpose. Catch that man doing errands for anyone!'

'You don't like him, do you?'

Lily stopped scrubbing for a moment and leant on her mop. 'Not like him? It isn't liking or not liking, it's the mischief he gets up to, walks over everyone, never a backward glance or a moment's remorse. Anything goes, as long as he gets what he wants. Never mind, you've slipped out of his clutches, haven't you? That's one blessing. Out of my way, there's some egg by your foot there.'

She gave Cleo a brisk shove, and Cleo took up a position by the sink. 'I'll miss all this in the autumn, Lily. Your mystifying conversations and the way you know far more than you ought to about what's going on. How do you know I've slipped out of Val's clutches? I can tell you, I'm beginning to think I'd like a night with him. He's certainly got something.'

'Stick to Luke, that's my advice. Really, Valdemar's not safe at the best of times, and in your case, oh dear, oh dear, that would be the worst of all. I suppose it was inevitable you and Prue coming here this summer, it had to happen, but it's nerve-wracking to watch. Heard from your mum recently?'

Startled at the change of subject, Cleo blinked. 'What? No, I haven't, actually. I wrote to her a few days ago, told her all about everything here. She likes to know what's going on, and I don't mind writing about it, not when she's so far away. Different when she's around, of course, got to keep your own space, although she's not an interfering mother. You'd like her, Lily, she's your sort of person.'

'Looks like you, does she?'

'No, couldn't be more different. Physically, anyhow, although people say I remind them of her. My colouring comes from my father, I never knew him because he died when I was tiny, and mum hasn't got any pics of him, I don't know why, but he was very dark with blue eyes. Like me.'

'Like you,' Lily echoed. 'Unusual, that hair and those eyes.'

'Not that unusual. Look at young Thomas; he's got black hair and smashing blue eyes. He's going to be a treat, that boy, when he grows up, a real heart-stopper.'

Lily became suddenly brisk. 'Now, I'm getting behind. You've got plenty of work to do, Cleo. Sylvester will want that lot he gave you out of the way now that all the festival business is coming up.'

'I'm going into the orangery,' said Cleo. 'It's too hot to go on working outside. I like it in there with all the plants, makes me feel I'm in some exotic country.'

The orangery ran almost the length of the house, with the library and the music room leading off it. It had a glowing polished wooden floor and pots and urns held shrubs and ferns. There was even an orange tree, with tiny little fruits beginning to form. You felt, thought Cleo, as though the plants were growing while you watched; it was alive with greenery. She put her papers down on a little table, drew up a chair, and gazed out across the lawns, thinking of Luke (of course), of the pleasure of sex with him, of how he was still pining for Sophie, of Prue and what was going to happen with Seton. Prue could do worse, in a material sense; he was older than she was, would be protective, no doubt, at least at first, plenty of money, nice house by all accounts, but was that life when you were only eighteen and hadn't even begun to live? Cleo thought not.

She opened the envelope which Valdemar had brought down from the castle and flicked through the papers inside. Sylvester wanted her to draw up a final programme for the printers.

'We've done a preliminary programme already, that goes out to everyone on the mailing list. But it always changes, so we do a final programme; that's what this will be. It'll need checking again at proof stage; we usually have to make some last-minute changes.'

'Where do you have the concerts?'

'Here and there, where we can. Churches, one or two big concerts in the cathedral, but we don't have to worry too much about those, thank God. Simon Praetorius looks after that end.' He rattled off the names of some local churches. 'Can be cold in the summer, so we just hope we're lucky. There's the great Hall at the castle, of course, and we sometimes have recitals in here in the orangery during the festival,' Sylvester had told her. 'Quite a good acoustic, here in the orangery and in the music room, you see architects then knew what they were doing. Not like today. I was playing in a college recently, in Cambridge, I can't tell you how appalling the sound was. Waste of anybody's money coming to listen in a place like that. Still, I mustn't grumble; they paid their money and clapped like mad at the end. Glad to get away, probably.'

It all seemed a dreadful muddle to Cleo, with items crossed out and programmes and venues altered unintelligibly. She sighed. Perhaps Prue knew about it; if she didn't, she might be able to make sense of it all, she had always had a knack for that kind of thing. In the distance, the phone rang. Cleo waited for a minute to see if Sylvester was going to answer it . . . no.

Cleo ran through the library to the hall, where the telephone lived in a little recess under the staircase. Sylvester wouldn't have a phone in the library or the music room, and he switched the one in the drawing room off when he was working.

'Hello,' said Cleo, slightly breathless. 'Yes, this is Midwinter 392, yes, England, of course it's England. Where else would it be?' Crackle, crackle, crackle. A voice came through for a moment, an American voice? Then more hisses and buzzes. 'Hello,' yelled Cleo. 'Can you hear me? Is anybody there?'

The drawing room door opened and Sylvester bounced out, much displeased.

'Cleo, it is too much. How can I possibly play with you making all this noise? What are you doing? Who is on the phone?'

'Your guess is as good as mine,' said Cleo cheerfully, handing him the receiver.

Sylvester put it to his ear and immediately held it away, wincing. 'There's something wrong with the line. No, wait a minute, it's cleared. Battery, yes, yes, you want to speak to Miss who? You have a message for her . . . Cleo, it must be for you, some lunatic from America by the sound of it, here she is. What? From her mother? Oh, really, now it's gone completely dead. Cleo, would anybody be sending you a message from America?'

'Only Mum,' said Cleo, a quick frown tightening her brow. 'And I don't think she would, you know what transatlantic calls cost. I hope she's all right.'

Valdemar had emerged from the drawing room, a look of impatience on his face as he observed Sylvester's and Cleo's antics with the phone. 'If there's a problem, no doubt whoever wants to yet through will try again,' he said dryly. 'It's high time they did something about this exchange. It's a disgrace the service they provide up here. You hardly need to make all that fuss, Cleo. You should know better than to disturb Sylvester like that when he's practising.'

Cleo made a rude gesture and a swift face at him as he turned to go back into the drawing room and Sylvester let out a deep, rumbling laugh as he returned to his cello.

Lily popped her head through another door. 'What's up? Who was on the phone?'

'We don't know,' said Cleo. 'It seemed to be from America. I hope there isn't anything wrong with Mum.'

'Don't fret,' said Lily comfortably. 'Why should there be anything wrong? I expect she just wanted to have a chat, see how you are and so on. She'll ring back, I should think.'

'It wasn't her, from what I could hear it was a message. Why should she send me a message?'

'A message doesn't sound very alarming. She'll be in touch if it's anything urgent. Prue's just come through the back door. Magdalena says have you done the programme yet, can she have a copy?'

'Good Lord, no, I can't make head or tail of it, it'll have to wait until Sylvester's finished. Perhaps he can sort it out for me.'

'What's the problem?'

'Names, I don't know the places, it's all been scribbled on, hopeless. I thought these festivals were all highly organized; chaos it'll be by the look of it.'

'Bring it all into the kitchen, and I dare say we can sort it out. Magdalena hasn't been able to do as much as she usually does. It's very much her baby, this festival, but of course with not being well, so tired, earlier on . . .'

Prue was sitting at the table humming happily to herself. She gave Cleo a smile of welcome. Goodness, she looks different, thought Cleo as she dumped the papers in front of her.

'You look very pleased with yourself. Been out again with Seton?'

Prue's eyes shone at the thought of him and she gave a sigh of pleasure. 'Yes, well, we're seeing each other quite a lot.'

'Been to bed with him yet?'

'Cleo!'

'That's enough of that,' said Lily sharply. 'Not everyone's made like you.'

'Bet you were, Lily,' said Cleo, with a swift, sly look. 'Bet you didn't just hold hands on the river.'

'Never you mind what I did or didn't do. Prue here is enamoured, look at her, leave her be. It'll pass, Prue, first time's the worst.'

'It's the only time,' said Prue with unusual firmness. 'I won't ever feel about anyone else the way I do about Seton.'

Cleo snorted. Lily shook her head a little sadly. 'That's what we all think, pet. Make sure you know what you're doing, though. Don't go tumbling into bed with a man because it's the only thing left to do with him.'

Prue was hurt. 'You don't understand. Seton isn't like that, he's wonderful. Oh, I am lucky. Just think, Cleo, if I hadn't bumped into you that morning, I would never have come up here, and I might never have met Seton.'

She liked saying his name, it gave her a frisson of pleasure. How different were her feelings for Seton from Cleo's for Luke.

'St Polycarp's Church,' Lily was saying. 'That can't be right, that lot wouldn't fit in there, a soloist or a quartet at most. Lovely little place, and there's a leg in the altar.'

'A leg?' said Prue, startled. 'Whose leg?'

'One of the Mountjoys. Lost it at Waterloo. All the Mountjoys in those days went off and joined in whatever fighting they could, before coming back to the castle and fighting each other. That one, he was a Valdemar, too, led some charge, got shot in the leg and they had to take it off on the battlefield. One of the soldiers wrapped it up for him, he wasn't in a fit state to do it himself, but the Mountjoys have never liked to leave bits of themselves anywhere, so he brought it home. It's in St Polycarp because he's the patron saint of legs.'

Cleo thought that was very funny. Prue didn't; how awful to lose a leg. She imagined Seton on the battlefield at Waterloo, in agony, dying, bravely of course, the sorrow of his widow when she heard the news; a lump came into her throat and she sniffed.

'It's so sad,' she said, 'to think of all those young men killed and wounded. I don't know how you can laugh, Cleo.'

'Some people lose all sense of proportion and all their sense of humour when they're in love,' said Cleo accurately but unkindly. 'I can't get upset about a leg lost a hundred and fifty years ago. I must tell Mum, she'll roar.'

Prue cast her a reproachful look and lapsed into a blissful daydream of Seton, alive and well this time, taking part in some colourful mediaeval pageant and covering himself in glory.

'Hopeless,' Cleo said to Lily. 'I hope she gets over it quickly, or she's going to be no fun at all for the rest of the summer.'

She turned her attention once more to the programme. 'This woman must be singing there, then, and these people here, in the Orangery, and then these concerts are in the cathedral. I'll go and type this out again, and Prue can take it back.'

Prue wandered out on to the terrace, revelling in the warm air, feeling sensuous in a way new to her; all her senses were tuned to a new pitch. She breathed in the rich scent of the roses which tumbled down the walls of the courtyard.

Valdemar caught sight of her from the drawing-room window; he leant back in his chair so that he could see further through the archway. He watched her intently. Her interest in Seton had transformed her; who was Seton to make a girl look like that? thought Valdemar irritably. Why hadn't he seen her potential earlier? Still, he had no doubt he could cut Seton out. It would be fun, if Seton was serious, to take Prue away from under his nose, bend her to his will, then discard her and see if Seton was still interested. He laughed, a pleasing prospect.

'Don't do that,' protested Sylvester. 'Don't laugh like that, Valdemar, you look as though you were plotting someone's downfall.'

'Perhaps I am, Sylvester, perhaps I am.' He rose. 'I'll go into the garden, Sylvester. Mind if I stay to lunch?'

'Tell Lily,' said Sylvester, absorbed again in his music.

Valdemar strolled out on to the lawn through the french windows and followed the path round and into the courtyard. Prue was leaning back against a wall, basking like a cat in the sun. She hadn't heard him coming, was startled when he spoke.

'Is Lily about? Tell her I'm staying to lunch.'

Prue looked at him with wary eyes. She was slightly pink from the sun and a blush, feeling dishevelled as she always did with Valdemar's critical eyes on her; off-balance, a tasty morsel.

Oh dear, thought Sylvester, putting his cello down. Damn it all, how could he ever get any work done with so much going on? Look at Val eyeing Prue; why couldn't he leave her alone? With a sigh he stepped through the french windows in his turn. These young people, no real work to do, nothing but intrigue and dalliance. He missed Gabriel, someone adult to talk it over with and laugh about it. Lily was no substitute this summer, prophesying woe all the time; how tiresome it all was.

Sylvester gathered up Valdemar through sheer imposition of bulk and explained to Lily that he was staying to lunch. Then he hauled Cleo out of the orangery, took the papers and bore Valdemar off, saying firmly that, since he was here, they could sort out one or two little matters. Did he remember what St Adolphus was like – dead, or a good sound? They hadn't used it before but the Bishop had asked for it to be included.

They vanished into the house and Lily turned on Prue. 'Off,' she said firmly.

Cleo protested. 'No, Prue's staying to lunch. You can't turf her out now.'

'I'm busy, Sylvester's busy, Val's staying to lunch and one extra is enough, thank you. Go with her, Sophie will give you something to eat, I should imagine. Tell Magdalena Sylvester's still going through the programme. Now, off with you both.'

Prue and Cleo toiled up the dusty track towards the castle, talking about Lily and Valdemar; Cleo reckoned Lily knew some dark secret about Valdemar's past. Prue felt that Lily simply didn't like Valdemar because he was so forceful and arrogant.

'Goodness, how hot it is, hotter and hotter every day, the ground all cracking up.'

'Yes, but why did she send us away like that?'

'Oh, doesn't like the look in Valdemar's eye. He's after you, you know that.'

Prue stopped dead. 'Me? That is so silly. Lily can't think that Valdemar is the least bit interested in me; he knows that I and Seton . . . well, he knows the way things are.'

'Probably why he's taking an interest in you,' said Cleo cynically. 'I must say, it doesn't half improve you. Must have got the hormones going, Seton; you're glowing with it.'

'Shut up,' said Prue with dignity. 'Why do you and Lily and everyone think you can pass comments on me all the time?'

'Sorry,' said Cleo. 'I wonder where Luke is. If I find him up at the castle gazing at Sophie with an expression like a witless sheep on his face, I shall be furious. What does he see in her? Why hasn't he got more pride? He's the laughing stock of the village. They all know she's got someone else. I expect they know who, too, which I don't, because there has to be something fishy about it, and if I knew it might put Luke off her.'

'Why should there be anything fishy?'

'Come on, Prue, be your age. If it was someone unattached, her own age, they wouldn't need all this secrecy. No, he is married, that's my bet, or he's one of the monks at that monastery the other side of Gossiby, who's slipping out for a bit of what he fancies.'

'Cleo, not a monk.' Prue's eyes danced at the thought. 'Can you imagine it! Monks are either short and fat and round, or tall and cadaverous. Attractive men don't become monks.'

'Well, it wouldn't surprise me, but my money's on a married man. Not at the castle, in the village, someone who goes away from time to time. I bet Julie knows, but she won't let on. One good thing, though,' she said, brightening. 'Oxford's a long way away. He won't be able to get his fix there.' She shaded her eyes, narrowing them as she looked towards the castle. 'Car coming in, I think it's love's young dream.'

'Luke?' said Prue.

'No, Seton,' said Cleo. She looked at Prue, who was standing stock still, eyes fixed on the approaching car. 'I expect he's come to propose.'

14

He had. However, he wasn't going to propose to Prue there at the castle, on alien territory. No, his own home was the place to do it; he would ask Magdalena if he could borrow Prue for an hour.

'Certainly, she's on her way back from the Hall now. Look, you can see her on the path there, with Cleo.'

Seton would rather Prue had *not* been with Cleo, but he made the best of it and went to meet them, walking back with them and making polite conversation; Seton's company manners were excellent.

Once in the courtyard, he took Prue firmly by the arm and removed her so quickly that she couldn't manage more than a wave in Cleo's direction. He bundled her into the car, reversed and turned with a flourish and roared off down the drive.

Cleo looked after them, shaking her head. 'I fear the worst.'

Magdalena watched the car as it disappeared round the corner. Then she shrugged. 'She has to make her own mistakes, we all do. Have you brought the programme back for me?'

'No. Sylvester's going to work on it. That's what I came to say.'

'It's a hot walk; why didn't Sylvester ring up?'

'Lily threw us out. Val's down there, and they're all on edge. Lily thinks Val's got his eye on Prue.'

'Damn the man!' said Magdalena, roused to a rare outburst of anger. 'Can't he leave anyone alone? Prue's such an innocent. It's only because Seton's taken a fancy to her.' She realized they were still standing in the courtyard. 'Have you had lunch?'

'No, but it doesn't matter. It's too hot to want to eat much.'

'Come into the hall for a moment,' said Magdalena. 'Mrs Grobbins is in there, it always has to have a good turn-out before the festival. It's the only time we use it except at Christmas, and weddings and christenings. I'm doing some work on a tapestry.'

Cleo hadn't been in the Great Hall before, and she stopped still in the doorway, amazed.

'I didn't know places like this still existed, not where people live, I mean. Except for royals and people like that. Look at the fireplaces, and the panelling. And those tapestries! Are they real, genuine, I mean, or are they modern copies?'

'Some of them are eighteenth-century, most of them are older. They were woven for this room, when the Mountjoys were rich and powerful. I'm afraid sooner or later they'll have to go.'

'Go? Go where? Why?'

'To be sold, to a museum, I expect. A castle is an expensive place to run.'

Cleo gave her a quick shrewd look. 'And not where you'd choose to live?'

Magdalena laughed, and knelt on a cushion lying in front of one of the tapestries. She was weaving threads into the pattern where the original ones had frayed or worn through.

'Not really, no. I find it cold and heartless, but of course it doesn't mean to me what it does to Mountjoy.'

'What are you doing?' said Cleo, watching curiously. 'Isn't repairing tapestries like this work for an expert?'

'Yes, but I know what I'm doing. I trained at the V & A; I never dreamt it would come in useful. It would cost a fortune if we had to send them away to be done; they'd just have to fall to bits.'

Cleo was surprised that Magdalena was so easy to talk to. She had been a little in awe of her, a much older woman who seemed rather remote. Mind you, thought Cleo, she's worn very well, much better than Mum, and she must be five years older at least. Magdalena's hair might have a few grey hairs, but it looked glossy and heavy, and her skin had a bloom on it that many a younger woman would envy.

Cleo liked her mother with her unmade-up face, which showed the little wrinkles round her eyes and mouth, but she felt that she would rather look like Magdalena when she was that old.

Her attention was suddenly caught by the scene which Magdalena was working on, and she looked at the tapestries properly for the first time.

'Heavens, look at that! Goodness, what do people say about those when they come for a concert? I shouldn't think they would concentrate on the music at all!'

They were joined by a cheerful Mrs Grobbins. 'Rude, isn't it? You should see some of the ones in the gallery up there. Suggestive, they are, very.'

'They're called the Eros tapestries,' said Magdalena helpfully. 'A lot of my work has been removing fig-leaves which some unusually modest Mountjoy ancestor had stitched on. It was crudely done, and the material underneath often has to be repaired.'

Cleo watched as Magdalena's deft fingers worked round the private parts of a very well-endowed satyr.

'They also hung curtains in front of them. Apparently, any servant caught looking behind it was dismissed on the spot, although I gather the then Lord Mountjoy used to spend a lot of time in here himself. I had the curtains taken down when I came here because I felt that they spoilt the hall.'

'How long have you lived here?' asked Cleo.

'I married Mountjoy five years ago. Yes, it must seem odd to you to get married at that age. When you're eighteen it seems unbelievable that anyone would marry at forty, doesn't it? I was married before, of course.'

'Who to?'

'A monster.' Mrs Grobbins' voice rose from a dark corner. 'I knew him, and he was a bad lot.'

'Yes, I have to say he was. I knew a few days after the wedding that I should never have married him. I was only nineteen so I hadn't understood what kind of a man he was.'

'So you left him.'

'Oh, no. My family didn't go in for divorce. We're Catholic, you see, and besides, it wasn't done. You could have a friend on the side if you were very discreet. Then you had separate bedrooms. It didn't matter, as long as on the surface you appeared to be a happily-married couple.'

'So what happened to him?'

'He died in a car accident.'

'Drunk, he was,' came the voice of doom from the corner. 'Drunk as a skunk, smashed into a wall, which was very good riddance, and no loss to anyone.'

'That was how I met Mountjoy,' said Magdalena, unperturbed by Mrs Grobbins' contributions to the conversation. 'Roddy crashed up here, you see, so I had to come up. For the funeral and so on.'

'Bits, that's all they had to bury.' Mrs Grobbins was a ghoul.

Cleo was silent for a few moments. 'That's awful,' she said firmly. 'To stay with a man you didn't like . . .'

'Nobody liked Roddy Lazonby,' said Mrs Grobbins. 'He was a

bad lot from the time he was a little boy, came from two villages along from here. We all knew about him and his little ways.'

'I'm not going to get married young,' said Cleo thoughtfully. 'I think it's risky, especially if it's the first man you fall for. Mum married young, I never knew my dad, but I don't suppose he and Mum would have lasted, she's much better off by herself, I reckon.'

'Didn't you mind not having a father?'

'Not really. You don't miss what you've never had, and Mum always had men friends, not all lovers, just friends, and we used to go out to the zoo and things. Mum could have married again, but on the whole she thought better not. When you hear about some people's stepfathers, I think it's just as well.' She peered up into the huge fireplace on the east wall. 'Is this Jacobean?'

'Yes. The other one's older.'

'Wonderful carvings. It's huge, you could move in here. Do you ever light a fire?'

'We do, very occasionally. They both smoke, which is rather a problem, because it tends to make people cough.'

Cleo stepped back from the fireplace and collided with Mrs Grobbins' bucket.

'Oh, sorry, Mrs Grobbins. Am I in your way?'

'Got to get on, some of us have work to do, which is not to say I'm suggesting you don't work, don't get me wrong, I know anyone who works for Sylvester earns their keep.'

Cleo was indignant. 'Sylvester's lovely to work for, he couldn't be nicer.'

'Even so, bet when you think about it, you've done a lot more work than you would in some office, nine to five. I've seen the lights on at the Hall and thought to myself, nine o'clock, and that's the room where Sylvester's girl works. My word, I wouldn't like to have his electricity bill!'

'Come and have a cold drink,' said Magdalena, getting up from her cushion. 'I've finished this section. And something to eat. I am sorry, I get absorbed with this work in there and forget to be domestic. I think Mrs Grobbins wants us out of here.'

'Since you mention it, Lady M, much the best thing just to leave me to it. You can brew a cuppa for me, I won't be long.'

'Isn't it too hot for tea?' asked Cleo as she followed Magdalena out.

'Never too hot for tea,' said Mrs Grobbins, drawing the huge door shut behind them.

Magdalena led the way back though a great panelled gallery – 'This is the Long Gallery,' she said helpfully; 'the Little Gallery is the one at the end of the hall' – along a stone passage and up a dark stone staircase. 'It's quicker this way, along the ramparts,' she explained. Another doorway, another austere passage with stone flags on the floor, cold even in such a hot summer, and they came out at the other kitchen door.

'Is Sophie here?'

'No, not this afternoon,' said Magdalena. 'She went into Eyot to get some special vegetables. I'm very hungry these days, and Sophie loves her cooking. When I wasn't feeling very well, she tried all kinds of dishes to tempt my appetite, but I didn't want to eat at all. So she's making up for it now. I wish Prue liked her food more. She doesn't seem at all interested in what she's eating. I wasn't at her age, I remember.'

As she was talking, she opened the fridge and found some cheese. She investigated various packets and unwrapped some cold meats.

'She's in love,' said Cleo, taking an appreciative gulp of the fresh lime juice which Sophie had thoughtfully left in the fridge. 'You aren't interested in food when you're in love. Actually, Prue's coming on, enjoying the good things of life quite a lot. You wouldn't believe the difference in her. I used to think she might end up a nun, but not any more.'

'Oh, no, not a nun!' said Magdalena, idly breaking off a piece of cheese. 'Not from the nuns that I know. What does Prue want to do with her life, though? She seems so intelligent, but I suppose in the end she'll just marry and settle down. She hasn't got a home any more, has she? That's very difficult for a young girl.'

'She's got me,' said Cleo defensively.

'Yes, she's lucky to have such a good friend, but then you'll be away at university, and she'll have to fend for herself. She can't stay on here at the castle after the summer, she knows that. We'd love her to, but we couldn't afford it.'

'What Prue really wanted to do, only her utterly ghastly aunt wouldn't hear of it, and Prue never disobeyed anyone in her life, you have to realize that, is to be a paleoanthropologist.'

Magdalena was incredulous. 'Oh, no, the poor child, like some very average little boy saying he's going to be a brain surgeon.'

'No, not at all like that,' said Cleo crossly. 'Prue is very clever, top marks in everything. She's much brighter than I am,' she added gloomily. 'I've always had to work hard to get good results; with Prue it's effortless. The nuns were furious that her aunt said no university. She's been fascinated with the subject as long as I've known her. She'd love to go and spend months in some utterly remote, hot uninhabited part of Ethiopia or Kenya or wherever they came from, scrabbling around in the dust for old teeth or a scrap of shin. But she couldn't.' Cleo looked thoughtful. 'Of course, she may be able to, now. Not this autumn, I shouldn't think, too late for this year, but next year. She'll get a full grant, no parents or guardian. Then she'd only have a year to cope on her own.'

Cleo's face darkened suddenly. 'Mind you, it's different now, now that she's met Seton and fallen in love with him. He's such a clunk. Oh, it's a terrible waste.'

'How unexpected,' was all Magdalena said, but she thought that all this boded ill for their future if Seton and Prue were to marry. Doubtless Prue would forget her intellectual dreams – one did, we all did, heaven help us – but in the end the personality didn't change. A young woman who dreamed of bones in a distant African plateau was not the right wife for Seton. 'Why, he can't bear abroad, the heat upsets him. He sits indoors grumbling about the heat and squashing insects. That's what Geraldine says.'

'Who is Geraldine?' Cleo was suddenly interested; was there another woman in Seton's life?

No, there wasn't. Geraldine was Seton's sister, Magdalena said. She was much older than he was, and treated him with a kind of amiable contempt. 'She married a strange man, not at all what you would expect. He makes clocks.'

Cleo wasn't interested in clocks. Her thoughts were on Prue. 'I know she's going to marry him, it's such a shame.'

Magdalena was amused by her vehemence. 'Tell her, then. You're her friend.'

'She won't listen, no one does when they're in love like that, it makes their brains go gooey. There's no room for reason or sense.'

'I wouldn't worry,' said Magdalena. 'Seton may be more elusive than you think. He's in his thirties; if he hasn't married by now, perhaps he never will.'

'He will,' said Cleo gloomily. 'I just know it. Oh, poor misguided Prue!'

Prue wouldn't have thanked Cleo for her sympathy; she was

extremely pleased with herself. From the time when Seton's car drew up outside the mellow red brick frontage of Feather House, to the actual moment when he asked her to marry him, looking down on her as she sat on the chintz sofa in the drawing room, Prue was enchanted. She stroked the dogs at her feet, fondling the labrador's black ears, unable to say anything.

Seton smiled. A new acquisition, one that would fit so well in the house. He hadn't felt so pleased about anything since he bought that new gun. Prue looked round the room which would be her sitting room; it was so quintessentially English, just like Seton. Faded blue chintz curtains, polished floor with shabby rugs, a disreputable old chair for the dogs and the slightly less disreputable sofa which she was sitting on. It was all perfect: to Prue this represented security.

Her natural taste distorted by her inclination to approve of everything connected with Seton, she decided she even liked the fearsome paintings on the walls: alert and sleeping dogs, stiff-looking brown horses, and a still life of two dead birds and a gun.

This was the ideal background for Seton. It matched his solidity and steadiness, was part and parcel of him, like the jackets he wore and his ready laugh.

Lucky me, she thought.

Seton, not being given much to thinking, had no idea of this. Not usually a restless man, he took a turn about the room. He felt he was taking on a new and important role: husband, father (in due course), head of a family. He was head of the family now, he supposed, but you didn't feel like it when the family was Geraldine and a very snobbish aunt with a nasty tongue. 'Your people,' he said. 'What about your people? Will they be pleased?'

'I don't have people,' said Prue. Oh dear, were people important? It was probably just as well that Aunt Josephine was dead. Prue had a suspicion that she wouldn't have gone down well with Seton. 'I told you, my parents are both dead. And so is the aunt who brought me up.'

'Yes, of course you did,' said Seton, who hadn't listened very closely to anything that Prue said. 'What about other family, brothers, sisters . . .?'

Prue shook her head.

'My little orphan,' said Seton, not unkindly. 'Never mind. What was your father's name? I'll need it for the notice.'

'Notice?' repeated Prue, puzzled. Something to do with the banns, perhaps.

'In the papers. *Times* and *Telegraph*. Hold on, I'll get some paper, may as well get it done right away.'

'Oh, yes, *The Times*, of course,' she said.

Engaged! She, Prue Pagan, was engaged! Quite possibly before any of the other girls who had left the convent with her. Cissie Jonxville was always bragging about how she was going to marry her cousin Rory the minute she finished at school, but the other girls said that was just Cissie showing off as usual, and, as everyone knew, Rory was going round with an amazingly beautiful black girl called Jane.

'He was called Piers,' she said.

'Piers.' He wrote it down. 'There we are, daughter of the late Piers Pagan Esq. – he didn't have any letters after his name, did he?'

'Letters?'

'Gongs, you know, OBE, that kind of thing.'

'I don't think so.'

'One has to get the details right, you know. What time do you finish tomorrow?'

'Oh, I'm not really sure. I work when they need me, not regular hours.'

'When Magdalena hears you're engaged, she'll let you have time off. She can't expect you to work full time from now on, you'll have a lot to do. I've got a ring, it was my mother's, it's a sapphire. A good stone, insured for quite a lot; you'll have to take care of it. We'll drive into Eyot and get it fitted. Ma was much bigger than you are, I expect it will need to be made smaller.'

Prue disagreed. 'I can't stop working full time for the Mountjoys just like that; I have to give notice. I was taken on for the summer, until the end of September.'

Seton wasn't going to be bothered with the niceties of Prue's employment. 'It's hardly a serious job, is it? I know what you girls are like, have to do something to earn a bit of pocket money and fill in the time. No problem. I've no objections to you helping the Mountjoys a little longer.'

Prue opened her mouth to explain, but then, already growing wiser about what Seton would and wouldn't understand, she shut it again. She would talk to Lady Mountjoy about it; she would deal with Seton. Seton paused by the window and looked out.

'I tell you what, I do believe the weather's going to break. Good thing too, disaster for the crops all this sun. I'll run you back now, Prue, a few bits and pieces to see to if we're in for rain. You don't mind, do you?'

'No,' said Prue, although she did. Why didn't he kiss her? Didn't he want to?

He gave her a friendly hug of an embrace, holding her more tightly now. Prue closed her eyes and pressed her mouth more closely to his, searching for his tongue. She could feel his heart beating, and there was a masculine smell about him that was extraordinarily appealing.

He broke away. 'Steady on, plenty of time for that. Now we're engaged it's different, of course. We can go as far as we want. Good thing, to get to know each other.'

Bed, thought Prue, as they drove along lanes that had been speckled with brilliant sunlight so shortly before and were now dark and forbidding. Oh, good, he means we can go to bed together. Soon! Before we're married. 'When are we going to get married?' she asked, caressing his sleeve.

'Careful, tricky road this. Next month, why not? You won't want a honeymoon, will you? I've got the harvest to think of, and I've already been away this year. We can get away in the autumn together, Scotland, perhaps, for the shooting.'

15

Water dripped from the leaves, it ran down the windows in fat drops; the gutters gurgled and sent little rippling floods across the terrace. Sylvester looked gloomily out at the sodden landscape and banged the copy of *The Times* he was holding down on his desk.

'Pompous idiot. Fool of a girl. Why do people do these things?'

He watched Cleo dash across the lawn clutching a cardboard box. Her hair lay wet and flat on her head and strands were plastered across her face. Her tee-shirt was soaked and clung to her.

'Papers,' she said, panting. 'I remembered that I'd left them in the summerhouse yesterday. The roof leaks, did you know?'

'My papers!'

Sylvester was longing to roar at someone.

'Not really,' said Cleo. 'Magdalena's papers, if anyone's. Festival stuff, and quite all right. Wouldn't have been by the end of today. It's a good thing I remembered the box was there.'

'Better still if you hadn't left it there. And Lady Mountjoy to you. All this first-naming, you and Prue have no manners.'

'Oh, pigs,' said Cleo, paying no attention at all to Sylvester. 'My sandals are sodden, and the strap's come away.'

'Damn this weather,' said Sylvester. 'I hate the rain.'

'It isn't very refreshing rain, either, is it?' said Cleo. 'Sort of tropical. Is it usually like this here in the summer?'

'What, here in the north? You must be mad, we're nearly in the Arctic here. Being of a full figure – no need to snigger, Cleo – I don't altogether like the heat, so I choose to live in the north. However, it's mostly so very cold and depressing that I spend my time wishing I lived in the South of Spain. Normally, Gabriel and I go away for the summer, but he's on tour this year.'

'Gabriel?'

'A friend, a special friend. I wish he were here, I'm sure he'd find a way out of this mess. Cleo, you're her friend; can't you stop her?'

'Oh, it's Prue's engagement that's getting at you, is it?'

'Yes, it is. One day I may meet up with Piers again, in another place, you understand, and what can I say to him? Hello, Piers, sorry I didn't do anything to prevent your daughter marrying that very uninspiring man who made her so unhappy.'

Cleo was touched by his concern. 'We all knew it was going to happen. No one should get married that young, but it may work out all right. Prue needs protecting, you know. Perhaps she won't be too unhappy.'

Sylvester quivered with rage. 'Protecting? What from? She isn't living in an African village, is she? Does she face disease or starvation? Is she in some Asian country torn by war? Does she live in a slum in an impoverished town? Does she have a mother who hates her, a stepfather who molests her? No, she does not. She is an intelligent, educated, healthy girl, just at the beginning of her adult life. How can she not be unhappy, married to a fool like Seton?'

Cleo perched on the edge of a chair, her chin in her hands, thoughtful. 'I don't think there's anything we can do. It's her decision. If she's an adult, which I suppose she is, she has to make mistakes.'

'This is a very big mistake, though,' said Sylvester. 'She's shutting the door on everything life has to offer, just to exist – because it will be an existence, nothing more – in a country village with a dull man who cares more about his dogs and land and guns than anything else. Children, oh, she'll have children, and then she'll be really stuck.'

Cleo and Sylvester looked at each other in silence; they could both picture Prue's life at Feather House.

'Horrifying,' said Cleo finally. 'What are you going to do?'

'Do? Nothing. There's nothing I can do, except offer to give her away, as an old friend of her father's. I suppose they won't wait, no family to consult, only themselves to please. Well, I tell you, as soon as the festival is over, I'm off. We'll go to London, Cleo. I won't be able to get a word of my book done up here, it's all too depressing.'

The damp weather and Sylvester's gloom pervaded Midwinter Hall. Lily was nowhere to be seen; this annoyed Cleo, who wanted to talk it all over with her. Luke was abrupt and unhelpful. How dare he, muttered Cleo to herself; he was still moping over that bloody Sophie, talk about lost causes. Well, he was welcome to her. Finally Peter paused in his work overhauling a generator – been saving this job for a rainy day, he informed her – to tell her that Lily had gone to Eyot on the early bus.

Sylvester was playing his cello now, a melancholy piece, slow and rich-sounding; it made Cleo feel sad. She couldn't settle to her work; she felt uneasy, out of place. Why had she ever brought Prue up here? If she hadn't bumped into her that day, she wouldn't have come here. All she would have known of Gossiby would have been a postcard from Cleo; she would have carried it into the law office where she would have worked all summer and probably beyond, any firm would have kept Prue on, and she would never have met Seton.

On the other hand, Cleo reasoned, perhaps she would. Not this Seton, of course, but another one. There were hundreds of Setons about, that was the trouble with him. A country solicitor would have come into the office, meeting his chum from university days, now a coming London man. 'Had lunch with old Julian today, same as ever, bet he's earning a fortune now. Nice girl he's got working for him, called Prue. Thought I might ask her down here one weekend. Lovely smile, fond of dogs, you'd like her, Mummy.'

Ugh!

Oh well. Cleo resolutely applied herself to the papers in front of her. For a while, she gave them her undivided attention. Then thoughts of Prue and Seton came back unbidden into her mind. Impatiently she pushed her hair back from her head and gave a dramatic groan.

'Groaning won't get you anywhere!' said a tart voice.

'Lily! I thought you'd gone to Eyot.'

'I had, but I didn't have much to do, and Seton gave me a lift back.'

'Don't mention that man to me. It makes me mad, that smug, boring . . . I suppose he'd been to Eyot to buy Prue a nice suit-able ring.'

'No, they're seeing about the ring this afternoon, he told me. He'd had to go in this morning to collect a bag of dog food.'

'Oh, Lily,' wailed Cleo, 'Prue can't marry that man!'

'She can, but it doesn't mean that she will. Or, if she does, that she'll stay married to him. Many's the young girl I've seen get engaged with stars in her eyes that's seen the truth about her fiancé before the day. Most don't, of course. There was Miranda, a cousin of Sylvester's. You'd like her, oh, she's a beauty all right. Married her childhood sweetheart. They'd been together since their schooldays, she'd never gone out with anyone else. He went to Cambridge, clever he was, which you can't say about Seton. He studied Maths, if I remember rightly. Evening before her wedding she came to me, tears, scenes. 'I can't do it, Lily, I don't want to marry him, but I have to.'

'"Why?" I said. She wasn't expecting a baby, but it was her family, everyone there, the presents, all the arrangements, quite a big wedding it was. I told her, "Don't". I said if she'd any doubts at all, now was the time to say no. Never mind presents and guests and the church booked, what did all that matter?'

'What happened?' said Cleo, fascinated.

'She got married, of course.'

'And lived happily ever after?'

Lily gave a very earthy chuckle. 'Yes, she did, but not with him, not with the one she married the next day. No, six weeks later she ran off with the best man. Got two children now, nice little things.'

'You do cheer me up, Lily. But somehow, I can't see Prue running away with Seton's best man. Apart from anything else, I bet his best man will be just like him.'

'Nicholas Gaskett, I expect. His oldest friend. Works in the Estate Office. No, he wouldn't be any better for Prue than Seton.'

Lily divested herself of her plastic mac, which was dribbling water on to the floor. She picked up the carrier bags and handed one to Cleo. 'These are for Sophie. She ordered them yesterday, I said I'd pick them up.'

Cleo looked into the bag. 'Exotic veggies. Lovely. Didn't know you could get things like this up here. Why don't we have them at the Hall?'

'Because Sylvester likes good solid English cooking, says he gets enough of this kind of thing when he's abroad. There's a shop in Eyot that gets all this stuff, Henry at Ghercombes nagged them into it. Your mind isn't on your work, duckie, so take this up to the castle and you can have a word with Prue.'

'Don't think I want to,' said Cleo disconsolately. 'I don't suppose Seton approves of me; I expect he thinks I'm Bohemian and a bad influence. He won't let me come near Prue once they're married.'

'I dare say Prue will keep up with her old friends.'

'No, it will be total commitment with Prue. It always is. What she does, she does thoroughly. If hubbie says he'd prefer her not to see Cleo, she'll agree.'

'And sneak off and see you just the same?'

'No, that's the trouble. She won't. Anything else for Sophie? How I hate that woman. Luke's in a real mood this morning, all because Peter told him Sophie was out again last night. I'm giving up sex, Lily, it isn't worth the effort.'

Lily smiled a wicked little smile. 'That's what we all say, until next time. Get along now, you'll have to be back before his nibs finishes his practising. There's a pair of wellies in the scullery; they'll fit and you'll need them.'

Cleo squelched her way along the path to the castle. It had stopped raining, but the air was heavy with thundery dampness. The castle looked as though it belonged in Transylvania, with great purple grey clouds massed behind it.

Thomas was in the kitchen, helping Sophie make a cake. At least, that's what he said he was doing. 'I don't see why you always have to put in the ingredients in the same order. Why can't I start with the eggs and then add the sugar and butter? I mean, they all get mixed up in the long run. I don't see why it should make any difference.'

'For some cakes it doesn't,' said Sophie. 'For this one, it does. It would come out heavy if you just mixed everything together. Careful with those eggs!'

Thomas was rolling two eggs towards the edge of the table and catching them as they fell off.

'It's all right, Sophie, I've got excellent co-ordination. That's what Sylvester says, and I have complete control over these eggs.'

He gave one of them an extra hard shove, missed it, and it smashed on the floor.

'Thomas! Please!'

'Sorry, Sophie. I'll clean it up. I know what to do, we did it in science. Egg is protein, and if you pour a lot of salt on it, it coagulates. I wonder if sand works as well? There's sand in the fire-bucket outside, I'll get some, and . . .'

'I've cleared it up, Thomas. Now, get another egg, and break them – carefully – into the bowl.'

Sophie went over to the sink and washed her hands, took a folded piece of pastry out of the fridge, manoeuvred a marble slab into position in front of her and flattened the pastry on to it.

'Can I work the mixer? I love doing that bit, making it go faster and faster until it all flies around.'

'I do not want cake mixture flying around.'

'Around the *bowl*, I mean, Sophie, not around the kitchen, although it would be fun to see how far it could go.'

'Thomas, do you want to help with this cake or not?'

'Sorry, Sophie. Mmm, yummy!'

'And get your fingers out of the bowl.'

Thomas shot her a look of injured innocence.

'And it's no good you flashing your big blue eyes at me.'

'That's what Matron says at school. I hate Matron. I wish you were our matron, or Prue. You'd be much nicer than horrible Matron Knickers.'

Sophie laughed and gave her pastry a determined last roll. 'She can't be called Knickers.'

'That's what we call her. Her real name is Pickering, Pickers, Knickers, you see. She's awful. Do you know what she does? She hides my socks, deliberately, and then I get into trouble for it. Honestly, she does.'

'Don't you like boarding school, Thomas?'

Thomas turned the speed on the mixture to full and then hastily down again as a piece of butter flew out of the bowl. 'Oops.' He picked it up and put it back in the bowl, licking his fingers. 'I don't mind it, I suppose. I like the singing. I'd rather live in a family, though, like Jellicoe does. He's a day boy. He lives in a super little house on an estate, really small. He's got a sister and his mum's great, really funny. His dad's nice, too; they've got a terrific train layout in the attic. He helps Jellicoe with it a lot. Wish I lived in a house like that. Wish I had a dad.'

'Oh, Thomas, you've got a home here!'

'It's not a real home, is it? It's a castle. The other boys think, gosh, he lives in a castle, but they won't come and stay because they don't live in castles and they think I'd look down on their ordinary houses. At least they've got parents at home. Well, Haversham has a parent in two homes, if you see what I mean.'

'His parents are divorced?' Sophie wrinkled her nose and rubbed it with a floury finger.

Thomas giggled. 'You've got a white nose now.' His face became solemn again. 'Separated, the Havershams are. They live apart, but anyway, George Haversham sees them both every hols because he goes to stay with them in turn. And they come and take him out at exeats.'

'You've got a mother.'

'Yes, but what's the use of that when she spends all her time in India?' asked Thomas reasonably. 'The headmaster loves it when Mountjoy and Magdalena come and take me out, because he's a Lord and old Puffy is a terrific snob, but it isn't the same, is it? It's not the same as your own mum and dad,' he finished sadly.

'Oh, Thomas,' said Sophie, her heart wrung. 'Thomas, would you like it if I came and took you out next term? You can go out on Saturdays after Evensong, can't you?'

Thomas's face brightened. 'That would be great. I can show you my dorm, and my special place in the bushes in Dean Woffington's garden. Then you could take me out to tea.'

'It's a promise,' said Sophie, returning her pastry to the fridge. 'The vicar sometimes goes to Evensong at the Cathedral on Saturdays, he can give me a lift.'

Thomas peered into the bowl. 'It looks a bit funny.'

'I think you've over-beaten it. Never mind, it'll probably turn out all right. And if it doesn't, we'll make another one. Mind your fingers!' She clicked the whisk out and removed the bowl. Thomas watched her as she deftly spooned the mixture into a tin.

'Do you think I could be a cook when I grow up?' he said. 'Is it a very long training?'

Sophie shook her head. 'No, but I don't expect you'll end up a cook, Thomas. You'll want to go to university, go into a profession.'

'Like Val?'

'Could be. Or the law, medicine; you've plenty of time to decide.'

'I'd like to do something with music best. Sylvester doesn't think I'm going to be a great performer because he says my music is too much mind and I don't have the attention to detail. But there are lots of other things you can do in music. Did you know Val wanted to be a musician?'

'No, I didn't know that. I wouldn't have thought that was his line at all. I know he likes music, but he doesn't strike me as an artist. Thomas, not your feet on the table, please!'

'Fuss, fuss,' grumbled Thomas. 'I just wanted to see if my legs would reach. I've grown a lot, have you noticed? I think I'm going to be tall, taller than Val even. Someone at the Cathedral told me about Val, a real old dodderer who comes into some of the services. He remembers Val when he was a chorister. Says it caused a lot of talk; apparently people like the Mountjoys didn't send their sons to Choir Schools in those days, thought it was common or something.

His mum chose the school. I think she was foreign, wasn't she? Val was one of the best they've ever had, and a terrific organist, that's what this chap says. Composer, too. But his dad didn't approve, and sent him to a very sporty school where they didn't let him do much music. His pa wanted him to go into the diplomatic service, but Val did engineering instead.'

'Just as well,' said Sophie. She gave the table a vigorous wipe. 'He's just about the most undiplomatic person you could meet. He'd have had everybody up in arms against us.'

'Third World War,' said Thomas appreciatively.

'Someone at the door, Thomas, go and see who it is.'

Thomas slid off his stool and opened the door. 'It's Cleo. Hello, Cleo.'

'Hello, Thomas. Is Sophie in? I brought some veg from Eyot for her.' She caught sight of Sophie as she emerged from behind the big fridge door. 'Here you are, Sophie. Where do you want them?'

'Bung them on the table, please. Thank you for picking them up for me.'

'Don't thank me. Lily collected them, not me. I've just brought them up from the hall. Is Prue about?'

'She's in the Muniment Room,' said Thomas politely. 'Do you know where that is, or shall I show you?'

'Is it the room in the big tower?'

'That's right. She's engaged, did you know? I quite like Seton, he's got nice dogs and he lets me go out with him sometimes. I don't know why she wants to marry him, though. She hardly knows him.'

Sophie and Cleo exchanged speaking glances, Cleo's hostility momentarily forgotten. 'From the mouths of babes . . .' she murmured.

'I quite agree,' said Sophie. 'I wouldn't do it. Still, it's her funeral. There's no accounting for tastes.'

'Exactly so,' said Cleo, with feeling.

Prue was whistling to herself through her teeth. She looked up as Cleo slunk into the room.

'Goodness, you look miserable, Cleo,' she said. Cleo looked glumly at her. For once her own energy was dimmed, while Prue was brimming with vitality. Prue gave Cleo a radiant smile. 'Kick those plimsolls over, Cleo, then I can get up and find you a chair. Bare feet on this stone floor are agony.'

Cleo handed her a pair of damp black plimsolls. 'These are disgusting,' she told Prue.

'Aren't they?' said Prue cheerfully. 'That's why I took them off. Magdalena lent them to me, it doesn't matter if they get wet, and it's wet everywhere here at the castle. I've got a rug under the table, so I don't need to keep them on.'

Prue made a face as she pulled on the damp plimsolls, then she cleared some boxes off a chair and pushed it towards Cleo. 'What are you doing here? Haven't you got anything to do?'

'Yuh,' said Cleo. 'Had to bring some things up for Lily, thought I'd drop in and see you. You look, well, I have to say you look all right.'

'Of course I do,' said Prue, surprised. 'Why shouldn't I? You don't mind if I go on with this, because I'm not stopping for any lunch. I couldn't eat anyway, Seton's coming to pick me up. Cleo, you should see my ring, it's beautiful.'

'Where is it?' said Cleo, looking at Prue's bare fingers.

'It has to be altered, it was Seton's mother's ring. Don't you think it's lovely to have a family ring rather than a new one?'

'No, actually, I'd rather choose my own ring, but I suppose it's cheaper that way for Seton.'

Prue was shocked. How could Cleo not be pleased for her? She couldn't be jealous because Prue was engaged. No, how ridiculous, you couldn't doubt Cleo's zest for making her own way, it would be a long time before she became tied down. Cleo didn't understand, she didn't want a new ring; much, much better to have something which belonged to the family. Look how little she had from her own family, a few papers and the french horn; it would be heaven to live somewhere that was filled with the possessions of generations of the same family.

'We've fixed a date,' she went on. 'I spoke to Seton on the phone last night, we talked for three-quarters of an hour!'

'His bill or the castle's?' enquired Cleo, idly looking through some of the old letters on the desk.

'Don't get those in a muddle,' protested Prue. 'I've only just got them straight.'

'What are they?'

'Eighteenth-century family letters. I haven't read them properly. Actually, they might be quite interesting. There's a girl who's engaged to a Mountjoy, and she writes to him about how he's not to fondle the serving women.'

Cleo laughed, and Prue grinned at her. 'Coming out of your black mood? Oh good, I'm so utterly happy. I want everyone else to be, as well. How's Luke?' she added.

Cleo made a face. 'Don't ask. I've given him up. He was writing a poem to Sophie last night, just after we'd been in bed together, too.'

'Cleo, no! How did you find out?'

'He went out to go to the loo. He thought I was asleep, but I wasn't, and I nipped out of bed to see what he was writing.'

'Was it good poetry?'

'No, it was not. Adolescent heart-burnings, I've had enough of it.'

'Cleo, you should find someone you really love, not just sex, but someone more permanent.'

'No, thank you very much. That's the last thing I want to do.'

Prue's thoughts were very much on her own affairs. 'I'm going to be married here, in the castle chapel, Magdalena says. On the day after the festival finishes, because there'll be a marquee up and so on.'

'Everyone will be worn out!'

'No, because the last three concerts are in Eyot, at the Cathedral, so it will be all right. Will you be a bridesmaid?'

'No, certainly not. Can you see me traipsing down the aisle after you, Prue? It would look ridiculous.'

Prue's mouth twitched, and then she burst out laughing. Yes it would look funny. 'Perhaps Thomas will be a page,' she said.

'Not if he's got any sense. I'm sure Seton will produce a little cousin for you, a Caroline or Sarah who'll look sweet in a bo-peep frock. You're going to wear a long white dress, aren't you?'

Prue flushed. What was the matter with Cleo? Of course she was going to wear a long white dress. She might not have any family at the wedding, but she wanted everything else to be just as it should be.

'Don't be so contemptuous, Cleo. Yes, I am. Magdalena's buying it for me. I've never had a long dress.'

Cleo was contrite. All very well for her to hit out at Prue because she was so concerned about her, it might end in tears, but Prue had probably never been so happy. Not surprising; by marrying she would belong somewhere. 'What do the Mountjoys think of all this?' she asked in a more normal tone.

'They are so kind, they are so amazingly kind. Magdalena's arranging everything, and Mountjoy is making lists and plans. Magdalena says he loves weddings.'

'Valdemar?'

'He's a bit sneery. I don't think he's very keen on weddings, said to let him know the date so he could be sure to be away.'

'That's rude, even for Valdemar.'

'Yes, isn't it? I think the Mountjoys were a bit shocked, but he's going to Hong Kong today. I expect he's got a lot on his mind.'

Lucky man, thought Cleo absently. Wish I were going to Hong Kong.

'Pass me that pile. Help, look at the time, I want to get these finished before I go. Seton's going to be here at half-past two.'

'It's twenty past now, you'd better lock up or whatever it is that you do.'

Prue gave a contented little sigh and got up from the table she had been working at.

'It's going to be strange, being married. Having a home of my own, that kind of thing.'

'Have you slept with him yet?'

'Cleo, of course not!'

'Of course not!' Cleo's mimicry was savage. 'Prue, how can you possibly, possibly marry a man when, oh, Prue!'

'Look, Seton and I are in love. It isn't a problem, that side of marriage,' said Prue with tremendous dignity. 'Now, I must go. I won't see you this evening, because Seton is taking me out to dinner.'

'Bye, Prue,' said Cleo, sadly.

16

As the plane came in to land, Valdemar jammed the report he was reading into his briefcase and gazed out of the window. A seasoned traveller, he rarely took any notice of take-offs or landings, but always, always, he watched as they made the descent into Hong Kong.

He loved watching the skyscrapers coming closer and closer, the swoop towards the city until it seemed that the plane was going to hurl itself into the centre, then the touch-down on the runway jutting out into the harbour. It never failed to enthral Valdemar, even after an eighteen-hour flight.

An unfortunate businessman, a pleasant man in the retail clothing trade, had been allocated the seat next to Valdemar. Every civil remark had been answered with a snarl. The businessman, rebuffed, had ostentatiously turned away from such a disagreeable travelling companion.

Shaming if he behaved like that when he was in Hong Kong, the kind of man who gave Britain a bad name. He took a quick look at the dark, angry face. Not another businessman, he thought. Too much character and intelligence for a merchant banker – he had considerable experience of merchant bankers and had his own, kept-to-himself opinion of them – a lawyer, perhaps? A consultant of some kind. They came in all shapes and sizes, and tended to have an authoritative way to them; certainly it would take a brave client to question this man's views.

A limousine was waiting for Valdemar. The businessman, waiting for his own more modest transport, noted it and nodded his head with satisfaction. Yes, an important man undoubtedly, but what an unpleasant one! He pitied his wife. Must be hell at home, he thought, as he collected the keys of his hire car and headed for his hotel.

Colwyn Henderson was waiting for Valdemar in his apartment.

'Val, good to see you again, marvellous that you could make the trip, wouldn't be the same without you.'

Valdemar greeted him in a friendly enough fashion, but his mind was obviously elsewhere.

'You must be tired,' said Colwyn apologetically. 'You had to fly down from the north before catching the plane, bit of a haul.'

'I've done it before.'

'There is a reception tonight,' said Colwyn uncertainly. 'If you're tired . . .'

His voice tailed away. Valdemar's energy was legendary; lesser men succumbed to jet lag or tiredness after exhausting stretches of work, but he never seemed to notice.

'Reception,' said Val. 'Where?'

'At Government House, actually.'

'God, have to go to that, otherwise the Chinese will all think I'm out of favour. I'll have a bath, meet you at the office in an hour.'

It was a dismissal, and Colwyn turned to go. 'CC is looking after you; you remember him from last time. He'll run you a bath. I expect he's already unpacked your bags.'

Val grunted and headed for the bedroom.

'I'll see you in an hour, then,' said Colwyn to the bedroom door, and made a thankful departure.

'Something's bugging him,' he reported to his colleagues at the office. 'Hope it isn't anything to do with us here.'

'So do I,' said a stocky, red-haired man. 'Remember last time when some silly sod had mucked about with his plans? Ouch!'

'Who've you got lined up for him tonight?' asked a taller, grey-haired man, 'womanwise?'

'They'll all be there, it's up to him. I hope he's tactful; won't do to remove some nob's bird from under his nose.'

'No, business first. Val won't do anything which endangers present or future contracts, you know that.' He looked out of the huge roundel window which overlooked a large swathe of Hong Kong with views across to the harbour. 'It's hot tonight. Let's hope the air-conditioning there is working properly.'

Valdemar was taller than most of the Europeans present, and he towered above nearly all the Chinese. He stopped to talk to one very tall man, representative of the government in Peking, who came from the north and could look him in the eye. He chatted briefly to the Governor. They had been to school together; Valdemar had loathed him there, now thought he had been promoted way beyond his level of competence.

'Let's hope they find someone a bit better than that when we get nearer to 1997,' he whispered into the ear of a slim and exceedingly elegant Chinese woman.

Martha Li turned on her expensive high heels and beamed at Valdemar. She tucked her hand under his arm.

'Val, I am so pleased to see you. Come and sit with me, and we talk, not business, just old friends.'

Martha Li, Oxford, Harvard Business School, daughter of a rich man and now incomparably wealthy in her own right, was one of the few women Valdemar had any respect for. 'Mind like a razor, no sentiment in business at all, straight to the point.'

He had come for the opening of the huge and impressive head-quarters which had just been built for her company. His firm, Mountjoy & Partners, had been the structural engineers.

'Did you see, in the ante-room, there's an exhibition of your buildings?'

'No, I didn't see that.'

'Come.'

She led him through the throng and waved a diamond-ringed hand at the pictures. 'You see? All yours. Quite an honour.'

Valdemar laughed. 'Yes, flying the flag tonight, aren't we?'

Martha Li's eyes wrinkled appreciatively. 'Will you take me out to dinner? Not tonight. Tonight, I think you need to sleep.' She raised a finger in rebuke. 'I know, Valdemar is never tired, but let me tell you, as a friend, that tonight you look tired. Tonight, you look your age.'

Valdemar grimaced. 'Thank you.'

'No, in China it is okay to look your age. With years come wisdom and serenity.' She shot him an affectionate glance. 'Maybe wisdom in your case, but not yet, I think, serenity. Of course, if you have something already arranged . . .'

Valdemar swirled the drink in his glass, he had hardly touched it. 'No, nothing. In any case, I would break a prior engagement to spend time with you.'

She gave a delightful, bubbly laugh. 'Is Sylvia with you?'

'No, she's in France.'

'Ah, one of her regular trips to keep her husband happy!'

'She's gone to visit her mother,' Valdemar went on. Then he realized what Martha had said. 'Mother. She goes to visit her mother. She isn't well.'

Martha looked at him, her eyebrows slightly raised. 'My dear Val, Sylvia has no mother. It's her husband she goes to see, everyone knows that.' She hesitated, puzzled by the expression on Valdemar's face.

'Val, you must have known, I wouldn't have said anything. How could you not know?'

'Bloody hell,' said Valdemar, rendered for once almost speechless. He drained his glass and swiftly hooked another off a tray carried by a passing waiter. 'Bloody hell,' he repeated.

Martha looked at him with concern. 'But Val, you must have realized. Why, she's been with you for years; she's never talked about getting married, not even hinted at it. Didn't you wonder?'

'I simply thought it was her good sense. A husband? So every time she goes off to France, it's to be with a husband! For Christ's sake, I don't believe this.'

'Val, calm down, you're beginning to attract attention.'

Valdemar took a deep breath. 'Yes, yes, all right.'

Martha skilfully propelled him to a sofa and sat him down. 'Val, this isn't like you, you're so sophisticated about these matters. You aren't in love with her, are you?'

'Hell, no, but I don't care to share my possessions.'

She looked at him, amused. 'I don't know that Sylvia thinks of herself as a possession, you know. People don't like to be a possession, it tends to limit them as human beings.'

'Don't preach, Martha.'

'I never preach. Now listen, Val, you're too old for all this. Why don't you marry, some nice girl, you must know dozens of them, good family, some money . . . then you can have some children. I can't tell you what a comfort it is to have children!' Martha's eyes misted as she thought of her own adored family. 'That's what you need, Val,' she said firmly. 'Children.'

'Children? Why should I need children?' Val waved his hand along the carefully-arranged photos and models, huge blocks of concrete and metal dominating their surroundings.

'These are my children, Martha. These are all I need.'

'Oh, Val,' she said, pity in her voice. 'Val, marry, find yourself

176

a young girl who admires you, a good girl, not a smart Londoner. Marry her and spend every summer up in that uncle's castle that you tell me about. Have children, become a human being.'

Valdemar's face and jaw twitched and then he gave an ironic laugh. 'I'll marry if I can find someone like you, Martha. What a pity we didn't meet twenty years ago.'

Martha looked grave. 'Oh, no, Val, you couldn't ever marry someone like me. Only men who like women marry people like me.'

'What are you saying, Martha? You're impossible. Are you suggesting . . .?'

'You like women for sex and to make you feel good, but you don't like women for what they are, as characters, personalities; you don't find them interesting.'

'Is that a criticism?'

'No, just a perceptive remark. You might have been different if you had grown up with a sister; better still, several sisters. Men with sisters are usually much more civilized where women are concerned, and they learn to respect them too, something you have never done, Valdemar, hey, confess?'

Valdemar was getting restless. This conversation was doing nothing for his vanity. He changed the subject.

'By the way, I've got a scheme in mind, you might like to come in on it, to do with the castle. Leisure is going to be big, you appreciate that.'

'I appreciate an old friend's thinking of me. Don't be cross, Val, no big deal for an old friend to tell you some truths, I don't think you get very much truth about yourself.'

She gave him a dazzling smile. Blast her, thought Val, she always manages to wrong-foot me. Reluctantly he smiled back, and leant forward to kiss her cheeks in farewell. 'I'll ring tomorrow, I want your help in choosing some material.'

'Aha. What kind?'

'Silk, naturally. For a wedding dress.' He laughed at her expression. 'No, Martha, nothing to do with what you've been saying. I never take advice, and I'm not making any plans. It's for a young friend of my uncle's; she's getting married at the castle. It's a present for her.'

'I thought, in England, the bride's mother sees to such things.'

'Yes, but this girl has popped up from nowhere, her parents

are dead, brought up by an aunt, but she's dead now as well, I understand. Magdalena asked me to do this for her.'

'Magdalena asked you to do it? Then of course, the very best. Telephone me and we will go hunting. I take you to the best places, without question.'

Valdemar walked to the shop where he was to meet Martha. He was restless, ill-at-ease; good idea to stretch his legs. He could hardly claim to be getting fresh air; at that time of the year, Hong Kong was filled with a sticky, humid heat. He liked the city, though, bustling with life and business, every lock-up shop and workshop teeming with busy workers. Usually a family, everyone from the tiny gran to the very young children with work in hand; Valdemar approved of the work ethic.

He strolled towards the ferry, paid the minimal fare and found himself a space on the packed vessel. The harbour, too, was alive with activity: sampans, junks, tankers making their way to moorings, a sailing boat tacking out towards the sea, tugs, a cruise ship on a round-the-world voyage.

Valdemar looked up at the Peak, misty at the moment; very different from his native fells. He thought of the quiet, muddy roads, the sheep, the uncommunicative northerners, the emptiness of the fells, a world away from this thriving, vital place. You could be dead, there, he said angrily to himself. Must get Mountjoy to buck up his ideas, get the go-ahead on the castle business, bring a bit of work and activity there as well. When I own the castle, Val thought (not wishing Mountjoy any harm, for he was fond of his uncle, but in the natural order of things he would one day inherit), I'm going to make a lot of changes.

His head was so full of plans – none of them very suitable for the staid northern way of life around Gossiby – that he only noticed that the ferry had got to the other side when his neighbour jostled against him as he tried to squeeze past to the exit.

Martha chose the silk for him, quickly and expertly. 'Describe this girl. Who is she going to marry, a relation of your uncle's, of yours?'

'No, no one in the family. A neighbour, good property but no ideas, a very dull man. Can't think what she sees in him.'

'Such men can make very good husbands. What does she look like? Dark, fair?'

Prue came vividly into Valdemar's mind. 'Fair,' he said. 'That slightly reddish blonde hair that goes with a few freckles. Blue and golden eyes, unusual, quite tall, very slim, not much figure but well-proportioned.'

Martha gave him a quick, appraising look, which he didn't notice. 'Is she beautiful, does she have character?'

'She's pretty, yes, in a Botticelli kind of way, Primavera, you know. Bit wistful. They say she's intelligent, can't say I've seen any signs of it.'

'You describe her very clearly.'

'Yes, well, she's been at the castle this summer, helping Magdalena. Now she's got herself engaged, I suppose that's what she came for, husband-hunting.'

'Perhaps she just fell in love with this neighbour. It happens, you know. Cream, and not white, of course, most English girls look dreadful in white, very common. Not off-white, either, with that colouring. Ivory, I think, yes, ivory.'

Martha chose a thick silk at a price which made Valdemar blink. 'Good God, that's far too good for her.'

'Are you paying? Or Magdalena? She will know that this would cost three times as much in England, if you could get it. You must always be generous when it is a gift for a bride, it is a natural courtesy.'

'Oh, very well. I suppose I might as well get her something while I'm here, save having to bother about it later.'

'A bag, these bags are lovely. What do you normally do when you buy presents, Val?'

'Get my secretary to shop for me, of course,' said Valdemar. 'All right, I know, typical male behaviour. That's the way I am, Martha, and I'm not going to change after all these years.'

He chose an unexpectedly lovely bag for Prue, which surprised Martha, and refused to buy a present for Sylvia.

'She's been making a fool of me. She knew I had no idea she was married, and she must have been well aware that everyone else knew she had a husband in France. I won't forgive her for that.'

'Careful, Val, it means you'll have to find a new mistress. I know you like to play the field, but you always need a steady one, don't you? A familiar base after your other, brief affairs.'

'How come you know so much about my private life?' asked Val with irritation. 'Have you had private detectives on my trail?'

'That is something I do sometimes, when it's a matter of business, you know. I like to have as much information as possible about people I am doing business with. Not in your case, Val. There is no need. We have a lot of friends in common, and you make no secret of the way you live. That's admirable, in its way, even if the lifestyle is not.'

'It suits me.'

'So you say. There, we have finished, they will send the material and the bag round to your hotel. Okay?'

Val was relieved that he was only in Hong Kong for two days on this trip. He usually left the colony with regret, always saw to it that he was involved in the Hong Kong office's contracts; this time, he was pleased to get away. Although he wouldn't admit it to himself, he was hurt by Martha's teasing words. He hated being criticized, always had done. Of course it was all rubbish, but still, he had a suspicion that he had been judged and found wanting – and by a woman.

He had intended to spend the day in London, sleep at his club, which he generally did when Sylvia was away. God, he'd forgotten; she would be away for good now. He wasn't going to share her with another man, though of course that was exactly what he'd been doing, unwittingly, for years. He wondered if her husband knew about her other establishment in London. What kind of a man was he, anyway, to let his wife go off for months on end like that?

Suddenly, London didn't have much appeal. He queued impatiently at passport control and walked rapidly through the baggage hall; he never took more than hand luggage if he could help it. He fretted and fidgeted in the customs hall and paid the tax and duty on the silk and bag, grinning momentarily to himself as he noticed that the bill, doubtless on Martha's instructions, was made out for very much less than he had actually paid.

It was warm and overcast outside, grey and depressing, he thought, as he stepped off the kerb in front of a taxi.

A strong hand grabbed his shoulder and pulled him back. The taxi driver swore at him and drove furiously off.

Valdemar turned to thank his rescuer, a shortish man, foreigner clearly, with a thin, merry, intelligent face and a pair of concerned brown eyes. 'No trouble, you were thinking of something else. It's a good idea I find to concentrate on cars when crossing the road. Leave the worry and fret for other times, hey?'

He seemed vaguely familiar to Valdemar; not like him to forget a face. Then he noticed what the man was carrying; a bulgy blue bag slung over one shoulder and a briefcase, and, in the other hand, a violin case.

'You're Geza Muronyi!' he said. 'The violinist.'

The eyes danced again. 'Yes, that is so. But I don't know you. You aren't a musician, are you?'

'No. I saw you play in Budapest last year, the Mendelssohn violin concerto.'

'Ah, that's a nice little concerto, and one I sometimes play extremely well.'

'You played it extremely well when I heard you. You're giving some concerts at the Summer Music Festival at Midwinter, aren't you?'

Geza was delighted. 'Yes, yes, indeed I am. I go there now. I stay with my old friend, the cellist, a very, very great cellist, Sylvester Tate. Do you live there? Do you know my friend Sylvester?'

'Indeed I do, I'm up there every year. My family are neighbours of Sylvester.'

'Then I will see you there. I'm off now, on the bus, to Central London, then I catch a train from King's Cross, another train at Eyot, and a little country station. Sylvester says a very nice girl with dark hair and very blue eyes, just like you, will collect me there. So, goodbye,' he held out his hand, 'and I will meet you again soon.'

'Cleo,' said Valdemar.

'Cleo?'

'Sylvester has asked Cleo to meet you. I've got a better idea. I was due to spend a couple of days in London before I went north again, but for various reasons I've decided not to. You can drive up with me.'

Geza smiled an exuberant smile. 'Very good, I like that. Your car is where?'

'Here. The car park's miles away from the terminals, though, not like Budapest. We catch a bus – over there.'

'First, I think we have to ring Sylvester, because now this Cleo need not meet me.'

'Stop on the way and do that. We'll be there before your train is due to arrive, in any case. It usually takes me about four hours.'

Four memorable hours, thought Geza, glad to get out of the car. The front door was flung open and Sylvester burst out.

'Geza, excellent, a good journey, I trust. Val, come in, how was Hong Kong? What luck, your bumping into Geza at the airport like that. Come in, come in. Lily!' His voice boomed across the hall.

Lily appeared, and firmly took control of Geza.

She'd discussed him that morning with Cleo. 'Hungarians aren't too bad. I have to be frank, Cleo,' she'd said, 'what I can't stand is the French. You never know where you are with a Frenchman.'

Cleo had been prepared to argue the point, having an aversion to Scandinavians; as it turned out no one, whatever their prejudices, could fail to like Geza.

'Nice man, that,' Lily said approvingly as she returned downstairs. 'He's having a shower. I'll go and make him some coffee.'

'Good, strong coffee,' said Sylvester. 'Continentals like a bit of taste.'

'I shall make it the same as I always do. I haven't had any complaints yet.'

'Coffee?' said Valdemar. 'Good. I'll wait for that and then I'll get along to the castle.'

'I didn't offer it to you, but I suppose Sylvester would,' said Lily. 'Looks to me as though you need more than a cup of coffee to revive you. Are you sickening for something? I hope you haven't brought any tropical diseases back with you.'

'He's had a long flight,' protested Sylvester, 'and then the drive on top of it. Have some charity.'

'He's the last person in the world who needs charity. Anyway, he's always flying here there and everywhere, usually arrives fresh as a daisy. Looks to me as though he's had a nasty shock.' She gave him a piercing look. 'Heard from Sylvia recently?' she asked, then gave what could only be described as a cackle and went back to the kitchen.

'What was that about?' said Sylvester. 'I must say, I have seen you look better. Is something up?'

'No,' said Valdemar shortly. 'Just a tiring flight, as you say. Pour me a drink, there's a good fellow, I could do with it. God, life's a bugger.' With which inspiring words he sank into an armchair and closed his eyes.

Prue clambered off the bus. She watched it trundle away into the distance and then crossed the road to the station. Cleo was sitting in the old estate car, reading a book. Prue got in beside her.

'Prue! What on earth are you doing here?'

'Doesn't it seem years and years ago that we arrived here, not knowing what to expect? Sylvester asked me to come, I caught the bus; there are only two a day, you know. This Hungarian musician you've come to meet isn't coming by train after all, he's driving up with Val for some reason.'

'Bother,' said Cleo, starting the car and reversing wildly into the hedge. 'What a waste of time.'

'Do you mind if we go back via Eyot? Magdalena wants me to do something for her, and I've got an appointment at the dentist. A filling's fallen out, I think.'

'I've already been there today,' Cleo grumbled, as she swung out into the road.

Prue explored her tooth with her tongue. 'Ouch. Near the cathedral, Magdalena says, so we can park in the car park behind the Deanery. She wants us to pick up some posters, they're in the Cathedral shop.'

They sat at the dentist's, Cleo scowling and not very talkative, Prue looking at Country Life.

The receptionist disappeared into an inner sanctum, leaving them alone in the waiting room.

'You've slept with him, haven't you?' said Cleo suddenly. 'I can tell.'

'That's ridiculous,' said Prue, reddening. 'What do you mean, you can tell?'

'You're very thoughtful, not like you were when you'd just got engaged. Something's changed.'

'I love Seton as much as I did.'

'*Qui s'excuse, s'accuse*,' said Cleo. 'Why are you on the defensive, then? What was it like?'

Prue looked out of the window, her head tilted on one side, looking at the grotesques on the cathedral facade.

'Okay.'

'Okay? Hold on, this sounds less than enthusiastic.'

'It was messy. I hadn't realized how messy it all is.'

Cleo gave a snort of laughter. 'Yes, it is messy, but is that all you can say about it?'

'I suppose you get used to it.'

'I knew he'd be useless in bed,' said Cleo under her breath.

'What did you say?'

'Oh, nothing. Did he talk to you? I can't stand men who chat in bed. You can't relax because they expect answers, makes life very difficult.'

'No, he doesn't talk a lot. And we were interrupted. His aunt telephoned.'

'His aunt? You don't mean to tell me he answered the phone, when you were making love?'

'Yes, he said it might be someone important. But it wasn't, only his aunt. When he heard her voice, he asked her to hold on and he rushed into the other room to put his trousers on.'

'Put his trousers on?' Cleo was trying very hard not to laugh.

'Yes,' said Prue gloomily. 'He said he couldn't talk to her with nothing on, she'd know.'

Cleo couldn't help herself, she burst out laughing. 'Oh, Prue, how funny. And was it all right after that? I mean, it hadn't given him the droops, talking to his aunt?'

'Given him the . . . oh, oh, I see what you mean. No, that was all right.' She sighed. 'I think he enjoyed himself. Afterwards, he said, "Jolly good."'

'Jolly good? Oh, Prue. What then?'

'Then he went to sleep.'

They looked at each other. Cleo shook her head. 'I'm not going to say a single word, Prue, not a word.'

Prue took up a magazine as the receptionist came back into the room.

'Mr Buncliffe won't keep you long, now, Miss Pagan.'

'Thank you,' muttered Prue.

She flipped over the pages: desirable residences, people in evening dress, endless photographs of country interiors. Just like Seton's house, thought Prue, only smarter. And what have I got to do with these dogs and chintzes and polished tables?

Tears formed in her eyes, and a single fat one rolled down her cheek. I can't spend the rest of my life in one of these. Nor in a boring nine-to-five office in London, waiting for another Mr Right to come along. Last night, for the first time since she had arrived at the castle, she had got out some of her books, much treasured, expensive books which she had saved long and hard to buy. Extremely dull books to most people. Fairyland to Prue.

'Are you in much pain?' asked the receptionist sympathetically, noticing the tears.

'Not too bad, thanks,' Prue managed to say. Where was her handkerchief? Why was she crying? She was engaged to a wonderful man; it was just because it was a change. You were bound to find it difficult at first. She felt Cleo's hand squeezing hers.

'Cheer up, ducks, it'll all work out, you'll see.'

'I suppose so,' said Prue unhappily.

'The dentist is ready for you now, Miss Pagan.'

'Thank you,' said Prue.

17

'The Bishop rang,' said Daisy.

'The Bishop?' said Jacob, 'Which bishop?'

'Jacob, don't be so slow,' said Daisy impatiently. 'Your bishop, the Bishop of Eyot. He's coming to see you. Don't get excited, he says it's a personal matter, wants to ask your advice about something.' She sniffed. 'I can't see what use your advice would be to the Bishop.'

'When is he coming?' asked Jacob, a slight frown on his face. He had a nasty suspicion he knew exactly why the Bishop was coming. 'It'll be nice to see Reggie again.'

'When so many of the senior clergy are old friends of yours from school and university, I don't see why you don't get promotion, at least a better living than this.'

'There are many good men looking for promotion and good livings,' said Jacob. He didn't mention the two excellent livings and the rural deanship that had been offered to him and which he had refused. He suspected that Daisy wouldn't understand his refusals.

'He's coming tomorrow. It's my day over at Fusby, helping with the playgroup, so you'll have to entertain him yourself. Sorry about that.' So was Jacob. Her playgroup days were his days off, over the hills and far away.

Jacob went into the kitchen to do the washing-up. He retrieved Daisy's empties from their hiding place and put them in the bin. Everyone in the village knew about Daisy; what was the point in being discreet? He used to take the bottles to the dump when on his visits, but hadn't bothered to do that for a while now.

He wondered if the Bishop knew about Daisy, too. If tongues had been busy about one thing, then they probably had about everything else, too. For a moment he thought he might go to his church and pray, but he grinned and told himself not to be a hypocrite. He had no intention of giving up what gave him most pleasure in life, not for the Bishop and certainly not for God, who surely had much more important things on his plate than an erring country vicar.

He didn't feel so cheerful the next morning after he'd seen Daisy off and done a bit of haphazard tidying. He tried to put some thoughts down for next week's sermon, but nothing came, and he knew he would, yet again, use a ready-made text. Nobody listened to the sermon, in any case. The music and liturgy were all right, but who wanted to hear his, Jacob's, thoughts on what St Paul meant when he said this or that, and how the text from this morning's Gospel reading reminded him of the story about the Welshman marooned on a desert island.

He was thoroughly depressed by the time the Bishop arrived, and his spirits weren't raised when Reggie sat with his cup of instant coffee balanced on his knee and gave him an earnest look. He was a rotund bishop, fond of his food and wine, and comfortable in the knowledge that at least in his robes he looked a fine figure of a man. Cassocks hide a multitude of sins. He was in mufti today, with only a purple shirt to show his rank and to indicate to Jacob that this was more than a social visit. There was an intensity about him which was impressive; in fact the Bishop had poor eyesight and too much vanity to wear spectacles all the time. The intense gaze came simply from focusing hard in an attempt to see what was in front of him. He leant forward.

'I told Daisy that I wanted some, um, advice from you, because I didn't want to worry her unduly.'

'Very kind of you.'

'I dare say you have some, um, suspicion of why I am here, Jacob?'

'Tell me, Bishop.'

He waved an episcopal hand. 'My dear Jacob, why this 'Bishop' business? We are, are we not, old friends?'

'I thought it might make it easier for you, Reggie.'

'Jacob, that is so like you. The problem is this, um, young woman you've been seeing. Um, it can't go on.'

'How do you know about this?' Jacob asked.

'Um, you don't deny it? It's an unfortunate business. I hate this kind of thing, Jacob, I really do,' said the Bishop with some vehemence. 'My chaplain, Cecil – you remember Cecil? – he saw you. With the, um, girl. Twice. In a wood. And you were, um, well, you, that is to say . . . Yes.'

'What was young Cecil doing in the wood?' enquired Jacob. Yes, he remembered Cecil all right, even the dimmest chorister knew all about Cecil, and when he'd come here to preach that Sunday, he'd had to remove young Sebastian from the vestry very swiftly. It seemed that Cecil's little ways the church could live with; his, plainly, they could not.

'Meditating,' said the Bishop, a little nervously.

Jacob burst out laughing, he couldn't help himself. 'Meditating!'

'Jacob, each Christian comes to God . . .'

'Reggie!'

'Do stop laughing, Jacob. Oh, very well, yes, I know, meditating in the woods . . . He is a very serious young man.'

'Not in such a deep meditative trance as to be unaware of his surroundings.'

The Bishop shifted in his chair. 'No, um, I think you were being rather, um, how shall I put it, conspicuous. Noisy.'

'Yes, we do get carried away a bit. We rather assume that no one will be there. It is a very dark and remote part of the wood.'

'Um, yes. Jacob, a wood, at your time of life? I don't presume to great knowledge, but a bed, perhaps . . .?'

'Thank you, Reggie, you're right, but for reasons which I am sure you can appreciate, neither my nor her bed is available for this particular activity. We do manage to get the occasional night away together, and then we eschew the woods.'

'Yes, um, Durham. Someone did mention something to me about the conference at Durham, a companion. It didn't sound like, um, Daisy.'

'My word, my fellow clerics have been busy, haven't they?'

'She's a parishioner, I understand. That makes it very awkward.'

'She lives in the parish, yes. But she doesn't worship in my church.'

The Bishop sighed. 'I am relieved to hear it.'

They were silent. The Bishop looked up at the ceiling. Jacob slowly drank the last of his coffee, now cold.

'Um,' said the Bishop at last. 'There is a living which has become vacant in Liverpool, St Cuthbert's. A thriving parish, a lot of good work for a first-class priest to do.'

Jacob bent down and put his coffee cup on the floor. 'I'm not a first class priest, Reggie. I'm not any kind of a priest.'

'My dear friend,' said the Bishop anxiously. He hated crises of faith; they were embarrassing, and either you made matters worse or, by luck, you managed to react in the right way, and then the person having the crisis was so horribly grateful.

'I think a period of retreat would be advisable. Of course if you are having spiritual struggles, these are so often reflected in our personal lives in a way we don't always recognize.'

Jacob got up. 'I'm glad you came, Reggie. You've made my mind up for me.'

'You'll take St Cuthbert's?' A relieved smile spread across the Bishop's face. 'I am so glad.'

'I'll ring you later in the week, if I may,' said Jacob, unwilling to get involved in what he felt would be a long argument.

'Of course. My secretary will put you through at once, or you can ring my private number, at any time. You have it, I know.'

At the door the Bishop paused. 'One thing, Daisy, does she know about this, um, unfortunate matter?'

'I don't know,' said Jacob, suddenly very tired. 'I don't know. I hope not.'

'Indeed, yes, we must hope not. Put this whole business behind you, Jacob. A new start, that's what you need.'

Jacob watched as Cecil, his eyes carefully avoiding him, held the door open for the Bishop and then bustled importantly round to the driver's seat. The Bishop turned round to wave, but Jacob had gone back into the vicarage and shut the door.

Jacob sat for a long time on the old bench in the garden. He was so quiet and still that the birds came and hopped around in a daredevil fashion. He was startled out of his reverie by an unfamiliar voice.

'Hello,' it said. 'Is it all right to come through? The front door wasn't locked, and Mrs Grobbins said you were in the garden, so I thought . . .'

Jacob stood up wearily.

'No, it's fine. What can I do for you? Let me see, you're one of the girls from London – the one at the castle. Prue? Is that right?'

'Yes, I'm Prue.' She looked doubtfully at him. 'Are you all right? You don't look very well.'

'No, I'm okay, just a bit tired,' said Jacob with an effort. 'What can I do for you?'

'This is from Lady Mountjoy. She said you'd need it, it's something to do with the music festival.' She eyed him uncertainly as she handed him the envelope. 'Are you sure I can't get you a glass of water?'

'No. I've had rather a shock. The Bishop was here.'

'The Bishop? Isn't that rather grand, a bishop calling? Oh dear,' she went on, with sudden perception, 'did he come to unfrock you?'

'Not quite, it takes a bit of time to do that, but basically you're not far wrong.'

'I am sorry. Unless it's what you want, of course.'

He pulled a face. 'It could be for the best, I suppose. My wife won't like it at all – you've met Daisy?'

Prue nodded. 'Does she like being a vicar's wife?'

'Yes, she does rather.'

'That's difficult, then.' She thought for a moment. 'Have you done something really dreadful, pinching the church silver or embezzling the funds? Or is it the kind of thing that's only wrong because you're a clergyman?'

Jacob looked at Prue properly for the first time, surprised at what she had said. She sat down beside him and tilted her head on one side.

'Well?'

He smiled, a genuine smile. 'You're a breath of fresh air, Prue. No, it would still be wrong if I weren't a clergyman, but it probably wouldn't cost me my job. I've been sleeping with someone who isn't my wife, and the Bishop has found out about it.'

'Oh,' said Prue. 'Trouble, then.'

'Yes and no. I can go to another parish, he's very kind, it's a good offer, and pretend it never happened. Or I can do what I should do and leave the church, my work here – oh, and my wife, and live openly with Sophie and put an end to all the deception.'

Prue's hand flew to her mouth. 'Sophie!' she exclaimed. 'You're Sophie's secret!'

Jacob was furious with himself. But why? he reasoned. Once one or two people knew about this kind of thing, it would be all over the village. 'Yes,' he said. 'I'm Sophie's secret, if you want to put it like that.'

'And you don't want to leave her and go off and be a good vicar and husband somewhere else?'

'No.'

'I think Sophie's very lucky, but it's hard on your wife.' Prue was thinking that if she were Jacob she'd prefer Sophie any day, for all her brusqueness, to Daisy's peculiar ways. It must be very difficult to be abused all the time, and since Daisy was so rude about Jacob in public, she was presumably horrid to him in private.

'She doesn't like being married,' said Jacob. He went on in a rush of honesty. 'I don't think she likes men at all. Not me, not any of us. She hates sex and always has done. I like sex. It's a problem.'

Prue was staring at him intently. 'She likes being Mrs Pugh, the vicar's wife, though.'

'Yes, that's about it.'

'Is sex so important in a marriage?' Prue asked, in what she hoped was a very casual way.

'Oh, yes,' said Jacob sadly. 'It is.' He remembered why he had heard Prue's name just recently. 'You're going to get married yourself, aren't you? To Seton?'

Prue nodded.

Jacob looked down urgently at Prue. 'Listen, Prue,' he said intently, 'if you've got any doubts, if sex with Seton isn't, oh, so wonderful that you can't wait until the next time, then don't even think of doing it – getting married, I mean. I tell you, not only from my own experience, but because of all the people I've counselled as a priest – though God knows, I'm hardly fitted to sort out their marital problems – I can assure you, it's always disastrous.'

'Is it?' said Prue, doubtfully. 'I thought, being a clergyman, you'd say marriage is more about friendship and making a home together and having children. That's what the nuns would say.'

'Nuns?' Jacob stared at Prue. 'What nuns?'

'The nuns at my school. I was at a convent school,' Prue explained.

'Don't you believe it. Sex may not be important to your nuns, but my God, it's at the heart of it for the rest of us. To hell with the nuns, Prue, and the Bishop and the whole pack of them. Follow your instincts.'

He grabbed her hand. 'Come on, I'm going to pour us large drinks, and we're going to drink to a future full of delightful sex – me with Sophie and you with whoever you find who really turns you on in bed, and, speaking off the record, I don't think Seton would cause the tiniest flicker in any woman worth her salt.'

Sylvester carried Prue up the stairs, a lightweight against his burly body. Geza came out of the sitting-room and watched with some amusement.

'Who is this?' he enquired.

Lily was following Sylvester up the stairs. 'It's young Prue Pagan,' she told him. 'She's been carousing with the vicar, what goings-on, and came home in a taxi, drunk as a lord.'

'Does she often do this?'

'I think,' said Sylvester, puffing slightly, 'I think it's the first time she's ever been drunk.'

'She's just a child. I thought in England you took better care of your children.'

'She's eighteen,' said Lily.

Geza laughed. 'Pagan. There's a name to remember. Sylvester, surely . . .'

'Yes, she's Piers Pagan's daughter.'

'No! The finest horn player I ever heard, and died so young. Is she a musician, this little one?'

'Sadly, not,' said Sylvester. He disappeared through a door and dumped Prue unceremoniously on a bed. 'Put her in here, Lily, I'm not carrying her up another flight of stairs.'

Lily pulled back the covers and rolled Prue into the bed. 'Leave the bathroom door open, she'll be sick as a dog when she wakes up.'

'That won't be for hours,' said Sylvester, casting an expert eye over her. 'We're lucky she had the sense to come here. Just think what Val would have said if she'd gone to the castle. Magdalena and Mountjoy have gone out to Henry's for dinner and Sophie's locked in her room crying her eyes out, Magdalena rang and told me, so he would have had to deal with her.'

Lily pushed him, still talking, out of the room, and closed the door. 'I'll make sure she's all right before I go to bed.'

'Has she been drinking alone, at the pub, this Prue?' asked Geza, as Sylvester lumbered down the stairs. 'I didn't quite understand what Lily was saying.'

'No, she's been drinking with the vicar.' Sylvester chuckled. 'Do her the world of good. Anything's better than spending time with the dull fellow she's engaged to.'

'Ah, the plot thickens,' cried Geza joyfully. 'Gossip. Above all things, I love gossip. Now, the vicar, he is the priest?'

'Yes.'

'And, being Protestant, yes I know a lot of English History, the Reforms, everything, he can have women, marry, that is? Have he and Prue been up to naughties tonight?'

Sylvester roared. 'No, they haven't. Mind you, I think the vicar has been up to naughties, as you put it, with someone; there are rumours, but not Prue.'

'Do you think the vicar, too, is in such a state?'

'That's a thought. Daisy's away today, she won't be back until late, often stays the night at Fusby, now I come to think of it. The vicar's more used to drink than Prue, of course, but I think we'll wander down that way. We could do with a walk, see that he's okay.'

'Yes, yes, and call in at the village pub on the way back. I love English pubs. Now, you tell me all. Who is this Fusby? Where is Daisy?'

'Fusby is a place, Daisy is the vicar's wife.'

'Ah, so the vicar is leading a double life. I expect his superiors disapprove. Who would that be? You don't have bishops, I know this, because Mr Cromwell beheaded them all.'

Sylvester appreciated Geza's version of history, but felt obliged to put him right. 'No, we do have bishops, far too many of them, if you ask me. One of them has been here today, visiting our vicar, so Lily tells me – Lily knows everything, you'll find that out – perhaps this is why he and Prue have been drinking to excess.'

'Let's go,' said Geza with enthusiasm. 'I love this, drunken vicars, naughties, Lily and her sharp tongue, little girls with dull fiancés, this is all very English.'

'Prue! Wake up!'

Prue rolled over in bed and opened an eye. She shut it again, quickly, and groaned.

'Prue, come on, wake up.'

'Go away, Cleo. I'm ill.'

'You aren't ill, you've just got a stinking hangover. Do wake up!'

With an effort, Prue hauled herself into a semi-recumbent position. She pushed her dank hair away from her face and tried opening her eyes.

'Cleo, what are you doing here? What time is it?'

'Late, and you're here, not me. That is, you aren't in your room at the castle, you're at Midwinter Hall. You got very drunk last night, with the vicar, and you came here.'

Prue opened her eyes a little more. Cleo giggled.

'You look like a delinquent mouse, Prue. Whatever were you drinking?'

'Martinis, Jacob said. Lots of gin in them. They were delicious, but I do feel so ill.'

'Lily says you were very sick last night, so I expect you'll perk up shortly. She's mixing you a pick-me-up.'

'I couldn't eat or drink anything. I just want to die!' She sank back into the bed and pulled a pillow over her face.

'Rubbish. Come on, Prue.'

Prue peered over the pillow. 'Go away, Cleo.'

'No.' Cleo perched herself on the bed. 'Seton rang.'

Prue groaned. 'Oh, no.'

'I told him you seemed to be going down with a bad cold and had gone to bed.'

'Thanks, Cleo.'

'He's going away for a few days, some emergency to do with the Farmers' Union.'

Prue began to laugh. 'Seton and the Farmers' Union, Jacob and the Mothers' Union.' She gave a nasty belch. 'Goodness, I feel very, very strange inside. And my head!' She shut her eyes again for a moment, and then remembered an exciting piece of news.

'Cleo, I've found out about Sophie's secret. It's Jacob Pugh, the vicar.'

Cleo was so astonished that she dropped the glass of water she had just poured out for Prue.

'Blast, look, water everywhere!' She dabbed at it ineffectually with a tissue, staring at Prue. 'The vicar! Prue, you're making it up.'

'Cleo, you know I never make things up. Cross my heart and hope to die. It's true, he told me last night. He said there was no point trying to keep it a secret, the whole village would know now the Bishop had been.'

'Bishop?'

'Yes, he came yesterday, to warn Jacob off, I think. But Jacob isn't going to be warned off. At least, I don't think so. He's going to leave Daisy and live with Sophie.'

'Well!' was all Cleo could say.

Lily had come into the room bearing a glass full of a horrid brown liquid. 'Drink this, Prue, and no buts.'

'Lily, I couldn't, if I had anything I'd be sick again, I know I would.'

'Nonsense, do as you're told, Prue, and get that inside you.'

Prue took a small sip and made a face.

'That's not the way; drink it down, all in one go. Now!'

Prue did as she was told. A look of panic came over her face, and she gave another violent belch.

'Oh, Lily,' she began, about to get out of bed and rush to the bathroom. Then she sank down into the pillows again.

'What's in that drink, Lily?' asked Cleo with admiration. 'It seems to work.'

'Trade secret. Never fails. Lie there for a minute, Prue, while I run you a bath.'

'Lily, did you hear what Prue told me, about . . .'

'About the vicar? Yes, it's open knowledge, all over the village. I've known all along, of course.'

'Lily, why didn't you say so?'

'If I went round prattling on about everything I know about other people, we'd all be in a dreadful pickle.'

'Wait till I see Luke,' said Cleo.

'He's heard,' said Lily, emerging from the bathroom. 'Get along, now, Prue, into the bath, and mind you wash your hair. You look like something from the orphanage.' She handed her a towel.

'Luke's in a terrible state, can't believe that Sophie could prefer a middle-aged vicar to him,' Lily went on. 'I've brought these clothes of yours for Prue to put on, I know you won't mind.'

'No, that's fine, although she'll need a belt if those are my jeans. But never mind that, tell me about Luke, I can see he must be feeling very put-out.'

'He's like an offended tomcat,' said Lily with scorn. 'What he can't see is that although he's got a strong body and plenty of action in all the useful bits, he hasn't got half the vicar's charm. Moreover, and this is what counts, young Cleo, as you'll find out when you get just a little bit older, the vicar's got a wonderful sense of humour.'

'Whereas Luke has none at all,' said Cleo ruefully. 'All right, don't rub it in, Lily. It was fun while it lasted.'

Lily darted over to the bathroom and popped her head through the door. 'No good just lying there, Prue, you haven't got all day.'

Cleo sat down on the bed again and tucked her feet up under her. 'What do you think will happen to the vicar, Lily? Will he lose his job?'

'If he doesn't want to give Sophie up, yes.'

'What about Daisy?'

'Ah, Daisy, yes. She hasn't got back from Fusby yet. I've got a feeling she may not be coming back. Vicar didn't notice, but she had a lot of luggage in the boot of the car.'

Cleo's eyes grew round with astonishment. 'You don't mean that Daisy . . . Oh, Lily, no, she couldn't possibly have a boyfriend!'

'Who said anything about a boyfriend?' replied Lily gnomically. 'Up you get, I want to strip this bed. We may be going to have more visitors. Who knows?' She gave a loud hoot of laughter. 'It's all happening, I can see it plain as anything now.'

18

Geza walked up with Prue to the castle. 'I must thank Val, so kind to drive me here, and this afternoon Sylvester and I are going to be playing, so it needs to be done now. Besides, I want to see this castle, where these strange happenings occur.'

'Strange happenings?' said Prue. She stopped and wiped some perspiration from her face. She still felt most peculiar, and the heat was building up again. There were a few clouds wispily covering the sun, but the rain and wind had blown itself off to Scotland.

'I don't know of any strange happenings. I don't think there are any ghosts.'

'No, but there are interesting people, and some dramas, Sylvester tells me. You know,' he went on chattily, 'everyone always tells about how dreadful the English climate is, but I come here, and it's beautiful, as hot as Budapest, but of course the scenery is quite, quite different.'

'What's Budapest like?' asked Prue.

'Budapest is like Budapest. It is unique. People say, it is like Paris or Vienna, but no, not really. Nowadays it is dingy' – Geza pronounced it 'dinggy', which perplexed Prue – 'and not brilliant as far as social life goes, but one day the Russian communists put on their nasty boots and go back to Russia, and we dispose of our own ones, and then we are all happy again.'

'It sounds a bit violent,' said Prue doubtfully.

'Do you like Paris?'

'I've never been to Paris. I've only once been abroad, to Belgium. With a school party. We stayed in a convent, so it wasn't very different from school here, except that the nuns wore extraordinary wimples, huge, stiff affairs. And the food was better. That's it, for foreign travel. I haven't even been to Scotland or Wales. Though I might be going to Scotland later this year,' she added, 'on my honeymoon.'

'Honeymoon, yes, you tell me about this dull fiancé.'

'Who said he was dull?' asked Prue. She hadn't the energy to protest, this conversation seemed so unreal. She had never met anyone quite like this Hungarian before. He came out with the most astonishing things; what you might think but never say. And he wanted to know everything.

'People,' said Geza vaguely. 'At the Hall, you know, and in the pub yesterday. Now, this pub is great fun. Many people there, villagers. One girl, very nice, very beautiful and sexy, red-haired, named Julie, she tells me a lot about people here, all very interesting.'

'Oh dear,' said Prue. 'I don't suppose it was very kind.'

'Kind?'

'What she said about people.'

'No, but truthful, I think. She has no time for your fiancé, says he has no sex. So you tell me about him, and why you are going to marry him if he has no sex. You like sex?'

'Mr Muronyi,' began Prue.

'Geza, Geza, please. We are all friends, and besides. I have a special link with you, because it was listening to your father play when I was a small boy, he came to Budapest, that made me want to be a musician. Not a gypsy violinist, but a classical musician.'

'I see,' said Prue weakly. 'Well, Geza, then, it's just that in England we don't ask people questions like that.'

'Like what?' said Geza in a surprised voice. 'All I ask are perfectly normal, okay questions.'

'About people you're engaged to, and sex.'

'Now, this is very strange. We Hungarians talk a lot about sex. What else don't you talk about?'

'Oh, money, I suppose.'

'That is even more strange. The first thing you want to know about someone is how much money they have, or how much they make. So, you ask them. They don't always say the truth, very well, but you can guess in other ways. Then, you want to know what kind of a sex life they have. This, also, is very interesting.'

'I wouldn't dream of asking people about their sex lives,' said Prue, going pale at the thought. Then she remembered the vicar. 'Of course, if a friend wants to confide in you, to have someone to talk to, if they have a problem, then that's different. But it would always remain confidential,' she added quickly, before this strange man asked for details.

Geza smiled his enchanting smile. 'So, I understand. Now tell me about the lord in his castle. Is he like Valdemar, this tall, kind, angry man who I am going to see?'

Prue couldn't help laughing at his description of Valdemar. 'No, Lord Mountjoy is quite like him to look at, but he's not so, how can I put it, powerful as Valdemar.'

'Virile, you mean? This Valdemar is very virile, I think.'

'No, that's not what I meant,' said Prue crossly. 'Valdemar's younger, that's all and he has a high-powered job, he's very forceful.'

'Bossy, you say in English.'

'We don't usually call men bossy, but, yes, he's bossy. Likes to have his own way.'

'Yes, I see. So Lord Mountjoy has a wife, and Sophie, who cooks at the castle, yes, I heard all about her in the pub, she sleeps with the vicar. Who does Valdemar sleep with?'

'I have no idea,' said Prue. 'He has a friend who was here until recently, but she's in France now. Otherwise I wouldn't know about his private life.'

Geza's thoughts had darted away on another track. 'You say you have never been abroad. This is not good. You are free to travel, no restrictions, you could go anywhere in Europe, or America – I love America – or to India, Africa, anywhere.'

'I could, if I could afford to,' replied Prue. 'Here we are. If you'll excuse me, I'm going to where I work. I'm horribly late today, and I must get some work done.'

Geza took her hand and kissed it gravely. 'Then, I see you later, beautiful little Prue. And I see Valdemar over there, in the delightful gardens, so I take my leave.'

Startled, Prue looked at her hand. No one had ever kissed her hand before.

Valdemar glared at Geza as he came along the path. What was he doing, kissing Prue's hand? And where had Prue been all night? Not in the castle; presumably she had spent the night with Seton. The thought of Prue in bed with Seton annoyed him intensely, and he greeted Geza brusquely.

Geza wasn't at all put out by this.

'Have you a sore head, as well, like Prue?'

'No, I haven't, and why should Prue have a sore head?' said Valdemar, interested despite himself, 'I've never seen her have more than a sip of wine, and Seton isn't a drinker.'

'Seton, the fiancé?'

'Yes. Sylvester been gossiping as usual, has he? I hope you're comfortable at the Hall. Sylvester is a good host.'

'Everything I could want, no, more, positive luxury. Tell me, this plant here, with the pinky flowers, what is this?'

'Haven't a clue,' said Val shortly. 'If you're interested in flowers, ask Magdalena, she knows all about them. She's my uncle's wife,' he explained, seeing a questioning look on Geza's face. 'Lady Mountjoy.'

'So. And who else is here at the castle, just a small family and this Sophie?'

'Yes. And Thomas, a young relation, he's about somewhere.'

As he spoke, there was a scuffling noise on the path and Thomas burst out in front of them, his face stained with tears.

'Talk of the devil,' said Valdemar resignedly.

'Val, please, you've got to help me. Sir's gone missing! I can't find him anywhere.'

'Thomas, where are your manners?' said Valdemar furiously. 'Say hello to Mr Muronyi, a distinguished musician who is staying with Sylvester.'

'I'm sorry. How do you do, Mr Mu . . . Muronyi,' said Thomas, wiping a grubby hand on his shorts and holding it out.

'Geza, please, not Mr Muronyi,' he said, shaking Thomas's hand.

Thomas turned back to Valdemar, desperation in his voice. 'Please, Val, he isn't used to being out. He could be in danger.'

'I haven't the least idea what you're talking about.'

'It's Sir, the rabbit. You remember, we brought him home from school, a big black rabbit.'

'I remember,' said Val. 'He peed in my car.'

'He didn't mean to, Val, he couldn't help it. He's the school rabbit, he came home with me for the holidays. He's escaped, he got away when I was cleaning his hutch, and I can't find him.' His voice rose to a wail.

'Oh, calm down, Thomas. What a fuss about nothing. I'll buy

202

another rabbit for you to take back, if that's what's worrying you. Now push off, I'm just going to take Geza to see Magdalena.'

'Val, you don't understand. I don't want another rabbit, Sir is special; he was just a baby rabbit when he came. I can't lose him.'

'You should have been more careful, then. If he's got away here, you'll never find him. He won't last long, anyhow; if one of the cats hasn't got him, then a fox will.'

'Val, please, you can't say that! Please help me find him, he can't have got far!'

Geza, who had been watching the man and the boy with fascination, intervened. 'Val, here is a child, very much upset. I think we go and look for this, what do you say, bunny-rabbit? Perhaps he hasn't gone far, he may be frightened, to be free, and so we will find him.'

'For God's sake, I've got better things to do than crawl around on my hands and knees after a bloody rabbit. Oh, all right, Thomas, do stop snivelling and wipe your nose. Where did this wretched creature go missing?'

Thomas ran eagerly in front of them, and showed them the empty hutch.

Geza waited beside Val, whose indifferent eyes swept across the lawn and rested on some bushes. 'There's an animal in there, Thomas, black. It's either the kitchen cat or your damned rabbit.'

'Val, you are clever,' said Thomas delightedly. 'I can see him now. I'll go round here and you go that way. Geza, you stand in front, to stop him coming out.'

'Catch him yourself, Thomas. Oh, don't start again. Come here, you crass animal!'

Although the rabbit was in principle quite ready to return to his hutch and his half-eaten breakfast, it was beneath his dignity to give in without a fuss. It took twenty minutes for the three of them to catch him, and when Val did finally grab hold of him and deposit him in his run, he got a deep scratch across his hand for his pains. 'Vicious brute,' he said.

Geza got up from his hands and knees, and dusted his trousers down. 'Very clever, Val. A good catch, as you say. Now, we go inside, perhaps, and clean up, and you dress that wound or it goes bad and you die.'

'No, Thomas, I'm not going to die of a rabbit scratch,' said Val, seeing panic on the boy's face. 'Be more careful in future. If he gets out again, he can go in a pie for all I care.'

He stalked into the house, followed by an amused Geza and a radiant Thomas. 'Magdalena,' he said, as he hurled himself into the kitchen. 'Do you know, Sir got out, and Val caught him for me, he was brilliant. This is Geza. He's foreign, I think. He helped too, it was great.'

Geza bowed, with superb grace. It was his stage bow, perfected over many years in front of a mirror. 'I do not offer to shake your hand, because, as you can see, I am rather dirty. And Val, he has a wound to his hand.'

'Have you, Val?' said Magdalena. 'Let me see. Not too bad. Run it under the tap, and I'll get a dressing for you.'

Val was a tremendous hypochondriac, and he loved being fussed over with medicines and bandages. 'It hurts,' he said. 'Perhaps I should see the doctor.'

'Don't be such a baby,' said Magdalena, cutting the tape with a small pair of scissors. 'There you are, that's clean now, it'll be fine. You know you always heal in no time.'

'Perhaps he should have a sling,' suggested Thomas.

'No,' said Magdalena firmly. 'He'll make enough fuss about it as it is, until he forgets it's there.'

She smiled at Geza. 'You must be Geza Muronyi. We are so pleased you can play at the festival this year. I have to say the sales of tickets for your concerts are excellent.'

'And I am so very pleased to be here. It is such lovely countryside, and such warmth, and I like very much being with my old friend Sylvester. Also, there is already a lot of intrigues here, and this I like extremely much.'

'Sylvester's been gossiping, I expect,' said Magdalena. 'You mustn't believe everything he tells you.'

'No, no, but I can see for myself there are things going on. For instance, this Prue, who came here with me, she isn't happy to be married with her fiancé, this I can tell. Then, I hear on all sides the scandal about the vicar. And, doubtless, here in this ancient castle, behind these thick walls, there are scandals, too.'

'No, hardly,' said Magdalena, looking into the distance. 'Thomas, take Geza to the cloakroom, and then go to your room, via the bathroom. Wash yourself, thoroughly, put on a clean shirt and then you can take Sir some extra lettuce. I expect he needs it after his little outing.'

'Okay, you're the boss. Did you know,' they heard him say as he led Geza away, 'that lettuce is a tranquillizer? If you ate enough lettuces you'd zonk out. Drugged! Me and Jellicoe, he's my friend, you'd like him, we tried it once. We ate four lettuces each, it didn't have any effect. I think you probably have to eat about a hundred lettuce. Do you know . . .'

'I need to go and clean up, too,' said Val. 'Thomas gets more exhausting every holidays. Thank God he's not mine.'

Magdalena gave him a strange look but Val didn't notice, he was too busy pushing open the kitchen door with his shoulder so as not to knock his injured hand, which he was ostentiously holding with his other hand. The door banged behind him.

Magdalena sighed and went back to peeling potatoes. I hope Sophie comes out of her dismals soon, she thought, how I hate cooking.

Prue was disturbed to find how little she missed Seton while he was away. She had thought of nothing else but Seton all this time; it was an obsession, the longing to be with him . . . How could it fade so quickly? All she felt now was relief that he wasn't there.

She had tried to have some enthusiasm for the wedding preparations, but she found it hard. She wanted a very small, private wedding, but Seton had been stubborn; we don't want people to think we've got anything to hide, and once you've asked a couple of chums you've got to ask the rest, otherwise they get sniffy.

Prue had pointed out that there would only be a handful of guests on her side of the church, but Seton had dismissed that; Prue would be sure to think of more people to ask, and his family and friends could always overflow.

Magdalena was organizing it all, and she was finding it very difficult to get any answers out of Prue. 'If you think that's right, whatever you think is best, I am sure whatever you do will be fine, I don't mind.'

Prue was aware that she wasn't being very helpful, but, to her surprise, she felt tired and depressed. There had been a scene when Valdemar brought out the silk he had bought for Magdalena in Hong Kong. Seton had been furious that Val had chosen the silk for his bride's wedding dress, and had huffed and puffed in what Prue thought was a ridiculous manner.

'What does it matter?' she had said wearily. 'I haven't got a mother to get it for me. It's terribly kind of Magdalena to buy it for me, I don't care if Val chose it.'

'To be accurate,' said Valdemar in his coldest and haughtiest voice, 'I didn't choose it. A friend of mine, Martha Li, who lives in Hong Kong and knows a great deal about silk, chose it for me. I merely described Prue, and then she did the rest.'

Seton swung round, his face even redder than usual with rage.

'If you think it makes it any better that it was chosen by one of your numerous mistresses, and a bloody Chinese at that . . .'

Mountjoy intervened. 'That's enough, Seton. You're upsetting Magdalena, and I won't have it. Forget it, Val, you did Magdalena – and me – a favour, and I'm sure Prue is more than happy with what you bought.'

'Yes,' said Prue politely. 'It's beautiful.'

She felt guilty that she wasn't more keen on the wedding, and guilty at the amount of work Magdalena was doing on her behalf.

'Don't fuss, I love organizing weddings, christenings, parties,' said Magdalena. 'And I don't have to worry about the festival, because wonderful Delia will be here any day, and then she does everything!'

Wonderful Delia was Delia Huntingdon, a civil servant in London, who spent a lot of her annual leave working for the music festival. A big woman, plain, slightly horsy-looking, with a loud guffawing laugh, she was a paragon of intelligence and efficiency, which, combined with a real love of music, made Sylvester declare that if he ever got married it would be to Delia.

Delia, who had long carried a torch for Seton, accepted the compliment, taking it for what it was worth.

'I wouldn't marry you, Sylvester,' she said in her earthy way. 'Even if we found a bed big enough for both of us, you wouldn't know what to do with a woman in it, now, would you?'

Sylvester's gales of laughter had matched her own, and they had worked together very comfortably ever since.

Prue's low spirits were accepted as pining for the absent Seton. Lily knew better. Realizes what she's let herself in for, she said; poor lamb, she's not out of the woods yet. Cleo, still smarting from

Luke's absurd anguish about Sophie, wished the festival and the summer were over and she could start a new life at Oxford.

'It isn't always easy, a new life,' said Lily, who was polishing the floor in the hall. 'I shall have to have a word with Mrs Grobbins; she did this floor last time, and look at it. Not to mention the banisters. A house like this needs more care than that. Cleo, what are you doing? If it's nothing, then you can start on the stairs.'

'Okay,' said Cleo. 'I need to talk to Sylvester, and I never can these days. It's jabber, jabber with Geza, though I can understand that, I could talk to him all day, and when they aren't talking they're playing.'

'Who's on the piano in there?' said Lily.

'Simon Praetorius. Sylvester rang him up last night and said he had to come, they wanted to play trios today. Simon's wife is furious, because she wanted him to look after the children.'

'That's what you get when you marry an artist. If you want a peaceful life, marry a man in a regular line of work, an accountant, a civil servant, someone you can set your watch by.'

'Yes, but who wants a peaceful life?'

'In the end, Cleo, most of us.'

Cleo rubbed thoughtfully at a roundel on the banisters. 'My life's far too peaceful just at his moment, no excitement at all. I'm through with Luke. Do you know, he's hanging round with Julie now; I'd never trust a girl with that hair and those slinky eyes.'

Cleo was peeved that Julie was far better at dealing with the emotional Luke than she had ever been, probably a marvel at handling any man, damn her eyes.

'I think I might have a fling with Valdemar, you know, that could be interesting.'

Alarmed, Lily sent her tin of polish flying across the floor. 'Now look what you've made me do, a great mark all across the tiles I've just done. You leave Valdemar alone, Cleo. You'd as soon go into a cage with a tiger as get entangled with him. And for you, particularly . . .'

'You keep on saying, me particularly. Why? Admit it, he's wildly sexy. What harm could there be?'

The phone rang, and Lily let out her breath between her teeth in a hissy sigh of relief.

'You get that, my hands are covered in this stuff.'

'It's bound to be Simon Praetorius's wife, she's already rung twice,' said Cleo, picking up the phone. 'Hello?'

She put her hand over the mouthpiece. 'It's the mystery caller,' she whispered. 'The foreign one. No, the line's gone dead. I wonder where they're ringing from? It must be somewhere where the phone system isn't very good.'

'Well,' said Lily prosaically, 'if whoever it is really wants to get through, they can always send a letter.'

Delia Huntingdon parked her Mini in the stable yard and walked through the main doors to the castle. 'Anyone at home?'

Valdemar came down one of the stone stairways. 'Ah, Delia, good, time we had someone here prepared to do some work. You can't leave your car there, it's blocking mine.'

'The same old Val,' said Delia cheerfully. 'Are you going anywhere?'

'No, not at the moment, but . . .'

'I'll be going into Eyot this afternoon. If you want to use your car before then, just give me a shout, no trouble.' She looked at the plans he had in his hands. 'That your castle scheme? Browbeaten old Mountjoy into submission yet? He'll hate it, you know, he's not like you. To you the castle's an asset which can be made to pay, but not Mountjoy. It's his home. I think it's cruel to spoil his peaceful way of life.'

'His peaceful way of life happens to cost a good deal of money, more than his income. And in any case, it's . . .'

'None of my business,' finished Delia, unperturbed. 'No, but I feel sorry for the old chap. He's a nice man, a real gent.'

'And I'm not?'

Delia gave her great guffaw. 'You're a monster, Val. Is Magdalena in her room?'

'Probably,' said Valdemar, thinking how much he disliked large, positive women with loud laughs. Bloody woman, bloody rude, he muttered to himself.

'Ta,' Delia said, and bounded off towards Magdalena's tower.

She shot round the turning on the landing off the spiral staircase and bumped into Prue, who flew backwards.

'Sorry, going too fast as usual. Who are you? New cook, has Sophie gone? Relation?'

Prue flattened herself against the wall and looked at Delia with alarm. 'No, Sophie's still here. I'm Prue Pagan.'

'I know, the girl from Mrs Dotteridge, you're helping Mountjoy with his silly old papers. I'm Delia, I help organize the music festival, for my sins.' She gave a loud laugh, which alarmed Prue even more. 'I gather you've snaffled Seton, saw the announcement in *The Times*. Lucky you, you couldn't marry a better man. Mind you look after him. Wish I were in your shoes. Nice to have met you, we'll be seeing a lot of each other, I expect. Must go now, though, got a lot to do.'

With which she hurled herself up the next staircase, leaving Prue feeling that a steamroller had gone over her.

Magdalena was genuinely glad to see Delia. She kissed her warmly, and told her to make herself some coffee. 'I know you've been managing everything splendidly from the London end, Delia. I don't know how you find time to do it, as well as all your own work.'

'Always time for what you really want to do,' said Delia gruffly. 'You're looking well, Magdalena. Put on a bit of weight, haven't you? You could do with it, you were looking a bit scraggy last time I saw you. Have you changed your hairdo or something? You look different.'

'No, it's been such lovely weather; I have a slight tan. It makes one look much better, don't you think?'

'No, it's not the tan, but it doesn't matter, as long as you've got over whatever was wrong with you. My word, Mountjoy was worried about you, wasn't he? I spoke to him on the phone when you were in hospital. What a dear old fusspot he is.'

'Thank you for the flowers you sent.'

'Need something to cheer you up when you're in hospital, must be awful. Never been in, myself. I'm never ill, haven't got time to hang around in bed.'

Having ground the coffee beans with great vigour, she made the coffee and poured two cups. 'Black as usual, no sugar?'

'No sugar, but milk in it, please.'

'Right ho, here you are.' Delia handed Magdalena her coffee and sat herself down firmly on the window-seat. 'Lovely to be back here. Grounds are looking a bit the worse for wear; drought, I suppose. Same everywhere. I bumped into a tallish girl on the stairs, Prue. She's the one who's marrying Seton? He knows how to pick them. Got style, that one.'

'Yes,' said Magdalena. 'It all happened very quickly. I hope you aren't upset, we all thought that one day, perhaps . . .'

'Never looked at me that way,' said Delia with unimpaired cheerfulness. 'Men are so stupid, they fall for the most unsuitable women. It's because they're too thick to know what's good for them. This Prue will make a terrible wife for Seton. You can see she's got brains, probably sensitive; imaginative, too, I dare say. Hopeless, no good at all for a man like Seton. She'll wither and die living out in the country here all year round, and after the first year Seton'll pay her no more attention than he does one of the house cats. I wouldn't let him get away with that if I were his wife, but there you are.'

She finished her coffee with a quick slurp, rose, put the cup back in the little kitchen, gave a long stretch and took a deep breath.

'Right. I know you've been dealing with the advance bookings, Magdalena, so hand it all over. You cope with the musicians, I can't be doing with them. Sylvester's been messing around with the programming, has he? I'll go down to Midwinter Hall a little later on and take that away from him.'

'I shall be glad to leave it to you,' said Magdalena truthfully, thinking how tiring it was being with Delia for more than a few moments. 'Particularly glad, because I feel I must give a party for Prue. She hardly knows anyone up here.'

'And the neighbours are all dying of curiosity, wanting to see what Seton's wife-to-be is like. She'll have to buck up a bit; she looked like a lost soul just now.'

'Seton's away, she'll be missing him. He rings her up, but she doesn't have much to say to him. She probably wants to hold hands with him.'

'More than that,' said Delia with a jolly laugh. 'Thanks, Magdalena. I'll put myself in my usual room, if that's all right with you.'

'Yes, I told Mrs Grobbins to make sure it was clean.'

'Bet the old wretch hasn't touched it. Don't worry, I'll get after her. You get on with the invites and so on. Let me know if I can help. Sophie going to do the works for you?'

Magdalena looked worried. 'She should, of course, but she's in a bit of a state at the moment. You'll hear about it soon enough, so I may as well tell you . . .'

'It's come out about her and Jacob, has it?' said Delia, much to Magdalena's surprise. 'Bound to, was only a matter of time. How's Daisy taking it?'

'I didn't know you knew about them,' said Magdalena. 'You might have said. I had no idea.'

'Not one for gossip, you know that.'

'Daisy's away, she went to Fusby the day the Bishop came, and she hasn't been back. She may not even know.'

'Staying with Jocasta Jones, is she? And the Bishop came? Wish I'd been a fly on the wall during that conversation. Poor old Reggie, he does hate that kind of business.'

'Of course, he's a cousin of yours, isn't he?'

'Yes, he was a pain when he was a boy, always siding with the real no-hopers. Offer a psychopath a lump of sugar, Reggie would. When are Seton and this Prue getting married – she doesn't come from these parts, does she? Is it going to be a London wedding?'

'No, Prue is an orphan. Her only family was an aunt, who's died, so isn't much use. I've offered them the chapel here.'

'Good, that'll suit Seton much better. Who's going to tie the knot? Can Jacob do it, in the circs?'

A look of consternation crossed Magdalena's face. 'Do you know, I hadn't thought of that. Lord, this could be difficult.'

'Would you like Reggie to do it for you? He knows Seton, he advises the Dean and Chapter about their land holdings; he'll do it if I tell him to.'

'That would be an excellent solution.'

'Yes, and I'll tell him to leave that pillock of a chaplain behind, too – you know,' she said, seeing that Magdalena was lost, 'Cedric, Cecil, whatever his name is. The one we had to warn Thomas about.'

'That one, yes, it would be preferable not to have him. But perhaps the Bishop needs him, to carry his mitre and so forth.'

'I'll see to it.' She pulled a fat notebook out of her capacious Liberty handbag and made a note. 'Ask Lily to help Sophie with the party, that'll put Sophie on her mettle. I'm sure Seton won't mind. Don't worry, Magdalena, nothing here that Lily and I can't sort out.'

19

Seen from Prue's tower, the landscape was pale and parched with the summer's relentless sun. There were forlorn little green patches showing on a raw and cracked earth. The trees were untidy and windblown; it was a barren, dusty prospect.

Prue sighed, and bent her head over her book again, holding it sideways to look at the diagrams of early human knuckle bones compared with ape ones. A bang on the door, and without waiting, Valdemar came in. He looked at Prue; wonderful hair, he thought, even better in the sun than it was by moonlight.

'Rapunzel, Rapunzel, let down your long hair,' he said in a mocking voice. 'What are you reading?'

Prue silently handed him the book and went back to looking out of the window, basking like a cat in the warmth.

'Good God,' he said in his usual explosive way as he read the title. 'What on earth are you looking at this for!'

'I'm not looking at it, I'm reading it,' said Prue without turning her head. 'It interests me.'

'You never struck me as a blue-stocking. I thought your friend Cleo was the one who was going to Oxford.'

'She is. I got a place at Cambridge, but I can't go, because my aunt didn't want me to.'

'Isn't that a bit feeble?'

'No. She brought me up; I didn't want to upset her, and she said there wasn't any money for it.'

'Students get grants, they manage.'

'Yes, they do.'

'So you're getting married instead. Do you think Seton will allow you to read this kind of book?'

'I don't suppose he'll mind what I read.'

'Yes, he will. He'd think you were cleverer than him, which wouldn't be difficult, I have to say, and he'd stop you.'

Silence.

Valdemar tapped her on the shoulder. 'Here, have your heavy tome back. Turn round, I've got a present for you.'

'For me?' Prue's eyes widened with surprise.

'A wedding present.'

'I see. Thank you very much.' She took the exquisitely-wrapped box from him.

He sat on the bed, long legs stretched out in front of him and gave Prue a quizzical look.

'Aren't you going to open it? It's from Hong Kong. I didn't give it to you the other evening because Seton made such a stink about the silk.'

Prue pulled at the bow with neat fingers and removed the wrapping paper. 'Oh,' she said, when she opened the box. 'It's beautiful.' Then she laughed. 'It's so exotic, it isn't like me at all. When ever could I use such a bag?'

'Not buried in the English countryside, certainly, Prue.'

He got up, stretched his arms behind his neck and moved closer to the window.

'There is an alternative,' he said.

'Oh,' said Prue, who saw a look in his eyes that was instantly recognizable, even to someone as inexperienced as she was. He wants to go to bed with me, she thought with surprise. Of course I can't, though I do wonder what it would be like, he's so different from Seton. And it is so warm, such an effort to resist . . .

She didn't. And, later, she was glad she hadn't. All she felt was amazement that making love, which with Seton had been so uncomfortable and awkward, could be so astonishingly pleasurable with another man. She didn't know that Valdemar, usually a selfish lover, had surpassed himself, for once thinking more of his partner than himself.

Valdemar was equally pleased with himself. Getting on, am I, Martha? There's one eighteen-year-old who doesn't think so. And that's your goose cooked, Seton, clumsy ass. She's far too good for you. I shall enjoy taking her to London, abroad. I've saved her from a life of total tedium.

'Ho,' said Geza when he saw Prue that evening. Sylvester had invited her to dinner, and they were sitting at the big oval table in the dining room at Midwinter Hall. It was a dramatic room, built out of a barn

that had adjoined the old house. It had exposed beams, high up in
the roof, and a minstrel's gallery ran along one end, with a curving
staircase leading down into the main part of the room. There was no
fire on this warm night in the great stone fireplace which Sylvester
had bought in Spain, and the stone-flagged floor, chilly in winter,
was cool at the end of a hot day. Geza loved this room; pastiche it
might be, but he appreciated the humour of it. 'What an enormous
suit of armour, Sylvester. Why, you yourself could fit into this.'

'Yes,' said Sylvester with a loud laugh. 'As soon as I saw it, I
knew I must buy it, for that very reason. Most suits of armour
are for such tiny little men that I don't know how they were able
to wallop anyone. They all needed good nourishing food; they
were probably vegetarians – that would account for their small
stature.'

'You look like the pussy-cat who has drunk the cream, Prue,'
went on Geza. 'I don't ask what have you been doing, this would
embarrass you at table. And your fiancé, this Seton, he is still away.'
He gave a little snort of laughter; Prue couldn't be offended, there
was such mischief in his face.

'What are you saying?' said Sylvester. 'Cleo, what did he say?'

'I didn't hear,' said Cleo. She shot a glance at Prue from under
her dark brows. Goodness, yes, she did look rather pleased with
herself. What had she been up to?

'Coffee on the terrace, if you've all finished your pud,' said
Sylvester amiably. 'Lily, where are the chocolates? Geza and the
girls will want chocolates.'

'I've got them here. Where are you sitting? I'm going to put them
out of your reach.'

They drifted out to the terrace, another hot and heavy evening
when they could sit out after midnight in the lightest of clothes, still
feeling enveloped by warm air. A small figure slipped out of some
trees and came across the grass.

'It's Thomas, the little boy with the rabbit,' said Geza. 'I like this
boy, so like his father.'

'I haven't got a father,' said Thomas, 'so I can't be like him. Or, I
could be like him, but I won't ever know. Mum might, but she isn't
saying.'

Geza sat upright in his garden seat, eyes bright with interest.
'There is no question, surely. You would have to be blind not to
see, because the likeness is so remarkable.'

'You mean Val?' said Thomas, helping himself to several chocolates at once. 'People who don't know always think he's my father. It's just family looks, though; my mum's his half-sister, you see.'

Geza was about to say more, but Sylvester got up, very quickly for a man of his bulk. 'More coffee, Geza?' he asked, taking his cup. He made a hideous face, and Geza, with quick understanding, asked Thomas about his rabbit instead.

The rabbit was fine, none the worse for his escapade. And what was Thomas doing here? Surely this must be past his bedtime; it was, but it was hot, and he needed some exercise. He wouldn't be able to sleep, and everyone at the castle was so boring, nobody wanted to talk to him . . . so.

'And I don't suppose they know where you are, so there'll be another hullabaloo if they find you gone, think you've wandered off on to the fells again,' said Lily. Reproving words, but spoken fondly; Lily was never cross with Thomas.

There was no answering smile from the boy.

'I don't suppose they'd care. I'm just a nuisance, it's nothing to them whether I'm there or not. I expect it would suit them best if I did go and fall off the gully, now that Magdalena . . .' He flushed and fell silent.

'Thomas,' said Sylvester, alarmed. 'What on earth's the matter? It's not like you to be in a mood.'

'Oh, nothing,' said Thomas. 'I don't suppose you want me, either. I'll go if you like.'

'You'd better go and ring the castle, Sylvester, and tell them Thomas is with us,' said Lily. 'Take the tray, and I'll make some more coffee. Get a cold drink for Thomas. We'll need some more chocolates, too, by the look of it.'

Despite his glum mood and having had a huge supper earlier in the evening, Thomas had plenty of empty space, to tuck the odd chocolate into. He gave Lily an appreciative look and slumped in the seat she had just vacated. Geza moved over towards him and looked over to where Prue and Cleo were sitting. They were deep in a fascinating conversation about Fiona in the Lower Sixth, whose picture had been splashed over the papers that morning, '*Three Dutchmen*,' said Cleo incredulously, 'all at once, imagine.'

'The nuns won't like it,' said Prue.

In a low, kind voice, Geza invited Thomas to tell him what was up. Thomas's fears tumbled out in the high clear voice of childhood; Geza's face darkened. What kind of people were these, what selfishness and unconcern for others? Adults might cope with such matters, but not a child. This was wrong.

Thomas felt much happier; better out than in, as his nanny used to say when he'd eaten too many baked beans. He managed a smile as Sylvester came back and helped himself to more chocolates.

'Sorry, Sylv,' he said. 'Just things were worrying me a bit. It's all right now.'

'Don't call me Sylv, you wretched boy. Geza, this scrubby boy, believe it or not, has a trained voice, and a good one. Let's go and find some music.'

Prue and Cleo's conversation died away, and Lily stood motionless as the soaring, faultless voice wafted out from the music room into the still evening air.

Another figure came out of the shadows and stood on the terrace. He, too, stood quite still, listening. The years fell away, and he remembered his own childhood, his own lovely voice, so pure and sexless, destined, like a rose, to bloom and have its day of glory, then to vanish forever. The music tugged at his heart. Very little had the power to move him these days, but this had caught him unawares.

Oh, bugger it all, he thought angrily. Suddenly, he didn't want to be with people. Thomas was safe there, they would bring him back. Why had he bothered to come and find him, anyhow? The boy was like a cat, always landed on his feet. He melted back into the darkness, unnoticed and therefore unmissed.

Sylvester had responded with huge enthusiasm to Magdalena's plan for a party. 'Invite everyone,' he said expansively. 'Good PR for the music festival, they're all the kind of people you'll want to ask anyway. I'll bear half the cost. No, don't argue. We can invite likely sponsors and so on. Good, that's very good, I love a big party.'

Despite the short notice, the turnout was impressive. Some people came because they weren't going to refuse an invitation from a Lord and Lady, and at a castle, too. Others were there because they were curious about Prue; the church contingent came because the Dean and Chapter never liked to miss out on what young Canon Feverfew incongruously called a good thrash; others accepted from a sense of social obligation; yet others because they were, or wanted to be, involved with the music festival. Some even came because they liked Mountjoy and Magdalena and could look forward to a pleasant evening among friends.

From first thing on the morning of the party, people were busy at the castle. Sophie, still in despair, had been shaken out of her torpor by an enraged Lily, who told her forthrightly to stop behaving like a spoilt child, dry her eyes, and get on with the work she was paid to do.

'But I may never see him again, Lily,' she wailed. 'He's said it's better if we don't meet for the moment, until things are settled. I know he and Daisy are going to go off to another part of the country, and I won't even know where's he's gone. I don't want him to have to leave the church, but I can't live without him.'

'What dramatics! At least Jacob seems to have some sense of propriety; unusual up here, if you ask me. You silly girl, he's trying to protect you, and you're behaving like a ninny in return. Pull yourself together. If he says for the moment, that'll be what he means, no less, no more. Now, get up, go and have a shower, because you don't smell very nice if you don't mind my saying so, not surprising if you've been lying around in bed snivelling, and get down to the kitchen. We've all got more than enough to do, there's no time for scenes.'

The marquee, gay with broad white and yellow stripes, had gone up the day before. It was to be used for the party and then for refreshments at the music festival concerts; it would remain up for Prue's wedding. Trestle tables were up, and Mrs Grobbins and Cleo were cutting lengths of banqueting roll to cover them. Luke, more Byronic and sullen than ever, was carrying stacking chairs and little tables from a van. Valdemar, energized by a night spent with Prue, was being forceful as usual and telling everyone what to do.

Seton arrived, carrying trays of strawberries in the back of his estate car. He looked and felt cross. Prue had hardly spared him a moment since he came back, pretty poor show just before their wedding, and he didn't know whether to believe her ready excuses about being so busy with the arrangements.

Delia pounced on him. 'You can carry more trays than that, Seton. Come along. Lily and Sophie are waiting for those, and then you can go and collect the food that's been ordered from Ghercombes. Henry and Patrick rang to say it's all ready.'

'Jolly extravagant, all this,' he grumbled. 'People only come for a free drink.'

'Come along,' said Delia, as though to a disobedient dog. 'No whingeing, Seton, I won't have it.'

Julie sidled into the marquee. 'Mum said I was to come and help. Hi, Cleo.'

'Hello,' said Cleo as she wrestled with some sticky tape that had twisted round and stuck to itself. 'The people who make this must be rich; for every bit you get to use, you have to throw yards away.'

'Give it to me,' said Julie, and with a few swift movements the paper was firmly taped in place.

'Thanks,' said Cleo.

'No hard feelings, eh?' said Julie, lolling against a central pole.

'Julie, get off that,' screeched Mrs Grobbins. 'You'll have the whole tent down on us!'

'About what?' said Cleo coldly.

'That Luke. I've had a yen for him for a long time, him and his silly crush on that Sophie. He's no good for you, he's got no sense of humour.'

'No, I wasn't really interested in his sense of humour.'

'Course not, I know what you were interested in, same as the rest of us. You leave him to me. You can always have a turn when you're at the university.'

'Thank you, but I don't think I'll take up your offer. Perhaps Luke will find another Sophie, only this time one who returns his feelings.'

'Shouldn't let it worry you either way. Plenty more fish in the sea. All the men you want at Oxford, ten men to every girl, that's what I've heard. And older men, too, if that's what you fancy for a change. Pick and choose, that's what you'll be able to do.'

Cleo wasn't listening any more, and Julie looked round to see what had caught her attention. The baker's assistant was unloading baskets of rolls.

'Lovely bum. Lovely thighs. Good shoulders, too,' she said appreciatively.

Cleo felt more cheerful. It was true, lots of men at Oxford. She made a suggestive gesture towards the baker's back, and she and Julie burst out giggling. He turned round and scampered away when he saw them, scarlet in the face.

Lily flew into the tent, chiding them for being idle, and told

219

Cleo to help Magdalena. 'You stay here, Julie, and do what Mrs G tells you.'

Julie snorted with laughter and Mrs Grobbins waved a huge pair of scissors in the air. 'Hasn't listened to what I've said since she was in her cot, Julie hasn't.'

'Then she won't get any pay,' said Lily.

Gradually, it all came together. Under Mountjoy's and Valdemar's supervision, coloured light bulbs had been strung from tree to tree, to be lit when the light began to fade. Magdalena and Cleo had done the flowers, armfuls of flowers from the castle's famous rose gardens, the pink and cream and white blossoms of Cuisses de Nymphes, Hebe's Lip and Maiden's Blush set off by silvery Hostas. Purple and white Turk's Cap lilies glowed against a background of Crested Lady's Fern; Magdalena was pleased with her arrangements.

By six o'clock she was luxuriating in a foaming bath, which smelt delicious. Kind Mountjoy had given her a jar of wildly expensive salts, and he sat on the edge of the bath chatting to her, delighted to have pleased her.

Prue had a quick shower and sat in a towel, deep in her bones.

Sophie went to her room to put on a print dress, which she covered in a huge white cook's apron before returning to the kitchen to put the finishing touches to the food.

Thomas hastily dragged on a pair of grey school trousers with a white shirt before racing back outside to help with the lights, as he put it, or to wreck the generator, as Peter saw it.

Valdemar shaved for the second time that day. He always had a shadow on his chin by the evening. He put on a dark suit with a white shirt, and, on a whim, an Old Chorister tie which he hadn't worn for years.

Cleo, who was helping to hand round and serve drinks, had put on a tight, minuscule black dress; she had wanted to add a saucy little white apron, but Sylvester, shocked, had vetoed the suggestion.

'You look like something out of a naughty French film as it is.'

Lily also wore black, and made a striking little figure with her hennaed hair piled on top of her head to give her height. Sylvester and Geza, who had decided to play as an appetite whetter for the festival, were in white tie and tails, Sylvester's cello and Geza's fiddle carefully stowed in the back of the big Volvo which Sylvester drove.

'Goodness, Geza, you do look smart,' said Prue when she saw him. He looked less approachable in his formal clothes, but the delightful smile was still there as he greeted her and expressed courteous admiration of her appearance in a a simple dark navy linen shift. Very *jeune fille*, he said, and added something incomprehensible in Hungarian.

At the vicarage Jacob put on an ordinary shirt and tie. He stared at himself in the mirror, and then with sudden resolution took them off and put on a clerical shirt and dog collar. They'll all be there, he thought. I'm not going to be intimidated, I am still a priest.

Daisy and Jocasta, both wearing their best hideous flowery summer frocks, jolted and jerked their way across the county to the castle in Jocasta's aged Morris Minor.

Unknown to all of them, an unexpected guest in the shape of Cleo's mother was even then clambering on to a bus at Eyot. It would bring her, after a rambling cross-country journey of nearly two hours, to Gossiby. From there, she planned to hitch. She wasn't dressed for any party, travelling us she usually did in jeans and a checked shirt, with a big rucksack on her back and a painting bag slung over one shoulder.

She enjoyed the journey and the company of her fellow travellers, who were vastly well-informed about Midwinter Hall, and pleased to meet Cleo's Mum. Cleo is Sylvester's young lady, who's helping him write a book, they told each other.

'You won't find her at the Hall,' one of the women informed her. 'They'll all be at the Castle. Young Greg'll be going up that way with the trailer, so he can give you a lift.'

So Gussie Byng arrived late, sitting in a trailer on bales of straw. Only Lily saw her arrive.

'You must be Cleo's Mum,' she said.

'How clever of you to know,' said Gussie, with her wide smile. 'Most people don't think we're alike.'

'She's got a photo of you in her room,' explained Lily as she took her to a guest bathroom. 'Favours her father, though, I'll agree with you there. I'll wait and show you where they all are.'

Gussie was sociable, and not at all disturbed at the thought of arriving at a party full of people she had never met. People had spilled out of the Great Hall on to the terrace and the lawns where the marquee was. There was a hum of mostly upper-class English voices all talking rather loudly, and Gussie looked round with interest.

'There's someone you know, I think,' whispered Lily in her ear, before she slipped away.

Gussie looked where Lily had pointed, and made her way through the throng. She attracted stares from the women because of her unorthodox clothes. The men looked too, for different reasons: Gussie had kept her figure well and had all Cleo's vitality.

'Hello, Valdemar,' she said. 'I thought it must be you. You haven't changed very much.'

Valdemar swung round as she spoke and eyed her up and down appreciatively; getting on, of course, but there was certainly something about her. He frowned. 'Who . . .?'

'I'm Gussie. Gussie Byng, Cleo's mother.'

'Ah. For a moment I thought I'd met you somewhere before.'

'You did, Val, in the fells, twenty years ago.'

A look of recognition leapt into his eyes. 'Linseed oil. You wanted to be a painter.'

'I am a painter. Also, a mother, or don't you remember that?'

'Can't say I do,' said Valdemar indifferently.

And then, before he had time to wonder at the contempt in Gussie's face, a tall attractive blonde woman with a particularly carrying voice caught sight of Magdalena.

'Magdalena, darling, I've been trying to get hold of you ever since we arrived. You look marvellous, absolutely marvellous. When's it due?'

20

The talk around Magdalena faded into silence. Then an excited hubbub broke out. Friends clapped Mountjoy on the back and congratulated him, people passed the news back to those who had been too far away to hear the remark. Prue wriggled her way through to Magdalena's side.

'Is it true?' she asked breathlessly, and when Magdalena nodded, Prue gave her a hug. 'Oh, I am so pleased. Oh, you must be so happy.'

Cleo was standing next to Sylvester and Geza. Geza was watching the scene with intent interest. 'I thought Mountjoy couldn't have children,' Cleo whispered to Sylvester. 'Not enough sperm.'

Sylvester rounded on her, a strong finger placed against his lips. 'Sssh, not a word about that, Cleo, please. My God,' he went on, most unusually for him, because he rarely blasphemed, 'My God, look at Val's face!'

Cleo had a glimpse of blazing fury before Valdemar turned on his heel and walked swiftly back into the castle.

Sylvester let out a whistle. 'He is *not* pleased,' he said.

'Why not?' asked Geza. 'Why should he be displeased? Is he worried for her health? She is not so young for a first baby, I think.'

Dr Mukherjee was passing, and she cast a disapproving look at Geza. 'These days,' she said repressively, 'there is little danger, provided the mother has proper medical attention. Which, naturally, Lady Mountjoy has, and will continue to have.'

Geza raised his eyebrows as she went on her way.

'That isn't what's got to Val,' hissed Sylvester. 'If Mountjoy has a son, and there's a good chance of it, because it's usually two boys to every girl in their family, back for generations, then the son will inherit the Castle and the title and, of course, any money there is. If it's a girl, then Val will become Lord Mountjoy when his uncle dies, but this Mountjoy can leave the castle and the money to a daughter, to go to her children in due course.'

'So. I can see why Val doesn't look so very happy. Is it such an important matter, though? I thought he was very successful, very distinguished in his own career.'

'He is, but the Mountjoys are all passionate about the castle and the land. Heaven knows, they've fought each other down the centuries: cousins, brothers, fathers and sons, you name it, for possession of it all. Val had ambitious plans for the castle, they'll have to be shelved. He won't like it, not one little bit. And of course, the irony of it is, I suspect that he's brought it all on himself. Lord, what a situation! I wonder what he'll do!'

Valdemar watched Mountjoy's car drive away from the castle. Jocasta's Morris had refused to start, despite the best efforts of Peter, unhelpful comments from Thomas and inexpert advice from the last few guests as they left. Wonderful party, Mountjoy, they said, terribly pleased about your news. Take care of Magdalena.

Seton, who did know about cars, had vanished earlier, captured by Delia who said he could take her out to dinner for a fling before he became a married man. In the end Mountjoy, courteous as ever, said he would run them home and get the AA in the next morning to see to the car.

Valdemar swept down the staircase and across to Magdalena's tower. She was alone in her room, peacefully brushing her hair, when he flung open the door.

'Magdalena,' he said grimly, 'I want a word with you.'

Magdalena's face was expressionless. 'I don't think I have anything to say to you just at this moment, Val,' she said in a pleasantly neutral voice.

'Is it true? Are you pregnant?'

'Yes, I am.'

'You'll have to get rid of it. Right away.'

Magdalena lost her poise, and dropped her brush.

'You're mad!'

'No. Practical. It isn't Mountjoy's, it can't be. He'll think it's an accident. You can say it's a miscarriage; that's likely at your age, anyway. I know a doctor who'll fix it for you, you can go to London next week.'

'No,' said Magdalena.

'Magdalena, you don't have a choice. God, how could you be so stupid? You said you were on the pill, and in any case, at your age . . .'

'At my age I'm delighted to be going to have a child, Val. And there's nothing you can do about it.'

'My God, there is. I'll tell Mountjoy as soon as he gets back just what his oh-so-devoted wife was up to when he was away for a few weeks. Ha,' he said, as he saw her flinch. 'That's made you think.'

'Yes, it has made me think how cold and inhuman you are, Val. Don't you dare tell Mountjoy. It will be your word against mine, and he'll believe me. And if you did tell him, *I* would tell him about your other children, and I think he'd be so horrified that he would never want to see you again – and he'd leave you nothing; the castle is his to do what he likes with. Even if I lost the child, I'd see he willed the castle to Thomas, not to you.'

'Other children?' Val sounded genuinely surprised. 'What are you talking about?'

'Thomas, and Cleo. There may be more, for all I know, there probably are, the way you leap into bed with women without ever bothering to take precautions, as far as I can see. And,' she added bitterly, 'without bothering about whether you're related to them or not.'

'Don't talk threadbare morality to me. If women want to go to bed with me, they can take the precautions, it's no business of mine. If they don't take the trouble and they end up pregnant, then it's up to them to do something about it.'

'You take my breath away, Valdemar, you really do,' said Magdalena, who couldn't help letting out a helpless shout of laughter. The vanity of the man. She had enjoyed going to bed with him; it had been a last protest of her individuality before she settled down for good to a steady country life, and the unexpected pregnancy had, after the first shock, been a joy. 'So Thomas and Cleo are merely unfortunate little accidents, which are nothing to do with you?'

'I don't know where you get your crazy ideas from,' said Val uncomfortably. 'Your hormones must be making you unbalanced.'

'Come on, your worst enemy never said you were stupid. Thomas is incredibly like you and you are pure Mountjoy; how could his looks have come from his mother? There have been rumours and hints about it ever since he started to grow up. I know you and

Hortense weren't brought up together, but, still, your half-sister! I wonder just where you draw the line.'

Valdemar was pale. 'I never heard such nonsense. Nobody knows who Thomas's father is. Hortense had a boyfriend; slept with dozens of men, for all I know.'

Magdalena looked Valdemar straight in the eye. 'Hortense wrote and told me, only recently, because her secret has been causing her more and more distress. I'm not surprised. And you must have guessed; you lack morals, not brains.'

'You're talking like an hysterical woman.'

'And all these years Thomas has longed to have a father, poor little boy, but of course that was nothing to do with you.'

He could hear the contempt in her voice.

'And Cleo? How do you pin that little piece of perfection to my door?'

'I don't. Her mother does. She was here not half an hour ago, we had a most interesting chat. When she got Cleo's letters, and realized that this older man Cleo was talking about was you, she was frantic. She couldn't contact Cleo on the phone, or get a message through to tell her, "Don't, whatever you do, sleep with that man, he's your father", so she dropped everything and came back to warn her. What a delightful woman. You should have married her, Val, as you said you would; you might have grown up to be quite human. As it is, while you've been fostering your wonderful and important career, she's been struggling to bring up that child single-handed. She hasn't aged as well as you have, Val. How surprising,' she added contemptuously.

Val flung himself into a chair. 'I'm not listening to this.'

'Put your fingers in your ears, and then you'll look just like Thomas, as well as sounding like him.'

Valdemar tried charm. 'Magdalena, please. We can discuss this, like reasonable people.'

'This isn't a reasonable matter. I do hope, by the way, for your sake as well as hers, that you didn't go to bed with Cleo.'

No, but it was a bloody near thing, thought Valdemar. Julie had saved him from that. Good God, had she somehow known about Cleo?

'Now go away,' Magdalena was saying. 'I'd take a long and honest look at yourself and think what you're going to be like in ten years' time if you don't change your spots. You'll end up having to pay women to go to bed with you. Who wants to sleep with a cold, cold man who's getting on, and only cares about himself – except for money?'

'God damn it all to hell,' shouted Val as he hurled himself from her room.

'And leave Prue alone.'

Magdalena's voice floated down the stairs after him.

Prue alone, Prue alone, echoed from the stone walls and in his ears as he headed for his room, a large drink and a very disturbed night.

Valdemar fled to London the next day, away from the whole ghastly business and so many emotional, unrestrained women. Menopausal, he said to himself furiously. Bloody hormones.

There was no comfort at his office. People were away on holiday; the only other partner there was Virginia Luthier, a formidable woman. Does she know about all this? he wondered. Could Magdalena have spread it around?

The flat was empty and lonely without Sylvia, no delicious meals or leisurely evenings at a favourite local restaurant.

He rang up his numerous girlfriends. Some were away, some too busy with their own lives to want to spend any time with him. How could this be happening? Veronica, married! To Philip, and quite happy never to see him again! He put a call through to Martha in Hong Kong, planning to fly out there; she was in Tokyo.

And not a word from Prue. She should be besotted with him; what was she up to? Did she know? Would Magdalena have told her any of this? Would she go ahead with the wedding, marry Seton? Was she back in Seton's bed? Bloody oaf was probably having a field day with her.

He tried to ring Prue but Magdalena answered the phone, and through some strange telepathy knew it was him before he said a word.

'If that's you, Val, no, you can't speak to Prue,' and the line went dead.

Prue was missing Valdemar, but she was too busy to have time to fret or mope. Seton, such a piece of luck, had fallen while out shooting and had sprained his groin very badly. He was the subject of much mirth among his friends! Watch out on your wedding night, old pal; you'll have to postpone the day if you don't get back in action pretty soon; and what were you doing when you got the sprain, as if we couldn't guess, ha, ha.

Prue couldn't believe her luck. Seton had been very attentive and amorous at Magdalena's party; thank goodness Delia had taken him off. How could she explain that what she had felt for him had faded so quickly, and that in comparison to Valdemar . . .

How could she explain it to herself, except to acknowledge that Jacob had been right. Poor Jacob; he might be right, but he'd managed to land himself in a terrible mess. She was in a terrible mess, too, she thought glumly. Oh, why didn't Valdemar come back, then she could decide what to do?

Meanwhile Sylvester, after consultation with Magdalena, had taken Prue on to the strength for the music festival, and she spent her days numbering seats and moving music stands; her evenings selling programmes and showing people to their seats.

She had only once in her life been to a concert, a performance of a sacred choral work while at the convent. Her aunt had never allowed her to go to concerts, too expensive, and inflaming to the young. Look what it did to her father. Since Prue's father had died with her mother in a plane crash, and before that had embarked on a successful and lucrative performing career, Prue wasn't sure on what her aunt's fears were grounded. She suspected that she simply didn't think music or musicians were at all respectable.

She loved it all. She was enthralled by the music, intrigued by the musicians; most of all she liked watching Geza play. The urbane, witty, nice man vanished, to be replaced by a commanding soloist, absorbed in the music but always in control, and basking in the limelight. She loved to hear Sylvester play, too; the music made her hurt inside.

'How can you take it for granted, Cleo,' she would say, 'doesn't it make you feel gooseflesh all over?'

'No,' said Cleo, 'it doesn't.'

Cleo's mother, staying at Midwinter Hall at Sylvester's request, and busy sketching the musicians for a series of paintings, was much more sympathetic.

'Enjoy it while you can, Prue. However much you love music, and however much you come to know about it, it will never be as intense as it is now. Make the most of it.'

Sylvester dug out an old and scratchy recording of her father playing, and they listened to it one evening after the concert. It brought tears to Prue's eyes. Sylvester and Geza watched her and said nothing.

'Very much of a waste, this wedding, Sylvester, I think,' Geza said later. 'We must stop her doing this foolish act, which she can only regret.'

'She's determined, and she thinks it's what she wants.'

'No. We will work a plan. I will think.'

Geza talked to her about her bones. 'I know a surprising lot about such bones, you see, because my aunt, an intellectual, teaches this at Budapest University. Her name is Dr Kati Csontvary.'

Prue's face lit up. 'She is famous, in this field. Her book is translated into English. I've got it here.'

'You come to Budapest, we make you very welcome, and then you can meet with my aunt, and have many interesting conversations about these old African people.'

'That would be lovely,' said Prue, drawing back into her shell. 'However, Seton doesn't care for abroad, he says, so I rather doubt that I will ever get there.' She giggled. 'I think he'd be frightened to go to Budapest, especially. He hates communists and would think they were going to lock him up.'

'Good, then let him come, and be locked up and they throw away the key,' said Geza to Sylvester.

Jacob overslept; he had set the alarm, but didn't hear it. His once effortless self-discipline was fast vanishing, he found it difficult just to get through the routines of his day, washing, shaving, eating . . . In addition, he had to shop and cook. He went to Eyot to shop. He couldn't face the locals at the moment, so that took more time. He missed Sophie, the sex, her bracing intelligence. He felt guilty about Daisy; surrounded by her things, it was hard to put her out of his mind.

'Haven't you heard from her?' Sylvester asked. He dropped in for a brief chat whenever he was in the village. Jacob appreciated that, although he found he didn't have much to say.

'No, not a word. Some busy-tongued soul has obviously told her about Sophie; goodness knows what she's heard. Have another chocolate biscuit. Sorry they're a bit soggy, I keep forgetting to put them in a tin.'

Jacob got himself dressed, and went downstairs to collect the post. Nothing from Daisy, from the Church authorities or from the Bishop; perhaps they had all forgotten about him?

He must pull himself together. It was the eve of Prue's wedding, and he had been invited to the castle for dinner. That was kind of Magdalena. He realized gloomily that he didn't have a clean shirt to put on. If he washed one and hung it outside, would it dry? Yes, but where had he left the iron? The cat yowled disconsolately round his ankles; he had yet again forgotten to buy cat food. He found a tin of tuna, opened that and forked the contents onto one of Daisy's prized Spode plates.

'Typical,' said a brisk voice. 'Jacob, what on earth do you think you're doing?'

I don't believe it, thought Jacob.

Daisy was back.

'She's leaving me!' Jacob told Magdalena and Mountjoy when he arrived at the castle.

'Not surprising, in the circumstances,' said Mountjoy.

'No, but that's not why she's leaving, or rather it's only part of the reason, because she says now she can hand me over to someone else to look after with an easy conscience. She was planning to leave me, anyway.'

'Don't tell me she's got a boyfriend,' said Magdalena, fascinated.

Mountjoy gave a snort of laughter. 'Let me guess, she's going to become a nun.'

Jacob shook his head. 'No, Magdalena is almost right, but it's a girlfriend. She's moving in with Jocasta, permanently.'

'Two women living together, perfectly respectable,' said Mountjoy. 'Still doesn't get you out of your fix, Jacob.'

'Oh, yes, it does. Theirs is a full relationship, she tells me. She says she isn't going to hide her true self any longer, she's a lesbian, only interested in women, and that sex with Jocasta is marvellous. In case I want to know, she's never enjoyed it once with me.'

'Sex with Jocasta, marvellous!' said Magdalena, awed.

Mountjoy was deeply shocked. 'Dreadful thing! Fancy having to put up with one of those all these years, Jacob. Shocking affair.' He brightened up. 'Tell you what; no trouble with the Bishop once he knows about this.'

Magdalena disagreed. 'He still committed adultery with Sophie, Mountjoy. That's not a criticism, Jacob, just a fact.'

'Mountjoy's right. My guess is that I'll be able to get a divorce and marry Sophie, and there won't be a murmur from the Bishop. They'll all be horrified about Daisy and Jocasta. They hate that, women, sex; that won't do at all.'

'Are you sure?'

'Definitely. Men, male homosexuality, that's okay, doesn't worry them a bit, they're used to that. But women? That's abnormal. So I'll get the sympathy and Sophie; Daisy and Jocasta will get the cold shoulder. No more garden parties at the Palace for them.'

Jacob's news enthralled everyone gathered at the castle. Only Seton wasn't there to hear the latest news. He was too full of painkillers to enjoy a stag night with his friends, so he had settled for an evening at home with the dogs.

'He could have come to dinner here,' said Delia cheerfully, 'but he didn't think it was correct, silly old chap. Prue, have another drink, you look as though you could do with it. Butterflies in the tummy at the thought of tomorrow? Chin up, it'll soon be over.'

Prue gave a slight smile. 'I'm not worried about tomorrow. I'm a bit tired, that's all.'

Valdemar isn't coming, she thought to herself. He said he would be away, but why doesn't he get in touch? She had tactfully tried to find out from Mountjoy where Valdemar was, but he was equally puzzled by his absence. Never been away this much in the summer before; strange fellow, though, goes his own way.

She pleaded tiredness and the need to get an early night to slip away. Affectionate good wishes were called out to her as she left.

'Poor child,' said Jacob compassionately. He was sitting with his arm round Sophie, who had joined them after dinner at Magdalena's invitation, waiting for his own chance to leave and make up for lost time with her. 'I hope she knows what she's doing.'

Prue walked slowly up the stairs to her room. Tomorrow, it'll be over, she said to herself. I won't belong here any more, nor anywhere else except Feather House. A tear trickled down her cheek and she brushed it away as she turned the handle on her door.

'Hello, Prue,' said Valdemar, getting up. 'I've been waiting for you.'

Cleo took off her high-heeled shoes and walked more comfortably across the grass to the marquee. She was carrying a bottle of champagne, one of the dozens put on ice for the reception.

'Pass a couple of glasses, Mum,' she said. 'Let's drink to Prue, wherever she is.'

Sylvester's bulk filled the entrance and he beamed at them. 'A glass for me, too, Cleo.' He balanced himself perilously on one of the fold-up chairs provided for the guests. 'What excitement. I haven't enjoyed myself so much at a wedding for years.'

'Sylvester, how can you be so pleased?' said Cleo. 'Prue doesn't know what she's let herself in for, running off with Valdemar.'

'I give it six weeks,' said Cleo's mother, sadly. 'If that.'

'Is Magdalena all right?' asked Sylvester. 'It must have been a terrible shock, not good for a woman in her condition.'

'She was seeing off the last of the guests just now, and the Bishop,' said Cleo. 'She's fine, said, "Good for Prue."'

Gussie's eyebrows went up; she had very expressive eyebrows. 'That surprises me, that really does surprise me. I wouldn't have thought she, of all people, could bear the thought of Prue going off with Val.'

'Better than Seton, anything's better than Seton,' said Sylvester genially. 'Got a bit of life in him, has Val, do Prue good. She's far too young to get married. Come on, Cleo, don't be mean with the champagne, fill up the glasses.'

Less than a hundred miles away, Geza was pouring champagne as well. 'We have much to celebrate, Prue. Here we are, eating a good lunch and then we go to bed together, then we get up and eat some more and then we go back to bed again, and enjoy lots more sex.'

Prue, very light-headed with the champagne and the exhilaration of not being married to Seton, giggled. 'I haven't said I'll go to bed with you, Geza.'

'No, but you will. You go to bed a lot with other people, it seems, so now you go to bed with me, which will be much better than the others, I can tell you.'

'Val was good,' she said dreamily.

'I want to hear no more about Val. I expect he is good at sex, he has had a lot of practice with sisters and aunts and I don't know who, but he is no longer going to practise with you!'

Prue's smile faded. 'I had no idea, why didn't someone tell me about him? Do you know, he asked me to marry him. I would have gone with him. He might have been serious, I suppose, but imagine, I might not have found out about his children and everything, not for years.'

Geza fed her a cherry. 'These secrets, they are embarrassing. People say, this is family business, not for outsiders. Then others say, Prue is very young, best not to know about such things.'

'Does Cleo know he's her father? Or Thomas?'

Geza shook his head. 'They will, in time, because big secrets are known in the end. But it will then be old scandal. People will have new gossip, so it doesn't matter so much.'

Prue's mind flashed back to earlier that day, when she had stolen down to the stables, french horn and suitcase in hand, to put them in the boot of Valdemar's car as he had told her to do. 'I'll be there at half-past ten. Put your bag in well before that, then you won't be noticed when you slip out. Don't be late, we've got a long way to go.'

Not so far, thought Prue. He would now be in London, humiliated and angry, furious with her, tearing up the note she had left tucked under his windscreen. And she was here, in a delightful house – it belongs to some good friends of mine, they are away, but they say, come whenever you want, Geza had told her – with a most delightful man, who she was longing to go to bed with, although she wasn't letting on about that. The cleverness of him, hiring a car to whisk her away from under Valdemar's very nose . . .

'I must telephone Magdalena,' she said. 'I hope she'll understand. I feel very guilty about the wedding, all her work, the food wasted, the expense!'

'I told Magdalena that I would not let you run away with Val, and she was pleased about that. I think the guests will all have eaten and drunk and enjoyed themselves very much. Who needs a bride and groom to have a good time? And Seton, now he can marry loud Delia, and he too will be very happy.'

'I hope so,' said Prue. 'How could I ever think of marrying him? Can I have some more champagne, please, Geza, and tell me all about Budapest.'